I0797129

Prologue

Sham smiled wickedly at the pitiful, cornered creature that bleated in agony. Initially, it resembled a winged lamb with white fur and feathers covering much of its body. The creature was not so white or winged anymore, Sham thought with a chuckle. He glanced at his new servants starting to nail the wings he had recently removed from the creature to a beam perpendicular to the main throne hall within his *palace.*

That thought immediately removed the pleasure from his mind and replaced it with the anger that had initially made him seek out the creature's pain.

It wasn't his fault that the king couldn't take a joke. Sham had simply whispered to his brothers that the king was extensively enjoying the blood wine that came with liberation day's festivities and they may see what was beneath his skin. While the king had always held that he wasn't projecting a skin and had retained his glorious visage after their initial break from the Creator, some didn't believe this assertion as nearly all shadows in the fallen legion hid their deteriorating bodies beneath a self-powered projection. Sham was absolutely not part of that group. Definitely not. Sham was extremely loyal to the king. Despite that, his legion brothers at the table were quick to try to gain their superiors' favor by bringing this harmless joke to their attention—the very next cycle, he was stationed at this remote garbage heap.

The creature's screams were a mild balm to his mind as he imagined his traitorous brothers screaming in its place.

Sham looked around once more at his new posting. He was in the center of a hall room with a single throne raised on a flat circular stone above the other chairs that lined

Cover design by: Ryan Ritchey
Printed in the United States of America

Preface

Warriors are called to unique battlefields. I am honored to carry my King's given skills onto the field to which He has called me. It is not the arena I had imagined, but I will not falter in the face of the enemy - even if that enemy is my own pride and internal accusations that stare back at me in the mirror.

____

This book is dedicated to my sons, Wulf and Bear. I pray that your use of Choice leads you to ultimate victory. You will face many battles in your life, but my hope is that you remember that all it takes is one good Choice to change your situation. Never forget that your father has your six and will love you forever.

To my wife, cheerleader, manager, and partner - Jihya. It is impossible to imagine completing this without you. Thank you for pushing me and helping me see the potential of my imaginative thoughts. Our nights of working side-by-side will forever be encased in my heart. There is no one else I would rather stack up with to clear the enemy's strongholds.

Thank you to those who reviewed my very rough, early versions and gave feedback to help produce what is on these pages: Micheal and Renee Harris, Jordan and Hannah Schaffer, Edgar Medina, and Ken Jacroux.

Eph 6:12

decrypt tables on either side of a large fire pit that held the room's center. Of course, he was sitting on the elaborate wooden throne decorated with Creator images and symbols, which often included a beautiful bird. The images and sense of the throne itself rejecting him seemed to seep into his bones as he sat upon it. He tried not to let the discomfort and unease he felt show to his servants as they moved around the room, attempting to make it more hospitable to one of his station. It wouldn't due to let these lower creatures think he was unworthy of the stupid thing.

The walls of his new hall were made of stone, and the roof, or what was remaining of it, was covered in rotting wood. It smelled of mold, decay, shit - and the fresh blood. The blood being the attempt to make it more to his liking, but it was doing a piss job of masking the other smells. He eyed his servants with contempt as they moved about the room.

While his standing as a captain within the legion warranted him the best servants the horde could provide, he was stuck with kreehauns. There wasn't even a bultun or marow to heed his call! Due to the suddenness of his departure, Sham was unfairly unable to bring a lowly stone with him. No, he was stuck with only stupid, smelly, ugly kreehauns.

Kreehauns seemed to enjoy taking ugly to another level. The creatures had sensitive noses that extended well beyond their face. Their lower jaw had obscenely large fangs protruding upward to cover their nose and mouth. It gave them the appearance of having been muzzled. Whiskers completed their ridiculous faces as they shot out between their protruding teeth to either side. Tiny, beady, black eyes were barely noticeable behind their ridiculous nose, but Sham assumed they were there.

All that said, the legion only cared about their small muscular bodies and dangerously sharp claws shooting out of their fingers and toes. With these and their inclination to be underground, they made excellent tunnelers that could be used in sieges and ambushes. Surprisingly, their bodies were covered in black fur, which was quite pleasant as a blanket. Few knew that since they were constantly covered in dirt and mud. At least, he hoped that it was dirt.... Sham now questioned where the smells were truly coming from. He may need to kill a few to lessen the smell.

Like all of the horde within this realm, the kreehauns were loyal to the new king and understood their place as much as their tiny brains allowed. They enjoyed the elimination and torture of the Kingdom's inhabitants, however rare that was. Due to that same rarity, Sham had considered it good tidings that on the day of his arrival, he had found the flying lamb creature stuck in the bowels of the hall. Since the kreehauns enjoyed digging so much, they were quick to hear it in the lower crypts of the outpost upon arriving, and Sham immediately investigated as he was eager to find anything of value. After a brief struggle, he captured it and used his weapons to sever the wings from its small body to both torment the creature and ensure it couldn't escape.

Sham's blades were immaculate and beautifully destructive. He was created with sickle blades that curved immediately from the handle, creating a half circle ending in a sharp point. The blades were razor sharp in the inner side of the curve, which enabled Sham to chop pieces off of his enemies. He gently touched the handles of the weapons strapped to his side in almost a reverent way. Considering that the Creator's images were no longer displayed on the blades or handles and instead gave off an inky black smoke, Sham often enjoyed worshiping his tools of chaos. Every shadow had a weapon representing his skill going back beyond liberation day, but Sham enjoyed his much more than any other he had met. He hardly missed the gifts the Creator had stripped away that so many other shadows bemoaned. Giving those up for true freedom was worth it,

Sham thought as he unconsciously reached for the severed gifts in his mind.

Shadow's blades also weren't always the black inky color with a dim red light glowing within that they were now. When Sham was a member of the Sword clan, it glowed with the Creator's light. The thought of that light brought a shiver to Sham's body. He needed to shift his thoughts quickly away from the light and onto more pleasurable things.

As his servants continued to nail his trophies to the center beam, he glanced around and imagined other trophies he might collect. There was nothing better to do now as his time in this wretched place slowly ticked by.

However, Sham would not sit idle in his time here. No, he would scheme and plot his triumphant return from this hideous ruin. He just needed something to get the king's attention, in a positive way.

While his outpost was far from the glories, pleasures, and intrigues of the castle and liberation city surrounding it, the small fort bordered other realms, including the Kingdom. Perhaps Sham could convince some of his former brethren along the border teams to join their war against the Creator? It had not been done since the great war, but Sham was obviously better equipped and more intelligent than other shadows who had worked the border before him. He could be as convincing as the king himself in the right circumstances. Alternatively, bringing back a few of his blue-skinned former brothers in chains would undoubtedly put him in good standing with the king. *Yes*, thought Sham. The king would be pleased to welcome another shadow to the liberated realm but perhaps even more thrilled to *play* with them instead. Sham could get anything he wanted! Screams of his legion brothers who had turned on him rang in his ears again, but the sound of them calling him general was just as sweet. Perhaps he would hear both? Sham laughed with glee at the imagined sound. The plan began forming in his mind, and the thought of rising from this dung pile to the upper heights of court gave him immediate gratification.

The cries of the creature brought him back to the current situation. While he wanted to prolong its suffering, he beamed with renewed energy as it was time to begin working on his strategy. With a quick step down from the throne and an even faster slice of one of his sickles, the head of the creature was separated from its body. He quickly ordered the kreehauns not to eat the body as both a punishment and the again hope of the blood masking the smell of his new hall.

In the far distance, a barely audible roar could be heard as the creature's blood poured over the immediate area of the hall, causing the rocks and wood to turn a bright red hue. Slower but no less steadily, it trickled down through the floorboards, stone slabs, and support beams. It made its way back to the crypt where the lamb was first seen and where something else began to stir.

1

COMMANDER Titus surveyed the training hall where his team was currently spread out, doing various exercises to prepare them for potential deployments.

In the center, there was a combat circle where they could test each other 1-on-1 or sometimes 1-on-many, depending on the training and the trainer. Currently, the latter was the case as his two sergeants, Killian and Kurian, or the twins as they were known, were taking on Private John in a no-holds brawl using only their gifted armor and primary weapons. It was an interesting tactical problem to consider as the twins should clearly have the advantage with their number; however, John's two-handed battle axe held the superior range against both Killian's knives and Kurian's bladed round shield.

Each member of the Host had a primary weapon used for close-quarters combat with an adversary, which was their preferred tactic when dispatching the enemy. Titus's team was unique in that no two primary weapons were the same type. It gave them more chances to train against odd fighting styles and weapons they could potentially face in the field, including the current scenario.

Or at least that is what Titus's team trained for. In truth, he and 1-1-8 hadn't been deployed since the initial attempted coup by some former members of the Clan. Titus could never understand why some of his brothers and sisters would ever abandon their King, but he had an extra measure of contempt for the traitors as it was his previous superior who helped lead the attack. Now, they lived outside the Kingdom and constantly looked for ways to hinder their Maker and His loyal subjects.

Re-centering his thoughts on his team's training, Titus watched as Killian tried a distraction maneuver of diving in, rolling, and leaping high to slash his knives at the taller and brawnier team member's eye slits. He continued his aerial acrobatics by flipping over his opponent's head. The maneuver was timed to his brother's attempt at a surprise attack on the left. Unfortunately for the twins, John wasn't distracted as he quickly tucked his chin out the knife's path and swung his ax with all his might at Kurian's shield. He *missed* and only caused a glancing blow to the edge, but the force was still strong enough to cause the smaller brother to step back. Unknown to his opponents, the hit was perfectly aimed as John's large framed body used the momentum of the deflected strike to swing around and deliver an acrobatic spinning high kick to the armored head of Killian. Both brothers were knocked back, and the game of cat and mouse continued. Titus wasn't sure yet who was the cat and who was the mouse, but it would likely be ages before anything was truly decided.

To his immediate left, Private Marcus was pouring over the latest information on the borderlands. Tactics used by the enemy, their strengths, weaknesses, supply lines, and some historical information on plant life, as well as a poem or song. While Marcus was awkward in his speech, Titus would rely on his thin yet extremely tall team member for intelligence as the team's knowledge seeker. When the time came for their eventual deployment, the information that Marcus provided could mean the difference between returning and going blue.

"Commander, can you please do something about that?" Marcus pleaded as he looked up from a fresh-looking scroll and gestured to the source of his irritation.

Next to Marcus was the complete opposite of everything the tall, quiet squad member encapsulated. Private

Amadon, more commonly referred to as Wit by the team, lay a few feet away snoring. Loudly. While members of the Host did not need sleep, it was an enjoyable experience for most, some a bit more than others. It was the team's belief that Wit not only enjoyed it but also reveled in the added perk of annoying his squad members. That said, he wasn't exactly quiet when he was awake, either. As the team's radio and communications expert, it was not surprising that he enjoyed speaking...frequently and at absurd volumes. He was also the team's trickster and overall clown, hence the nickname.

"Wit - stop pretending and start reading," Titus yelled without even as much of a glance towards the private.

"How did you know, Commander?" Wit called out as he shot up with a bemused look on his face.

"You actually snore louder when you are asleep."

"I do?" Wit replied with barely contained glee.

"Stop pestering Marcus and help, or you'll have next with John in the ring."

"Yes, sir! Right away, sir!" Wit yelped as he came over and grabbed a few scrolls off the top of the pile.

Marcus gave him a quick smirk, and Wit elbowed him in return.

While the smaller framed Wit would likely not enjoy a bout with John, or any other brother for that matter, the truth was that any one of them could hold their own in the ring against any opponent, at least for a time. The Creator saw fit to make them experts in warfare. Each one of them was unique in most ways, but they typically were grouped together within a skill set that made them valuable to the mission. The simple and undeniable fact was - they were warriors. Their entire existence was encapsulated by two things: serve their King and win wars, in that order.

Physically, his brothers and sisters within the clan all had the same teal-colored skin and eyes that shined like fire with orange and red hues. Additionally, the Creator's energy was constantly running throughout each of their bodies. His energy sustained them and caused them to glow slightly, with flashes of light periodically showing in their veins. The visual made each of them appear as though they were barely containing a lightning storm just beneath the surface. Observant eyes would notice that this is where their physical similarities ended. Some were tall and thin, whereas others were short or wider. Titus himself would be considered average among his peers, with only his brown curly hair and perfectly trimmed beard to set himself apart, but even those characteristics were not rare among the clan. What set him apart was being a Leader.

Leaders were given a small measure of extra strength at creation and a unique brain capable of taking in all information around them to come up with battle strategies within a single heartbeat. While they couldn't actually control time, as creation and control of time was a power held by only the King Himself, their perception of time seemed to slow as their brains raced to add information and decide on tactics.

Titus and his fellow Leaders were rare within the clan as each one typically had a minimum of five brothers or sisters under them, with the average being closer to twenty. As they fought and some members took the blue, others were shifted around to ensure each team was capable of completing missions assigned to them. Since no new members had ever been created, they were slowly becoming a smaller force, and team leads were similarly growing scarce. While each loss was painful, the clan understood that this was a temporary status. Once they take the blue, each member would sleep as an indestructible, statuesque blue form until the Creator decreed it was time to finish His work and unite all realms under His single banner. When the final battle horn sounded and the King took his place on the battlefield, the Clan's sleeping brothers and sisters would awake with renewed energy once more. They would fulfill both of their purposes in serving their Creator by cleaning the realms of the filth that has infested it.

Even as uncommon as team leaders were, there was one other group that was rarer yet with such unique skills and talents that they instantly stood out from all others. Members of the Scout and Long-Range Termination, or SALT group, were so highly skilled with their ranged gifts that it was as if they were actually their primary. Titus felt truly blessed by the Maker to have his second be a member of such an elite group.

Lieutenant Shay was the epitome of professionalism and warrior mindset. Shay knew how to take charge in any situation but would defer to Titus's decisions immediately. Titus knew that he depended upon his second a bit more than what would be considered appropriate in other teams, but he also knew that it would be folly to ignore such a resource.

Currently, the SALT team member was honing his impressive skill just to the right of the combat ring. Titus looked on as Shay lay quietly among simulated grass. His tunic was set for camouflage, so his rifle and clothes blended in with the surroundings so perfectly that it appeared as though grass was growing out of the prone warrior. If it wasn't for Shay's choice to forgo his hood and the fact that the lieutenant had his black hair in a ponytail down to his mid-back, Titus wasn't so sure he would have seen his second.

As soon as the commander spotted him, Shay took a single shot from his long rifle at a simulated target in a forest down range. The simulation also provided a storm with constantly changing wind directions and speed. Shay's shot was quickly followed by five more, each a small light of pure white energy. He didn't have to see the target at an unreal distance to know that every shot was perfect. Titus watched Shay's body dim slightly as the energy needed to make such shots took a toll, but he almost immediately returned to his typical bright teal coloring. Being within such close proximity to the Creator made energy drain almost non-existent for the Swords.

Having scanned his team, Titus took a moment to review his own weapon and gifts. Drawing his double-edged sword from the sheath at his back, he once again marveled at the beauty of his weapon and the love that the Creator poured into it. Within the clans, each weapon was designed for the user as a perfect tool of war and a beautiful work of art made by the ultimate Artist.

Primary weapons were not necessarily a gift to them but rather created *with* them. Each Sword was literally built with a weapon in their hands. It wasn't a tool outside of themselves; it was a part of who they were and represented their own uniqueness. The weapons were intricately designed with various Host signs and Creator-honoring images. Some of them, including Titus's own sword, even depicted the warrior fighting in the final battle that has yet to come.

Titus felt chills at the thought of the final battle and the glory that would radiate from his King. All members of the Host knew not when the battle would come, but they prepared for it with every moment of their existence.

The commander's ranged gift was a simple rifle. While nothing truly was simple about it, his rifle was the most common ranged gift. A command from within his mind brought the weapon into his hands. The barrel was made of black material, but the guard surrounding it and the stock, grip, and trigger were pure white with etched golden artistic images spread throughout, including the majestic bird that often symbolized their Maker. That said, stunning beauty wasn't ideal on the battlefield. Every Sword knew that when they camouflaged themselves or were in a battle, the ranged gift casing would also change to adapt to the environment and circumstances.

Since both ranged weapons and armor were presented to each Sword after their creation, they were called gifts. Both are dependent upon the Maker and the individual Sword's energy. Without a direct connection to the Creator and the energy within themselves, their gifts would no longer function. Since their own life energy was connected to the King, it was slow to regenerate outside of the Kingdom. This meant that each Sword needed to use their gifts sparingly in battle or risk taking the blue.

"Attention!" Wit called out loudly, and all motion ceased instantly outside of the squad entering a position of attention. Titus was able to spot General Tomaltach and a member of the Voice clan quickly and entered into the same position as his squad.

As soon as the General was within hearing range of the squad, he called out to them. "As you were, Swords. Commander, we need to speak with you."

"Yes, sir." Replied Titus as he quickly marched towards the pair.

While the general was similar to Titus physically, outside of a short and clean mustache, his mind was created by the Maker to be a leader of far more than a squad. Much like the ability to think quickly on the battlefield given to team leaders, generals could plan out every angle of a campaign. They were strategy and logistical geniuses who ensured the gears of the Sword clan moved quickly and efficiently to do the bidding of the King.

However, the General's current partner was very different than any Sword. Unlike members of Titus's clan, the Voice clan was as easy to spot in a crowd as eagles standing among cats. Due to their exposure to the King's presence, each Voice member glowed brightly in their body, especially their face. If Swords looked as though they barely contained storms, Voice members were pure lightning. Additionally, their voices were so beautiful in song and speech that it was known to cause some to weep in joy at the sound. And if this wasn't enough to set them apart, they did have giant wings and were about four hands taller than Swords.

The Voice clan got their name for their melodious voices and the fact that they spoke for the King. But, it wasn't as if they spoke in their own voice on behalf of the King; they were more like conduits of the King's voice. Each Voice was capable of passing along the Maker's voice and commands within themselves. That said, getting a visit from a Voice typically meant only one thing to a Sword: deployment.

"Good day, Commander. I am Eimear, and I come with word from the King."

Titus turned to the Voice and spoke back the appropriate response, "I am my King's Sword. I am honored to serve Him."

Eimear responded in her stunning voice, "Kneel, for your King speaks."

Titus and Tomaltach bowed their heads low to the ground in both reverence for the words that were about to be spoken and to ensure they weren't blinded.

Eimear opened her mouth, and pure golden energy flowed out as her face became akin to a sun. Then, a powerful yet loving voice that was clearly not her own spoke:

"SOMETHING OF IMMEASURABLE VALUE IS FORMED. IT SHALL NOT GO UNPROTECTED. YOU ARE CALLED TO SERVE."

Eimear closed her eyes and mouth, both of which immediately shot back open in a gasp. The joy she felt was evident in her radiant smile and face, even though it was still hard to look at. She had served her King in bringing Titus His words.

In light of those same words and the thought of fulfilling his own purpose, Titus couldn't stop his own smile from spreading across his face at one undeniable fact: Sword 1-1-8 was going to war.

2

WHILE the King gave orders and knew that they would be fulfilled, the details of deploying were known by leadership and worked out within the clan. Having understood precisely what the King referred to and where Titus's unit was to be deployed, Tomaltach outlined the situation with Titus and the rest of the squad as they surrounded a table within the training hall.

"Your squad will be transported to an old fort on the other side of these border realm mountains." Using a projection scroll that detailed the area, the General pointed to a southeastern mountain range that helped form a border between the Kingdom and a legion-claimed realm. While no space was truly outside the authority or reach of the King, He did provide room for those to live with the Choice they had formed. Within the lands outlined on the map, the traitors and the horde roamed free to destroy and wreak havoc on any who did not have the protection of the King.

The horde. Titus couldn't help but touch his sword at the mere thought of them. They are a ceaseless threat to the beloved creations of the Maker. While all good things were created by the King, the horde is the antithesis of what He represents. In His ultimate show of love and devotion, the Creator gave some creations a powerful force that He called Choice. Creations were able to use it in two ways: return the love and faith given to them or create something wholly outside of the Creator. Since the King represents all good and love, creating something new could only result in evil. By rejecting their Maker in the use of Choice, some of the created gave birth to new entities. These unique creations were abominations of such pure evil and chaos that their minds held little thought outside of a constant need to destroy. While totally incapable of entering the presence of the true Maker, the horde is a deadly blight to any who exists outside of the Kingdom.

Due to their capability of employing tactics and following orders of those they deem more chaotic, the fallen legion makes use of the horde as their personal slaves and cannon fodder. Their loyalty could not be counted on as the horde would break rank and disobey if their hunger to kill overtook them. There are reports of them turning on their own, or even their would-be leaders, if nothing else is available. Destruction purely for the sake of destruction is enough to ease their constant need for chaos.

Looking back at the map that the General was discussing, Titus refocused and saw the squad's destination as a tiny structural note on the map within a breath of a mountain range. The fort was close to the center of the range and in the shadow of its tallest peaks. It was so near the mountains that Titus's tactical mind suspected that at least one side of the fort made use of the sheer cliffs as part of its defense.

Tomaltach tapped on the fort's note, and the map adjusted to show a slightly more magnified look at the structures and adjacent areas. To his surprise and dismay, Titus saw it wasn't using the existing rock walls but was instead on a slightly raised plateau inside a glade—the mountain cliffs were just to the west of their destination. The fort had dead trees encroaching it on all sides with slightly healthier-looking pines as you traveled in any direction out from it. A look from above gave an eerie appearance of the structures being the center of an open wound with flesh dying as dark necrosis spread from the core.

The structures within the walls comprised several small buildings sprawled out within the walls and a main hall at the center. There were towers in the northwest and southeast corners, but their current condition made them more of a problem than a usable defensive position. The walls also had clearly seen better days with gaps and crumbling areas so vast that an entire herd of bullans could walk shoulder to shoulder through.

“Due to the fort being so near the mountains, don’t expect long-range communication to be consistent or effective. Outside of occasional Arrow patrols and provisions, we airdrop to your location; you and your squad will not have continuous support.” The General looked up at the Commander to emphasize his point, and Titus gave his superior a firm nod. There was never a doubt that they would take the mission and be glad for it. However, the General clearly conveyed that 1-1-8 could not rely on Sword command as a failsafe. As always, the King would have known of the situation and planned accordingly, but it was up to the Commander to ensure it was done with as few casualties as possible. Titus knew that his skills as a tactician and leader would be tested to their limits.

“Our scouts have seen cave openings near the fort at the foot of the mountains. You will likely either find kreehauns are in the fort itself or will converge on you from the immediate vicinity.”

Tomaltach expanded the map out more and stated, “There hasn’t been any major legion activity in the area, but in almost every direction, there are concentrations of horde groups. If they hear of your location and mission, it is possible that the legion could gather them together as a larger army.”

Titus responded to the explicit warning, “We will be prepared, General.”

“Intelligence is minimal in this area as the mountains

make it difficult to patrol. Your first priority is the mission, but holding and annexing this land would greatly benefit future deployments."

"Understood, General. We will hold the fort. What exactly is our primary objective, sir?"

"The Creator is forming something special in the fort in anticipation of annexing the surrounding area. His creation will grow beneath the main hall inside a tomb. If all else fails, you will hold that position at all costs. There is no moving the creation, so the tomb will be your final position. I do not recommend you be pushed into it."

Titus understood immediately what the General meant. To get pushed into the tomb would essentially mean all hope was lost. Being trapped underground with enemies pinning them in would likely result in mission failure, not to mention the fact that he and his brothers would almost certainly be taking an early blue. He would not let that happen.

Seemingly having provided all the relevant information, the General straightened up and looked to Titus before adding, "We are naming this mission Operation Dúneinri."

Titus would have preferred a more apt designation. Off the top of his head, maybe traitor's grave? It certainly looked the part of a graveyard. Additionally, he and his squad intended to make it the final resting place of any that challenged them.

Tomaltach rolled up the map as the projection winked out and handed the scroll to Titus. "You have an Arrow transport prepped with supplies and ready to take your squad."

"Thank you, sir."

In a more serious tone, Tomaltach said, "The Maker has given you this task. How well your unit does and how many of your squad make it back will depend on you. I wish you wisdom in your Choices, Commander."

The General then looked at the rest of the squad and,

with a knowing smile, said, "Happy hunting."

As one, they responded in loud, joyful voices, "Hura!"

After the General's departure, the team discussed options for entry and decided to go in quietly as the number and composition of the enemy were unknown. For that, they would exit the transport high above their objective and move in stealthily on the ground to catch as many of their enemies off guard as possible. The state of the fort would allow them entry without any real issue, something they would need to remedy soon after evicting the current tenants. No deployment timeline was given, so Titus planned on being there for the long haul. Upgrading and repairing what little defenses the fort offered would begin immediately after securing their objective.

With the plan agreed to, the warriors all felt the thrill of energy course through their bodies like electricity as each made a Choice to move forward. Making use of the power often created a physical reaction within an individual member of the Clans. Titus didn't need to know what each of them chose as it would have been impossible to prevent any of them from going. It was their first deployment since the traitor's war, and they were all itching to perform the task they were created for.

Due to their constant state of readiness, Titus and his team were headed to their transport within two marks of receiving their orders. The short briefing provided by the General and the subsequent team planning was the only delay outside of renewing their energy and checking the supplies that would be loaded into their transportation. Arrows were perfect at their work, but Swords always ensured that they reviewed supplies given as they needed to know exactly where certain items were stowed. Plus, for this mission, Arrow support would be infrequent at best. Titus and his brothers may not have another chance to tailor what supplies are dropped in for quite some time.

Arrows were members of the Sword clan but were

typically not in direct action roles. While some did provide air cover and transportation in and out of deployments, they mainly played the pivotal role of support and logistics. Every Sword element had at least their number in Arrows working behind the scenes to ensure the King's orders were fulfilled. Even though Swords and Arrows had a friendly competition, they also had a sense of fellowship and understood that the mission mattered most. They would always support each other and do whatever it took to fulfill the King's orders.

Titus had heard from spies and scouts that the camaraderie was not carried over into the legion. Arrows, or stones as they were called in the legion, were seen as second-class citizens and often treated as nothing more than servants. The Commander had very little sympathy for anyone who would attempt a coup against their King. As far as he was concerned, they had made their bed, and he personally intended to make sure that as many as possible had a painful death in it.

When he and his squad got closer to the airfield, Titus thought once again how transportation ships within the Arrow armada reminded him of an enormous pregnant bird, representing the bird of the Maker. Short wings jutted out from either side of the craft with a large round cargo area beneath a beaked-head-looking cockpit and above the landing legs. The rear had a large door that opened from bottom to top, exposing the craft's interior that now held his team's supplies. While not made for comfort, it had everything a Sword squad would need to deploy. It was easy to confuse the ship for something weak and slow, but even the Kingdom's enemies would never describe one of the ships that way. Wicked-looking guns were hidden just beneath the wings. Titus knew from experience that the barrels could rotate around the ship to any exterior point, which ensured no angle was safe from the righteous destruction that this 'bird' was capable of dishing out. That said, the weapons used the same energy as traveling between the realms. Just like a Sword's internal energy powered his gifts, the transport was only capable of so much travel or firepower before it would plummet from the sky.

As 1-1-8 finalized their supplies and started to board the transport, a jovial feminine voice came over their communication link. "Welcome to Arrow 5! My name is Captain Ailey, and I will be transporting you helmet heads to the most luxurious vacation of your dreams. I hear there are rocks to eat, monsters to hunt, and former brothers to stab you while you sleep. I am certain you all will love it!" Titus smiled along with his squad as they took their seats in the back of the transport. Swords had even designations, and Arrows had odd, and odd they were. The cockpit where the Captain and her gunner were starting the aircraft was above the cargo area where the Swords were seated. Supplies in nicely bundled packages were between them and the rear door. Other Arrows responsible for maintenance and dropping the supplies laughed out loud at their Captain's comment as they went about their final checks.

Wit chimed in over their link with, "Thank you for your generous offer, but is there any chance you airheads could drop us off somewhere with fewer rocks? I already had some for breakfast."

Everyone aboard had a chuckle or groan at Wit's comeback as the final preparations were complete and the transport lifted off. Titus looked to his brothers. Each face had various levels of the same emotions - determination, calm, and joy. He felt the same, except for the added level of anxiety that came from knowing his decisions could lead to any one of his brothers going blue. He knew no Sword feared it, but the King had gifted him the responsibility of using the resources provided to the best of his ability. This included his brothers.

That said, the King had asked for him and his squad. Confidence from this one thought released much of the anxiety the Commander felt. The transport shook as it entered a speed capable of traveling between realms. Titus quietly thought that it was time to earn that confidence.

3

THE sudden halt to Wit's snoring was the only warning they all got as they entered the border realm. Their transport shuddered slightly as they reduced speed. Titus saw the cargo Arrows starting to move about and doing final checks on the supplies.

"Commander, this is Captain Ailey. Please join us in the cockpit."

Titus unstrapped himself and used the ladder to climb into the cramped cockpit just to the right side of the ship's gunner and behind the Captain. A gentle touch to Ailey's shoulder let her know he had arrived, and she pointed at the peaks off in the distance. "Just over those mountains is our destination. We will come in high from the northwest of the objective. I understand you want to do a drop into the southern forest."

It wasn't a question as the Captain was fully briefed on the plan, but Titus responded with an affirmative nonetheless.

"We don't doubt you helmet heads, but we will do a long u-turn to get some intel of the area and give cover if things get hairy in a hurry down there."

"Roger that, Captain. We appreciate it. Just make sure you get back home and keep it warm. It doesn't hurt to have some help from above."

Ailey gave a wink and a nod before going back to her instruments.

The Commander turned around and looked down on his squad, who looked expectantly at him with their orange eyes.

"Lieutenant. We are half a mark out. Get them up and ready."

Shay responded quickly by unstrapping himself and beginning to bark out orders. Each squad member immediately got up and checked their weapons quickly before strapping on their wings. While Swords didn't have the wings to fly like their siblings in the Voice clan, they could glide and slow their descent using their attachable 'wings'. When used high in the air, they would shoot out four energized glowing wings that enabled a slow and controlled descent. If the Voice clan had wings like an eagle, the Sword's packs would be more akin to a dragonfly's. Even though they were one use, they were incredibly effective for infiltration. Plus, if Titus had to admit it, they were fun.

As the team got each other ready for the drop, Wit looked towards Private John and, with an incredibly straight face, said, "Has anyone ever told you that you will make a beautiful blue statue?"

John stared silently at Wit before giving him a thumbs-up as the other brothers burst into laughter. The large Sword had taken the vow of babel as an offering to their King. He would not speak a word until the King claimed ultimate victory. Since communication was vital in combat, he used various whistles with different meanings when needed. Outside of that, the vow would not permit him to say a word. It wasn't common among the Swords, but it was a true testimony to John's devotion to their Maker.

Even though the clownish private's comment was meant in jest, each brother knew that this might be where they go blue. However, a bit of humor helped break the tension of the high-stress moment before a drop. Titus had to admit that Wit did have his uses.....occasionally.

Immediately after Shay signaled to Titus that the team was ready, the Captain announced they were coming over the drop zone. A countdown was initiated, and the back cargo door opened. When the timer reached zero, an Arrow hugging the right wall released a lever, and all their supplies were released. They would be dropped closer to the fort as they had the capacity to hover longer in the air and only come down after Titus confirmed they were on the objective.

When the last of the supplies were released, there were only a few heartbeats before a bright green light popped on, and Titus was running for the open air. First in and last out was not a requirement, but that particular type of leader was what the Maker had created Titus to be, and He never made mistakes. Titus and his brothers were literally created for this mission and, the King willing, more.

1-1-8 gathered in the free-fall to ensure no one was lost and landed in the same general area. Starting with Shay, one by one, they activated their wings. Titus went last to ensure his full squad would land safely and that he wouldn't need to rescue one of his men from becoming a dazzling blue crater.

Being the last to activate his wings, the Commander was the first to land. Without detaching his wings, he did a quick scan of his surroundings. They had indeed made it into the green, dark forest just south of the fort as he could make out the structures uphill and beyond dying trees. Even though it was night and dark, Titus was able to detect fresh prints on the ground a few hands in front of him. With sword drawn, he tapped into his team's link, which was their internal communication channel that allowed each member to speak to each other over short to medium distances. He didn't speak and instead gave the tap code that enemies were near. Five taps responded to confirm silence and awareness. The sixth tap wasn't heard, so Titus slowed his mind to start forming strategies for search and rescue that wouldn't delay their push toward their objective.

Just as he confirmed his strategy in his mind, two different sets of beady eyes appeared out of the darkness behind a copse of trees. Titus immediately identified them as kreehauns and that they were likely scouts from the fortress. Making their rounds and circling back, the enemy's luck just happened to put 1-1-8 in a tight spot.

The Commander sensed he was in trouble, tactically. While these two barely posed a physical threat, Titus knew the fort would be alerted to their presence if he used his ranged weapon. On the other hand, if he attempted to engage them with his primary, they would be able to shout a warning to the fort before he closed the distance. Either way, their element of surprise was about to be lost.

With their sharp claws and pointed tusks, the kreehauns pointed toward the Commander and looked as though they were about to cry out. However, before they took a step or could utter a scream, a very fast-moving form dropped straight from the sky and directly on top of the monsters. Twin daggers flashed in the moonlight as each blade found a home in either of the creature's skulls. Their bodies actually cushioned the fall of the flying object as it landed and twisted to make use of their now lifeless corpses.

Titus jogged over and gave Shay a hand up. "You good, LT?"

"Yes, sir. I saw these two from the sky." Shay continued as he wiped the black acidic ichor off of his blades to sheath them, "I moved to intercept after hearing your radio silence command, but the wings were slowing me down. Had to cut them off to reach them in time."

The Commander smiled at his second and gave the other team members the signal to rally on him using a circular motion with his raised hand as he whispered, "Of course you did."

As the team gathered, Titus could hear a few whispers and some barely audible mentions of SALT. That said, his team was professional, and they quickly took up positions in a circle with weapons trained outward and scanning for potential enemies.

With Titus in the center of the circle, he whispered out orders on their link. "Primary weapons only outside the fort. Save your energy and stay quiet. Armor has limited approval as we enter the confines of the fort itself. Move out."

Moving as one body with multiple parts, the team fanned out into an inverted "V" with Kurian at the apex, Shay on the right tail, and Killian on the left. Kurian's shield made him perfect to take point as he could respond to ambushes quickly and with protection. On the other hand, his twin and Shay's more nimble weapons made them invaluable as flankers who could spread out immediately upon contact. They had practiced movement like this since their creation, so no orders were even necessary as each member filed into their position with practiced ease.

The terrain wasn't too difficult to circumvent. Dead trees weren't much use as cover or concealment, so the team opted for speed as they exited the greener portion of the forest. With a quick hand gesture from the Commander, the team started to run. Unlike their enemies, who exude chaos in everything they do, a Sword unit ran with a precision that mimicked water. They flowed over obstacles and worked in perfect sync to close in on their objective.

As Titus had hoped, they reached the outer wall without any signs of their presence being detected. They had spied a breach in the wall that appeared to be hidden behind one of the outer structures. Similar to how they moved in the open, Kurian went in first quietly with his bladed shield raised. Following quickly behind were the heavy hitters of John and Marcus with their weapons raised. Titus and Wit followed after a brief hold to give them room to retreat or fight in a new area. Finally, Shay and Killian gave the same hold time and scanned their rear once more before following their brothers through the breach.

The Commander pointed to a tower in the southeast corner of the fort to their immediate left: "Lieutenant, I need you up high. Hold fire unless absolutely necessary, but ensure no one gets out."

"Roger."

Just like that, Shay disappeared into the darkness and was gone.

Titus continued giving orders to the rest of the team, "Alpha team will clear the outer buildings in the west of the courtyard and move to make entry into the main hall from the front. Bravo to the east, and we will hit the back. Move silently and kill everything."

Under the leadership of Titus, Alpha team consisted of Kurian, Wit, and Marcus. Shay would typically lead Bravo, but Killian filled in as the next ranking brother and would lead John. Both groups separated and began moving to their designated positions.

Inside the walls of the fort, the four small buildings on either side of the courtyard were in worse shape than even the intelligence had predicted. There was only a well set in the center of the courtyard, so Alpha team continued to move along the wall to get to their area of responsibility. By using the wall's shadows as cover, they also gave themselves the opportunity to clear the gate and small gatehouse.

Kurian led the way and held up a fist to halt the team just a stone's throw away from the gatehouse. No light emanated from the small stone structure that sat just inside and to the east of the gate, but after only a few heartbeats of waiting, the sound of claws clicking on stone floors could be heard.

The team's engineering and explosive expert held his shield hand up and gave the signal for two enemies ahead. While Titus was sure that Kurian, aka Boomer, would love to toss an energy bomb into the room in accordance with his namesake, it would not be the most subtle of ways to announce their presence. Instead, the Commander gave the signal for a silent takedown to Kurian. He nodded his acknowledgment and moved quickly to the entrance.

Some may have thought that a bladed shield was not the best option for close-quarters assassination. Titus guaranteed that those same dissenters had never seen a true master of the weapon at work. Kurian spotted both of his targets by peaking through a window. After confirming only two kreehauns were inside, he moved to make entry. Instead of using the door, which may give away his presence too early, he saw an opportunity and jumped through the window. Leading with his shield, he hit the first short kreehaun in the head with the center of his weapon, knocking it to the ground and unconscious. Using his forward motion, the sergeant rolled up and swung the bladed edge of the shield upward, eviscerating the second kreehaun from groin to chin. Before the gore and black acidic blood hit the ground on the dissected foe, Kurian had already turned and brought down the edge of his shield on the throat of the first, decapitating the foul creature. With no other targets, Kurian exited through the front door and continued leading Alpha to their assigned buildings. Not a single drop of blood had touched his tunic.

Both Alpha and Bravo had come to the same conclusion that none of the outer buildings were occupied, save the two sentries at the gatehouse. Nonetheless, while they cleared the buildings, it was obvious that no creatures would be in the buildings due to the fact that most were without roofs or had collapsed entirely.

"Alpha. This is Bravo. How copy? Over."

Titus responded, "Bravo. This is Alpha. Solid copy. Are you in position and prepared for entry? Over."

"Roger that, Alpha. Bravo is in position and can make entry through a hole in the northeast corner of the building. It appears to lead into a separate room with no visible sentries. We are ready to move on your go. Over."

"Alpha is in position and moving to enter in the main entry. See you on the other side, Bravo. Go, go, go!"

Simultaneously, both teams entered the hall on the final word. Alpha wasn't as lucky as Bravo in that there was no partitioned area for the main entryway. The second they entered, a half dozen kreehauns moving about the hall doing various tasks and minor repairs immediately turned to stare at the intruders.

Kurian took the center as usual with his shield as Marcus and his hammer moved right while Wit's wicked-looking spiked mace looked for enemies on the left. Titus filled in the rear with his sword as he would support whoever needed it.

An unlucky kreehaun to the right met Marcus's hammer in an almost comical way as he swung low to strike the unfortunate horde creature's abdomen. The result was something akin to squeezing the bottom of a full pudding cup with full strength.

Marcus continued to hammer at two other kreehauns as Wit engaged his first enemy. Titus nearly stopped his advance to the center of the room as he heard Wit begin talking to his mace.

"Good hit, Macey! Don't worry about the blood; I will clean you up later." He glanced up and muttered in glee, "Oh! Look! Another one is coming."

Wit dodged under a wide swing of the kreehaun's razor claws by sliding on his knees with his head going back and nearly touching the wood floor. He rose with a jump and flung himself against a wall to continue his momentum right back over the beast. Driving his mace into the head of the confused kreehaun and dragging its body down with him, ending the brief fight.

"Did you see that one, Macey? We are such a good team. Let's go find more things to kill!"

Titus quickly realized he was needed with Kurian as he was fending off three of the ugly beasts. His shield was a blur as it moved to intercept blows and even strike at a few limbs that got too overextended. While Titus did not doubt that Kurian would come out on top of these three, or even more, they needed to be done with this fight and secure the objective.

Without a word, Titus moved up behind Kurian, and they began syncing their movements instantly. Kurian slammed his shield down and broke off the claws of one enemy as Titus swung his blade in a circle above the knelt brother's head and cut the throats of two at a time. The third came in from the left, and Kurian high-blocked its attempt to stab the Commander. This time, Titus ducked down and stabbed into its gut. It gave an ear-piercing screech before Kurian's shield ended the sound by cutting the creature's windpipe.

After the beast's scream, there was suddenly a cacophony of grunts and clicking claws on floorboards. While some came from the east side of the building, the majority seemed to be moving in from the west. Just then, John smashed through a wall on their right and was followed by Killian, dodging swiping and kicking claws. Kreehauns poured in after them, and soon, the combined group was surrounded by the foul-smelling creatures moving in from both sides.

"Sir, I humbly request to go loud," Killian asked matter-of-factly. He may have been first, but the glint in every present member of the squad was clearly evident. The threat wasn't quite high enough, and they currently had no way of replenishing energy. On the other hand, time was working against them. Securing the objective had to be done now, and the element of surprise was already lost.

With only a barely perceivable smile, Titus replied with, "Granted. All gifts are authorized. Use at your discretion."

What occurred next was nothing short of a slaughter. With John, Marcus, Wit, and Titus himself opting for their Creator-powered armor that made them almost indestructible at the cost of their own energy and the twins choosing their ranged gifts, 1-1-8 turned the hall into a death trap for their enemies. The closest enemies were cut to pieces by the juggernauts in a semi-circle, and the mid-ranged threats were dealt with using Killian's rifle and Kurian's shotgun. Unfortunately for those in the rear who couldn't see what was happening, their forward push towards the Swords only served to force their comrades further into the meat grinder.

The battle did not last long, as there were only a hundred or so kreehauns within or underneath the structure. Titus and the Alpha team moved through the bodies and dispatched any that were still moving while Bravo moved to clear out the rest of the side rooms. A calm voice came over the radio.

"Commander. This is Shay. I have a group of kreehauns and what appears to be a legion member moving towards the mountains. I am attempting to engage now. Over."

"Copy on all. Don't let them get away. Over."

"Roger that, sir. Over and out."

4

SHAM had just laid down in his quarters to the left of the main hall when he heard the first scream. Knowing that his servants looked to him for strong leadership, he quickly ordered some of his servants to go see what was happening. However, before the three kreehauns could take a step, Sham heard something he had not in an eternity. Creator gifts.

Immediately, he used his brilliant tactical mind to determine that it was time for a hasty retreat. Using the three kreehauns, he ordered them to dig a hole out of his quarters to the outside. It took them only moments, and he was out.

The next objective was to get as far away from here as possible. And warn the legion, he added as an afterthought. It was the only sensible thing to do.

Holding to the main hall's western wall, he and his servants moved to the rear of the building. He then used a break in the fortress's outer wall to escape the danger zone. It was at least two mils to the foot of the mountains, and the tunnels he knew were there. At a dead sprint, he could make it there in no time.

With a quick kick to one of the worthless creatures, they started sprinting, and it wasn't long before they were within reach of the thicker woods. The feeling of safety was just creeping in when a brilliant white light struck the lead kreehaun in the back of the head and exited the front, along with most of the head's contents.

Sham dove to the right immediately as another two

energy projectiles ended his remaining kreehauns. Only after a few heartbeats did he hear the reverberation of a ranged gift. They were already well over a mil away from the fort! That could only mean one thing. This squad had a SALT. Sham prided himself on never truly fearing anything but couldn't quite get his body to believe the same thing as a paralyzing sensation took hold of him. The thought of the deadly ranged killing machine taking a bead on him crept up his back and seized his heart. He knew it was only a matter of heartbeats before the Sword would have him in his sights. Fighting down the fear, Sham knew he had to move, but he needed to be smart.

With all his energy focused on not dying, Sham's projected skin began to fade, revealing ugly red scars glowing under his ashen, decaying flesh. While the ash color would be perfect cover under the night sky, the red glow gave him away easily. He had to pull himself together if he was going to survive this nightmare.

Sitting behind a thick tree, Sham grabbed a limb on the ground and attached part of his tunic. Slowly, he stood up and held the scarecrow in front of him. After slightly leaning it to the right, towards the bodies of the kreehauns, and giving his final bit of concentration to covering his glowing skin once more, he let go of the stick and let it fall to the ground. Immediately, he ran out to the left towards a thicker stand of trees. Hearing a shot instead of feeling one gave Sham the confidence to sprint the final hundred hands to freedom with a grin.

Once he reached the relative safety of the thicker forest, and knowing that the caves were near, Sham slowed his sprint a little. Even with that assurance, he couldn't stop completely as he felt eyes watching him. He told himself it was just the phantom feeling of the SALT watching him from a distance, but there was something different about it. When he spotted two shiny, floating orbs in the forest, he again told himself that he wasn't afraid of anything. His body only slightly betrayed his lie as his feet once more began moving at a sprint.

****

Shay cursed to himself as he realized the ruse too slow. His energy would likely allow him a few more shots at this range, but he knew the enemy would be much harder to hit as he was aware of his hunter. It wouldn't be wise to waste his energy when he may still need it to pursue or continue the fight here in the fort.

"Commander. This is Shay. Three kreehauns dead, but the shadow is in the wind. Last seen moving towards the foot of the mountains. Requesting permission to pursue. Over."

"Understood, LT. Negative on the pursuit. Regroup with us. We will attempt to deal with the shadow once we secure the objective. Over and out."

The lieutenant did not like failing, but he could learn from it. He still had a job to do and the trust of his King to see it done. It was time to switch gears and continue with the mission.

Feeling the energy of Choice made, Shay dismissed his rifle and began climbing down from the tower. He drew his curved long daggers as he used the darkness to stealthily move towards the main hall. While he trusted his brothers to have cleared the buildings as they had passed, ensuring no enemies had relocated during the skirmish inside was prudent.

Satisfied that there were no hidden enemies waiting in ambush, he quickly moved to the main entrance. What he saw inside almost made him lose his typical cool composure. Literal mounds of bodies were stacked all around the hall. It was obvious from the sounds outside that a battle took place, but the visual was something to behold. While it would have taken his squad days to clear out the bodies, the acidic nature of horde blood did have one small positive quality upon their death. Slowly, they would dissolve themselves over the next few marks. Removal of the bodies would not be necessary, but some slight repairs of the floor could be in order with so many of them in one place. Shay could already tell that a number of the bodies near the bottom of the piles were in various phases of decomposition thanks to their brethren stacked on top.

The layout of the main hall had a fire pit in the center with benches on either side. Directly beyond the pit was a raised dais with a basic wooden throne chair. Immediately to his left and right were doors, and Shay could tell that they both led to a hallway with potential rooms based on the giant hole in the wall to the left. This made sense as the main hall room was a bit small compared to the overall structure.

In the main room, the Commander was speaking with Wit about attempting to get a line to command as soon as possible. Although unlikely due to the area's geography, communication with command could mean the difference between all members coming back or none. Shay was about to interrupt when their link pinged in their ears.

"1-1-8, this is 5. How copy? Over."

"5, we read you loud and clear. This is 1-1-8 actual. Over." Titus replied.

"Good to hear you are still kicking, Commander. Are you in need of support? Over."

"Negative. We hold the fort and no blue. Requesting intelligence on our surroundings and neighbors. Over."

"Roger that, sir. We did a sweep and will send down a scroll with our findings along with the rest of your supplies. It looks like you will all have some rowdy neighbors. I advise you not to stir up the nest. Over."

"Appreciate the info and advice. We had some legion company down here, and it appears they got away. It may not be possible to keep things calm. Over."

“Legion? Way out here? I read you, Commander, and will advise command as soon as we return. Over.”

“My thanks, Captain. We are working on getting communications up here, but at best, it will be hit or miss. Over.”

“Understood. Good luck out there, and come home with your handsome hue, understood? Over.”

Titus chuckled before responding with, “Handsome, huh? I will take that under advisement. Safe travels 5. 1-1-8 actual, over and out.”

Shay was near and appeared a bit depleted, both from energy use and for missing the shadow. They would need to have Killian set up their energy bridge ASAP to ensure they could all replenish. As for the mental frustration, that would clear itself here soon. It would be impossible for the lieutenant to stay down for long. Titus needed his team to be on point as their current status was behind enemy lines with no immediate support, unknown enemy positions or composition, and an unmovable defense position that was crumbling around them. There was a lot of work to do.

Titus was about to set Wit and Shay out to bring down supplies when Killian came over the radio, “Commander. You may want to come to the southeast corner. John and I have found something in the tomb below the main hall that you may want to see.”

“Copy that, Boomer. I am on my way.”

Titus set Shay in charge to begin directing Alpha team to tasks and made his way through the door to the far right of the main entrance. As he went through the door, a long hallway was to his left, with doors all to the right. The hole that Bravo had used to make a dramatic entry into the main hall was further up the hallway. Bravo had been sent to clear the remaining rooms after the battle.

The first door led to a spiral wooden stairway, which had a single hallway with a right turn leading them to a tomb immediately beneath the main hall. There was a hardened wooden door that put the main door upstairs to shame. Titus thought the enemy would need a battering ram to get through. If this was indeed the final position, he didn't think it was as bad as it could have been.

Just inside the door were Killian and John. While there was plenty of space within the cave-like crypt, the two junior brothers stood to either side of the door so Titus could see the majority of the room. Directly in the center lay a single stone casket adorned with intricate scenes and Creator images.

Titus could see them all clearly within the tomb, not due to his impressive night sight but rather due to the red flame that simply sat, unmoving, atop the center of the casket. It was beautiful yet no larger than a tiny candle. The red flame didn't act like a normal fire that danced and provided heat. As if the flame was dead in all normal ways, it simply stood still and existed as a light within the cold and eerie room.

Where the flame sat, a small bowl was carved out of the center of the casket. Clearly, the flame was meant to be housed within the bowl where it sat. The bowl's center held a beautiful star shape made from pure diamonds. The rim of the bowl, too, had a line of diamonds that helped capture and expand the light in the larger room. Based on the positioning of the flame on the casket and the small pinhole just above it, he knew that the flame was just beneath the center fire pit in the main hall above. Due to the chimney above the pit, Titus realized that there was a small but direct line from the flame to the sky.

If Titus had to take an educated guess, he would say that they had found what they were sent to protect.

Wit came over the radio and broke the silence of the moment: "Commander, we have our supplies and the intel from the airheads. You will want to come see this, sir."

"On my way." Titus switched to the team channel with a thought and sent out an order to regroup in the main hall.

As the Swords left the room and strange flame, they didn't notice the tiny black vine cut into the very stone of the casket. Even if they had noticed it in the far right corner, they were gone when it sprouted a thorn.

5

IT was 4:23 AM on a Saturday when the warmth was ripped away from him. The soothing, rhythmic sound he had known his whole life was gone and replaced with a cacophony of noises that seemed to assault multiple senses. Strange things prodded him and held him tight. Quickly, he screamed and moved every ounce of himself to fight against the unknown assailants. However, that only seemed to cause those around him to restrain him in a tight cloth.

When all hope seemed lost, he heard their voices. The same voices that had comforted him and spoke to him for all of his existence. He recognized them, and suddenly, everything didn't seem as scary as it once was.

The masculine voice said, "Here he is! Our Henry is here, Arlene. You did such a great job, my love!"

"Honey, he looks just like you," came the feminine reply.

Henry didn't understand what was happening but was glad to latch on to something familiar. While nothing made sense, he knew that the comfort that these two provided was all he needed at that moment.

Arlene spoke down to Henry as she held him in her arms, "Welcome to the world, my little miracle."

The loving woman's husband, Carl, was giddy as he stood next to his wife and newest son, "We love you, little man. Your older brother Jace and sister Jules are excited to meet you."

"Let's just enjoy this alone time with our son. There will be time to introduce him to the rest of the family soon enough."

"Yes, of course, love," Carl responded before taking a breath and continuing, "Look at him. He is perfect. God is good."

"Just what I would expect a pastor to say," Arlene responded with a twinkle to suggest teasing.

"My congregation just expanded by one, so I must be doing something right," Carl said with a wink.

Within two hours of Henry's birth, the delivery room door swung open, and a brand new set of doctors entered.

"So soon? Does it have to be now," Henry's mother questioned the new doctors.

The lead looked at Henry and responded, "Congratulations, but I am afraid so. The cancer is aggressive, and while I understand your decision, we have put off treatment long enough. Your son is born, and it is time to start thinking about yourself."

Henry felt tension in the room as his mother handed him to Carl, which made him cry for a moment before the comforting sounds of his father talking to him began to soothe him again.

"Your mother and I love you so much, Henry. No matter what happens, know that we will always pick you over ourselves. She proved that many times during these last months."

Henry didn't understand anything, but he felt at ease in his father's arms and listened to the sounds he made as he continued to talk to him.

"Mommy is very sick, but she refused to put you in danger. Now that you are safe, she has to start working on getting herself healthy. Sound good, right buddy?"

"Don't you worry," Arlene said from the bed and added, "Either of you! Cancer is nothing to me or God. This sickness chose the wrong person to mess with."

"Your mom is one tough lady, Henry," Carl said, but the look and firm hold he gave Henry was not as confident as his words. It was clear as day that Arlene was in for a major uphill battle.

Whether it was that thought or something exiting his body, Henry started to feel upset. Maybe both. Either way, the outcome was clear as he only had a single response to anything at that point in his life - cry.

Carl moved to change his son's diaper as the doctors continued to work on getting Arlene ready for treatment. It seemed as though Henry's mother would not be leaving, which made him happy as he instinctively knew he needed her.

After his diaper was changed, Henry felt a new sensation that he had never had before, and it was one he didn't like. Of course, he had to let others know.

"Sounds like he is hungry," Arlene said.

"I got it," Carl quickly responded as he pulled out a fresh bottle of donor milk.

"Carl," Arlene hesitantly started, "maybe I should hold off for a bit more to give him mine.."

She was immediately cut off as Carl said, "No. Absolutely not. We are not delaying a moment longer. Besides, we have donor milk and formula. We looked into it and discussed it. Our child will be healthy and happy either way, but he needs his mother."

With a sigh, Arlene nodded in agreement. Her kids needed her, and that meant starting treatment immediately.

As Henry's mother started her treatment, Carl took Henry out into the hall to walk and attempt to lull him into sleep. During the walk, Carl spoke to his son in a calming tone on many topics. He told him stories of his own past and hopes for Henry's future. Carl was not always kind or the best at making good choices in his previous life. During the military, he made extremely poor choices, which led him to one of the lowest points of his life in which he contemplated suicide. If it were not for a friend who had realized the path that Carl was on and had directed him to a local church, it is a very good possibility that Henry's father would have eventually gone through with it. With God, the young soldier had found meaning and a new understanding of the world. After separating from the military, he went on to seminary school to become a pastor. It was actually in school that he had met Arlene. Together, they grew in faith and love, which eventually led to marriage not long after graduation.

After the conversation and walk, Henry was fast asleep, and Carl had a hard time keeping his own eyes open. He walked back into Arlene's room and placed his child in the bassinet next to his sleeping wife before walking over to the tiny bed that always seemed to come in these types of hospital rooms. While he didn't look forward to the uncomfortable foam mattress, the army had definitely taught him to sleep just about anywhere. This was proven as he immediately fell into a deep sleep when his head hit the tiny sterile pillow.

Henry didn't like his bassinet and needed to alert someone right away. Still only having the one ability so far, he cried. His mother came into view as she picked him up and held him close, which helped. However, it was her song that helped calm him the most. Not knowing it at the time, it was the same song she had sung to all of her children and the same one that his grandmother had sung to her. Apparently, his mother had never claimed to have the best voice, but she did often lead worship at their small church. Later, she would tell Henry that God viewed worship as a reflection of the heart versus how good the voice was.

After she laid Henry back down into the bassinet, Arlene gave a quick kiss to her sleeping husband before returning to her own bed just as she felt the pain starting to return. Thankfully, she had a strong stomach that helped her avoid most of the vomit that often came with her cancer treatment. More than anything, she knew that getting quality sleep was key. With that thought in her mind and a prayer for Henry, she started to drift off. Unfortunately, what awaited her in those first dark hours of the night were nightmares - full of monsters.

6

1-1-8 wasted no time in fortifying their new home. After bringing down their supplies into the large courtyard, which had a well in the center and two decrepit buildings to either side, Titus started issuing orders to his team.

"LT, I still need you up high and on overwatch. Work on repairing the tower in the northwest corner while keeping an eye out for unwanted guests. I suspect that the closest horde group is likely in the mountains."

Shay was already moving at the final word spoken as he gathered the needed supplies and confirmed his orders. Some of the devices they had brought were strictly for construction and were marvels in their own right. Some could repair an entire house by themselves, whereas others helped make the precise work of Host members that much easier. The lieutenant had grabbed one of the repair devices that would work autonomously as he ensured that no enemy caught them unaware.

"John and Marcus, I need you to clear out the dead trees within a mil of the fortress and stack them in regular groups just outside the heavy tree line. We need to be able to see everything within range of this fortress."

The shorter but heftier of the two stood with his axe and gave a nod before grabbing a trailer and heading outside the gates, quickly followed by the taller private. While the Creator had given them incredible strength that would allow any of them to easily carry one or two trees by hand, the trailer would allow his team to stack more than ten large trees and move them with barely a thought.

"Doc, I need an energy bridge right away."

Killian responded with, "Understood, sir. I know just the place to set up. Leave it to me."

Due to the fact that Killian was their battle healer, it was an obvious inevitability that he would get the nickname 'Doc'. Depleting their energy in either wounds or in the use of their gifts would cause them to go blue and take them out of this fight, as well as future fights leading up to the final battle. It was Killian's duty and responsibility to ensure that the team stayed in the fight for as long as the King willed it. Outside of direct orders from leadership in a battle, Killian had the authority to order even Titus to fill himself or stop using energy. The energy that the Creator gave was an abundant resource but extremely precious.

Killian set out to set up a single point of contact with the King's energy and realm, also known as a bridge. Since they were outside of his overwhelming presence in this realm, they would each need to spend time near the bridge to refill their internal stores. The sergeant is trained to locate the optimum location for the device, both for best connectivity and tactically. If they were to lose their bridge in a heated fight, their time would be measured in marks, not cycles.

With Killian off, Titus turned to his twin - Kurian. The similarities between the two were extremely striking, Titus thought. Of course, all members of the Host were brothers and sisters, but they also were very unique. Kurian and Killian were nearly identical in shape and looks. While they both had almost completely opposite expertise, they knew that they worked well together and didn't mind the nickname of twins given by their brothers. In fact, they were quoted once as saying, 'Creator made me and saw that it was good, so He made another me!' It was unclear which one spoke it at the time, but the team took to calling them the twins soon after.

"I need these walls repaired, Boomer. Use the building

materials around the breaches, but only use these internal buildings if needed."

"Copy that, sir. It will be done."

As the engineering expert, Kurian had a deep understanding of not only how to take things apart but also how to put them together. During training, he would often create magnificent structures and towers that were truly works of art. However, a real smile lit up his face when he made them collapse with tiny, well-placed charges or, his favorite, one huge explosion.

After Kurian gathered what was needed for his newest construction project, Wit stood next to the Commander, looking out over the various team members with almost a wistful expression, "They grow up so fast. Am I right, sir?"

Titus's quick, stern look was all it took to snap Wit back into professional mode.

"I know what you are going to say, but I already got started. The communications station is fortified in the second building on the right in the courtyard," said the communication expert as he pointed to the most solid-looking building of the four outside the main hall. He continued, "As expected, communication is finicky at best, and I haven't heard anything since the airheads took off a few marks ago."

Titus surveyed the building and saw the hint of a communications tower sticking out of the roof. Wit had assembled the station and even constructed some formidable cover within the building in case it was hit with any type of artillery. Even though Wit could be frustrating at times, there wasn't a doubt that he was simply the best at what he did. Titus suddenly felt very humble that the Creator had seen fit to place him in charge of such elite warriors.

"Sir. Requesting permission to find snacks."

Elite warriors. Right.

Without a response, Titus began moving towards the

communications building with Wit in tow. As he moved closer, he felt his own internal link grow stronger and was searching wider for similar connections. Confirming what Wit had just reported, the mountain range to their west and north was bouncing his request back to him. When Titus attempted to stretch his mind to the east and south, there was only darkness and anti-life in that direction. He knew that one of the legion's primary cities was not incredibly far to the east, but the darkness to the south somehow surprised him. It was unexpected that their reach had gotten so far.

"Wit, you did excellent work. I need you to continue by helping Boomer with the walls." At the first statement, Private Amadon beamed, but Titus saw how the second quickly stole away his enthusiasm.

"Roger that, sir."

As the private walked away, Titus returned to his previous thoughts regarding his team. He knew that Wit would do as commanded, and there was never a doubt he would do it to the best of his ability. Jokes aside, he was an elite warrior - snacks or no snacks.

The dark feeling to the south made Titus re-review the intelligence that Arrow 5 had provided with their supplies. He brought the scroll out and rolled it onto a table near the communications tower. Immediately, a map appeared, and his team was blinking as tiny blue lights outside of the extremely detailed rendering of the fortress as it was last night. A hundred red lights that likely represented the kreehauns were spread primarily in the main hall with a few outside of it, which were likely the two that Kurian had dispatched in the guardhouse. A single black dot was in one of the secondary rooms within the main hall. Why was the legion here in the first place? What did they hope to gain? Did they expect the King's creation ahead of time? Was it dumb luck? Unfortunately, Titus didn't have the answers to these questions. He needed more information and thought he might know where to get answers.

The Commander spread his hands in an expanding way over the map, and it zoomed out to make the fortress just a small structure. Just as it did when he and the team first looked at the map, it shocked Titus to see the extent of red dot concentration to their southwest, south, southeast, and east. In summary, with the mountains to their west and north, they were surrounded by potential thousands of horde creatures.

Looking south, there were fewer dots, but they appeared much larger than the others. They could be one of the larger siege monsters, but there was a small indicator on them that they were moving. Bullans could be stampeding through the area, which would spell trouble for 1-1-8 if they decided to continue north, but it could just be turtairs or farhatches migrating slowly to find something to crush. Titus hoped it was the latter as it would give them more time to prepare. He would have Marcus give the scroll a more thorough review later to try and confirm.

As Titus moved the map, he saw a smaller but more threatening collection of tiny dots only a few mils east of their current location. Those dots were known to all Swords, as their size meant they could only be one thing—bréag. He would need to prepare his brothers for that fight, and soon.

To the southeast were decrypt structures on the shore of a body of water that may have been a great lake but appeared more like a swamp now. Seeing how these were the only other standing structures in the area, they were his target as potential sources of information. That said, the fact that they were the only structures was not the only reason it had piqued his interest. The collection of red dots in that area seemed more concentrated than in any other on the map. It was almost as if they were protecting something or hiding it. Either way, it would be rude not to introduce themselves to their neighbors.

Lastly, the few golden dots to the north were a mystery for which none of them had answers. However, they also did not feel threatened, as many of their King's creations in the realms were mostly peaceful. They had found the remains of one such creature in the main hall and provided a proper burial for it.

After finishing his latest review of the scroll, Killian was next to announce that his task was done and the energy bridge was available in the main hall. Titus went to check where he had placed it and began filling his own stores. He would rotate his men through as they all had used Creator energy in their fight.

When he entered the main hall, he was a bit surprised to see Killian had set up the bridge at the foot of the small throne. Titus had expected to find the sergeant in the tomb, as that would be their final defensive position anyway. Clarifying, he explained that the tomb was no good as the connection underground was weak. After reviewing the options and weighing tactics against connection, Killian had decided that the throne would be the optimum position. It had a strong connection with their King and was in the middle of the last defensible building. Should the enemy push them into the tomb below, a weak bridge wouldn't help them. Tactically, it made the most sense to have it in the strongest connection position so they could fill themselves quickly to get back in the fight.

The bridge did indeed have a strong connection as Titus felt his stores of energy filling rapidly. Killian had already filled himself, but he would have had very little to fill anyway. As their assigned healer, he would reserve as much of his energy to share with his brothers in desperate times. The battle last night had hardly drained him as his smaller ranged gift did not use as much energy as others.

Once the Commander had received his fill, he went to relieve Shay while sending Killian to do the same for Kurian. The bridge would only fill one Sword at a time, but

Doc's placement had ensured that the restoration process would be quick.

Titus moved towards the tower in the northwest and noticed that it had nearly been fully repaired. While the construction devices would repair just about any structure, it was limited to what resources were available. It appeared as though the tower wouldn't be fully enclosed as it likely once was, but it had a strong-looking roof and a waist-high stone wall near the top. Shay would be put to deadly effect in such a perch.

After climbing the tower, he approached Shay from behind as he kept watch towards the mountains. Even though the Commander had not made a single sound while approaching, the SALT spoke to him without even turning his head.

"Commander. You seem to be filled. Doc has the bridge up." Not really a question, but it was just a little unnerving to have his team member know so much without even glancing in his direction.

"Correct. I came up to relieve you. Head on over so we can get everyone back up to full strength. Come back when you are done, and I will go relieve another."

"Roger that, sir." But before he began the climb down the new internal tower ladder that Titus had just used, he added, "Keep an eye on the mountains. That is where the enemy will likely come from."

The Commander thought that was interesting, as Shay was there when they first reviewed the intelligence that was provided by their Arrow. It was obvious that there were horde groups closer, and nothing had pinged from the mountains.

"Last night, the Shadow moved towards the mountains even though the legion city is to the east."

"Perhaps the mountains were just the more defensible position? He did have you breathing down his neck."

"Right, but he didn't know about me before making his

move towards the mountains. I don't put it past a shadow to make a quick retreat, but he made a deliberate Choice to not go directly toward his foul brothers for support. It is my opinion that there is a great force hiding in the caves at the foot of the mountain."

"That is quite a leap in theory, but I hear what you are saying, LT. What is your suggestion?"

"We need to secure our back before we move forward. I don't know what is in there, but I say we don't let it leave."

"Work with Boomer on a solution and give it to me. He is moving to meet you at the bridge. See what you two can come up with. I agree that we can't be surprised, but it may be more important to handle the enemy we know of before going after the one we don't. There are Choices being made by forces outside our control that will undoubtedly impact our fight. It is our duty to be prepared for all of them."

"Understood, sir."

With that, the lieutenant was gone, and Titus was left to keep watch and ponder his next steps. If Shay was right and there was a contingent of enemies with unknown composition just two mils to their north, it was a threat that had to be dealt with before dividing his forces to explore and gather more intelligence. His defensive plans were already in motion, but they did require a small reprieve before the next contact with the enemy.

A few short marks later, Shay returned and outlined his and Kurian's plan. It was good and wouldn't require the full squad. Titus gave permission to move forward after the full squad was re-energized and had finished their assigned tasks.

Titus trusted his brothers and gave them a large amount of freedom to accomplish tasks or change their tactics as they saw fit. He would be responsible for the overall strategy and give detailed instructions when needed, but each brother was an absolute expert in their assigned areas. It would be foolhardy of any leader not to trust them to get things done in the most effective and efficient way.

It wasn't long before the team had finished all of the defensive upgrades. The walls were repaired and improved to the point that Titus doubted the enemy could even put a dent in it with even their largest abominations. Kurian had even repaired the smaller southeast tower, which was roughly the same construction as the northwestern tower that Shay had repaired with the machine. Not to be outdone by a machine, Kurian reinforced the upper half walls and made ports for them to engage the enemy with their ranged gifts in relative safety.

All the ugly dead trees were cleared for a mil in every direction around the fortress and stacked in groups at regular intervals at the edge of each clearing. It would be nearly impossible for any type of monster or shadow to sneak up on them.

With the tasks complete, Titus agreed to have Shay and Kurian set out to enact their plan to deal with the potential threat to the north. Splitting such a small group like 1-1-8 could be disastrous, but there were no immediate threats, and Shay would ensure both he and Kurian remained silent. Besides, there always needed to be a few brothers available to defend their assigned objective. Failure to uphold the orders of their King and leave their objective undefended was simply not going to happen.

He wished his two brothers well and began assigning out new tasks and rotations of watch. The strategy was sound, and the reasonings were pure, but there was something that kept nagging at him that not all was well here, within the fortress itself and in the air. Something was telling him that separating was a mistake. Almost as if there was already an enemy among them, and he would need every Sword hand, and more, to fight it. Titus trusted his feelings, but the strategy eventually won. However, that didn't stop him from ordering the team to be on high alert and move Killian to the tomb as he watched Shay and Kurian disappear into the woods.

7

IT was 2:43 PM on a Friday when Henry went to his first-ever birthday party. He was becoming a big boy, according to his parents. At the age of 4, he didn't feel like a big boy compared to his brother and sister. They got to do more exciting things like go to school, have slumber parties, and even stay up much later than him. He didn't understand why they would call him big, but he didn't look any bigger when he looked in the mirror. He just hoped that we would be big enough one day to take down his older brother, Jace, when they wrestled. Henry always seemed to lose until Daddy showed up to take them both down.

Henry loved to wrestle and play with his dad, but lately, Daddy was always very tired and wasn't around the house very much. Jace tried to play with him sometimes, but he didn't make up fun rules like Daddy did and couldn't throw him into the sky.

For Henry's first big party, Jace and Jules had stayed behind with their dad. Henry had asked his dad to come, but Mommy wanted to see her sister and get out of the house like Henry did. A special date with Mommy did help make Henry feel better about the choice. He and his mommy didn't get out much, so he was sure they would have fun together.

When they got to the giant playground where his cousin was having the party, Henry couldn't believe his eyes! There was a bouncy house, a man making balloon animals, lots of sweet snacks, and a ginormous pile of presents. He was so excited that he didn't even know where to start.

After letting go of his mommy's hand and taking off at a sprint, his feet decided for him as the bounce house was where he got to first. His cousin, Kurt, was already inside and yelling with joy as he bounced around a group of kids Henry had never seen before. He quickly stripped off his shoes like the other kids had done and started crawling into the inflated play structure.

Arlene had yelled to Henry to be careful as he ran off from her, but it was evident that her son was too excited to hear anything she said. She approached the pile of gifts and placed their small gift bag among the hordes of others. As she walked towards her sister, she noticed a few glances in her direction. It was not uncommon, as the new round of treatment had made her bald once more. While it never felt good to be pitied, she had made peace with the stares long ago and would not waste her precious energy on social anxiety.

Elizabeth saw her sister approaching and called out to her, "Sister! I am so glad you and Henry could make it. We haven't seen you all in ages!"

"Thank you for the invitation! Henry has been cooped up lately and is in desperate need of some social time."

Arlene did not mention that Henry had primarily been at home because of her. With Carl working two jobs of pastoring and construction in an attempt to stay on top of her medical bills and her lack of energy, Henry wasn't able to go out much anymore. While she missed her husband, Henry often lamented how he wished he could see his daddy more, and both she and Carl understood that sacrifices had to be made. Money was especially tight as the church had been losing members at a steady pace. She prayed that things would change once she beat cancer again. That said, it did break her heart to see her baby boy trapped at home every day without a present father and an energy-less mother.

Henry was a trooper, though, and was a big help to her.

They did everything together, and she just knew that she would cry her eyes out when he started school. She looked towards her little companion as his face lit up with joy in the bounce house.

As the party progressed, Elizabeth called for all the kids to come to have cake and open presents. Henry followed his cousin out of the bounce house and went to get his shoes. A boy who looked much larger and older than him was reaching for an awesome-looking pair of shoes with dinosaurs on them when suddenly he stopped and pointed at Henry's shoes. "Yuck! These shoes smell terrible." He lifted Henry's shoes up for emphasis as he continued, "They are so old they have holes in them! These must belong to a poor person."

A poor person? Henry didn't understand what that meant, but he knew by the reaction of the other kids that it wasn't good. He suddenly felt very ashamed and didn't want to claim them as his. However, his cousin didn't have that reservation and tried to be helpful by pointing out Henry as the owner. While not out of bad intentions, Henry couldn't help but wish he didn't have a cousin at that moment.

Face completely red from embarrassment, he walked over to the boy and asked for his shoes. The boy threw the shoes in disgust toward Henry and asked, "Why don't your parents buy you a new pair? Are you so poor you can't afford shoes? Maybe you shouldn't ever leave the house, poor boy." Henry didn't quite understand all of what the bigger boy was saying, but the reaction of laughing from the other kids made him all the more red.

Kurt's mom yelled again for the kids to hurry up, and all the children quickly forgot about Henry and took off toward the outdoor structure that housed the sweets and presents—all of them except Henry. He stood there, looking down at his shoes, and began crying. It wasn't long before his mommy came up to him and hugged him. Between gasps of air and tears, Henry looked at his mother and asked one question: "Are we poor?"

"Where did you hear such a thing, my love?"

"The other kids said my shoes were gross, and we are poor because I don't have nicer shoes."

"Shoes and things do not make someone rich or poor, sweetheart. We may not have all the nice things that other kids do or parties like your cousin, but we have something of great value worth more than all those things put together."

"We do?" asked Henry excitedly.

"Of course! We have the love of our Father in heaven. He gives us everything we need and more. Our family is very blessed with love for each other and from God." Henry already didn't like that answer at all, but his mommy continued, "What you are experiencing is called envy. It digs deep and breaks us down from the inside out. God doesn't want us to break down. Instead, He wants you to be happy with what He gives you and what He has blessed you with. You don't have to think about what other people have. God has already given you a lot to be thankful for."

Once she stopped, Henry realized that he really didn't like the answer. He wanted newer shoes and fun parties. Even at 4, he knew that what Mommy was saying was that he would not get what he wanted.

With only a hint of embarrassment and a lot of frustration, Henry responded with, "I want new things! I don't want to be poor!"

After emphasizing his point with a stomp of his foot and throwing his shoes into the bushes nearby, Henry turned and ran away. Arlene didn't have the energy to chase him, so she opted to get his shoes out of the bushes. A kind parent saw her struggle and offered to get Henry, who was hiding behind a nearby wall. She politely refused but did take them up when they offered to fetch the shoes that were further into the bush than she could reach.

Henry cried for a while before the thought of cake made him want to get up and join the others. Eventually, he calmed down and nearly forgot about the shoe incident.

Once everyone had gotten their fill of cake, it was time for presents. Henry's cousin had so many kids at the party that it would have taken him all day to open half of the gifts given to him. Kurt's parents opted to have him open just a few, so he chose the biggest ones there. Each one he opened was better and greater than the last! First, it was a new batting cage for practicing his T-ball. Next, it was a giant T-rex robot that moved and made sounds while shooting balls from its back cannon. The final box contained a brand-new car that he could drive himself!

Henry had never seen toys like this and instantly wanted to play with all of them. Every kid there was begging to play with that toy, but the parents decided it was time to go home. Henry couldn't believe it! They had just seen the best toys ever, and he couldn't even play with them? He wanted not only the toys but also the party, the nice shoes, and even Kurt's mom! She was giving everything to her son. Why couldn't Henry's mom do that for him?

As Arlene and Henry got into the car, she asked him if he had a good time. After a few moments of silence, Henry asked, "Can I have a party like that when it is my birthday? With a bounce house, balloons, and all those cool presents?"

His mom smiled at her boy, but there was sadness in her eyes. "No, honey. We can't. I am sorry."

"I wish I was Kurt. I wish I wasn't poor." As he spoke, Henry took off his shoes and threw them out the open car window.

8

SHAM'S stay was short in the tunnels as he needed to move out and move on. It was now his sacred task to bring news of the Sword team taking the outpost to his king. Sham would, of course, ensure that his leader was aware of his martial combat prowess during the fight and that he had literally no choice but to pull back in order to warn his king. After defeating a few Swords himself, naturally.

Sham repeatedly practiced his conversation with the king as he traveled across the terribly boring prairie to the east until he absolutely believed the lies. He knew that any good lie was simply the truth to someone else. Besides, there wasn't much else he could do to entertain himself as he couldn't even bring some of the kreehauns from the caves. They were slow to begin with but nearly blind out in the open as well. He would have had to practically carry them himself if he wanted any of them to come along.

After entering the caves and tunnels at the foot of the mountain, Sham immediately took command of the kreehauns he found hiding there. It was not an inconsequential number of horde creatures living beneath the mountain. He had known about it after watching a large group of his servants appear from there once they had smelled blood from the dumb winged creature he had tortured and killed. Sham's brilliant mind had deduced that there would be more where they came from. He was not disappointed after his arrival.

However, it was clear to Sham that even with this larger force, he would still not have enough to remove the now-embedded Sword team. He needed to get to liberation city for reinforcements. The king would surely give him an army or at least a company of shadows and stones to retake the territory. Upon his return, he would bolster his forces with the hidden army in the mountains to ensure victory. Sham had always known he had superior intelligence over his brothers, and this reality would soon become even more evident to everyone. He just needed the stupid creatures not to give away their position. Before leaving to deliver his report to the king, he gave orders to their leader not to leave the caves for any reason. Well, he thought it was their leader... Sham did have to slaughter a handful to get his point across to the others. He had assumed the leader was the tallest of the hidden creatures and had spoken to it directly, but who knew how these odorous monsters decided anything among themselves. Maybe it was the smelliest among them? Either way, he believed they had gotten the point.

Sham's mind was turning and plotting against all possible outcomes as he ran across the prairie towards the sea and his passage into liberation city. It was easy for him to miss the camouflaged skin of something that was shadowing his movements at a distance.

****

Shay and Boomer moved up through the forested hills towards the mountains at nearly a dead sprint. While they moved as fast as the wind, no sound or evidence of their passing was left. The sergeant did his best to keep an eye on his own steps and on the SALT leading him, but it was sometimes an impossible task. He would cast his glance to the ground as he leaped over a fallen tree, only to instantly look back up and realize he had lost his superior. It had become a common enough issue that all he had to do was slow his pace for Shay to make himself known. Kurian would once again take up the run as they acknowledged each other.

The tunics they wore allowed for a change of color and pattern to conceal themselves. They activated this as they ran up through the hills. Each member of the Sword clan had tunics that covered the majority of their body with a small measure of extra cloth hanging between their legs forward and back. That said, not all tunics were the same. Some of his fellow brothers and sisters had differences in their attire, such as sleeves that covered their arms or shorter pants. Kurian himself had shorter sleeves but longer pants. In His infinite wisdom, the Creator had taken it to another level with the members of SALT. It was said that each one was covered from head to toe in an invisibility cloak, but that was only said by those who had never met one of the elite force. Kurian knew that, in actuality, they simply had their tunics extend from head to toe. A hood covered their head with a half mask covering their face from the nose down. Longer sleeves extended to their wrists with small straps of the cloth, even wrapping around their knuckles and between their fingers, exposing only the fingers themselves. With that level of camouflage available, it was a wonder he could keep eyes on his lieutenant at all.

Of course, it also didn't help that there wasn't a small amount of explosives strapped to Kurian's back. He comforted himself with the fact that he may have done better keeping up with the SALT if he didn't have to worry about blowing himself up and probably half the forest with them.

As they climbed higher, they started reaching boulders and rocky outcroppings, which signaled that they had reached the mountains. After only a few moments of searching, they located a cave opening that was clearly made by kreehaun hands. Boomer started getting to work after they cleared the opening of any potential enemies. He set explosives at regular intervals down the cave opening that would only explode after the trip wire that was set at the entrance triggered. Their plan was not only to seal the tunnel but to cause maximum damage to any number of enemies attempting to come out by collapsing the ceiling backward from the entrance.

While Kurian was doing his thing in the cave, Shay was doing his by scouting the area. It was evident that he was right in his initial assessment of the threat. Not only were there a multitude of various claw prints surrounding the area outside the tunnel, but in his quick scouting around the area, there were no less than ten other entrances. He used his internal link to alert Kurian of the situation and to let his brother know that he would be scouting further to discover if there were more. Shay silently hoped that the explosive expert had brought enough bombs. He doubted they would get a second chance at their plan.

****

Titus felt it in the air long before his body started reacting to it. The body of a Sword was meant to handle some of the most extreme environments and was immune to all sickness and most poisons. Even as his eyes began inexplicably watering, and his breath was stolen from his body, Titus couldn't escape a sense of familiarity with the toxin. He was sure that he had never felt this before, but something beneath the surface of the wrongness spoke to him.

The first of them to report the symptoms was Doc himself. It wasn't long before they all fell victim. The mystery of the problem only added to the foreboding that hadn't stopped dogging the Commander since his second had set off with Boomer.

While it was an annoyance, there was no true threat to the sickness. It was identified as an airborne substance when Doc performed an analysis of the environment upon feeling the initial symptoms. Marcus had reviewed all the scrolls on horde creatures and tactics of the legion, but nothing recorded matched the description of what they were experiencing. That said, Titus was not going to take chances. He recalled all members from their tasks to place them in a defensive posture while sending John with Wit to clear the fort room by room. Killian was also performing more tests, so Titus took a position in Shay's tower, which was in the northwest portion of the fort.

Once in position, Titus noticed that his symptoms had lessened after exiting the main hall. Doing some quick thinking, he told Killian to sprint out of the fort's entrance about five hundred hands and run a test there. After he was done, Titus told him to do a similar test to the west and east of the fort. When Killian returned, he confirmed what Titus had feared. The substance was weaker outside the fort but grew stronger as time passed.

Considering that Killian was the first to feel its' effects, both he and Titus returned to the tomb beneath the hall. Upon opening the door to the crypt, the thickness of the airborne substance was to the extent that it could literally be seen. Yellowish-green spores floated and combined in the room, making the entire tomb cast in a putrid color. While the flame above the stone coffin continued to burn red, it actually only added to the sickening atmosphere. Titus felt as though sickness itself had come to claim the tomb.

To ease their discomfort, Titus authorized the use of their armor within the room. Both he and Killian felt instant relief, but tiny bits of their energy were constantly being drained, and their armor lit up as though they were being attacked by an army of microscopic enemies. Not wanting to waste their energy more than needed, with weapons in hand, they quickly began scanning the room for any potential sources of the attack.

Only after a very detailed search did they locate the strange black-thorned vine that seemed to be growing from the very base of the coffin. It pulsed like a diseased heart that spread poison instead of life. Touching it directly seemed to have the same effect as the airborne spores but a more extreme dose. The amount of energy it zapped from them made it clear that they would not attempt to touch it a second time. Seeing how it was directly carved into the side of the coffin, attacking it or cutting it out seemed impossible without damaging the very thing they were there to protect.

As inexplicable as it had started, suddenly, the pulsing stopped, and the spores began clearing. Within moments, both Killian and Titus dismissed their armor without discomfort. Perplexed, they emerged from the crypt, and Titus discussed their discovery with the rest of the team as Killian refilled his energy using the bridge.

"What do you think it is, Marcus?" Titus asked their knowledge seeker.

"As we previously discussed, there is no mention of this in the enemy scrolls." Before Titus could interject with the obviousness of the statement, Marcus continued, "If we rule out horde and legion, there are very limited options of what it could be. We could be witnessing a natural creation of this realm." Again, Titus was about to interject, but Marcus quickly added, "However, the fact that the direct source had such a negative effect on you and Doc leads me to believe that it is not anything the Creator has made." Marcus went silent for a long pause, almost like he expected Titus to respond, but eventually wrapped up with, "In summary, Commander, I have no idea what is going on."

"Thank you for the report, private," Titus responded a little tersely.

With nothing else for it, Titus dismissed the team to return to heightened security positions, in addition to moving Marcus down into the crypt with Killian. Something was not right, and even though the spores were now fully dispersed, Titus's knot within his chest refused to let go. Now more than ever, the Commander felt he needed his team here and ready for battle.

****

Shay had located four additional caves and tunnels above the initial ten. True to his name, Boomer had indeed brought enough charges to make their plan work. They were in the midst of rigging the final cave, which was actually the largest they had found, when the Commander came over the internal radio, albeit a little broken. Being close to the mountains was messing with the communications, but the signal was still reaching them.

"Alp... eam.... Come in. Ov.."

"Bravo team to Alpha team. We copy, but you are coming in broken. Over," Shay responded to the communication and hoped his response was making it back to their leader more clearly than what they were receiving.

"Bravo tea... do you have.... Red... breathe.. ver."

Trying to use their best judgment and combining with the strange symptoms that they both experienced a few moments ago, Shay's gut started screaming to him of trouble as he responded with, "Alpha, you are still coming in a bit broken, but we did experience symptoms of red eyes and shortness of breath. How did you know? Over."

"RTB. Repea... Retu...base! Ov..."

"Roger that, sir. We have one more cave to remove and will RTB shortly. How copy? Over."

Just then, an unmistakable noise sounded off in the distance - Boomer's charges going off. Not just one, but a cascade effect that shook the ground as every one of the tunnels began exploding and collapsing simultaneously. All of them, except one. The one they were currently standing in front of.

Deep into the cave, a sea of beady eyes glowing a sick green were moving towards the duo. Without a word or order from the senior, Killian engaged the charges in the cave, even though he wasn't finished. The explosion made the cave unstable, but it wasn't enough to collapse.

Without a word, Boomer and Shay started running down the mountain. The thunder of claws on stone was the first thing to catch them as the chase began. Like ants defending their home from an invading force, a flood of kreehauns poured out of the cave opening and ran downhill in search of prey. Typically, this type of horde creature was not known for its speed, but they seemed possessed. Not caring if they crushed their own beneath their claws and equally dismissing any personal injury, they simply screamed and ran.

Dismissing the thought of hiding in the woods and not liking the odds of two versus potential thousands, Shay stayed close to Kurian and encouraged the junior to keep running. Using internal communications, Shay attempted to warn the rest of the team about what they were bringing with them.

Suddenly, one of the kreehauns hurdled out of the air and nearly impaled Shay with its claws outstretched. If it were not for the quick actions of Kurian using his shield to block the attack, it could have led to an injury that slowed them down. At this point, slowing seemed like an early way to go blue.

Shay was slightly confused as there was absolutely no way that a kreehaun should have been able to catch up to them by running. Their stubby feet made it an impossibility. Risking it, Shay turned around to see how these short monsters were able to reach them so quickly. Just then, two more came flying towards him. He made short work of both using his daggers and dodged another as he picked up the sprint with a new understanding based on what he had just witnessed.

"They are rolling!" Shay shouted to Kurian as they made their way through the forest and slid through the trees.

While the bulk of the forces seemed to be running at a faster pace than intelligence suggested was possible, a group of the forerunners was aligning their path with theirs and tucking themselves into balls to roll downhill like spiked boulders. Some of them were impaling themselves on rocks and tree limbs, but others were making it down and traveling at incredible speeds. It almost seemed like they were attempting to slow them down instead of actually engaging them. The strategy was obviously crude, but Shay had to admit that it was effective. He questioned whether or not they would make it to the fort if they needed to engage the rollers while also outrunning the vanguard. Shay could make it by himself as he moved quicker and with more fluidity between the trees than his brother, but that would mean abandoning Boomer. Since that was not an option, this was going to be a close race to the finish line.

"Bravo, this is Alpha. Do you copy? Over."

"We read you loud and clear, Alpha. Hundreds, if not thousands, of kreehauns are scratching at our back. We are coming in hot. Over"

Titus's response was deadly calm, "Understood, Bravo. Come straight to the north wall near the northwest tower. We've got you covered. Over."

"Copy that, sir. We are moving to the north wall. Over and out."

With their orders clear, they pushed their bodies to the limit as they broke free of the forest. The fort looked beautiful as a bastion of protection as they sprinted. Just as they thought they were clear with very little downslope that would allow the kreehauns to use their trick to catch them, one final kreehaun bounced above them and landed just ahead of Kurian. With a dying rage-filled swipe, it clipped the sergeant as he passed, causing him to trip and fall.

Without a second thought, Shay ran to his junior and yelled, “Roll!” Immediately understanding what Shay was commanding him to do, Kurian laid flat on his back with his feet pointed toward the running lieutenant. As Shay approached, he actually jumped on top of the sergeant in a somersault. The move was perfectly executed to grab Kurian’s tunic leg and roll towards his shoulder, thereby picking up the junior onto Shay’s shoulders. Using his momentum to instantly continue the sprint. Now, with Kurian’s arms on Shay’s left and legs to his right, the lieutenant drew one dagger. A kreehauns barreled in their direction, and Shay changed his right dagger hand grip to perform an uppercut that forced the dagger through the bone and tissue of the approaching creature’s extended nose and jaw. With half of its face sliced off, the creature slowed, and Shay was able to continue his run unfettered.

As they ran, Shay felt a sudden jolt as Kurian used his shield to dispatch a kreehaun who had gotten too close to them on the left. Unfortunately, it wasn’t enough as more started closing the gap on the burdened runner. When it was looking bleak, the light show began.

The SALT ranged weapon was one of precision. A fine needle that helped poke out key pieces from the field of battle. However, Private John’s was more on the opposite of that scale. Being the heaviest of the team, John was their designated Battle Integral Gunner - or Big for short. The amount of energy he was able to store allowed him to make use of his armor for an extended period, but it also enabled him to shoot a very large volume of energy. John’s weapon had multiple barrels in a cylindrical shape that rotated with each shot fired. The amount of white energy dispensing from the Creator’s gift was simply beautiful. It appeared as a laser that cut down any that it touched. Which was exactly what it was doing to the massive army of kreehauns as they emerged from the forest.

With Titus and Wit providing more precise fire to cover their retreating brothers, Shay and Kurian were able to make it to the wall where a rope was waiting. Marcus and Killian were there to pull their brothers up. Killian quickly took a look and began healing his twin while Shay and Marcus summoned their ranged weapons to join the fight. While Shay was not as effective in this type of battle as John, he still made his talents known as he started taking down 2 or 3 with a single shot of his rifle.

The improved defenses proved invaluable as the flood of enemies broke upon the walls of the fort. Some of them started to dig beneath the walls, but Kurian's updates to them ensured that they were only met with disorienting sounds that caused them to veer off their underground attack.

Their victory was an inevitable outcome, with the enemy not having any ranged capabilities and no path inside, but the battle still took most of the day due to the sheer volume of the attackers. Titus was about to give the order to dismiss their gifts and allow Doc to begin triaging team members and prioritizing their turns back to the bridge when the final stragglers emerged from the forest. From the look of it, most of them appeared injured, which would align with Shay's report of the 'rollers' who had wounded themselves in an effort to slow his team's retreat. These, too, were dispatched quickly, but the actions of these horde beasts made no sense. Even these creatures should understand they were beaten and pulled back to fight another day, but it seemed as though they didn't care. Between the glowing green eyes they all witnessed and the unfettered rage that pushed them directly to the fort, it was obvious to the Commander and his team that something was controlling them. Or, perhaps even more concerning, calling them.

9

JOHN was first to the bridge as he had used a continuous amount of energy compared to the rest of the team. Killian suspected that John had gone close to the edge, but he would recover in time. Due to his energy stores being larger, he would take the most time. It was a bit dangerous to have the rest of the team as low as they were as the only defense, but Titus deemed it worth the risk. Plus, the mountain seemed very quiet after the all-out attack from the kreehauns. With the behavior of the enemy fresh in his mind, Titus highly doubted that any enemy actually remained in the mountain tunnels.

Once the team was back to full strength, Titus would need to send Bravo to fully clear the caves and tunnels. Based on Shay and Kurian's after-action report, it seemed as though their traps had worked to cut the enemy forces down significantly as they exited. If it hadn't been for their plan, the battle could have gone differently, defending against an even larger force.

During their meeting, it also became clear that the spores produced by the inky-black vine on the coffin had caused the symptoms of the team, which was the likely culprit behind the sudden, brutal attack by the kreehauns. The timing of the attack and the symptoms felt by Bravo at the tunnels were too close not to see the connection. Titus questioned Marcus, but he had no answers.

"Could that shadow have done something to the coffin before it left?" Shay asked.

"Anything is possible at this point," Titus responded.

They truly did not have any information on this new threat. It was frustrating not to know, but it didn't change their mission.

"Marcus, I need information." The Commander looked to his knowledge seeker, "Where do we start, and what do you need?"

Knowledge seeker were not only the record of all information known but excellent detectives in their own right. They seek answers and dive into the realms that their Creator has made to understand the majesty of their King while also studying the enemy to ensure they can provide their leaders with details that develop better tactics.

Marcus thought for a good long minute before responding, "I will go into the tomb to study the coffin in more detail. We also need more information about the reaction of the vine's spores on the enemy."

Titus waited a bit longer before attempting a response as he understood Marcus's method of thinking often involved long pauses. As he was about to ask follow-up questions, Marcus jumped back in with, "I think we need to capture a horde beast. Specifically, a kreehaun."

Not giving Marcus the chance to interrupt him, Titus quickly asked, "Why specifically a kreehaun?"

"Did you not notice? No other horde creature in the area came at us during the attack. If you recall, Commander, the scroll showed at least a bréag not that far from the fort. It likely would have been closer than the creatures in the tunnels, yet we saw no sign of it."

That was a chilling thought. If the bréag had joined the fight, it might have had a completely different outcome. Marcus's point was correct, though. To their knowledge, the only creatures affected by the spores were the kreehauns. It added a new layer of complexity to the situation.

"Go. Take John with you after you fill yourself at the bridge." Turning to the rest of his team, he said, "That is an order for all of you. For now, none are to be alone in the crypt, and all are required to be filled with energy before going in. Understood?" All members present nodded and voiced their agreement. Titus told Marcus to bring John up to speed on their findings and his orders.

Titus dismissed his men to keep watch as he felt the familiar thrill of Choice being used. Suddenly, his mind went back to the sensation he had first felt during the release of spores from within the crypt. Something about that sensation and the use of Choice was connected, but he still had no idea how.

Deciding to ponder it later, Titus held Shay back after ensuring his team was moving to their assigned positions. Getting right to the point, Titus told his second, "We need a kreehaun for Marcus to study. Any chance you left any alive in the tunnels?"

"It is possible, but I would call it unlikely."

"Take Bravo back up when you are ready, I need you to go in and make sure. If there are any left, they would be in there."

"Roger that, sir. I would need Boomer and all of Bravo to make sure we get out of there in one piece."

"Agreed. I will pull Marcus from his studies to man the walls with Wit. I will guard the tomb myself."

"Disobeying your own orders, sir?"

Shay had him there, but there wasn't anything to do about it. They needed a minimum of two brothers on the walls, but someone needed to watch/guard the tomb as it was their objective.

"I will keep the crypt doors open and guard it from within the tunnel leading to it." It was the best option, and Shay knew it.

"We will head out as soon as the team is renewed. That should give Marcus enough time to start his study of the evil-looking plant."

Titus snorted in agreement with the description before

he got a serious look on his face and told his second, "Bring them back."

"Absolutely, sir. Is there something else going on? Why the sudden concern?"

"Something is telling me that we are just scratching the surface of this assignment. Between the shadow getting away, something in the fort seemingly commanding horde creatures, and the inability to reach command - something else is going on here, and we don't yet know what it is."

"True. But, another way of thinking about it is this - the King knows exactly what is happening, and he sent us. Swords have a zero-fail mission. The Creator, in His wisdom, chose us. He never makes mistakes. The harder this gets, the more I am proud to serve with my brothers. You will find a way, Commander. We all have faith in our King, and that means we have faith in you."

Bolstered by his second's words, Titus smiled at Shay and replied, "You buttering me up for a promotion, LT?"

"Sir, you couldn't pay me enough to lead this disaster." They both laughed before returning to a serious note and going over the details of Bravo's return to the tunnels.

Before they set out, Titus had Kurian help create a cell in which they could keep a potential prisoner. Due to the digging capabilities of the kreehauns, they needed to place it within one of the outer buildings in the fort's courtyard as they had stone floors. Over time, the stone wouldn't prevent the creature from getting out with its claws, so they would likely need to remove its claws when they caught it. It would also likely help in the transport of the monster if they didn't have to worry about the razor-sharp appendages.

Marcus hadn't found out much more than they already knew during the short study of the dark plant, which is what they all began calling it. The knowledge seeker took detailed notes of its position and measurements. While he confirmed that the plant was actually carved into the coffin, he also believed that it, simultaneously, was indeed a plant. It was a carving, and it was alive. There also was no way of removing it with any of their weapons or tools. Titus watched as Bravo headed out and hoped that they would be successful. Perhaps once they had a kreehaun, they would be able to discover a way in which they could defend against these types of attacks in the future.

Bravo made quick time of moving up the hills towards the tunnels. While they didn't go out of their way to make noise, they also didn't disguise their movement like Shay and Kurian had done the first time. Getting one of the kreehauns to attack them in the forest would have made their job much easier. Going into the enemy's home was not ideal, but neither was the thought of an ambush. Opting for speed as the middle ground, they ran towards the final known cave that was still standing.

As they approached, the silence was deafening. No birds or forest creatures and no monsters running out to greet them. What did welcome them was the black, quiet stillness of the cave mouth. With the stalagmites and stalactites around the tunnel's entrance, it appeared that the cave was actually a monster simply waiting for its prey to walk into its maw. Swords are never prey, and Shay intended to show whatever awaited inside the word's true meaning.

Using their enhanced night vision, they set out on their spelunking mission, with Kurian, as always, leading the way with his shield. They would need to tread carefully as the cave was unsteady from Boomer's previous charges. An accidental sealing of the cave prematurely would likely lead to a long, slow descent into the blue.

It wasn't a difficult path to follow as the thousands of kreehauns coming out of the cave had made a very clear and flattened path. What soon made it complicated was the variety of paths that began to emerge. Not willing to separate the team just yet, Shay had them stick to the larger, more traveled path in the hopes that they would find their future prisoner. That plan became untenable once he saw more tunnels continuing to branch, and the path became less clear as to where the majority of their enemies had come from. Shay realized it was time to go hunting separately; otherwise, it would take them far too long.

Taking Kurian with him on one path and assigning Killian and John to another, they descended further into the cave system. He gave permission to use armor if needed but ordered the other duo to stay on a linear path and mark their progress. With their communications not working inside the mountain, they set a rendezvous time and place to meet back up. If one of the duo wasn't back on time, the other would follow the marked path to try and quickly provide support.

After descending further, Shay and Kurian felt as though they were circling back in the direction they had come. They decided to take the far left path at each of the junctions they went down. Reaching a massive lake within the interior of the mountain with no paths around it, they had to backtrack and try the previous fork.

Shay had only just started to question if the mission was possible when they arrived at a well-worn path toward a wall of collapsed rock. It was one of the lower entrances on which they had recently set trip charges. It was clear that a large contingent of kreehauns had come through and died in either the explosion or subsequent collapse. There was enough of their acidic blood to have melted more than a few of the rocks. Shay noticed a slight smile on Kurian's face as he examined his handiwork.

Suddenly, a half-painful moan and half-furious noise emitted from the right side of the rock pile. Kurian approached warily, tapped on the rock, and was met with a yell that was definitely more on the furious side. He turned to his senior with a new bright smile, "I think we have a survivor."

"Excellent. Let's get the others and dig it out."

Shay had considered leaving his junior behind to ensure this packaged gift didn't get away, but he knew that they shouldn't be alone in these tunnels, and it was unlikely that the kreehaun would get out at this point. It was almost time to regroup anyway, and the others may be in danger, so returning to get Kurian would waste more precious time.

Moving quickly, they made their way back to the rally point. As it turned out, the others were already there waiting for them. After giving them a brief recap and ensuring they had everything they needed, they moved back to their prisoner.

Digging the creature was not difficult as it was relatively close to their side versus the exit. Once some of the boulders were out of the way, Bravo was able to see how the creature had both survived and not been able to get out. A rock below and above had pinched the creature's legs. Due to the positioning of the above boulder, it had actually sheltered the monster from being crushed like his brethren.

The kreehaun attempted a few swipes at them with his impressive claws, but it was a futile effort. A single kreehaun was barely worth the effort of any Sword, let alone four of the best. John used his axe and three quick strikes to sever the three free appendage's claws. The only threat was the creature's teeth and the stuck foot, so the team used rope to tie the mouth closed and carefully avoided the protruding fangs in the front. Its long snout was almost comically easy to close and seal shut. Just in the nick of time, too, as the monster's furious blood-curdling screeching was starting to annoy the team.

Once the threats were removed, they released the creature's foot from the boulders. It attempted one more time to kill its enemy by kicking at John, who held the top boulder up on his back. With lightning speed and incredible strength, John lifted the boulder up further to raise his leg and stomped on the swiping claws. There was a sickening sound as not only claws but the bones within the kreehaun's foot shattered. Shay looked at John with a quizzical expression at the feat of strength he just witnessed, and the silent brother simply shrugged.

Using more rope and a pole, they hog-tied the ugly creature and started their return journey. Their steps were sped by the feeling of completing their objective and the fact that the kreehaun was still annoying with its feeble attempts to get out and attack them. Shay used their communications link to inform their leader that they were bringing back a guest.

"Good work, Bravo. Over and out." Titus responded to Shay's report. He hoped that the creature would provide more answers, but he doubted they would learn much. Horde creatures weren't capable of speech, but they had some level of intelligence. That said, Marcus wanted the creature for experiments more than communication. Titus needed every edge he could get in this mission.

With the possibility of getting more intelligence and gaining an edge, his thoughts turned to the structures to the southeast. Once Bravo returned and Marcus had time to examine the kreehaun in connection to the dark plant, he would need to get a group together to go explore. Titus would love to lead the exploration team, but it would be a waste not to use Shay's talents as a scout, which would require Titus to stay in command at the fort.

Between the two new avenues of gathering information, Titus prayed to the King that something would reveal itself that actually helped him in his use of Choice in this hellscape. Failure was not an option, and all routes led to victory for the King, but Choice is hardest when the path is unclear. Titus continued to have more questions than answers the longer they stayed in this place, and his next moves were shaded by the unknown.

10

MARCUS couldn't determine as much as the team had hoped, but one interesting discovery was that the kreehaun's bloodlust had abated. Well, it was back to the original level of bloodlust expected of any 'normal' horde creature. As anticipated, the creature doesn't communicate outside of screeches and attempts to bite Marcus. The knowledge seeker needed to knock the creature out more than a few times using his hammer.

After some initial review of the kreehaun, Marcus shifted his approach and reconcentrated on the crypt, the carved plant growing on the coffin, and any connection they shared. Unexpectedly, once he arrived with John, he had difficulty not marveling at the flame that rested on top of the coffin. It was strange and beautiful in a way that Marcus couldn't quite put his finger on. The color showed bright red, as one would expect from a normal candle flame, but a closer inspection showed that it was truly just red. Flames should have some color differential from white to orange; however, this particular one was set to one specific color of red. Marcus measured with his eyes and noted the flame's width and height once more on his scroll, but there was no change.

Moving to the black plant, the feeling was instantly different while staring at it. Unlike the flame, the carved black plant gave off a vibe of evil that made it hard to want to study it closely. Regardless of feelings, there were questions that needed answering, and he would find those answers. The Creator had built the knowledge seekers as insatiably curious. A mystery like this was another battle, one in which he was uniquely qualified to fight.

Using his vision once more on the plant, Marcus instantly became aware that it had grown some since he had first measured it. In fact, the plant seemed to have grown branches along with more thorns. Each thorn looked sharp enough to cut even the flesh of his brothers, and he almost believed it would if he attempted to grab it. The knowledge seeker knew that was ridiculous as it was carved into the coffin, meaning it couldn't hold a point. Even the confidence in his mind of facts he knew didn't stop the warning that screamed in his mind.

Gathering all of his findings, including his own feelings of discomfort, he and John left and found the Commander to give a report and findings in a scroll. After giving all the details, Titus waited to ensure Marcus wasn't about to add more context before speaking, "Good work. I don't imagine we will learn more here."

Marcus responded with, "Agreed. I assume you will be sending me with Bravo to learn more from the structures to the south?"

Titus was only mildly surprised that Marcus had deduced his next plan of action. His knowledge seeker had a fascinating brain that could work out facts from the smallest amount of information, so he didn't even bother asking how he had figured out Titus's next order.

"Correct. You are taking John's spot and will leave at sunset to make use of the night."

"Roger that, sir. I will be ready."

"Bring me some answers, private. That is an order."

"Understood, sir. I won't let you down."

"I know you won't. Dismissed."

Marcus left to prepare and ensure he had his energy full before embarking. Titus was left alone once more in the radio room, which had become his command center, with intelligence and scrolls organized on a nearly perfect desk that Kurian had made in his spare time. He rolled the scroll out again, displaying the map with horde creatures identified. Looking at the ruins to the south with red dots spread around the area. Shay would know what he and his team were walking into, but the weight of sending half of his squad into an enemy-controlled area with many hostiles was not a small thing. However, Titus understood this was the best option and immediately had the sensation that came with making a Choice.

The marks flew by quickly, and it was time for Bravo's departure. Swapping out John with Marcus in this mission made the most tactical sense. John had proven to be valuable in defending the fortress against a larger force, and Marcus was needed for any detailed intelligence gathering. Killian was the team's medic, so he would be valuable if the smaller group was caught behind enemy lines, and Shay would lead.

Once again, Titus watched his brothers leave with the growing frustration of someone making Choices in the dark. He knew that the King would be victorious in the end regardless of his use of Choice, but he desperately wanted all of his brothers to return.

****

Due to their number and moving into unknown enemy territory, Shay decided to travel mainly in a stacked single-file formation, with himself out front and his two brothers bringing up the rear. If Shay ran into anything, he would have time to warn his team and divert their path accordingly. Additionally, walking over each other's footprints enabled them to hide their number should an enemy pick up their trail. It wasn't a new strategy, as they had all trained in various combinations of 1-1-8 brothers and in various war scenarios. Killian and himself were comfortable with Marcus in their group, and Marcus, in turn, fell right into step with the others.

Swords often trained in various scenarios and attempted to develop new ones to test their limits. From fighting solo in whiteout conditions to blindfolded marching in a full battalion, there were very few, if any, battle situations that a Sword would not feel comfortable in or have perfected. Mixing up the squads to accommodate a given task was hardly worth a second thought.

Shay kept his camouflage up as they moved through the wooded area, and his eyes were constantly scanning. He was both the leader and the point man, which literally meant that everything boiled down to his focus and use of Choice. Luckily for him, being a SALT meant scouting was a natural part of who the Creator had made him to be. His eyes pierced the darkness, and his mind began cataloging the rhythm of the forest. By the laws of the King, each place had one. It was how the creatures interacted with each other and intruders. It was how the plants grew and what could cause them to fall. It was how the limbs and grass lay when not disturbed versus when something had moved over them. It was even how his brothers moved through the forest, just ever so slightly outside the natural law of this place. He analyzed and understood each of these details to become one with the forest's rhythm and to know instantly when it was disrupted. Anything not part of the natural flow would be as obvious to him as a fire roaring through a meadow.

While the ruins were not close to the fort, they made good time as they wanted to make the most of the night. Some horde creatures did have impressive night vision, but nothing close to what Swords had. Even though the legion did retain their night vision after their rebellion, Shay wasn't concerned as the intelligence had made it clear that no shadow was within close range of the fort - outside of the one that got away. That reminder caused fresh frustration to Shay as a miss was wholly unacceptable.

Shoving the frustration down and re-concentrating on the current task, Shay quickly pushed to reach a hill cliff that overlooked their objective. Looking down, he began mapping the area in his mind. While it was obvious that there was a settlement of some kind at one point, what remained was barely the bones of a civilization. Some half-stone walls and partially collapsed buildings were strewn about in a half-circle. After a few moments, it became obvious to Shay what this once was. A fishing or water town once on the edge of a giant lake. Partially decomposed posts in the ground, along with one pier, made it clear that there was once a large body of water closer to the structures. What remained of the water made the area a swamp instead. Small flying creatures abound, but the area seemed eerily quiet.

The only point of interest that caught Shay's eye was a large stone building on a slightly raised hill in the center of the town. With his impressive vision and scan of the remaining structures, it was obvious that if there was anything of interest in this place, they would find it there. It was also obvious that if they were to run into enemies, it would be there as well.

Returning to his team, he outlined what he saw and their next steps. They would move together and clear the northern structures first, which would help secure their quick retreat if needed. After clearing the primary building, Marcus would get to work investigating anything of value while Killian stayed to guard him. Shay would move to a position to cover them both from as many avenues as possible. It would be a stealth mission, as they didn't want to kick the hornet's nest this far from their other brothers. A quick reaction force wasn't coming for them, so discretion and stealth were their best advantage.

With their primary weapons at the ready, the three warriors began clearing the empty walls and decomposing structures. As expected, there was no resistance and no visible enemy. They pushed forward, moving quickly and quietly toward the stone building in the center.

As they approached, Shay was almost taken aback as the doors for the structure were still solid and looked very strong. Additionally, Creator images were chiseled into the wood and stone of the archway. After working the large doors open, they entered what appeared to be a large gathering room with benches and tables spread out. There was only a single door to the right, which Shay moved to with Killian to clear.

Killian's knives and Shay's daggers were perfect for close quarters of a structure, while Marcus's hammer made him ideal for area denial. That said, Shay had seen Marcus wield his giant war hammer with expertise in the smallest of spaces that would put some of the best knife fighters to shame. Regardless, they played to their strengths, and the two shorter members moved to clear the interior.

Once Shay got the door opened, Killian looked at him with a quizzical and astonished look. Shay didn't have to be a mind reader to know what he was thinking as he was having the same feeling - recognition.

Shay and Killian saw a spiral stairwell leading to an underground area. Right as they expected, there was a crypt beneath the structure. As soon as they were done clearing it, Killian switched with Marcus so he could come to investigate. While the crypt was close to their own back at the fort, this one did actually have differences. The biggest was that the coffin in the center was fully wrapped in thick, thorny black vines. As Marcus approached, Shay grabbed his arm and said, "Do not touch it and be prepared to activate your armor at a moment's notice. Do not hesitate. Something is very wrong with this one, and I don't intend for you to fall here."

Marcus thought of a quick comeback, but it died on his lips as he saw Shay's concern while staring at the black vines. Instead, he nodded in agreement and slowly approached to begin his study.

Shay had Killian join Marcus outside the crypt as a guard before moving himself to find a perch. A remnant of a bell tower nearby was still solid enough, albeit not as high as it was probably meant to be. He climbed up and did a radio check before settling in.

“Marcus, you have one mark before we move out. Over.”

Barely disguising his disappointment, Marcus responded, “Copy that, LT. One mark, and we are returning to base. Over.”

“Doc, keep an eye on him and pull him if anything smells off in there. How copy?”

“Roger that, sir. We will be ready to move in a mark. Over.”

“Keep your wits about you, brothers. Something smells off here, and it isn’t the swamp. Eyes up and weapons sharp. Over and out.”

For Marcus, time flew way too fast. Concentrating on the crypt as the likely source of the most information, he stayed close and studied it closely without touching it. Despite his innate curiosity, he felt the same unease that Shay so obviously felt. The dark plant was in full bloom around this coffin, and after some measurements, the coffin seemed a fair bit lower than their own back at the fort. It seemed like the vines were pulling the coffin into the ground.

The other thing immediately obvious to each team member was that there was no flame. Instead, the plant itself pulled in the light, making the room feel much darker than possible with their eyes.

After gathering fascinating data, Shay came on the radio and warned them of their upcoming departure. Marcus had finished putting most of the data into a scroll and was packing away his supplies when a distinct sound came from the coffin. Unsure of what it was, Marcus got closer and heard it again, but faintly. The sound was similar to a moan of pain and anguish. Risking it to understand what was happening, Marcus drew just a little closer to the coffin, bringing his ear a hair away from the rippling black darkness plant. This time, it was very clear. A moan of such torment and pain reserved for only the enemies of the King came deep within the coffin. It shook him to his core, to the point where he didn't hear anything as Killian approached.

"You okay, Marcus? What happened?"

The suddenness of Killian so close without Marcus realizing it startled the knowledge seeker, and he lost his balance. Spinning away from Killian, he reached out for something to balance himself. Unfortunately, the only thing within reach was the coffin itself and the pure black plant surrounding it.

Instantly, Marcus's body convulsed as though a lightning bolt had struck him. The plant attacked the energy within his body, and he screamed. Within a heartbeat, Marcus was beginning to turn blue.

Doc acted without hesitation as he tackled the private, breaking his connection to the coffin and the vines that encircled it. He rolled his taller brother onto his side and began assessing him while simultaneously alerting Shay to the situation.

"LT, Marcus is down. He touched the black plant and is now dangerously close to blue. Over."

"Understood. Moving to your location now. Over."

Because the vast majority of injuries a Sword sustained were actually repaired internally using their Creator energy, the team's medic's primary responsibility was to ensure that each member had enough energy not to go blue. As such, they had a unique ability to share their own stored energy with other Swords to heal injuries. However, there was no external injury that Killian could find on Marcus. It seemed as though the plant had specifically targeted the energy within the Sword.

Since there was no injury to heal, Killian Chose to share

his energy with Marcus directly. By the look of the taller brother, it wasn't long before what little energy in him would be gone, so he needed to act quickly. Placing his own forehead on Marcus's, he breathed energy into the wounded Sword. Sharing a breath of a brother placed Killian in danger as Marcus may not be aware of how much he was pulling from him. Like a drowning man pulling his savior underwater, a Sword may pull more than necessary from a healer. Fortunately, it appeared Marcus retained some of his sense as he pulled back after a few heartbeats. Killian's energy was down significantly, but they both should barely have enough to return to the fort.

Shay arrived quickly and just in time to see the color return to Marcus's glowing eyes and body. The yellow energy pushed the blue back into a strained but closer-to-normal hue. Giving his brothers a moment to catch their breath again, Shay asked, "What happened?" He knew that Marcus would never deliberately disobey a direct order, so something else had to have happened.

"Sorry, sir. I heard a sound from the inside the coffin." Marcus nearly shuttered, thinking about the sound again. Shay waited a minute for the private to gather himself and was rewarded by Marcus continuing with, "A sound from the very depths of pain came out of the coffin, and I lost my balance when Killian approached. My hand touched it, and Killian rescued me."

Looking at Killian now, he could tell that he was also significantly low on energy. Shay knew immediately that the Doc had done his job by sharing his life's energy with Marcus. He nodded his appreciation towards Killian and was about to ask more questions when there was a distinct sound of something wet peeling from stone up above.

Instantly, Shay gave the signal for silence and drew his daggers. Both the injured brothers drew their weapons, but Shay ordered them to stay. They weren't in a condition to fight at the moment.

The team lead ascended the stairs and peeked out into the larger room. Doing a quick scan of the room from behind the door, Shay saw nothing. Silence was the only thing that greeted him as he checked right and left. His advanced eyesight was the key to spotting the warning, which saw a partially dried wet footprint. Leaping and rolling to the left as a poisoned-tipped spear pierced a chair he stood in front of a heartbeat earlier, he spun and threw one of his daggers. It buried itself to the hilt into the head of a giant amphibious-frog-like monster attached to the wall above the doorway he had emerged from.

As the beast fell, Shay jumped over the corpse and ran down the stairs, careful to avoid the yellow streak across the horde creature's back, which was the source of its poison. He was berating himself every step for not seeing it as soon as they got to the settlement.

The image of their intelligence scroll showing the area and local horde creatures came to his head. In his mind, he overlaid that image with his own internal map of the area. The many red dots on the scroll showing horde creatures were not directly in the ruins as they would expect of kreehauns; they were in the swamp adjacent to the structures. He and his two weakened brothers were in a loskang nest.

11

IT was 12:35 PM on a Monday when Henry was having a great time playing king of the hill with his friends at recess. There was a small grassy mound just to the right of the play structure and before the foursquare pad that had a distinct rise above the grass surrounding it. With it being a good three feet high, his fellow third-grade class members quickly made king of the hill into a favorite game to play after lunch.

"I am the king!" Shouted Henry's friend named Aston. He was the biggest in the class and the best at almost everything. With cool clothes and cool cars that his parents took him to school in, everyone wanted to be his friend. Inexplicably, he had taken Henry under his wing as soon as he joined the school last year. Since then, they had spent every recess together and had a few play dates at Aston's house. Henry didn't like having people at his house since there weren't very many fun things to do.

Even though his mom had gotten better, his dad still had to work at least two jobs to try and keep their family from *going under*. His mom and dad never argued in front of Henry or his older siblings, but they heard them when they would have their talks at night. Dad refused to let Mom find work as he wanted to make sure that nothing disrupted her health or added stress. Mom said that the work Dad was taking on was too much and that it was all because of her. No matter what, it was Henry who seemed to have it the worse. He didn't even have the newest video game system! How was he supposed to invite Aston over when they couldn't even play video games together?

Henry charged up the hill with a single objective to push his friend off and claim the top spot. With a bit more force than he probably should have used, he lowered his shoulder like his brother taught him and knocked Aston to the ground.

"Oh my God, dude! You trying to kill me? Shit!" Aston looked up and stared at Henry with accusing eyes. He often used words like that, and it made him sound so cool. Henry offered his hand to his friend and considered how he wasn't allowed to say any of those things. His dad would always say the same thing, "Henry - let the words of your mouth be a reflection of your heart. Every curse you say is like poison on the lips. Is that what you want coming from your heart?" What his dad didn't understand was how he stood out from all the other kids because he couldn't talk like them - especially Aston.

"Sorry, dude! I didn't mean to hit you that hard."

Aston quickly turned his frown around and smiled as he pulled Henry off of the hill again.

"I am king again!"

After a second hesitation, Henry said, "Shit, dude!"

Aston stared at Henry like he had grown a second head and laughed before responding, "I didn't think you had it in you to say *shit*. I thought the pastor's kid was too good to use those words."

Part of Henry felt bad about saying it, but another part felt liberated. He didn't change, and God didn't strike him dead. It felt good to say whatever he wanted and be like the other kids. If they could all say things like that, why couldn't he? No teacher had ever talked to Aston about him using bad words, and he did it in class every day! His parents weren't ever talking to him about his language and his heart or that God's name is precious. It was just a word, right? Why did it matter so much, especially since every adult said the same words? Every adult except Henry's parents.

"No way, dude! I say stuff like that all the time."

"You ever say it to your parents?" Aston asked with a mischievous smile.

Henry hesitated but wasn't about to back down now. "Of course! They say it too, but just not around other people." Aston smiled at him again, which spoke volumes of how much he believed his friend.

"I dare you to say it to the teacher today."

Henry balked at the thought but was already in over his head and didn't want to lose face with his friend, "Sure, but only if I get called on or something."

Thinking he was safe now as he didn't usually get called on in class, and there wasn't a need to curse, Henry went back to playing and running around on the playground. Unfortunately for him, it wasn't long before the bell rang, and all the kids headed back to class. Along the way, Aston gave Henry a nudge and a wink to confirm that his friend had not forgotten their little agreement. Henry winked back, but nervousness and anxiety shot through his body.

After recess, the next subject was math, and it went by slowly in Henry's mind. Thankfully, he didn't get called on and let a small knot in his stomach unravel.

Next was vocabulary, and Henry actually enjoyed that subject. Different words could have similar meanings, but all sounded unique and cool. It helped that he was one of the best in class with words since his parents liked teaching him new ones regularly.

Mrs Olsen called out one of the words they had been working on recently and called on Aston, "Can you please spell it and give the definition?"

Aston put on a serious face and thought for a long time before replying, "I am sorry, Mrs Olsen. That is a hard one for me. I don't remember it." Before the teacher could reply or tell him to sit down, Aston added, "But Henry knows! I bet Henry could do it." He began chanting Henry's name again and again. Soon, the rest of the class had picked it up, and the teacher quieted them down. With a smile, she turned to Henry and said, "Well, Henry? How about it?"

Henry was as white as a piece of paper, and sweat beaded on his forehead. Aston had deliberately set him up. Henry was either going to be a coward in his friend's eyes or show that he could talk like the other cool kids.

With determination, he stood up and said, "Damn, Mrs Olsen. That shit is hard for all of us."

Everyone in the room stopped and stared at Henry. Instead of being white, he immediately became as red as a ripe tomato. Shock was on every single person's face, including Mrs. Olsen.

The room went from silence to laughter as all the kids began hooping and hollering. Aston laughed and clapped Henry on the back, letting him know that they were laughing with him and not at him. For someone who felt very different from the other kids, he suddenly had a small taste of what it meant to be cool—and he liked it.

However, there was one person in the room who not only didn't laugh but who looked very disappointed. Mrs Olsen shushed the room again and asked Henry to sit down. She moved on to another student, but Henry couldn't help but notice a small change in her demeanor. He wasn't sure why, as she hadn't yelled at him or even told him never to use those words, but he sensed the change in her, immediately making him want to apologize.

Quickly, those feelings of shame were washed away as Aston seemed to revel in the event. He talked about how awesome it was and how he always knew that Henry was just like him. It made Henry feel good, as if he was now fully accepted.

The rest of the school day flew by with only one other subject after vocabulary. Aston and Henry were talking and playing with Aston's latest new toy in the gym as they waited for their parents to pick them up. Usually, only the gym teacher and the principals were managing and calling kids up to go home, but Henry noticed that Mrs Olsen was waiting near the entrance today. When Henry's mom came to pick him up, she walked over and started talking to her. Immediately, he knew what they were discussing and wanted to get over there to interrupt or say it was all a lie. But it was too late as the shadow seemed to pass from Mrs Olsen to his mom. When she looked over and locked eyes with Henry, the sadness within her gaze made him want to cry or look for someplace to hide.

He was called over, and his tears were on the verge of pouring out by the time he reached his mother. His heart sank with each step as she led him to the car without saying a single word. They both got in and buckled into their seats. She started the car and pulled out to head home. All while under the heavy blanket of silence.

The pressure was too much for Henry, and he blurted out, "Aston made me say it! This was his fault and idea! He always says those things and said we couldn't be friends if I didn't too." Without taking a break to breathe, he continued, "Why can't I say those things?! Everyone else does. Why do I have to be different?"

Arlene continued to sit there in silence, so Henry launched back into his emotion-filled tirade, "If everyone else has a dirty heart, I don't see the big deal if I do!"

Sitting in the back row of their car, Henry couldn't see his mother's face but only felt the weight of the silence that emanated from her. Not being able to take it anymore, Henry shouted, "Oh my God, Mom! Say something!"

His mom slowed the car down to the side of the road and stopped. She turned back in her seat, and Henry could see the tears in her eyes. Before he could say anything to try and appease her, she reached back her hand and, for the first time in his entire life, slapped him.

Though her voice nearly cracked, Henry's mother very calmly said, "You will never again use our Lord's name in vain."

The rest of the ride home was in mutual silence, and Henry was immediately confined to his room. As he sat there, a new realization and panic began setting into his mind. If mom was willing to slap him over what he said, what would his dad do? It was extremely rare that he or his siblings were spanked, but they were never forgotten.

Deep down, Henry knew he had messed up something big, but a part of him didn't care. He kept the memory of everyone cheering him fresh in his mind. In fact, he determined that even if he got a spanking, he would continue to talk like the other kids. Maybe he would be more careful about where, but he felt accepted now, and that was all that mattered.

Carl got home, and the house got quiet again. A few minutes went by, and Henry's dad entered his room. He walked over and sat on Henry's bed beside his son.

"Hey, son. Having a rough day?"

Henry began to cry into his father's arms. The shame and disappointment he felt was too strong to ignore anymore, no matter how much he tried to hold onto the defiant part of himself.

After a few minutes, Henry calmed down, and his father began by saying, "Do you know how much your mother and I love you?" It being a rhetorical question, he continued, "We would do anything to see you grow into a man who is strong, wise, and good. We would also do anything to ensure you didn't grow into a man *you* truly don't want to be. Do you understand?"

Henry nodded his understanding before his dad continued once more, "I know you are pretty sick of me saying this to you, but the words that come from your mouth are a true reflection of your heart. If you can't control your words, how can you control yourself when it really matters?"

"But dad! Aston and the other kids talk like that! Even

their parents use wor..." Carl quickly cut him off with a wave of his hand.

"You don't have the right to speak about others in that way. You are responsible for your words and your choices. For good or bad, the only person who is responsible for what you do is you. Cursing is like a poison that starts in the mind, spews from the mouth, and corrodes the heart. If you speak about others, including your friends and their parents, who's poison is it?"

With a grumble that was barely coherent, Henry responded with, "Mine."

"That is right. I love you and will always want you to make the right choices. I can't force you, and I will not always be around to correct you. It is up to you how you want others to see you."

"But, Dad! That is just it! I want to be cool like the other kids."

"I understand, son, but they are not the judge of who you are. They don't get to decide if you are a man of integrity. Only by your choices and how God judges those choices will you be what you are meant to be."

At the mention of *God*, Henry winced a little. Carl noticed it and asked his son a question, "Have you ever heard of the story of the sun and the boy?"

Henry shook his head, and his father started the story:

There once was a boy who loved the sun, and the sun loved the boy. Every day, the boy would greet the sun in a bow, and the sun would shine down his warmth on the boy. As the boy grew, he lost interest in bowing to the sun as he could easily get warmth from his own fire and clothes. The boy no longer cared to honor the sun and instead saw it as his equal. He would stare at the sun in greeting every morning instead of bowing his head. The sun begged the boy to stop and told him he wanted what was best for him. However, the boy became even bolder and began trying to stare down the sun even longer to show that he was just as good as the sun. Soon, the boy's eyes faded, and he became blind. He yelled at the sun and said, 'How could you do this to me? Are we not friends?' The sun responded by saying, 'You saw only what I gave you, not what I truly am. Without respecting who I am, how could you claim to know me?'

Carl looked at his son and asked if he understood the moral of the story. Henry said that it was stupid of the boy to stare at the sun as everyone knows that will cause you to go blind. His father agreed but continued, "Using our Lord's name in everyday conversations causes us to lose sight of what that name represents. Every time you say His name casually, you are minimizing how awesome and powerful He is."

Henry realized what his father was getting at and said, "Like staring at the sun and forgetting it will make you blind?"

"Exactly! You must respect the sun as it is powerful. It brings warmth and comfort, but if you think it is nothing more than that, you will go blind."

"I think I understand Dad. I won't say it again."

"Good."

"Am I going to get spanked?"

With a chuckle and a slight touch to his son's cheek, Henry responded with, "I think you got your punishment already." Henry sighed in relief, but his dad didn't stop, "There is something I would like to do, though. I want to pray with you and ask God to keep working on your heart. I know you have a good one in there." Carl said with a smile as he tapped his son's chest.

Once they both closed their eyes, Carl began with, "Our Father in heaven, holy and honored is your name....."

12

SHAY gathered his two weakened members, and they set out immediately towards the east. They needed to take the longer route back as they were not in a position to fight a large force. Attempting to return the way they had come would be too great of a risk, considering this enemy would likely have found their trail and were already lying in wait.

Loskangs were ambush hunters as they were not physically that strong. What they did lack in strength, they made up for in camouflage and cunning. Their limbs were lanky, with most of the force generated from their legs to help jump impressive distances and heights. Stretched out straight, they were roughly double the height of a Sword, but they walked in a crouched way with their legs bent at an angle that made them a head shorter than Host warriors. Their eyes bulged out above their heads with nose holes just above a flexible mouth. Like a snake, they could swallow large victims whole into their expandable stomachs. They had excellent camouflage all over their body, except for a single streak of yellow that appeared randomly on each of the monsters. Unfortunately, the streak was not a biological mistake that made them easier to see. In truth, it created the poison that they used to debilitate their foes, including Swords. While immune to almost every poison, one of the few that could slow a Sword was a loskang's. Combining their poison with an impressive use of spear-like weapons, they were not a foe to be taken lightly.

Due to their jumping power and poisoned spears that

they carried, these would be a far more challenging foe than the kreehauns to push back from the fort. Shay and his team needed to avoid ambushes and hurry back to the fort to help defend it.

"Alpha, this is Bravo. Do you copy? Over." Shay let his brothers rest for a moment on the outskirts of the ruins while he attempted to raise the fort team on their communication link.

"Bravo, this is 1-1-8 actual. I hear you. Over."

"Commander. Marcus gathered information from the ruins of the settlement but was injured, and Killian shared energy. They are both dangerously low. Additionally, we have confirmed the presence of loskang in and around the ruins. Over."

"Are they aware of your presence? Over."

"Unclear, but likely. I had to eliminate one. They will know of our incursion soon, if not already. Over."

"Understood. We will be ready here, but I need you all back here ASAP. Over."

"Roger that, Commander. We are on the move but may need to take an alternate route to the east. I will check back in one mark from now. Over"

"Solid copy. Over and out."

Shay gave Marcus and Killian a nod, and they gave their acknowledgment. They were ready to move.

Picking up the same column formation that they adopted on the way to the ruins, Shay took point to scout for any ambushes ahead. If anyone on the team could spot a loskang before it was too late, it would be him. However, even Shay wasn't confident enough to say that it was a guarantee. Being this far away from help, having two injured brothers, and an unknown number of loskang in front and behind was a new scenario for him. He would need to remember it to add to the various tests Swords gave each other. Of course, he could only do that if he didn't go blue.

* * *

****

After getting Shay's report, Titus immediately began instigating his plan to defend against the jumping monstrosities. With limited brothers and a large area to defend, it wouldn't be easy.

It was unlikely that a loskang could jump the entire height of the fort's walls, but that wouldn't matter much as each loskang was capable of sticking to surfaces. They could simply jump and crawl the remaining distance. Titus planned on using some of their supplies in a unique way to ensure their enemy didn't have an easy climb.

His plan was fairly simple, but most tactical plans were. Force the enemy into a position where their numbers and preferred tactics were useless. The first step was denying the enemy the ability to surround them inside the walls. They would accomplish this by coating the top half of the walls with an oil-like substance used in their earlier construction. Oil would ensure they couldn't climb the walls and force them to move through the front gate, where they would be waiting to ambush them. Titus planned to let these wannabe fighters know who the true masters were.

Titus outlined his plan to his brothers and set each member to their assigned wall. They would use most of their oil, making construction difficult later, but Titus needed to take one battle at a time. Being stingy on resources now may allow them to do more later, or it may also ensure there was no *later* for them to experience.

With his brothers running to prepare for the coming battle, Titus went to fill his energy at the bridge. When he entered the main hall, a familiar feeling tickled his intuition. Something was not right. He moved to the doorway that led to the crypt and opened it to walk down the stairs. There wasn't a need to go a single step further as he instantly felt shortness of breath, and his eyes became watery.

Closing the doorway, he turned and started running while mentally activating his radio with all of 1-1-8, "Spores! Spores! Spores! Prepare for contact!"

With his team acknowledging his warning and moving as fast as possible to prepare, Titus ran towards their makeshift prison to make sure their prisoner was not escaping in a green-eyed frenzy. When he opened the door, he was shocked. Instead of the snarling and chaos-driven beast he had expected, a snarling, churlish kreehaun sat in a corner. No green eyes, and it wasn't acting like his horde brethren had the last time the spores were launched into the air. Just to make sure, Titus sat and watched him to ensure the spores hadn't reached it yet. After a few more heartbeats, his team started calling out similar symptoms. It had clearly reached far enough to touch this one, but the only reaction was the kreehaun sniffing the air and giving almost a feral smile at the Commander.

Titus's unease increased as the questions mounted in his mind. He again felt like something was missing, and it was just within reach. Whatever it was, he was sure that it would help them complete their mission, and not knowing would jeopardize his team.

Closing the door behind him and moving to get into his position, Titus silently asked the King for wisdom and the safe return of his full team. Something was out there, and it was coming for them inside and outside these walls.

****

Shay knew there was an ambush ahead of them, but they couldn't avoid it completely. The loskang had prepared and knew of their movements. If they attempted to go around them, they would waste valuable time, and their enemy would simply relocate ahead of them again.

Unfortunately, the loskang had chosen a position well. Bravo would either need to climb down into a creek bed on their right or climb out a small cliff on the left to avoid the ambush waiting for them around an outcropping of boulders ahead. Neither option of avoidance is ideal, with their enemy able to relocate to the high ground quickly to rain down spears on them. Seeing how their Choices were limited, Shay opted for the third option of all the above and felt the familiar sensation of Choice being used.

Killian would move right to flank, and Shay would ascend the cliff to cover from above. Marcus, unfortunately, would be the bait to spring their enemy's trap. He would be easy to spot by their enemies due to his height and limited camouflage. If the enemy was bloodthirsty enough and they fell for the single-column formation ruse, they may think only a single Sword was out scouting.

It was a risky plan, as neither Marcus nor Killian had enough energy for armor or ranged gifts without going blue, but Shay knew they needed to fight through the ambush if they had any hope of getting back. With Shay being the only one with enough energy for ranged gifts and his unique abilities, it was bad tactics for him to spring the trap instead.

Before they separated to execute the plan, Marcus grabbed Shay's arm, "I need you to give this to the Commander." He proceeded to hand Shay a scroll. It was the intelligence he had gathered from the tomb within the lakeside stone structure.

"Give it to him yourself when we get back."

"That doesn't make logical sense, sir."

Shay knew he was right. Whoever had the best chance of returning would need to be holding the information. If it didn't make it back and they lost brothers, it would mean that their mission was a complete failure and a waste of resources.

The lieutenant stuffed the scroll into his tunic belt and

looked into the junior's eyes, "We are getting back and getting home. You hear me?"

"Understood, sir! Let's pave the way in their blood, yeah?"

Shay gave him a nod and began climbing. Killian had already moved back to cross the creek bed further away from prying eyes, so Marcus waited for both to confirm they were in position to begin flanking their ambushers. None of them could have anticipated what happened next.

As Shay was nearing the top, he heard the croaking deep-throat war cry of a loskang. He peered down through the forest and saw the flashes of loskangs moving quickly toward Marcus. It was almost inconceivable. Why would they give up their power position to charge straight at them? It went against everything they knew about their enemy.

Without stopping his climb, he opened his link to Marcus and Killian to try and warn them. It was too late; Marcus was already fighting for his life, and he was all alone. Killian and Shay were too far away to provide the help that he needed.

"Killian, cross the creek and come in behind them. I will get into a position to offer range support. Marcus.... Hold on, brother. We are coming." Only grunting and the sounds of battle were returned through the link.

Marcus fought like a bull. Using only his hammer, he crushed one after another that charged him. They came at him with unbridled fury and familiar green eyes. Some were throwing their spears while others charged in to begin stabbing at the lone Sword. He avoided the thrown weapons as much as possible while spinning and launching enemies to the right and left while crushing others into the ground. His concentration was solely on the battle, and he heard only the rhythm of the fight. Responding to anyone on the link would break his flow, and he barely computed what was being said.

One loskang charged in from the right, and Marcus raised his long leg straight up and brought it straight down on top of the creature's skull, crushing it into the ground. Showing his flexibility, he next bent backward to avoid two spears thrown from the horde creatures on the outskirts. He continued into a backflip that used his hammer as the grounding point. Swinging it back off the ground, he crushed another that charged in. He began swinging the hammer in a wide circle to fend off the close enemies, but the horde monsters didn't seem to care for their own well-being. They jumped at him from all directions, uncaring of their own immediate death waiting for them.

One of the monsters dived at the lone Sword and grabbed his right hand. Twisting the creature's arm and snapping it in one motion, he turned to face another coming at him. Unfortunately, his right arm moved sluggish. Instantly, he understood that the loskang that had grabbed him did so with his yellow-striped hand. The poison was working quickly to slow his movements.

Even one-armed, a Sword was no easy prey. He expertly wielded his hammer in one hand by smashing legs and arms to debilitate those close to him while enabling them to remain standing as body shields for the spears that continued to harass him from a distance.

With the bodies beginning to pile around him, it was an inevitable outcome, but Marcus eventually stepped on a yellow stripe of a dead loskang. His foot and leg went numb, limiting his mobility and galvanizing the loskang into pushing their advantage. Using one good leg, he started spinning his numb leg on one end and holding his hammer with his left hand on the other. Appearing like a spinning T of death, he pushed the enemy back again. However, the poison was now moving through the rest of his body, and he couldn't summon the speed needed to fend the rest of them off.

One loskang charged him with a spear held high, and

Marcus knew he couldn't get his defense up in time. Marcus started to summon his armor, preparing to use his final energy to destroy the remaining enemy. Just before it was too late, the loskang head exploded in gore and black blood. Through weary eyes, he saw Killian charge out of the forest with quick knives that flashed and ended the spear-throwing nuisances while Shay's energy projectiles quickly silenced a number of the closer screaming green-eyed creatures.

After clearing the initial attacking group, Killian approached Marcus and pulled him close, getting ready to share more energy. Marcus used what little strength he had and pushed him away with a hushed statement, "You will not go blue for me."

"Let me help you, Marcus. I have enough that we can both get back."

Marcus heard the half-truth in the statement. Killian may have enough to share, but it would be unlikely they both would make it back.

Shay came down off the cliff quickly and joined his team. "More loskang are coming from behind. Marcus, let's get you up. Can you walk?"

Marcus chuckled and said, "That is about all I can do, but we don't have time. You both need to get out of here. I will hold them back long enough for you to reach the fort."

Shay wanted to protest. He wanted to tell Marcus that there was a grand strategy in which they all made it back. But there wasn't, and he couldn't protest against the only plan that would work. The tall private would likely go blue if they stayed and fought, and Killian may not be far behind.

"I can still share more energy. We can do it!" Killian protested against the idea.

"You know you can't. It wouldn't be enough to get you both back." With sorrow, Shay grabbed Marcus's forearm and looked him in the eyes, "It was an honor, knowledge seeker. I look forward to fighting beside you in the final battle."

Marcus nodded and responded with, "Honor was mine, SALT."

Finally resolved with the choice, Killian took Marcus's other arm in a similar embrace as Shay. "We will meet again, knowledge seeker." After nodding toward the approaching enemy, he finished with, "Take them all with you."

"I wouldn't be a good Sword if I didn't, healer."

They pulled their brother into a standing position between the two swords and handed him his war hammer. They embraced their taller brother quickly and set off towards the fort in a dead sprint.

Marcus turned on his communication link for all of 1-1-8, "Brothers, fight well and bring honor to the King." With a serious tone, he continued, "I look forward to hearing how you completed this mission. Be prepared to answer my many questions."

The loskang was approaching. Marcus saw the limbs of the trees shake in the distance as they jumped from tree to tree. Just as the first green-eyed loskang leaped towards him, he summoned his armor. Curing his sluggishness instantly, he started stacking their lifeless bodies up high as they came at him with frenzied abandon.

However, it wasn't long before the loskang overwhelmed him in sheer numbers. They piled on top of Marcus and stabbed at him, trying to find gaps in his armor with their poisoned tips. Not a single tip touched his skin through his impenetrable armor. The energy required to maintain his gift pushed him beyond saving. With a last swing that crushed three of his enemies, Marcus felt the blue overtaking him. He knelt as if he were in audience to his King. The last of the Creator's energy left him, and his armor was dismissed. Like a wave of the ocean starting from his feet, the color of his skin cascaded into a sharp blue. As it changed color, his body took on sharp edges reminiscent of stone.

Spears were thrust at the now fully blue Marcus and even smashed against his head, but his body was now impenetrable, and the loskang only broke their weapons against the statuesque body. They quickly gave up and moved to chase their other prey.

Soon, the clearing grew silent. The sun peaked through the forest and shined upon Marcus's body as it rested in humble acceptance. Light reflected from him and illuminated the horde bodies strewn in a circle around him. Mounds of decomposing monsters lay as a testimony to his skill as well as the fierce love of his brothers. As a warrior, he couldn't have offered a better tribute to his King.

13

TITUS was positioned near the front gate when the first of the loskang was seen sneaking around the perimeter. While they were obviously more aggressive in their tactics, they still appeared a bit more in control compared to the kreehaun's previous attack while under the influence of the dark plant. There was no doubting the influence as their green eyes darting around in the woods were obvious, even at this distance.

The rest of the team was in position to execute the plan. They were simply waiting for the signal. While the news of Marcus taking the blue may have been seen as a hit to morale, the truth was that his team was eager to extract their controlled vengeance.

Wit was in the northeast tower, watching the rear and left walls, with Titus in the southwestern covering the other two. The private spotted the first attempt at climbing their walls as loskang began with a flanking attack. Multiple of the horde beasts stealthily approached the wall and started their climb. Wit commented how comical the first time a loskang reached the slick-oiled section of the wall was. It reached up with both hands and, not finding the expected grip, fell backward with arms windmilling and a confused look still on its face - until it hit the rocky ground.

It disappointed Wit that not more of them attempted to jump over the slicked part. Others on the wall just gingerly touched the oil, a bit confused. Alternatively, their surprise came from the energy projectiles piercing their bodies from Wit's rifle. They were easy shots, but Wit held himself back from wiping them all out, leaving one or two to throw spears back at him while they climbed back down and retreated. So far, so good.

Various loskang groups tried to climb other sections of the walls. Some even endeavored to jump the entire height of the wall in certain sections where the wall appeared lower. They didn't make it and would slip back to their doom. Loskang could jump extremely high, but they required something to grab hold of at a certain height, as it was possible for them to kill themselves on their return to the ground. Suicide by jumping too high was a humorous thought.

"Excellent work on the walls, Kurian. Prepare for step two." Titus announced over the team channel as he watched another of the larger loskang attempt a jump, only to be shot down by his quick shot.

Kurian responded, "Roger, Commander. John and I are ready."

As expected, the loskang settled on throwing spears at Wit and Titus's positions with no hope of actually hitting them. The frustration was palpable from their enemy as the dark plant's spores were whipping them into a frenzy, but their instincts told them it was fruitless to continue throwing themselves at the walls.

Suddenly, the gates to the fort opened. The enemy saw this and instantly jumped to try and take advantage of the opening. To them, it must have seemed like something had gone wrong inside, and their enemy had made a fatal mistake. Loskang's drive to get inside and their instincts snapped together into a single driving purpose - get to the gate before it closed.

A hundred raging loskang ran through the gates to a silent and still courtyard with stone piles to their left and right, almost like it was guiding them forward. The rocks were not tall or slicked, so loskang could easily get around them. However, before more could make it to the gate, the doors closed as suddenly as they had opened. All those within whipped their heads back to where they entered to see Kurian re-locking the gate. Quickly, the Sword dove back to his original hiding place in the corner of the entrance with a wall to his right and the closed gate to his left. Some spears were thrown, but the brother tucked himself into a ball behind his shield.

Seeing an enemy trapped in a corner and appearing to huddle in fear behind a shield, they all turned to attack. As they circled in, up and around the piles of rock that enclosed the entrance, a shout came from the back of the shield. "Fire in the hole!"

As the hidden explosive devices went off under the piles of rock, the force broke each stone into hundreds of tiny projectiles. Those near the rocks were practically disintegrated, while those *lucky* enough to have fellow monsters between them and the explosives were simply shredded into bits of gore and acidic blood by flying debris.

Kurian, safe behind his shield and in the farthest corner away from all the explosions, finally peeked out to survey his handiwork. He was not disappointed. No loskang were left standing, and no sounds were heard as the courtyard returned to silence.

"Objective complete, Commander. No enemy left inside the fort."

"Good work, Sergeant. Prepare for phase three."

"Roger that, moving to phase three."

Titus smiled as his plan continued to unfold. How do you handle ambush hunters? You ambush them.

From the outside, the loskang that had been behind the initial group who made it into the fort had stopped outside the gates. They had heard the explosion but weren't in a position to see the cause or aftermath. After a few minutes of silence, the doors suddenly re-opened. Inside, they could only see small crevices in the ground but no sign of their brethren. Much more cautiously than the first group, the new loskang huddled together and checked their surroundings as they entered. Nothing showed signs of explosive traps as they carefully walked forward, including behind the doors.

Before the second wave of loskang dispersed, a different type of trap was activated. John opened up with his ranged gift from a concealed and protected position within one of the ruined buildings to the right of the entrance. Grouped and cautious as they were, the enemy couldn't have made it easier for him. With just a few extended bursts from his weapon, the entire group was down. His field of fire was perfect for the ambush as his position was in the upper right corner of the kill box, giving him full visibility of the gate. The clearing of the rubble and stones had made sure that there was no cover or escape routes. It was over in a few short heartbeats.

Kurian emerged from the gatehouse and went through the carnage to ensure all the monsters were permanently down. After giving John the thumbs up, he radioed Titus to give him the good news that their second trap was a complete success.

As Titus was about to congratulate the team, Wit interrupted the team communication, "We have enemy in the fort! Repeat, enemy in the fort!"

Without asking the questions that quickly ran through his head and he easily dismissed as unimportant at the moment, Titus responded immediately with new orders for his team. "Kurian, secure the gate and coordinate with Wit to hunt the enemy inside. John, fall back from your position and secure the tomb."

Now that his team was moving, he asked his communication expert for details: "How many and where, Wit? Do you see how they got in?"

"Negative on their entry point, Commander. I saw three near the hall on the ground and five on the northwestern corner, but exact numbers are unclear."

"I believe I can answer the how, Commander." Shay's voice piped in on the team link. "It appears as though they are throwing their spears into the corner of the northwestern wall and using them as grips to climb just outside your field of vision."

Clever, Titus thought. While it was good to hear his second and know he was close, the information brought about new challenges. Their ability to ambush the horde depended on funneling them through the gates. Their positions were no longer defensible, with loskang in the fort and capable of attacking his brothers from behind.

"Any chance you can provide support from outside, Lieutenant?"

"Sorry, Commander. We are being hunted by roughly one hundred loskang, and Killian is low on energy."

"Understood. Get here any way you can so we can hold them off together at the main hall."

"Roger that, sir. We will get through their line and rendezvous with you at the main hall."

Both the warriors left the unspoken thought of *easier said than done* out of their communication. Being chased down was one thing, but forcing their way through a line of enemies at the same time seemed near suicidal. However, their mission was the tomb, so there was no such thing as running and fighting another day. If they had any chance of success, it was together as a team.

Titus shifted back into the moment and revised his orders for all members to fall back to the hall as he began to see even more loskang climb over the walls on all sides. Their best shot was forcing their enemy to fight in close quarters of the hall and bottleneck them in the entrance.

****

* * *

Shay shouted to Killian as they moved together, “Stay right on me and run straight to the western wall. We will use the enemy’s tactic and our primaries to scale the wall to come in behind them.”

Killian nodded without questioning the plan, but they both knew the issue was not about how they would climb the wall. Shay had neglected to say how they would get through the small army between them and the wall while avoiding the other small army directly behind.

The SALT prepared himself and took off out of the woods directly towards the group of loskang waiting at the bottom of the wall for those climbing ahead. It took them longer than Shay had expected for one or more to notice the two lone Swords charging towards them, but it would likely have been nothing any one of them could have ever considered. These monsters didn’t have the type of communication the Swords did, so this group would not have known that their own brethren were chasing them in this direction.

While they were able to close a significant amount of distance, it wasn’t quite as much as what Shay wanted. The loskang on the ground quickly organized into two groups. One was charging them, and another began to throw spears.

“Keep running straight. I will clear a path.” Shay shouted back to his junior as he drew his hand and half-curved daggers in each palm from behind his back and called his armor. He suddenly sped ahead of Killian as he showed the special gift of his light armor. SALTs didn’t have the true protection of heavy armor that other Swords experienced. Instead, their armor increased their speed to almost ten times their original.

Both loskang charging him and his brother behind were shocked as it seemed as though the running warrior just disappeared in front of them. However, his speed made his movements hard to track with the naked eye.

As he hit their charging line, Shay gracefully deflected spears and flowed through the enemy, leaving nothing but bodies. His earlier momentum wasn't slowed as he seemed to still be sprinting ahead, but a three loskang wide path suddenly cut through their line. He was cutting them down while still running at the regular speed of a Sword.

Shay channeled his anger for losing a brother into his footwork as he spun and cut arms, legs, and throats. He poured his frustration at not seeing the charge at Marcus before it was too late into his hands as he stabbed rapidly into heads, stomachs, and backs. He moved so quickly that some of the spears that were thrown at him pierced loskang instead.

Suddenly, Shay and Killian were through, and the wall was ahead. Opting to ensure his junior made it first, the lieutenant quickly dismissed his armor so as not to waste more energy. He placed his back on the wall in a crouched position with his hands intertwined. Killian ran towards him in full sprint and stepped into his makeshift foothold. Using both Killian's leg power and Shay's arm strength to launch, the healer was close to the top before he drew his knives and stabbed them into the wood. Quickly, he began to ascend the wall, and Shay started his own climb using daggers.

Killian was about to grab the top of the roof when a spear from the line of charging loskang pierced his arm. Losing his grip, he fell backward to the rocky ground with nothing to slow him.

Shay saw it happen from his lower position on the wall. Thinking quickly, he pulled his feet up to place them between himself and the wall while using his dagger's grip to hold his entire weight. Right before Killian's body passed him, the lieutenant launched himself out in parallel from the ground and directly into the falling body. Using the forward momentum out from the wall to turn an inevitable death fall into a survivable roll, the two Swords crashed to the ground.

Checking to ensure Killian was still alive, he pulled the healer behind a small boulder as more spears began raining down on them. Shay summoned his ranged rifle and began firing at any loskang attempting to push their position. It was a delaying tactic, and Shay knew it. Killian could not attempt another climb, and the gate was closed. With no way in, they were now between a wall of spears and a literal wall.

Shay looked at Killian, and they both shared a moment. No escaping the inevitable, but anger at missing out on finishing the mission. Is this what Marcus felt in his final waking moments?

Just as they were about to say their farewells, Killian's mouth opened in surprise and pointed behind Shay into the sky. He turned to look, and a beam of light came from the sky to land on the main hall's chimney. The light pierced down from the clouds and danced with the life of fire. It was a violet color and was no larger than a finger, but the amount of light and energy it produced showered all present with power. Shay instantly knew the sensation. Something other than them had used the power of Choice.

****

Titus and the rest of the fort's defenders fought back the loskang at the hall's entrance. There seemed to now be an endless supply of the hideous monsters as the team was constantly assailed by poison and spears. It would only take a single misstep or accident for one of them to succumb to poison, and their defenses would begin to collapse.

The green-eyed loskang were beyond frenzied as they were within range of the dark plant, the source of what called to them. They stabbed and bit, kicked and punched at even each other to get at the defenders.

Looking at the situation, Titus considered whether it was time to fall back to their final position inside the tomb. The hall just outside the crypt would limit their enemy's ranged capabilities, giving the defenders one more advantage.

Choosing to order the retreat, Titus opened their communication link to give directions to his remaining Swords. Suddenly, a beam of violet-colored light appeared through the roof in the center of the main hall and landed in the fire pit directly above the tomb. Fighting stopped, and the room grew quiet as both parties looked at the spectacle of a light that had manifested from the sky.

The beauty of the light was stunning. The energy coming out of the beam was immediately recognizable as Choice, but Titus had never felt another's use of Choice before. It was both familiar and foreign at the same time.

Horde monsters, the declared enemy of beauty and order, drew back from the light but soon pushed the attack even more fiercely to try and destroy their enemy and whatever was creating this insult to their senses.

Alpha team felt invigorated by the energy, but it didn't provide them with true Creator power. It was more like seeing reinforcements coming over the hill during a battle. While heartening, it wasn't actual rest. Titus resumed his thought process of getting his team to the tomb. While beautiful, the light could potentially be a hindrance if it distracted them from the battle in front of them.

With the clearest signal 1-1-8 had experienced since their arrival, a familiar female voice came over their communications link, "1-1-8, this is Arrow 5 and 7. We see your beacon. Does anyone copy? Over."

"Arrow 5, this is 1-1-8 actual. We copy you loud and clear. Good to hear your voice, Captain. Over."

"You too, Commander. Looks like you rock-eaters could use a little help from above. Over."

"We will take all the help we can get, Captain. The fort's interior needs to be cleared, and air support due west of the Sword beacon, which is about to be placed outside the walls by my exterior team. How copy? Over."

"Solid copy, Commander. 7 take the western wall and cover the Swords there. Leave the interior to me. Over."

A new voice responded with, "Understood, Captain. 7 moving to western wall. Over."

Titus told Shay to place his light beacon out for the Arrows to see, and soon, confirmation of the stranded Swords' position was announced over the link by the new Arrow pilot.

"Roger that, 7. You are weapons-free. Over."

As both Arrows began their attack, it was clear that nothing would escape the destruction that rained down from above. Each Arrow was capable of more precise targeting and large-scale bombardment. Arrow 5 used the former method of clearing the fort's interior, while 7 used the latter outside the walls. Both were effective, but the more precise attack inside left the buildings standing, and the exterior shelling was quicker.

While a few spears were launched up at the flying creations, there was no danger to the ships themselves. Such small projectiles were not even a nuisance to the Arrows due to the height at which they flew.

Within half a mark, the fort and outside were clear of all enemies, and the entirety of the team was back together - minus one.

Once the Arrows made a few final runs around their position to be sure all of the infected horde was destroyed and dropped off much-needed resources, Titus asked them for one more favor. Their fallen brother needed to be returned home to lay with the other warriors who had taken the blue.

After giving their condolences and assurances that Marcus would be treated with honor, they began traveling back home. However, as they were about to leave, Captain Ailey asked Titus, "How did you get that beacon up right as we approached?"

His response was simple, "We didn't."

Confused but understanding that there were no real answers to her question, she wished them goodbye once more, and the two Arrows began their return flight with their precious cargo aboard.

During their after-battle discussion, Wit bluntly asked, "Okay, so what happened? Who sent that beacon? Don't get me wrong, sir. I loved it, and the airheads it seemed to have manifested certainly helped a ton, but where did it come from?"

Titus looked to his second, and they had nearly a telepathic conversation with simple nods in which they agreed and had come to the same conclusion. They responded simultaneously with, "The tomb is using Choice."

14

FINALLY! Sham thought as he reached the water. Just across the small ocean, he could move into the realm of the legion and directly into liberation city. After accomplishing that, he would seek an audience with his king and gather an army to crush the Sword unit that had pushed him out. The glory he saw in decorating his new home with blue statues kept him going and ensured that the ocean before him seemed like a minor inconvenience.

It was funny how Sham now considered that wretched hall his new home. In truth, he hated it. However, there was poetic justice in changing a punishment into a masterpiece rivaling a great castle in his mind.

He liked the idea of turning his fort into a new den of pleasure for only a select few to come and enjoy. The thought of blue statues everywhere and his fellow shadows indulging in every whim and fantasy greatly pleased him. And why should he not be allowed to prop up his shabby home into a castle that any shadow would envy? After defeating a whole Sword unit, he would surely be rewarded handsomely.

Sham took these thoughts with him as he began moving south along the beach, hoping to find the means to cross the ocean. There was always some sort of horde beast around that would likely bend to Sham's will and take him across. Also, there were some watercraft around that would serve him in crossing. Sham would build his own raft and simply cross on his own power if he had to. He wasn't against hard work as long as he saw the payoff as worth it. Long gone were the days in which he would do whatever he was ordered to do without payment. Sham had broken those chains along with the other legion members.

Unfortunately for him, there were no beasts or crafts as Sham continued his journey south. The more he walked, the more frustrated he became. As cycles passed, he started to engineer a watercraft in his mind that he would need to start building to reach the barrier to liberation city. To his disgust, there weren't any living trees or other resources nearby that he could use for his designs. Instead, the beaches turned to prairie land with nothing for mils.

His frustration was to the point where he would need to kill something very soon to slightly satiate his anger when he saw smoke rising in the distance. It was southeast of his location and hidden by some rolling hills. Sham smiled as he thought he might have both of his desires in one place: something to kill and transportation.

As he got closer, more and more smoke trails were seen. Sham slowed and crawled over the last hill to understand what he was walking into. He would never put himself in a situation where there was no chance of getting something he wanted or getting out of it in one piece.

When he crested the hill and saw what was the cause of the smoke, he was both delighted and gravely disappointed. An army was camped out in the prairie. Not just any army, but the western army of the legion. His *brothers*.

Sham was happy to see that his revenge may be closer than he even realized, but the glory would go to the renowned leader of this army - general Neart. There was no hope that Neart would simply give Sham his army, and he doubted that the king would be happy that Sham simply bypassed the current army at the enemy's doorstep to bring news to him personally.

The shadow crawled back down the hill and began thinking furiously through his options. There must be some way in which he could come out on top and get everything he wanted. How would he get the army? No, that was not what was important. The real question was how was he going to get the glory. If Sham was honest with himself, he knew Neart was far better equipped to lead a battle against a Sword team. Sham needed to ensure that glory came to him instead of the general.

As he was nearing some potential strategies to get what he wanted, a wicked-looking sword was placed under his chin and across his throat. The shock was hard to remove from Sham's face as he slowly looked up and into one of the most beautiful smiles he had ever seen. Unfortunately, that beauty did not extend to the sword holder's eyes as they screamed insanity and violent intent with the red-colored darkness that was a hallmark of the legion.

"And who might you be?" said the newcomer in a whimsical and almost bored voice. Before Sham could respond to the ethereal shadow, the sword bearer continued, "Wait. Do I care? Hmmm, I don't think so."

The sword started to move up and into a killing blow, or at least an extremely painful and long recovery for a shadow. Thinking as fast as he ever had before, Sham blurted out, "Swords are near!"

As he had hoped, the evil-looking sword stopped in its path to behead him and hovered just along his throat once again. Sadistically, the sword slowly got closer and closer as the new shadow teased with Sham. As the blade touched his skin and soon began biting deeper, the energy within his body began dripping out along the sword.

"I swear! A full unit took my fort. They are held up there now."

The sword continued its slow, painful journey through Sham's neck, but the look on the bearer's face suddenly turned to concern. "Oh my! That must have been horrible for you!"

His tone could have easily confused anyone for true

concern, but the way the sword kept slicing into Sham's throat showed the true mockery that the shadow was performing.

"It is true! They even have a SALT with them!"

With that one word, the sword halted as Sham's energy continued to slowly trickle out along the blade, and the cruel shadow said, "Did you say a SALT was with them?"

"Yes! I had escaped from the fort and was over a mil out before he took out my horde servants. He would have gotten me too if I hadn't used my skills."

Laughing at the last bit, the sword bearer pulled his sword away. "I believe you, small one. You must have very impressive *skills*."

The silent and insane shadow simply turned and began walking away. Sham called, "Aren't you going to take me to the general?"

Turning back to shine a brilliant smile at Sham that made his veins turn to ice, the shadow simply said, "You can find your own way. Something out here is hunting you, and it seems far more interesting than anything you may have to say."

With that final confusing comment, the shadow simply disappeared. If something was truly hunting Sham, which he doubted, maybe they could kill each other. Sham sincerely hoped he would never see those cruel eyes ever again. He didn't think he would survive the meeting.

****

After reviewing the scroll that Marcus had given everything for, it appeared as though the knowledge seeker had agreed with Titus and Shay. Titus would never say that it was worthless to send Bravo out to the ruins, as that would dishonor Marcus's work, but it was a bitter pill to swallow, knowing that both teams had come to the same conclusion at the end of the mission.

However, Marcus's scroll highlighted more details about a potential true objective and what they needed to do. As Marcus had put in the scroll, the key was to protect the casket and to ensure the flame stayed lit for as long as possible. He was convinced that the thing within the casket had the potential of life and Choice, and without the flame, the darkness plant would pull whatever it was into a forever darkness that Marcus had vividly experienced.

In his report, Marcus described how he experienced what the being within the tomb felt after touching the covered casket momentarily. The knowledge-seeker described it as an eternity of pain and darkness within a heartbeat.

Titus took this information and made his own study of their crypt. Looking at the situation through new eyes, he wasn't convinced that the flame kept the plant at bay. The flame's color was still the soft red of a normal candle, whereas the beacon that appeared in the sky was violet. As the Commander moved his hand over the flame, he felt no heat and nothing that felt like it was physical, just as they had noted previously. While he didn't deny that the flame played a vital role, at this point, nothing was certain outside of three things: something was making Choices, they had to protect the tomb from the enemy, and the dark plant was designed to make their task harder.

Without the ability to separate the plant carved into the stone, Titus needed to understand what the enemy wanted from it. They obviously wanted to get inside the tomb, but why had they not done so earlier? Did something change? Was it 1-1-8's arrival or something else?

Regardless of what he knew or didn't know, Titus could use the spores as an early warning system. Truth be told, there wasn't anything he or his team could do to protect the coffin from itself. Marcus took the blue to ensure Titus had all the information available, but it wasn't enough to fully grasp the situation. Now that the team was down one brother, their ability to gather more information or do reconnaissance was severely hampered.

All that said, there was one more thing that they had discovered in the latest attack. Not all spores from the plant were equal, and that it could call specific monsters. Because of this, Titus headed towards their prisoner after emerging from the crypt. Walking into the room with the kreehaun, it charged at him with nothing but hate and murder in its eyes. Titus quickly drew his sword without ceremony and separated the monster's head from its body. He couldn't do anything about the enemy attached to the crypt, but he would not stand to have another enemy in their midst a heartbeat longer than needed. His King had commanded them to purge the chaos from his land in every fight, so keeping this one alive for more than necessary would be as close to sacrilege as a Sword could get.

As Titus made the rounds to check on his brothers, it was clear that they were disappointed that Marcus was no longer with them. Taking the blue was not shameful or dishonorable, but it did hamper the overall unit's mission. Without Marcus, a key resource and a deadly fighter would no longer be available for the mission, and the team would feel that loss. Titus encouraged his brothers and jokingly lamented about having to answer every question that Marcus would immediately have once he woke up. The truth was that Marcus likely wouldn't immediately be looking for answers as he would only be awakened once the final battle horn was sounded. All who slept in the blue would awake and immediately be sent to finish off the enemy once and for all. After that, he and his brothers would have plenty of time to catch up and begin a new life within a new united Kingdom of their Maker.

When the Commander reached Shay in his northwestern tower, he had a harder time raising the SALT's morale. The lieutenant was second-guessing some of his decisions during the retreat and thinking through what may have worked.

"If only I had stayed with Marcus and..."

Titus interrupted with, "Staying with Marcus would have been the more reasonable and tactical decision?"

"No, but.." Shay's rebuttal died on his lips.

"We may never know the repercussions of our use of Choice, but I know now that you were able to get back with Doc to fight another day. Only our Creator can say what our Choices will reap." Titus paused to look into Shay's flame-colored eyes before looking out over the fort as he added, "Our existence is a unique tapestry made up of individual Choices. Some big and some small. Those Choices will weave others into our story in ways only the Creator understands. My Choice put you out into the wilderness, but don't doubt it was your own that saved you. It is in us to make a beautiful design that is joined with others in complex and imaginative ways. We must honor Him through Choice and strive to make our life worthy of His eyes. Learn from your mistakes, as I will, and honor the fallen's sacrifice by making it a turning point in your own tapestry."

Shay looked back at his leader and nodded. He knew the truth of his words just like he had made the only Choices he could have. It still stung that one of his brothers went blue on his watch, but he would not dishonor Marcus's sacrifice.

"Thank you, Commander. I appreciate the words and perspective."

Returning his junior officer's nod, Titus began his climb back down. As he reached the ground floor, Kurian came over the link and confirmed that the defenses were reset and fortified once more. Titus had set the sergeant to the task almost immediately after the Arrows provided additional material. Kurian had set multiple traps and hardened the fort against larger attacks using what they had. While not invincible, the fortress was better equipped to handle future onslaughts like they had recently experienced.

Their fort's gates were now fortified with metal instead of solely the wood that was part of its original construction. The walls were reinforced with sturdy beams in strategic spots, ensuring they would fare better against siege monsters such as farhatch or turtairs. Titus's team always mentally prepared for any type of attack and would work tirelessly to physically prepare their position for as many threats as possible.

One of the more ingenious improvements that Kurian had cooked up was an early warning system two mils out from the fort. A series of hidden tripwires would actually tap into their own communication link to provide an internal audio warning. The enemy would be unaware that their presence was already detected and that the Swords knew exactly which direction they were approaching from. While it may seem redundant to have another warning system, as the dark plant partially did that work for them, that warning method would not be trusted. Besides, every Sword knew the rule: one is none. Having redundancy was the only way to provide resilience in a system.

The team came together in the main hall to discuss potential improvements to their defenses. Suggestions ranged from blowing up the entire fort as a last-ditch effort to digging trenches from the main hall to the gate and using the natural incline to roll boulders at invading forces. Some were implemented, and others were not due to a lack of resources or problematic engineering.

That said, one of the ideas that quickly became a hot topic came from Wit. Well, his half-thought-spoken-out-loud and half-wise-crack. As the team was talking about fighting position improvements, Wit blurted out, "We still have a bréag to deal with. I wish we could stuff it into a box and blow it up." The comment had inspired Kurian.

While getting a monster like a whole bréag inside a box

was not exactly likely, luring it into a room or building? That could be plausible. Kurian ran through options and outlined his plan to rig their prison building with a large number of explosives that directed energy blasts to the interior. The explosion would not only incinerate everything within, but it should also bring the roof down on top of the ashes.

Shay interrupted Kurian's presentation with, "We know that the beast will likely go for the crypt. Why not do part of the hall or the entrance to the crypt instead of an exterior room?"

Titus answered, "We don't know what the beast will do. It was around the fort for two rounds of the cursed spores and hasn't come running yet. There is no evidence that it has any interest in the tomb - yet. None of us doubt it will come, but what it will be here for is the question. Will come for us or at the beckoning of the dark plant?"

"We need to plan for both outcomes," Kurian said. After bringing up the fort's interior layout on a scroll, he continued, "I will place some charges within the makeshift prison but reserve some for placement on the path to the crypt below the main hall. We are dividing our resources, but I should be able to rig enough to bring down the exterior structure while still creating a wall of flame in the crypt's hallway."

"Will it cause a collapse and seal off the crypt?" Titus asked.

"No, I will place them on a makeshift wall pointed back towards the stairwell. The tunnel will remain intact."

Titus was relieved at the confirmation as it would be impossible to protect the objective if buried underground. Unfortunately, his relief was somewhat short-lived as Kurian continued, "Sir, I am not sure if either explosion will be enough to end the bréag. By dividing our resources to cover both possible strategies, we risk not finishing off the enemy in either position."

"What is your estimation of success?"

"I suspect we have an eighty percent chance to kill it if we split our focus."

The room went silent as they all looked at Titus. Eighty percent was better odds than he could hope for, but it kept the door open for the creature to drag itself away and regain strength. If it did that, the same tactic would no longer be effective against it as it would be more wary of such traps.

"Do it."

Outwardly, the team barely registered even a heartbeat before Titus's response, but the Commander had taken all the information and ran through a multitude of scenarios in his mind. Splitting the charges into the different potential avenues of attack was the best strategy, even if the percentage of success wasn't the best.

Kurian took Wit and John to implement their traps and tactics while the remaining team members dispersed to go back on watch or complete other needed tasks. It wasn't long before the trio had completed a chest-height wall of explosives in the crypt's hallway and moved to the exterior courtyard building. As they passed Titus on the way to the second trap position, Killian came over the link from his position at the front gate, "Commander, you may want to get here. Now."

1-1-8's leader ran to the gate, and Killian, who was just inside the closed gate, instead of his watch post on the wall. The junior Sword was crouched, facing the wall away from the approaching Commander. With the keen senses of a warrior, Doc stood and turned at his approaching senior. Pierced at the end of his held knife was a small, lifeless creature with black fur, four legs, and a tail. Its overall size was no bigger than a small fist, and the legs didn't end with toes but had hooked claws like miniature scythes. Its nose and whiskers extended over protruding fangs, and the tail had similar hooked barbs sprouting from the end. The black fur hid additional hooks that could be retracted or extended. While this particular tiny creature had his eyes closed, Titus instantly knew they were bloodshot red. As final evidence of the creature's true nature, black, acidic blood ran down the healer's blade.

The bréag had come.

15

"BRÉAG inside the wall! Kurian, I need that trap set yesterday. Shay, go high and begin scanning for it within the fort. John and Amadon pair up and search the main hall, starting with the crypt. Killian and I will take the exterior. Use of armor is authorized if necessary. All Swords confirm," the Commander ordered over their link.

"Shay confirms, and I am moving to the tower."

"Kurian confirms, and I am setting up as fast as possible."

"Amadon here with John, we confirm. Moving to search the interior of the main hall."

Wit nodded towards John, and they sprinted towards the crypt, leaving Kurian to finish up the trap within the makeshift prison cell. As he ran, the communications expert began recalling all he knew about a bréag. None of it was very promising, but that only made him smile. Nothing was more thrilling than pushing oneself to the limit while performing the function the Creator had made them for. His grin may have seemed a bit out of place, but his partner running beside him seemed to catch on and returned just a hint of a smile.

The trouble with a bréag was that it was extremely hard to finish off completely. It wasn't actually made of one entity but rather an entire swarm of small, vicious creatures. While a juvenile bréag wasn't too difficult for a Sword unit to handle, the more mature clusters with hundreds or thousands of creatures were far more of a threat. Even if the majority were destroyed, just a handful of the vile creatures escaping would still allow it to repopulate into a larger threat once again. The additional fact that it had a long memory and held grudges ensured that it would return with a vengeance. Of all the horde monsters, this one had caused the most Host brothers and sisters to take an early blue.

After Wit had cataloged what he knew about the threat, he began thinking to himself that there was no way he could go blue today. Blue really was not his color. He was more of a warm yellow. Plus, all the naps he planned on taking and the pranks he had in the works that, if he were honest, would just be hilarious and awesome. His calendar was way too full to take time out to go blue. It was settled. He would just need to kill the thing.

As they reached the crypt's stairwell, Wit took the lead and moved down with Macey in hand while scanning every possible angle to ensure nothing was waiting for them. Circular stairways were designed to help defenders against an attacking force from below. It allowed the retreating fighters to swing weapons down at attackers while limiting the same attackers from fully swinging weapons back up. Wit appreciated the design, but it also meant that surprise attacks from below would be extra surprising as he moved slowly down and hugged the exterior wall to give him the best visual angles.

Clearing the stairs and seeing nothing, Wit and John walked side by side through the hallway to the tomb's door while avoiding their earlier set explosive trap. Through a quick hand signal, they opened the door and checked the tomb itself. Nothing. If the creature wanted to get here, it would have been here already. The additional fact that the vile plant didn't have spores spewing out of it meant that the creature wasn't summoned, unlike the others. It had seemingly just come to kill them, which was a surprisingly comforting thought to Wit.

"Commander, this is Amadon. No bréag in the crypt and

no spores. Permission to leave John to guard the crypt and search the main hall above?"

"Permission granted, but keep your link open."

Wit gave John a smack on his behind and a wink as he left, but the larger brother simply grunted and prepared himself behind the explosive trap. One of these days, Wit would get the big, silent grump to loosen up. Granted, it was likely that some, if not all, of them were about to go blue, but that didn't mean they couldn't enjoy themselves - right?

In a reverse of Wit's earlier slow pace down the stairs, he nearly sprinted back up the stairway. While the design of the circular stairwell was against him, as he was technically the supposed attacker in the situation, two facts prevented Wit from worrying about it. First, he had already cleared the stairwell moments before, and it was unlikely that any enemy could be waiting so quickly. Secondly, he was a Sword. The structure's design didn't matter; he would be the deadliest thing within it. Probably.

Having come in through the main entrance and not seeing anything initially, Wit decided to clear the right side of the building and associated storerooms since he was already in that hallway. He moved with both stealth and speed to clear each of the rooms. As he approached the second to the last room, he heard a barely audible chittering from within. Due to his enhanced hearing as a communications expert, he picked up sounds that no other brother or sister would have likely heard, which probably saved him from the attack that immediately occurred.

Wit dived to the side just as the door he was standing in front of flew off its hinges straight out into the hall, smashed to pieces against the opposite wall. He quickly recovered from his roll to turn and face the creature that walked out of the now-opened room. One would not immediately think of a swarm of small creatures as *walking*, but the bréag was not deadly because of the individual creatures - rather what they became together. The swarm had a single hive mind that controlled all the tiny beasts as one, and they used their hooks and claws to form a single entity. What walked out into the hall was a large golem made up of the individual monsters scurrying across the body while connecting their claws and even their teeth together to hold a massive shape. As the bréag approached Wit, the large arms and legs swung and moved like any other bipedal beast with bright, unblinking red eyes made up of multiple rats constantly staring at Wit with an almost physical feeling of intense hatred. Black, acidic blood continually dripped off it due to the beasts digging into each other to hold the shape. It was an enormous and ominous enemy that screamed death.

"I found it, Commander!"

"Understood, Wit. We are engaged with one here as well," Titus responded.

Two! How could there be two here?!? Bréag did not share, and they never traveled together with other horde beasts. The only answer was that they were dealing with a truly ancient swarm that had more than enough individual monsters to make two golems controlled by one mind. This was not good. If they didn't take out both simultaneously, at least half of the swarm would immediately try to escape.

Almost like he sensed Wit's thoughts, the Commander came back over the link with, "Try to get yours to the tunnel and hold it. We will trigger the traps together. Over." The way the Commander was breathing heavily meant that he was in the thick of it.

Unfortunately, the unspoken question of how long Wit would need to entertain his half wasn't about to be answered as it charged him. A fist made of nothing but teeth, claws, and acid-filled flesh swung low, so Wit went high. He jumped and swung his mace at the beast's head where its eyes were located and felt the satisfying crunch that comes with his mace connecting with flesh. Roughly ten of the tiny creatures flew down the opposite side of the hall and lay lifeless. Almost immediately, the creatures reformed, and a new set of eyes appeared. While the bréag didn't have a mouth, Wit could have sworn it grinned at him. Wit, having never backed down from being cheeky, grinned back. Regardless of whether the monster had smiled, it very obviously did not like the attitude that Wit was giving it. Being an older horde creature used to its victims being filled with fear, it did not appreciate this Sword seemingly laughing in its face.

The golem reared back and slammed another fist at its condescending opponent. While Wit was fast and ducked to the side, the fist was too wide, and Wit was too close to allow a second miss. He went flying and slammed hard against a wall. The wind knocked out of him was enough for him to question his own relaxed attitude.

Jumping back up, Wit swung at the larger foe's leg, hoping to slow it down. His attack wasn't hidden or subtle, so the bréag watched as the mace came in low and simply moved its smaller creatures out of the way. As his mace passed through where the leg had been and hit nothing but air, Wit got backhanded with another fist. The razor claws sliced up the junior Sword's face, sending him flying again.

Slamming into his second wall in just as many heartbeats, Wit slumped to the ground. He tentatively reached up and felt the slashes in his cheek. They began to heal instantly as Creator energy flowed out into the cuts, alongside a multitude of internal injuries. Attempting to get his wind back, Wit rose up, using the wall to steady himself, and began thinking through the strategies for dealing with the threat. However, he didn't have time to formulate a plan as the bréag wouldn't allow it. In almost a throwing motion, it launched a stream of the smaller beasts at him. They landed and immediately began clawing and biting. Hundreds of the beasts were holding fast to his body and tunic, doing whatever they could to burrow themselves into his very flesh.

Almost instinctively, Wit summoned his armor. In a flash, the tiny creatures on the Sword were turned into a black mist of gore and blood. Those lucky enough not to be touching his body at the time scurried back to the main golem and reformed into the creature.

Standing in the hallway while staring down the bréag in his bright armor and a smile, Wit whispered just loud enough for the monster to hear, "My turn."

Wit was never the fastest, but he knew he was quicker than most in their armor. He moved quickly, but in an exaggerated way, towards the throwing arm that had recently been diminished due to the creatures that had perished on Wit's armor. At the last moment, he dived to the ground and swung his mace hard. Smashing through both of the monster's legs where they touched the ground, the bréag's body dropped the span of a hand. The result was not only the death of any creature that the mace struck but also the creatures just above them as the entire golem's weight unexpectedly came crashing down on top.

Not stopping his momentum, Wit continued his swing in a full circle to come back and launch upwards between the crushed legs. His mace severed the golem into two seething halves, with tiny dead creatures flying up into the ceiling.

"Nice work, Macey!" Wit shouted joyfully as he witnessed the two parallel halves float there momentarily. Before he could react, and with speed that should not have been possible after being cut in half, each side reached out and grabbed the Sword into a crushing hug without fully reforming. Wit thought that was a bit unfair as he attempted to untangle himself from a sea of gnawing, angry creatures.

The amount of energy being used to hold his armor and repel the attack was quickly becoming worrisome. Kicking and striking with everything he had, Wit felt himself nearing a precipice internally. The feeling of his armor weakening seemed to only emphasize the fact that he didn't see a way out. Wit's one-on-one fight with the creature had barely lasted a handful of heartbeats from discovery to his current situation. He would have to apologize to Macey later.

As Wit was trying to come up with some jokes to help his apology go down when he awoke from the blue, a beam of white light suddenly outlined his body perfectly. Enough space between him and the bréag was created, so he whipped his mace up in a circular strike that severed the last lines of creatures that held him in place. He was free without a moment to spare.

At the end of the hall, John stood with his ranged gift in hand. The Sword had fired so accurately that, for a moment, an outline of Wit was carved into the bréag. Begrudgingly, Wit complimented his brother's shooting. Internally.

"You're late and almost hit me!" Wit shouted at John.

The only response was a very sarcastic thumbs up that clearly said 'You're welcome' without words.

Not wanting another taste of John's weapon, the bréag melted into a swarm of creatures that flowed back towards the larger brother like rushing water. Spreading themselves out to prevent his ranged gift from taking out groups and instead forcing its new opponent to either shoot and waste energy at individual creatures or abandon the use of ranged weapons altogether.

In response, John dismissed his ranged gift and, instead, summoned his armor. He didn't have the agility of Wit, but he was built similar to a tank or juggernaut. Like an unstoppable rock slowly rolling downhill, John stepped up to meet the swarm.

Not bothering to use his axe, John started stomping and crushing the swarm as it neared. Without pause, the beast soon formed once more and attempted to strike John with a heavy fist like it had done to Wit. Unlike Wit, John simply punched back at the fist swinging towards him. For a moment, it appeared as though the bréag had simply formed around John's arm, but a pile of dead creatures soon fell from the outstretched arm of the monster. With a shriek, the bréag began rapidly assaulting John. While the larger brother held his own, Wit sensed it was taking a toll on him.

Charging in from behind, Wit expected to catch the beast off his guard. That was not the case as a third arm sprung out from the back of the golem to smack Wit against the wall once more. As he recovered quickly, Wit considered how tired he was of smashing into walls in this particular hallway. Maybe he would choose another hallway for his next fight.

When Wit re-engaged the backside of the bréag, new eyes formed that were now facing him, giving the monster the appearance of having two bodies held together at the center. While this particular bréag seemed to have a large supply of the creatures to call upon, the Swords were slowly cutting the swarm down.

"Wit. Be ready. We are getting ours into position. Should be any moment now. Over," the Commander announced over the communications.

Not knowing exactly how much time they had, both Wit and John began pushing the attack with all the strength and agility they could muster. They had already pushed the bréag into the corner, with John blocking off the main entrance and Wit preventing the monster from returning back down the hallway where it had originated from. The only avenue of retreat for the beast was through the stairwell and into the crypt.

Everything seemed to be going well for the defenders, and the bréag was starting to push into the stairwell's doorway when disaster struck as an explosion was heard from outside. Whether or not it was an accident or planned, the exterior team had detonated their trap.

Instantly, the golem took on a more defensive posture and began trying to escape via a handful of the tiny creatures attempting to sprint past Wit and John. Both Swords did their best to kill any of them that moved away, but the golem made it difficult as it would lash out in defense of the tiny creature's attempts at escape.

Just like before, when John appeared, the swarm suddenly collapsed, and it became a free-for-all as the tiny creatures ran in all directions. Having no true way of stopping them all, John and Wit killed as many as they could. Within a heartbeat of that strategy, it was clear that it would not work, and a majority of the beasts would get away.

Quickly thinking of anything that would help, Wit thought back on when he first encountered the beast and its apparent disdain for his behavior. Willing to try anything, Wit began laughing and taunting the beast.

"Look, John! See how the mighty bréag runs for its life like a little child?" His laughter was not quite infectious and a bit forced, but John almost immediately caught on and began pointing and chuckling.

"Look at the tiny little creatures running in terror! Run, bréag! Run from us, the superior warriors!" Wit continued as he flexed his muscles in a show of arrogance.

All the tiny creatures stopped moving immediately and were instantly pulled back like they were attached to a single leash. They immediately reformed themselves into a golem. It launched itself at them with a rage that both John and Wit had never seen before. They, in turn, ran.

As the seemingly enraged beast chased them down the stairwell, the two Sword's dismissed their armor. It was no longer going to be a hand-to-hand fight. They had already used too much energy for that to be a winning strategy. Their trap was either going to work, or they were about to join their fallen brethren in the blue.

When they flew from the bottom step and dashed down

the hall, they could feel the creatures right behind them—the red eyes of hundreds of angry monsters singular in their purpose to kill them.

Neck and neck, the Swords raced to their half wall in the center of the crypt's hallway and leaped over. Wit activated the trap, and the crypt was ablaze in white energy and light. The pure energy directed back at the chasing enemy was so intense that scorch marks could be found at the bottom of the stairwell and all throughout the tunnel immediately after.

A small handful of the beasts had survived by leaping onto the Swords at the last minute. They attempted to scurry away and back towards the stairwell, but a few quick blasts from Wit's ranged gift made short work of them.

Wit looked around at their handiwork. Ash floating in the air, a putrid odor filling the tunnel, gore all around them, and both the Swords covered in unhealed cuts and bruises at the very brink of going blue. He turned to his brother and said, "Now that wasn't so bad, was it?"

John mustered up just enough energy to punch him.

****

Neither Sword caught sight of the final individual bréag, slipping past them towards the crypt and pulling itself under the doors.

Almost hesitantly, the tiny monster approached the tomb. It sniffed the air and circled to stay out of the light of the flame. Seeing the etched vines, the bréag took the final few steps to get closer. As it touched the vine, a single thorn made of blackness stuck into the creature and almost immediately drained all the acidic blood out of it. In a heartbeat, the monster had become a husk that quickly dissipated into dust, destroying all evidence of its presence.

A new, thin vine of blackness carved itself into the tomb from the main branch and moved around to the side of the tomb. Almost as if in pleasure, the plant slightly shook as its grip on the tomb grew tighter.

16

IT was 8:20 PM on a Sunday, and Henry was sitting on his bed after returning from a week-long church camp a few hours ago. His mom had picked him and his older siblings up from the church parking lot and taken them out to eat dinner. She wanted to hear all about what they did and catch up with her three children. Since eating out was always a special event for their family, none of them complained about the constant questions thrown at each of them.

When they got home, their father greeted them as he was waking up. Due to the decline of their church, Henry's dad was forced to quit being a pastor and go full-time into road construction. Unfortunately for his family, that meant he needed to work a lot of early mornings and even late nights to accommodate traffic.

Henry knew that his dad was in pain from all the long hours and the demanding labor, but they finally had enough money to pay off their debt and even go out to eat on occasion. While he missed his dad a lot, Henry did enjoy the benefits of finally being able to afford some of his own clothes and newer things.

When they got home, they needed to repeat the same answers given earlier during dinner but now to their father, who wanted to hear their experiences directly from them. Henry complained that he had already said everything and wanted to go to his room. One stern warning glance from his mother was all he needed to begin retelling the stories about his adventures at camp.

"Each morning, we would wake up and get ready for the day. We would eat breakfast and then play some games outside before it got too hot. After that, we would have lunch and go swimming in the lake. We would do a bible study and worship at night," Henry rapidly spoke. "Happy now?"

The last bit came out more harshly than Henry intended, and his dad looked crestfallen and confused. He merely said, "Yes, sounds like a good trip. Why don't you head to bed?"

Henry sensed the disappointment and knew that his dad just wanted to see them after being gone for a week, but Henry was too excited to care. He just wanted to get to his room and check out what was hidden deep in his bags.

"Thanks," Henry said as he went to his room. But, before he could make it a few steps, the shame he felt caused him to stop and add, "I will fill you in on all the details tomorrow after school. Okay, dad?"

Carl nodded to his youngest son before turning to his daughter and asking more questions. Before Henry reached his door, he heard his dad ask Jules about boys, and she responded with a loud 'Dad!' that almost echoed down the hall.

As soon as Henry entered his room, he shut the door and locked it. Quickly throwing down his bags on the bed and sitting next to them, he began ripping out the clothes that were shoved into his large blue duffel bag. His room was not normally clean, but the large pile of clothes on the floor would definitely send his mother into a frustrated rant. However, his mother was absolutely the last thing on his mind.

Finally, after pulling out nearly all the clothes and lifting up the small plastic panel at the bottom that helped keep the bag's shape, Henry pulled out a magazine. There was a very beautiful woman on the cover, but unlike anything he had ever seen before this week, the woman wasn't wearing anything over her chest. Just above the woman, in large letters, the magazine's title was prominently displayed: *PlayBunny*.

The mere sight of the woman excited Henry and made him feel good. She was seductively posed and licking her lips. From experience at camp, he knew that a lot more was in store for him within the magazine itself.

Earlier, when Henry was explaining what he did during the week, he obviously left out the part about the boys' cabin coming together at night to look at the magazines that a counselor had stashed away in his bunk. The older man of 25 who was in charge of Henry's cabin had a few of these magazines hidden away in his bunk. He never showed them to the boys directly, but they had found them while trying to play a prank on their cabin's leader.

After discovering them, the boys in his group swore not to tell anyone about it and would sneak in and look at each one during the night meetings all the counselors attended. Once they had looked through one, they would put it back where it was and run back to their bunks. The excitement of the discovery and the shared secret made them all giddy, and they would often laugh as soon as their cabin leader returned. While some of the boys felt bad about it, the majority was quick to silence the dissenters through peer pressure and threats. Henry had not been one of those who objected.

He was immediately captivated by the images in the magazine. They would flash in his mind as he lay in his bunk, and they were all he thought of during the day when everyone was doing activities. By the end of the week, he knew he would take one home. Sure enough, on the last night, a couple of the boys agreed with him and took their favorites hidden away in their bag.

The theft of the magazines was the perfect crime as the councilor wouldn't ever report what was stolen, and they would never see him again. Henry was sure that their cabin leader would get more anyway.

As for the nagging feeling of remorse from hiding it from his parents, he could smother that quickly enough using the desire he felt. He *wanted* to look and do other things.

That thought suddenly brought the memory of his dad having THE talk with him not too long ago. It had started with his dad taking him out for ice cream, just the two of them. While not exactly unheard of, it was enough of an oddity that Henry had thought there was something afoot. After their ice cream, his dad drove him to their church's parking lot, and they sat there for a few minutes before he asked the first awkward question of the night, "Do you know what sex is, Henry?"

The blood rushed into Henry's face, making him bright red as he turned to his father. Hoping to stave off the conversation and show his dad how mature he really was, he responded, "Yes, Dad! I already know about all of that and how it works. We don't need to talk about the *birds and the bees*."

Henry did, in fact, understand how a man and a woman physically came together. Television shows and biology class ensured he fully understood what went where and how.

Almost as if he had read the very thoughts of his son, Carl nodded and replied, "Yes. I do believe you understand the performance of it. It is a shame on me as your father that you would have already been exposed to such things in this world."

Exhaling a sigh of relief, thinking he had forestalled the whole conversation, Henry started taking more bites of his ice cream.

"What is your responsibility as a man in sex?"

Having caught him mid-swallow, Henry started choking a little at his dad's question. The blood rushing to his head was not all from the cold substance caught in the back of his throat as he thought through the various scenarios he had seen on TV or the movies he had silently watched from afar when his older siblings rented them.

Once he was composed, Henry didn't look at his dad as he turned his head and almost whispered his answer, "Please the woman?"

In the following few seconds, the car grew so silent that cars 200 yards away seemed to be driving right next to their parked car. But, after only a brief pause, Henry heard his dad start to laugh louder and harder than he ever had. It wasn't an accusatory laugh but one that welcomed Henry into it. Still unsure as to the cause of the laughter, Henry couldn't help but join his dad. It felt good, and it was one of the most memorable moments in his life so far.

After both of them calmed down, Carl responded, "Yes, son. That definitely is one of your responsibilities." He then wiped a few of his laughter tears off his face before stating, with a more serious tone, "But that isn't your main responsibility."

He continued, "As a man, it is your responsibility to protect women and honor them as partners in fulfillment of one of the very first commandments God ever gave us."

Henry was confused. He had thought they were talking about sex, but now his dad was bringing up the Ten Commandments?

Seeing the confusion on Henry, Carl elaborated further, "When God created us, He told Adam and Eve to be fruitful and multiply. That was one of the first things he ever told us to do. Can you imagine that? God was telling these two people to have sex."

"That is actually kind of funny."

"Right? God wanted us to enjoy each other and the creation of life," Carl elbowed his son with a wink before continuing, "Of course, there are roles, responsibilities, and rules in place to help us make the most of each other."

"What kind of rules and responsibilities?"

"Well, as a man, you are responsible for protecting

women until they reach their husbands. To ensure you fulfill that responsibility, you will treat each unmarried woman like they *could* be your wife or are someone else's wife."

"Huh? What does that mean?"

"Well, would you be very happy to hear that a man had sex with your wife?"

"No! I would be furious."

"Would you be ashamed if you had sex with a married woman? Could you face her husband? Could you defend your actions?"

Henry shook his head in the negative as the thought of it was hard to imagine.

"There is someone out there for you, Henry. A woman so good and beautiful that she will make your heart sing. Someday, you will meet her, fall in love, and get married, God willing. In the meantime, there will more than likely be a number of girls that you get to date and hang out with. Each one of these girls could be your wife, but they won't be until the day you are married. Until then, you need to understand that they could also be someone else's wife."

"What?!? Are you saying I am going to be dating married girls? Dad! I would never do that!"

With a smile, Carl responded, "I am glad to hear that, and no - I don't imagine you will be dating married girls. But you need to understand that one day, they *could* be married to someone else. It is your job, as a man, to ensure you can look eye-to-eye with her future husband and retain your honor. However, even more importantly, you need to be able to look into your wife's eyes at the altar and tell her that she was worth waiting for."

Seeing a chance to return the earlier jab, Henry elbowed his dad and said, "Like you did with mom, right?"

The car grew quiet once more, and there wasn't a smile or a laugh this time as darkness seemed to set over his dad at that moment. With sorrow, he looked at his son and replied, "No, son. I didn't get the honor of telling your mother that."

The car was silent once more as Henry grasped the meaning behind his father's words.

"I made many mistakes as a young man, and I was not the man I should have been for your mother. That said, God has forgiven me, and your mother has too. I still feel the regret, which is why I want you and your brother to be better than me - better than I ever was. My prayer every day is for you both to do just that."

Henry sat there with this new information for a while before he had a thought: what if women made his dad do it? He verbalized the question to his father.

"No, son. That was not my situation. It can happen to either boy or girl, and it is terrible when it does, but I made the choices that got me into the situations."

"What if the woman really wants to? It is kind of like her choice, and you go along with it?"

"Let me ask you a question. If you were a lifeguard at a pool and someone jumps in to try and drown themselves, do you jump in to drown with them, or do you try to save them?"

"I would try to save them, but you know I am not a good swimmer, Dad."

Carl laughed at his son's unintended innuendo but quickly confirmed his son's choice, "Of course you would! The same can be said of a woman you care about. She may want to do things that could be bad for her, but it is your job to defend her and save her - even from herself. Lust can fog anyone's mind into not seeing the dangers or consequences ahead."

"I understand, Dad. Don't worry. I want to look my wife in the eye and tell her she was worth the wait."

With a hint of a tear in his eye, Carl said, "Few things would make me more proud, son."

After that, they sat, ate ice cream, and talked about

sports until they finally drove home.

Sitting on the bed now with his magazine out, Henry didn't see how this would affect his ability to look his wife in the eye on their wedding day. He considered this to be like research since the magazine told him how to approach girls, too, right? It was a weak excuse, but his mind grasped for any and took hold of what was offered.

Flipping through the magazine, he reached the end for the tenth time. On the back, a full-page ad for a website seemed to offer even more content. Henry almost immediately started scheming as to how he might be able to get the family computer all to himself. He felt like he *needed* to see what was on the site.

17

SHAM was glad he didn't have to walk to the general's tent with the insane shadow. All his legion brethren were cruel, and they took pride in their ability to inflict pain, but it was not usually directed at each other with such intensity. Within the legion, shadows used politics and infighting to move up in the social hierarchy, but rarely physical violence. It wasn't exactly the wisest move to torture or attempt to kill something nearly immortal who also had a proclivity for vengeance. That said, Sham could almost believe that this particular brother would welcome the attempt as an excuse to return the favor.

Trying to shake off the memory and foreboding words the shadow had left Sham with, he started walking toward the army's camp. Sentries at the camp entrance would soon see him and direct him toward the general's tent. There was very little time to plan, so Sham decided to do something that went against the very nature of a shadow and tell the truth - up to a point.

Once the general knew that a Sword unit was in his vicinity, it would be almost impossible for him to ignore it. Sham would give the general all the information he needed but leave a few details out. With Sham's luck and skill, the general would falter at some point, and he would step in with his leadership and intelligence to ensure a victory.

Sham smiled at the thought of him rising to save the day after the famous general Neart had faltered and failed. It would be a glorious event that would rocket him into a position of authority just under the king himself. All he needed to do was give the general enough true information to get him invested but not enough to lead to a victory.

Sentries, made up of two bullans and a stone, challenged him as Sham got within shouting range of the makeshift gate, "Who goes there?"

"I am Sham, lord of the western fort, and demand to see the general immediately!" Sham shouted his response with authority. His title wasn't exactly accurate, but he had taken it for himself anyway. Unfortunately, none of them seemed to take him seriously.

In a mocking tone, the sentry replied, "Forgive me, my lord. I just didn't expect such an illustrious guest to arrive at our humble camp with no escort, tattered clothes, and bleeding energy."

Sham touched his throat at the last comment and felt the cut skin. Looking at his fingers as he pulled them away, the red lightning in liquid form coated his fingertips. A reminder of his recent encounter outside the camp.

Trying to turn the situation around, Sham responded, "Of course I am tattered, bleeding, and have no escort, you idiots!" The sudden ferocity of the response perked the sentries up a little. Good. Now that he had their attention, it was time to get some respect.

"I have just come from battling a Sword unit that invaded my fort. I fought alongside my valiant horde warriors until I was the only one left standing." Warrior was a strong word for the imbeciles he was given, and valiant was an absolute joke, but Sham knew his words had struck a chord with the bullans posted here as they stood a bit taller and reassessed him. They would likely spread the word that Sham respected the stupid beasts throughout the horde side of camp. Nothing was further from the truth, but he may need their loyalty fast.

Bullans were not the most intelligent of the horde, if any of them could really be associated with that term at all. Still, they were not exactly stupid either and were one of the more dependable fighters in a battle.

Each bullan towered over shadows by several hands and would likely get close to the height of the Voice clan wretches. Their heads were topped with horns, and they had elongated faces with short hair covering their entire bodies. Snouts stuck out from their face, ending with a large, typically black nose. Unsmiling mouths under the nose hid rows of blunt teeth that could easily break bones. Both of the bullans standing guard at the entrance to the camp had golden rings pierced through their noses, indicating that they belonged to someone important.

The creatures' bodies were nothing monstrous, outside of hoofed feet that bent at the knee in the opposite direction. However, they were all extremely muscular in their humanoid arms and chests. Everything about them spoke of mostly controlled violence, even if you took the well-maintained weapons out of their hands.

Not wanting to break his momentum, Sham continued, "I barely escaped," gesturing to his bleeding throat, "and ran without stopping to get here." He finished his theatrical performance by spreading his arms wide to display his tattered tunic. If the shadow believed that his recent injury came from a battle that supposedly took place hundreds of mils away, he was more stupid than he looked. That said, he needed to recruit this stone to his cause, and teasing his imagination with thoughts of glorious battle wouldn't hurt.

To ensure the sentry didn't have time to think through Sham's story, the beleaguered shadow pointed to a tent on a hill near the center of the camp and asked, "Is that where the legendary general is? We need to get him this information as soon as possible so that we can move to crush our enemy quickly." Using inclusive language and putting urgency behind the request would help manipulate the sentry further into doing what Sham wanted. To top it off, he added the physical element by not pushing past the stone but rather wrapping his arm around him and starting to walk side-by-side.

He didn't doubt his manipulation skills, but even he was surprised by his plan's effectiveness as the sentry started walking with purpose alongside Sham. It was lucky that this one had sentry duty at the time of his arrival. The sentry position was not a punishment; it was rewarded only to those with keen senses and intelligence in a war camp. Sham continued to pour honey into his ear as they marched towards the general to ensure the stone didn't have time to engage that supposed intelligence. He spoke to him of battle and how urgent the general would want to hear his story. Just because he had the simpleton by the throat didn't mean he would let up.

Along the way, Sham had started slyly positioning himself and adjusting his posture in just a way that gave the illusion that the sentry was more of a proper escort for one of his station. Even in his tattered clothes, having a sentry walk like a bodyguard next to him would give every shadow in the area the distinct impression that Sham was someone of import.

As they neared the tent, Sham realized he may need to actually learn the sentry's name. The poor fool could be useful later as he planned on how to push his agenda with the other legion soldiers in the camp.

All things considered, Sham thought that he had salvaged the situation fairly well as he entered right behind the sentry into the giant central tent. Those feelings scattered like the wind when he first gazed upon general Neart.

Unlike all shadows, the general did not use energy to project a skin. He displayed himself as he was when the legion first rejected the King for their own path and glory. Ashen skin with bright flashes of red lighting streaking throughout Neart's body. Scars and sunken eyes gave the impression that the general was barely alive. However, he was far larger than any shadow Sham had ever seen. The general's strength was evident in the rippling muscles covering his body under his clothes. Even the earlier bullans could be put to shame next to this monster. Yet, those same muscles seem to be peeling off his bones as if they were rejecting the body that they were attached to.

Sham didn't doubt that Neart had been one of the more handsome Sword generals prior to throwing his lot in with their new king. The fact that he didn't even care enough about his looks to put on a skin made it evident that this was not someone who would be trifled with. Sham almost changed his mind completely at that moment and gave Neart everything. Almost.

The sentry that Sham never learned the name of spoke first, "General, sir! This is lord Sham of the western fort, and he brings word of a Sword incursion."

Looking up from an extremely large map of the area spread out over a table in the center of the tent, the general glanced past the sentry at Sham and gave an appraising glance. Without taking his eyes off Sham, the general responded to the sentry in a calm voice, "Report to the punishment post for a hundred lashes."

Sham's jaw nearly dropped. One hundred lashes with a legion whip would make the sentry nearly useless for the next thirty cycles! He was glad that the sentry had gone ahead of him, but the evil look on the stone's face as he passed Sham clearly indicated that the ally he sought had now become an enemy.

Neart stared at Sham in utter silence for several heartbeats after the stone had exited. It stretched a bit longer, and the general's blood-red eyes bore holes into Sham like kreehauns tunneling through soft ground. Finally, he addressed his guest with a single word, "Speak."

After seeing the general and his interaction with the sentry, Sham changed his approach immediately. Going from a shadow of authority and importance at the entrance to the camp, he transformed his demeanor into something closer to a meek servant. Sham bowed before responding, "My lord general. I come to you as your humble servant to bring news of an invasion in your land by a Sword element."

It almost pained Sham to refer to the general as a lord and call his territory the property of another, but his ability to adapt and survive won out against his ego - at least for now.

Hearing no immediate response, Sham raised his head and continued, "I was given the privilege of holding a border fort at the base of the mountains. Only a few cycles ago, I was attacked in the night by a small unit of Swords that overwhelmed my defenses and kreehauns. We could not hold the fort, my lord."

Neart continued to stare at Sham as he spoke with a face that was nearly unreadable due to the constant decomposing and healing nature of his true flesh. Sham paused to get a read on the general to see where he needed to adjust his story. Instead of a response, the tent was again filled with a palpable silence.

Feeling no other choice, Sham continued by adding more details to his escape and the SALT's attempt to cut him down from an extreme distance. He did leave out his quick stop in the mountain and the kreehauns he had posted there but detailed his travels to the camp where he found himself. Having reached the point in the story where he arrived in that very tent, Sham stopped and waited for a response. What followed was simply more silence.

Torture was no stranger to Sham, but the silence inflicted by the general on him was starting to drive the shadow crazy. What was he thinking? Did he not believe him about the Swords? Sham felt he needed to say something more, but he didn't know what the general wanted from him.

With nothing else to do, Sham broke the silence once more by saying, "I will do whatever you say, my lord. My only ask is that you let me fight beside you to repel the vile Swords from your land and regain the fort. And my honor."

The legion did not care for honor, but Sham was throwing everything out in the hopes that something would stick.

To his great relief, Sham seemed to have finally hit the target, as Neart finally responded with a simple request: "Show me your weapons."

Happy to be out of the silence but very confused, Sham drew his scythes into each hand and displayed them to the general. While inspecting the blades, Neart asked his first question of the entire interaction, "Which one do you favor when fighting?"

Sham was even more confused, but he answered the question honestly by saying his right. The general told Sham to put his blades back and walked back over to the map he had been reviewing when Sham had first entered.

"Point to where your fort and these Swords are now."

Walking over to the table more confidently, Sham used his right hand to point to the mountain's base with a small building displayed. "Here."

"Indulge me. Point to it with your left hand."

Warning signals went off like fireworks in his mind, but Sham switched hands and slowly pointed to the same building outlined on the map without seeing any other choice.

In the blink of an eye and with no way to prevent it, Sham watched in horror as the general drew one of the largest swords he had ever seen off his back and swung it through his extended wrist. Instantly, Sham screamed in pain as angry red energy poured out of his arm where his left hand once was.

Using the same calm tone he had used in every word since Sham's arrival, the general directly addressed Sham as the injured shadow held the stump of his hand: "I accept your offer of aiding me in the fight to come. " Turning back to the table and the map, he continued, "Never lie to me, and never enter my tent without permission."

Sham pulled himself together and started to shuffle out of the tent when the general stopped him and asked, "Was there a tomb in this fort, and did it have a flame above a casket?"

"Yes, there was a tomb," Sham responded through gritted teeth, "But I am not aware of any flame."

"You are dismissed."

Sham nearly tripped over himself, trying to exit the tent as fast as possible, not giving his hand on the table another thought. In contrast, the general stared intently at the appendage with a single outstretched finger pointing directly to a solitary fort at the base of the mountains.

18

ONCE Wit and John regained strength, Killian ensured his 'twin' visited the bridge next before taking a turn on watch. As per usual, Kurian took the brunt of the attack during the exterior fight with the bréag's second golem. Doc constantly had to remind his brother that the shield he carried didn't make him invincible and that his constant need to defend them all would pull someone into an early blue.

According to Wit, with John's silent confirmation, the interior fight had been fierce and nearly catastrophic when the first charge went off prematurely. They didn't blame anyone or point fingers, but they both were a bit extra cocky in describing the brilliance of pulling the creature into their trap after the initial explosion had gone off. Well, mostly Wit was cocky as John just stood there.

Truth be told, they had every right to be, as it was no easy feat to change the very instinct of a forewarned, intelligent swarm of creatures and lead them into a tunnel built for their death. The exterior team had trouble containing the creatures in the smaller building, and Kurian had been the bait in his own trap. Having just set the charges, the engineer had held his ground within the cell to pull the golem in. Titus and Killian had brought the creature, but Boomer held it in place nearly single-handedly.

Seeing that Kurian was in trouble with only himself and the golem in a small confined room, Titus had ordered him to get out and trigger the trap. They all knew that the second golem was not yet in position, but Killian could tell that Titus wasn't ready to lose another brother so soon.

All that said, their brothers in the main hall's interior had done what all Swords do - fight until the end. Killian was the first to see both of them in their final state, and he knew they were likely only a few more hits away from blue. Wit was, of course, smiling and wanted to immediately tell him of his exploits, whereas John only gave a tired nod of acknowledgment to Killian's order to seek the bridge. Killian wasn't sure if the fight had tired the larger brother or if it was the walking chatterbox next to him. He thought it was likely the latter, as he noticed that John's step got an extra pep when he left Wit behind.

Killian returned to the present and sped up to catch his twin, who had finished at the bridge and was moving to the gate. As he approached, their similarities once again comforted him as they fell into an identical step. They had minuscule differences in both height and facial features. With average builds for a Sword, nose-length chins, almond-shaped eyes, and short blond hair that was more wavy than straight, they both didn't stand out too much from the crowd. But when placed next to each other, even they may have trouble telling themselves apart. Team members constantly commented on how they had similar facial expressions and quirks. Wit had even once joked that the Creator pressed the copy button when making the twins. Killian had agreed but added that the Creator needed a double dose of handsomeness to balance the scales after Wit was made. The team, and especially Wit, had roared in laughter.

While they physically were near copies of each other, their functions and even attire were wholly unique. Killian's tight, self-cleaning, long-sleeved tunic and pants allowed him more coverage when performing triage in the field or stealth attacks aligned with his primary knives. Kurian's shorter-sleeved tunic ensured he had an easier time manipulating his shield in combat and less concern about his tunic snagging on a trap he had just set.

As Killian walked alongside his brother, Boomer nodded and gave a barely noticeable side head tilt toward the front gate. Killian gave a quick chin raise, and just like that, it was settled; they both would keep watch at the front together. Having been together since creation, communicating and anticipating each other was almost too easy.

When they reached the gate, they both climbed to the top of the wall and separated. Killian went left to the tower, and Kurian went right to begin pacing the wall's top. The engineering-minded twin would inspect the wall for minor but potentially deadly faults while keeping an eye on the surrounding area. Killian's eyes would constantly scan more of the exterior to watch for scouts or any movement.

Switching to a direct communication link with just Boomer, Killian started by picking a topic they would discuss, "Choice?"

"Perfect," Boomer said in response.

Seekers were not the only Swords who were curious and enjoyed the mental exercise of trying to understand the realms and the work of their King. The brothers would often discuss various topics and bounce ideas off each other. While they couldn't possibly fully understand their Creator, it was a pleasure to try and understand a fraction of what He was and what He did.

Kurian began their discussion by asking, "Do you want to know what confuses me? Why would our brethren use Choice against their Creator? They know Him like we do. Yet, they use Choice to abandon His gifts and their calling. It makes no sense."

Killian's initial response was silent contemplation, but he eventually responded, "Since we are not insane, I am not sure we could fully answer."

A small chuckle was Kurian's response, but Killian

continued, “Choice is a power that is given to few creations. I believe our Maker is working towards something, or someone, that will use the power for something greater.”

Kurian looked thoughtful before stating, “Interesting thought. I had never considered it in those terms. In a way, it makes sense from an outside perspective. Horde beasts were not created by the Maker, so each of the Creator’s creations serves a functional purpose. What if there is a function that only a creation with Choice can fulfill?”

“Exactly! What if a function is yet to be filled and the King is still building a creation or waiting for it to make the Choice?”

“So you are saying there could be another creation above us? I don’t mind, provided I still get to do my job.”

Killian smiled as he knew the truth of what his brother said. They may not have been the answer to a specific function within the Kingdom, but they had deep-rooted purpose and loyalty. Every remaining Sword would gladly fight and die for their King. They were devoted to Him and only desired to see His wishes fulfilled. Their Maker cared for them, and they wished to return that love with devotion.

To continue their conversation, Killian asked, “To answer your question, do you believe that the legion could not accept service under another creation?”

“Possibly. But how could they have known ahead of time of such a thing? Who could have told them? Someone who had to be close to the Creator to understand Him and powerful enough to use Choice for separation instead of communion. A being like that could potentially sow discontent among our traitorous brethren.”

Kurian didn’t need to say the name, as they both knew he was referring to the false king who now led the legion in a constant war against their Creator. As difficult as it was to imagine his brothers and sisters rebelling, it was nauseating to think that a lord of a realm would reject his Maker. To know who their King was and be in His direct presence, yet use His own power of Choice to attempt a coup - it was insanity.

"Choice is a precious gift that enables many of the King's subjects the ability to serve and to have potential. Some will reject that potential for a false hope of something better."

Before he could finish, the commander abruptly interrupted them with the announcement, "All Swords, we have spores! Prepare for contact."

Killian looked to his brother, and they again had a flash telepathic conversation that ended in another head nod. It was time to do what they did best, their function, and how they worshiped their Maker.

The Commander listed each team member and ordered them to move to their assigned position with slight deviations to accommodate their current locations. Each brother acknowledged and quickly found their places along the walls, with the Commander guarding the objective.

Each of the squad moved quickly and was in position within heartbeats of the initial warning, ready to take on whatever came. As arrows loaded into a bow, they were all tight and eager for a fight.

However, a very different flowing entity came at them. Instead of a charging army attempting to rip them to shreds, they saw a heavy, thick fog rolling towards them like a slow-moving tidal wave.

The fog enveloped them completely within a few heartbeats, with visibility reduced to maybe a few arm lengths in any direction. Somewhat like the spores, a sense of wrongness emanated from the mist. However, it didn't have the same power to actually hurt any of the team, which was a relief to Killian as he had no idea how he could attend to everyone simultaneously.

There was no doubt that something evil was behind the

fog, but there was no attack or ill effects of the mist itself other than a loss of visibility. All members of 1-1-8 were left scratching their heads a bit. Had the spores called the fog? If so, why? When would it dissipate? How could they remove it? Killian greatly missed Marcus and his ability to decipher such mysteries at that moment.

Lieutenant Shay eventually announced that the fog was not hiding an army. His abilities allowed him better sight, and his higher position in the tower ensured a less obstructed view.

After holding their positions for nearly an entire cycle and the spores long gone, the Commander summoned everyone to the main hall, except for Shay, who needed to remain on watch. Once everyone was gathered, the Commander asked, "Thoughts? Opinions?"

Killian was the first to break the silence, saying, "Sir, we have no idea what is happening, but it isn't good."

"Agreed, sergeant. However, we need solutions and answers as this fog will make things difficult for us."

Using a bit more serious tone than the team was used to, Wit added, "Communications are taking a hit in this fog, sir. We previously had limited communication with Command, but this fog makes long-range links impossible. I doubt we would have access to our internal network beyond the fort's immediate vicinity. If any of us go outside the walls, they won't be able to get support from those within."

Shay jumped into the conversation via their team link. However, almost to emphasize Wit's point, his voice came through a bit broken as he commented, "We can't rule out that there isn't an enemy hiding in the fog. Any army would be easy to spot, whereas a small group could get close enough to infiltrate."

Boomer responded, "That is true, but wouldn't that smaller force make themselves known by now, LT?"

No one seemed to have answers, just more questions.

They looked to their leader, and Titus took a moment to consider all that was said. After appearing to analyze everything that was known, he laid out his orders and strategy, "I will continue to guard the tomb, and Shay will stay in the tower and continue to monitor our exterior. John and Wit, you will be on the walls patrolling with Shay, who can direct you to areas that are harder for him to see. Use your ears as much as your eyes out there."

"On it, Commander. We just took out a bréag, so it's not like we can't handle a little fog, right big guy?" Wit announced with an elbow to John's rib.

Killian swallowed a chuckle when he saw John's disgruntled face as the Commander moved on to the final two members, Kurian and himself.

"Doc and Boomer. I need you two to go hunting. If something is in the fort already, find it and kill it."

"Understood, sir," Kurian answered for the both of them.

Soon after, the team disbanded and went out to perform the assigned tasks. Killian and Kurian began their search at the gate. Due to the Commander guarding the tomb, it seemed best to start at the possible entry points versus the potential goal of an invader. However, after closely examining the gate, it was apparent that nothing had gotten through.

Moving together, the twins began working clockwise around the fort to inspect each crevice and crack that would allow one of their enemies into their midst. Unsurprisingly, there wasn't much of anything due to the perfectionism of Kurian when it came to his work. However, when they were nearly back to the gate on the eastern wall, one crack appeared slightly larger than the others. It wouldn't allow entry by anything larger than a mouse, but it also wasn't there previously. Kurian inspected it thoroughly and reported to the Commander, "Sir, we have a possible entry point. Over."

"Any idea what we are dealing with?" came Commander's

slightly broken response.

"No guarantees, but I only know of one creature that could make it through a hole this size and evade Shay's sight," Kurian looked to his twin for confirmation before giving the answer they both knew was right, "Killian and I agree that we have at least one réama inside the fort."

Réama were no less vicious than their horde brethren, but they were more wily and often used as spies or assassins for the legion. While no Sword or shadow could conversate with any of the horde, these creatures could provide detailed maps or drawings to their legion masters. Having one among them would be a significant disadvantage if the legion made to attack the fort. They would have to find it and destroy it.

That said, like all horde beasts, finding and destroying them was easier said than done. Réamas were made entirely of a liquid-like substance with a small orb that could be described as a brain or heart. However, describing them simply as a moving puddle would vastly underestimate the lethality of what they truly are. Much like other horde creatures, a réama would take a humanoid form but typically smaller. They create empty pockets in a head-like bubble for things like eyes or mouths, giving them a ghoulish appearance. While they attempt to form appendages like legs and arms, the result is streams of liquid extending out from their center in a general shape of limbs with no discernible hands or feet, completing a jellyfish-like effigy. With no teeth, claws, or direct offensive weapons, it could be seen as one of the weaker members of the horde. However, what it lacked in direct weapons, it made up with clever tactics and almost sadistic attacks.

As its sole method of attack, a réama slowly drowns and digests a victim inside itself. The core inside the liquid not only controls the creature but also releases a toxin that gives the victim false pleasure. While inside the creature, it is said that a Sword feels like they are bathing in love and would sometimes fight to remain inside the monster.

Réamas were not difficult to kill as all you needed to do was destroy its floating core. It would make it as difficult as possible by hiding or constantly moving it around within its liquid, but its natural defense was holding victims and taking them apart, a little at a time.

Since their prey left little to no trail, made no sound, could move through any crack or hole large enough to fit a small pebble, was practically invisible in the mist, and there wasn't even confirmation that it was here, the twins had their work cut out for them. Regardless of the monumental task, Titus confirmed the order of tracking and killing the monster. Without much to go on, they decided it was best to keep in constant contact but split up to cover more ground. Typically, this would be a tactical blunder, but with a small search team and multiple hiding places available for a moving target, they had to take the risk. Finding a moving needle in their haystack would be a Maker's blessing.

Choosing to search the courtyard and surrounding buildings first, Killian took the western side, and Kurian took the eastern. They were in constant communication, letting each other know where they were and if the area appeared secure. Both Swords pushed their senses to the limit as they searched, but they quickly realized that the creature could easily have moved from one hiding spot to another without them being the wiser.

"We need this fog gone," Kurian called out to his brother.

"And we need a lot more Swords, brother," Killian responded.

Having reached the end of his side of the buildings, Killian alerted Boomer that he was moving to inspect the exterior of the main hall. Kurian confirmed and said he would begin searching on the opposite side when he finished with the last of the rubbled buildings in the courtyard.

Killian moved to the exterior, updated the Commander, and asked if the other team members had spotted anything. Each responded with a negative, so he switched back to a direct link to Kurian.

"Brother, have you moved to the exterior of the main hall yet?"

Silence was the only response.

Not wasting a moment, Killian alerted his team while sprinting back to the final building where Kurian had last confirmed his location. It was empty.

Running as fast as he possibly could, Killian ran around the entire main hall, hoping to locate his brother. He was nowhere to be found. Boomer had been taken.

19

AN immediate search of the area revealed nothing, and Shay confirmed that there had been no movement outside of the walls. Titus took charge of the search by changing the positions of each squad member, moving Wit to Shay's lookout position and John to guard the objective. Shay would be the best choice for tracking and sign-reading, with both Killian and Titus as a rescue force.

There was no doubt there would have to be a rescue since it was impossible for Kurian to have simply left. It was unheard of for a Sword to be in dereliction of duty after the legion had decided to forgo all responsibilities and honor. Since choosing to leave was impossible, the team understood that Kurian was in danger and likely being slowly devoured by a réama. Time was their enemy in this deadly game of hide and seek.

Shay started from Killian's last confirmed position on the east side of the courtyard and quickly identified his tracks. After only a few heartbeats, Shay outlined the initial movement of Boomer, "He walked over from between those two," pointing to two large boulders near where Titus and Killian both stood, "and did a typical circular search pattern starting counterclockwise and eventually ended here in the center." He emphasized his point by pointing at the ground where the lieutenant now crouched. A quizzical look came across the SALT as he turned and intently stared at the ground behind himself. Not wanting to interrupt his process, Killian remained silent along with the Commander.

The silence was finally cut when Shay said, "It shouldn't have been possible for any enemy to completely surprise Kurian without him being able to send out a warning to the team." Shay pointed at the ground with seemingly small clumps of dirt and rock, saying, "Here is where he was taken. Boomer turned suddenly to the south, potentially at a distraction, but was then quickly pushed from behind." Motioning to a scuff in the dirt, he said, "The tracks disappear there."

"Disappear? How is that possible," Killian responded in frustration.

Shay turned away from them once again and reached into a small hole made by a rock propped by a fallen wood beam. He pulled his finger out and licked it. Immediately, he spit and looked like he wanted to force himself to vomit.

"Réama," Titus said between gritted teeth.

Shay responded with a head nod, still looking slightly ill. While both Killian and Kurian had suspected as much, this was the true confirmation of what they were fighting and who had their brother.

"I assume there are no other tracks or signs you can follow, LT?"

"Correct, sir. The slimy beast leaves no footprints and hardly any trace," Shay responded, but seeing the dejection that began to form on Doc's face, he quickly added, "The good news is that the monster can't hide in small places while it has Boomer. It will need a hiding place large enough to hold Kurian within itself as it siphons off his energy."

While a dark thought, it was helpful because they no longer had to search every crevice in the fort. They could now concentrate on hiding places that would hold a full-size Sword. It helped narrow down their search, but time was still a factor. The longer it took to find Boomer, the less chance they would have any hope of saving him.

Knowing that the creature had already taken one of them

and couldn't hold two, Titus ordered them to split up to cover more ground. Titus returned to the gate and started slowly working back to the courtyard, while Shay went to the main hall with fresh eyes. Killian was left to sweep the buildings in the courtyard once more.

Killian stopped at the well in the center of the courtyard and peered into the darkness as he moved to clear the buildings he had already cleared once before. He had already scanned the well, but he needed to be thorough. Shining a light into the hole, he saw the same thing he had previously—shallow, dirty water.

As the team's healer, he understood the consequences of long-term exposure to a réama, which meant he also knew they were running short on time. It wouldn't be long before they would only be looking for the statuesque blue form of Kurian.

Turning away from the well, Killian switched his communication back to his direct link with Kurian and almost whispered, "We need help, brother. Give us a signal. Give us a chance."

The silence was deafening as Killian simply stood in place and hoped beyond hope for some sort of response. After waiting longer than he probably should have, Killian could only hear the night sounds around the fort and water lapping in the well.

When he reached the radio building and began searching, something wasn't sitting right in his mind. He knew something was wrong, and he was missing it.

Realization hit him like a boulder rolling down a mountain as he started running and bringing up the team's link, "The well, Commander! They are in the well!"

Water in a well doesn't move to make any sounds. The gentle lapping of water he had heard emanating from the well could only mean one thing: something was in there, and it had moved. He wasn't sure how it hid in such a small space, but he knew they were down there.

Being the first to arrive, Killian drew his knives and didn't hesitate to jump in. He used his feet and knives to slow his descent. The blades shot sparks as he moved in what one could only describe as barely 'not' free-falling. When he reached the water, he expected to land in knee-high water based on the rocks jutting from the bottom. To his surprise, the rocks were smoothed in such a way that they acted like a slide. Before he knew what had happened, he was submerged and nearly underneath the east courtyard buildings.

There was no panic at being under the water in new surroundings. Swords didn't panic, and Killian was focused on finding his brother. An intense need to save others was embedded in all healers, but he also knew that his connection with his *twin* was greater than the average team connection. Something about them being so similar, yet different in just the right ways, made them a brotherhood within a brotherhood.

Before making any moves in the new surroundings, Killian surveyed the area he found himself in. Surprisingly, there was light as bioluminescence fungus grew in the water and on the cave wall. Even though he could see, the first thing he did was release a small amount of air to quickly determine his positioning. The bubbles went past his eyes, confirming that he was right-side up. Additionally, the same bubbles dissipated above him, helping to show at least a sign that there was space for him to surface - which he moved to do so.

Slowly, his head broke the surface. Killian resisted the urge to seek air and only let his eyes come out of the water, letting the bottom half remain submerged. He wanted to keep the element of surprise and give only the smallest of targets. Using the little available light, he was slightly shocked at what he saw. It wasn't necessarily what his eyes told him but how their intelligence could have missed it.

He was in the middle of a small lake with pebble shores

in every direction. Enormous stalactites hung above him, and the light-giving fungus grew sporadically on them. The result was shadows that gave the impression of fanged beasts on every side. However, the only beast that Killian cared about was the one holding his brother.

Spotting some movement near the shore on the far side of the cave, Killian took a small breath through his nose and went back underwater. He swam until he was just a few hands away from the shore and slowly walked out of the water with knives at the ready. A large stalagmite blocked his view, but he knew his enemy was on the other side. Carefully placing his feet, he side-stepped to get a better angle on what was hidden.

Fury coursed through him as he was finally able to see around the obstruction and witnessed the réama's jelly-like body hold his brother inside of itself. Only the head of Kurian was outside of the beast, and a tiny orange ball with a black center moved rapidly around the Sword inside the liquid body. The head of the monster was just above Kurian, and it held the shape of a humanoid with the Sword's own legs and arms, giving it more structure. Overall, it appeared as though Kurian was the bones of a beast, and Killian was seeing through its flesh.

As Killian studied it to find an opening, the movement of the eye-like ball started to convey excitement as the light within his brother started to dim. He needed to act quickly but also needed the element of surprise. It would be difficult to destroy the creature once it was aware of Killian.

Suddenly, two quick splashes could be heard as Killian realized backup had arrived. Unfortunately, the disturbance also alerted the réama, who immediately moved the ball towards the sound and stared directly at Killian.

With a half-gurgle cry that echoed throughout the cave, the réama charged. The brain-like ball immediately circled behind the head of its hostage for protection, which meant that Killian had no clear shot to take it out. Additionally, the jelly-like substance moved up behind Kurian's hands and arms. Not sure what to make of this, Killian dove to the right and summoned his ranged gift to attempt a shot at the creature. Seeing a small opening, he fired. With a loud *ping,* the energy ricocheted and flew into the cave roof, causing some debris to fall. Kurian's own shield had blocked it.

Had Kurian given in to the ecstasy that the réama provided? Was he doing whatever he could to stay within the creature? Killian looked at his brother again more closely.

Kurian was not moving, and his eyes were not open. He hadn't given in but was too weak to fight back against the réama. It didn't yet have his mind, but it controlled his body like a puppet.

Killian ducked quickly as his brother's shield sliced through the air at his head. The réama was quick, but Killian knew his brother was still in there and doing everything he could to slow the puppeteer's movements.

Another attack came in, and Killian acrobatically used a thin stalagmite as a pole to swing out of the way and deliver a kick to the poorly formed creature's head. Nothing happened as the head simply reformed, and the shield attacks started to come in faster. The only way to put this monster down was to pierce the core of it, the small floating ball.

Range gift dismissed, Killian went back to his knives. Like any good healer, he could perform surgery anywhere and was adept at using his small blades to hit vital and key areas of his enemy. Killing or healing was one and the same to him, as he would use his weapons to fight the ruthless enemy of his King and heal the land of their blight. He now needed to do both simultaneously: kill the parasite quickly and heal the patient fast.

Maneuvering so that he had his own back to the water and the creature facing it, Killian fainted and struck in a way that caused the floating orb to shrink back and hide behind Kurian, temporarily blinding it to his movements. As quick as he could, Killian attempted a desperate attack by sliding underneath the legs of the beast and stabbing his right knife up between the legs and straight at the hidden weak point.

Unfortunately, the jelly-like substance slowed his attack, and the ball simply switched to the front - avoiding the knife completely. It now had a solid grip on Killian's right arm. While it couldn't absorb Killian like it had his brother, the réama could still hold his arm and trap it within itself temporarily.

The creature didn't realize that Killian had done everything with expert timing so that the ball floated right into the view of one of the deadliest marksmen the King had ever created the second he exited the water. Without a heartbeat's hesitation, Shay's projectile passed just over Kurian's shoulder within the monster and struck the ball as it tried to swing back to Killian's side. The hit was just grazing, as Shay's angle was a bit off. However, the subsequent stab from Killian's left blade was a direct hit, piercing the creature's only organ.

Almost as if a balloon filled with water was pierced, the creature burst as liquid gushed down around the twins. Slowly dripping a small amount of black acidic blood, only the small orange ball with a black center was left at the end of Killian's knife. Quickly grabbing his brother as he collapsed, Killian began his assessment as Titus and Shay approached.

"How is he doing? What's his status," the Commander asked.

Killian didn't immediately respond as he was checking Kurian over. When he did, he knew there wasn't much time. "It's not good, sir. He was in there for too long,"

Killian eventually said as he began estimating his brother's remaining time against the distance they would need to travel to get him to the bridge. There was no way they would make it. Almost to emphasize his point, the light within Kurian began to flicker.

There was no time left, and Killian didn't have enough of his own energy to share. Kurian would need a large amount to stabilize, and the fight had taken Killian's down just enough to make it impossible to only share. It became a Choice: Killian or Kurian.

The healer looked towards his Commander, and Titus instantly understood the dilemma. Tactically, Kurian was more of a priority as he would be invaluable in a siege or assault. Killian understood that - just like he knew the Commander would never order his healer to self-sacrifice for another.

"It was an honor to serve under you, Commander. I look forward to seeing you again."

"The honor was mine, healer. You fought well and tracked admirably. Your service to your King and your brothers will forever be remembered. I look forward to fighting beside you again."

With a final nod to both of his superiors, Killian turned back to the prone, near replica of himself lying on the cave floor as the familiar feeling of electricity in his body confirmed his use of Choice. He knelt down next to Kurian and pulled the still unconscious Sword to a kneeling position opposite him. Just as Killian got them into position, a blue wave began climbing Kurian's body.

Seeing his chance to save his brother slip away, Killian touched his forehead to Kurian's and *breathed*. As the energy transferred out of his body, the blue halted at Boomer's waist but did not recede. His twin might have been too far gone, and he was now simply throwing his lot in with him. There was still time for Killian to pull back and not go blue.

Killian breathed harder and pushed all his energy into his brother. By sheer will, he would fight the sleeping death, attempting to overcome Kurian. However, exhaustion from the fight with the réama and the mental drain of trying everything to save his twin nearly overwhelmed him. He was at his breaking point when the healer felt a touch on his shoulder. A jolt shot through him, not different than what Choice felt like, but intensified. The blue that had merely halted on Boomer began fading back. Soon enough, the team's engineer was starting to regain some of the light within, which was the Creator's energy flowing in their bodies. On the other hand, Killian was experiencing the same blue wave that had threatened his twin just a heartbeat ago.

As his body transformed into an impenetrable statue, Killian quickly attempted to glance at what had touched him and helped push him beyond his limit to save his brother. Expecting to see the battle-hardened hand of one of his superiors, he was dumbstruck by a pure white bird that was gently resting on his shoulder. Not having time to process the magnitude of seeing the magnificent being, Killian made peace with the enemy he had fought against for his entire existence - the blue.

20

KURIAN awoke to a sight he had hoped never to see. His brother, his twin, was a blue statue next to him. Without needing to ask anyone, he immediately knew what had happened - and he wept.

The Commander and the lieutenant were nearby, letting him experience the emotion in silence. Neither moved to comfort him nor pushed him to soldier on and leave the cave. They both sat near their friend and were simply there in his pain. Each knew this wasn't a final goodbye, but it didn't diminish the sorrow of missed time with a beloved brother. In Kurian's case, it was doubly painful as he knew that his brother had given his time in exchange for his own. He should have been the blue statue in this cave, not Killian.

Time had no meaning in the cave, as there was no daylight. All three of the Swords held their position for both an eternity and only a heartbeat. The remaining team members held their defensive positions and made no complaints.

Finally standing and wiping the tears from his eyes, Kurian nodded to his superiors as both an acknowledgment of their support and a confirmation that he was ready to get back to work. Titus returned his nod and began planning to get their fallen brother out of the cave.

When a brother took the blue, it was not an absolute necessity that he should be returned to the Kingdom to rest with the others who had fallen. When the time came for the final battle, their Creator would call all to his banner -

regardless of where they rested. While all Swords took pride in attempting to bring back their blue brothers and sisters, it was a matter of honor rather than a requirement. Additionally, each knew the blue didn't allow the sleeping to hear what was said, but some Swords occasionally enjoyed visiting their brethren who were waiting to awaken back inside the Kingdom.

After coordinating efforts above and below, they were able to haul Killian's body out of the well. Soon after, Titus asked Kurian to seal the well as they didn't need any more surprises. The explosive expert knew that a small charge would likely have sufficed in the right spot within the well but opted for a more *complete* seal by collapsing the entire cave.

Disgusted with what the réama had done to him and to Killian, Kurian took his anger out on the cave that had hidden the monster. Wide-spread charges made for a massive explosion underground, but they were placed in such a way as to retain the integrity of the ground above it. The Commander never once commented about reserving the charges for a real fight or preserving his time and energy for other tasks.

Once the caves collapsed, Titus approached Kurian and said, "Your brother made use of Choice. He gave you the ultimate sacrifice because he believed you would contribute more to our King's objective." After briefly pausing, he continued, "Bury your anger and grief in that cave. Now, give me everything. Complete our mission and prove him right."

Kurian mentally started to compartmentalize the distractions of anger and sadness. He imagined them in a box and watched as they buried themselves into the ground. Taking his brother out of this place was enough; he wouldn't weigh himself or his team down with the baggage he knew came with losing Killian.

With a deep breath, Kurian turned to Titus and said,

"Hura, sir," as a confirmation and expression of gratitude. He was determined to give his team his all and ensure his brother's sacrifice would not be in vain.

Boomer provided his report on what happened in the main hall with his superiors and the rest of the team listening in on their communications, but it was still hazy to him. He remembered searching the ruins and hearing a sound behind him. Turning towards the sound and seeing something move, he was about to call out to the team when everything went dark. The only sensation afterward was one of pleasure but of a diluted kind - never fulfilling like the joy they received from their Creator. The next image was Killian kneeling before him with only a cold and unemotional visage as their foreheads touched.

Titus listened to the information and sat with it for a moment. He eventually asked, “Was the movement you witnessed in the ruins caused by a rock or something thrown?”

Stopping to really consider what the Commander was asking before responding, Kurian answered, “No, the movement was unnatural. Even though it was hidden in shadow, I believe it was the réama.”

Next, the Commander turned to his second, “You are sure of what you saw and the tracks? Kurian was hit from behind?”

“No doubt, sir,” Shay responded.

“Then it is settled; there is at least one more in our midst - if it has not escaped. We will begin an immediate sweep.”

Kurian understood the Commander’s thinking. If he had been taken by one, a second had initially distracted him. He would not fall for the same trick twice, and they had just removed the only possible hiding place a réama could take a Sword. From here on, the hunted would be the hunters.

Beginning with a close inspection of the main hall and moving Shay back into his position overlooking the surrounding area, the team began a thorough search. They found evidence of the liquid-like creature in the main hall and even in the tunnel under it, but it appeared as though John's presence had stopped it from entering the crypt proper.

Continuing to follow the minuscule trail of evidence that their quarry left behind, they realized that the creature had inspected their entire fort. Using the cover that the fog provided, it had fully and completely scouted their position. The end of the trail was at the gate, where it had simply squeezed through the bars that Kurian had added and slipped under the large wooden doors.

Killian had traded his skills as the team's healer for the team's engineer. A healer would be a major asset in a single battle to get the team back into the fight. However, an engineer would be invaluable in the event of a siege. Judging by the fact that they were just scouted and their enemy now knew everything they could possibly want to know about their position and composition, Kurian had to admit that Killian's love and foresight may have just saved their mission.

****

Neart loved war. The idea of pitting your skill against another and emerging as the victor thrilled him like nothing else. It was as his Creator had made him, right?

All Swords were made for one thing - battle. With that in mind, prior to the legion's break and use of Choice to abandon their King, there was also no adversary for the Swords to fight. Neart remembered pondering that in frustration as the general of an army with no enemy. His new king had seized upon that frustration and had shown him there would only be one true glory in Neart's life: to claim victory over their Creator. War with the ultimate warrior would stretch the general's skills and prove his genius in combat. The more that their king had spoken to him, the more he had to agree. The Creator had made them for war but didn't give them an enemy. It only made sense that they would eventually create a war themselves. One that Neart planned on winning.

Neart had learned much after forsaking the King and helping to form the legion. With his new tactics and army swelling with horde beasts, Neart had yet to find an opponent to match him in combat. Of course, as the general, he would only take to the field himself once the battle was all but finished. It was his tactics and strategy that helped ensure victory. That said, Neart wasn't against getting his hands bloody - the general thought with a smile. He had personally seen to it that full Sword squads had gone blue. Few, if any, in the legion could boast such an accomplishment. Fewer still spoke of the casualties associated with those victories, but those were of little concern to the king and their objective.

Shadows used their own internal energy to heal themselves and enhance what power they retained after cutting themselves off from their Creator's energy. It was possible that they could be destroyed and turned to ash if their injuries far outweighed their ability to heal or restore themselves. However, it was extremely rare as their energy seemed tied to their own self-perception. They no longer needed bridges or healers to restore energy but instead reached into the angry red flame of their pride that burned inside. Enough damage would greatly diminish them, eventually turning them into a black statue. Unlike their former brethren, their statuesque form would not be solid and almost instantly collapse into ash and dust. Some believed that they would be reformed from the dust on the day of the final battle, but that was a sad hope. This mindset led to a lifestyle of seizing pleasure and living for the moment.

Neart despised the shadows that gave into their fleeting desires and lost sight of who they were - warriors. Order and discipline were required to wage war, but some of the legion had forgotten that and needed constant reminders, which led to the general's current task of whipping one of his subordinates and executing two horde beasts.

As the crack of the whip sounded throughout the camp, it was quickly followed by the scream of the shadow tied to the post near the command center. Neart smiled unconsciously as he circled the whip tipped with wicked-looking curved needles over his head. He had lost count again, but the shadow looked like he probably could take one more hit before going beyond his breaking point.

Punishments were always carried out personally by the general. He didn't want to be seen as someone above interacting with his soldiers.

The scream from the shadow during that last strike wasn't as satisfying as the previous ones, so Neart decided to go for just one more. As the needles dug into the skin of the shadow and ripped pieces from it, Neart realized that the skin of this shadow was no longer displaying, and he was whipping the true body of the shadow. Good. He hated the fake look of skins and preferred the natural terror that was his new body.

Fierce red energy was pouring out of the shadow's back. The unlucky soldier who was tied to the post suddenly stopped screaming and immediately turned black. Almost as an afterthought, Neart swung the whip one more time, and the shadow's black statue was blasted apart as pieces dissipated into the wind. While it was an unexpected loss, Neart consoled himself with the thought that he wouldn't need such weakness in his army anyway.

The general turned to those gathered and used his commanding voice to say, "An unorganized army is a defeated army. Let this be a lesson to all of you. Never set your tent where it doesn't belong!"

Seeing the stunned faces of those shadows gathered flickering between their real face and skin due to shock, he knew he had probably gone a little far in the application of discipline - again. Without knowing the reason for their punishment, the general quickly drew his bastard sword and chopped off the beaks of the giant bird-like bulturs. They were there for some offense, but he never bothered to remember it. Neart started walking to his command tent without a second glance back at his handiwork.

The shadows who remained watched the humanoid creatures with bird heads writhe in agony as their own acidic blood started dripping down onto their bodies, causing more wounds and eventual death. It was important that the general provided some sort of entertainment after such a shocking death of another shadow.

They had been on the march for twenty cycles, and it would take another twenty to reach the fort and the Swords that protected it. Neart summoned his three advisors to review their information and the battle plans.

"Speak," Neart said as he pointed to the shortest shadow across from him while looking down at the map.

"The enemy will have fortified their position long before we arrive," the shadow said.

Neart gave the shadow a look that spoke violence if he had nothing more than the obvious to say.

Following up quickly while breaking out in a cold sweat, the advisor stated, "They will have fortified, but they will not be expecting us so soon. No Arrow patrols were flying near us to have spotted our position, and they couldn't have known our guest would have found us so soon," the shadow stated as he pointed to the pouting Sham in the corner and summarized with, "In short, we are a larger force with surprise on our side."

The general nodded as he looked at the map, causing the short advisor to give a sigh of relief. Being an advisor to the great general had many perks, but it was like constantly dancing on a razor's edge. Some of his advisors didn't even want the position due to the sadistic nature of their leader, which was hiding underneath a facade of discipline.

Neart cast his gaze toward the one-armed Sham and asked, “What is the composition of their forces?”

Fighting the urge to curse at the general and spit in his face, Sham responded in veiled fear, “I would say a single squad with the typical roles attached to a Sword unit.” The advisors nodded as they knew exactly which roles would likely comprise an expedition Sword unit. That said, they all understood that a single unit was enough to hold back their army for an extended period. It wouldn’t be an easy fight, even with their far superior numbers and the tactical brilliance of their leader.

Neart ordered a squad of scouts to go to the fort and recon the area for their main force. Just before the orders were sent out, Sham decided to shake up the advisors by adding to his earlier statement, “There is one other thing about this squad. I believe they have a SALT.”

Expecting the shock or even slight dismay to pass over the gathered leaders of the western army at his revelation, Sham himself was shocked when they all actually smiled. He thought of repeating himself but held himself back as these were not simple shadows. They must have something up their sleeve that even Sham had never considered.

“Sham, what do you use to fight a fire?” Neart asked with the voice of a teacher correcting a student.

Hoping against hope that the question was rhetorical, Sham stayed silent while portraying a genuinely puzzled expression.

Neart didn't disappoint. He quickly answered his own question with a predatory smile, "You fight fire..... with fire."

21

STANDING on the wall and staring into the thick fog encompassing the entire area, Titus took stock of his team and their mission. It had felt like they had deployed here just moments ago, yet it had been many cycles. He had lost two of his brothers in the defense of...something. Without clear direction from Command, they were in the dark as to how long they needed to wait or what it was they were actually waiting for. He never questioned his resolve to complete the mission, but he began to question whether or not he could have made better Choices if he understood more. Quietly, he whispered his questions into the air as the wind blew his words away - was there a way he could have saved Marcus? Doc? Are there answers to why they were sent here just beneath his nose?

The Commander of 1-1-8 shook his head to clear the thoughts that plagued his resting mind. He was a Sword serving his King and would not dwell on the past. It was up to him to make the most of what he had to accomplish his mission. Knowing that their Maker never made mistakes in Choice gave him confidence. He would trust that truth and see the mission through, no matter the price.

Shay had swept the area to try and locate the trail of their missing spy, but the mist's thickness had made it an impossible task. However, the SALT's expedition into the surrounding area had brought some interesting information. The mist that encircled them seemed to be centered on the fort itself. It stretched in a perfect circle around the area with a three-mil radius. From the timing of its arrival, Titus didn't need his knowledge seeker to know that it had been the spores from the black plant. Unfortunately for them, their internal enemy seemed capable of more than just bringing fighters to their doorstep. Titus lamented on how this new obstacle was not an enemy they could simply kill as he frustratedly took a stab at the surrounding mist-filled air.

Concentrating on what he could fight, Titus switched his mind to the coming battle. He understood their work wasn't done and, therefore, knew what was coming. The réama would find allies, and a legion force would march on them. A large one. He needed to get his brothers ready.

After deciding to risk it, Titus called for a team meeting in the main hall and began addressing his brothers, "There is no telling when the enemy will be at our position, but they are coming and in far greater numbers."

First pausing to gauge his squad's resolve, Kurian surprisingly responded with, "Let them come, sir. We will show them why we are called Swords."

Wit and John both clapped the engineer on the back and grinned. Titus gave a nod before continuing, "We don't know yet how much time we have, so here is what I need from each of you: Kurian, I want this fort a death box for anything they can throw at us - legion or horde."

"Understood, sir. I have an idea of how to make our numbers count. How extreme can I get with design?"

"As extreme as you need."

"Roger that."

"Shay, I need intelligence. Get out beyond this hell-spawned mist and report back on anything. We are blind in here," Titus said to his second-in-command. He would have preferred to send at least one other with him, but there simply wasn't enough of them anymore.

"You can count on me, Commander," came the lieutenant's answer.

"John will help Kurian prepare, and Wit will be in the

tower listening for any threats. I will take the tomb."

Everyone immediately understood that Titus wasn't avoiding work or the enemy but, in fact, was taking on the most difficult task among the warriors. He would be alone in the tomb with no support. While Wit might be able to hear an enemy approaching, that was not a guarantee with the large area they had to monitor. Since the mist nearly cut off all communication, even in the fort, guarding their objective could mean that the Sword's leader is the only and last line of defense. If an enemy got past his squad, which was not beyond the realm of possibility, he was the objective's sole protector.

With his orders relayed, each squad member dispersed to complete their tasks and assigned positions. He watched Shay take off in a run and disappear into the mist just outside the main door within a heartbeat. John was listening intently to Kurian as he relayed the instructions to start gathering some materials needed for some contraption or another, but the details were lost in the mist as soon as the pair was only a few steps out the door.

Turning to move to his position down in the tunnel beneath his feet, he nearly ran into a grinning Amadon. "Was there something else private?"

"No, sir. Just excited for what is coming."

"Excited, huh?"

"Absolutely! Macey and I can't wait for another fight." Titus was about to ask the young private about his odd proclivity for speaking to his weapon but immediately thought otherwise, realizing he probably didn't want to know.

In a sudden shift of character, Wit spoke to his leader in a more serious tone, "Never forget, sir - we are warriors, and we never fail our King. Blue or not, we were made for this."

Taken aback, Titus questioned whether it was possible that Wit's hearing was powerful enough to have heard him questioning himself on the wall earlier. After watching the clownish private turn and start skipping away, he decided that it was likely the fickle nature of his communications expert.

Either way, he had a job to do. It was time to strategize how he would keep the rest of his team on this side of the blue while accomplishing his mission of protecting something that seemed determined to destroy itself. He would have plenty of time in the tunnel just outside the tomb.

He walked down and immediately started running through siege and infiltration scenarios. Reducing the number of defenders in his mental war games tugged at his heart and simultaneously reduced his options. His men were superior in every way to their legion counterparts, but it didn't make them any less a threat. It was known that a shadow's physical and mental capacity was diminished when they cut themselves off from the King's energy. Not only did they give up their gifts, health, and beauty, but also their future. Even if they lied to themselves, there was only ever one outcome to this war.

Titus re-concentrated on his battle strategies. He understood that the war was a forlorn conclusion, but the coming battles were not. He had to stretch his ability to plan and devise tactics and counter-tactics. His team was depending on him.

After several marks, Titus barely heard a crackle over his communication link while deep in his thoughts. He listened intently, like he was willing the message to come through. Eventually, his patience was awarded as Shay's broken voice came through, "Sir.....in. Can y......me? Ov..."

"This is Titus. You are coming in broken, Shay. Over."

"Roger, si.... I have foun....outs. Repeat, I have found enemy scouts west of our position and moving towards the fort. Over."

"Understood, LT. I read you—enemy scouts in the area.

Stand by for orders. Over."

Running quickly up the stairs and out the main hall to get the best possible reception to the rest of the team, he physically shouted while opening up a communication link to the team members who had stayed behind to maximize his chances of being heard, "1-1-8, rally on me!"

It took a few more shouts to get Kurian and John, who were outside the walls, but eventually, the remaining members of the fort came running to the Commander.

"Shay has located a group of scouts outside our walls. Kurian will stay and continue his work on the fort. Wit and John, I need you to join LT and wipe them out in the field. It is unknown what they may have seen so far, but we will deny them every piece of information. Understood?"

"Yes, sir," they all responded in unison, with John's silent nod.

"Get it done. Leave none alive."

As the professionals they were, they took off at a dead sprint out the gate. Like diving into a cloud, the mist enveloped them once again. While finding the lieutenant would be difficult in the fog, Titus didn't doubt that the SALT would find them as he relayed his orders to his second and forewarned him of the coming reinforcements.

Before retreating to his defensive position outside the tomb, he listened as best he could to Shay's description of the scouting force. Apparently, it was made up of both shadows and various horde creatures. Due to this, it was clear that a larger force was incoming and was likely not far away. Wiping out the scouts would put a damper on the planning of whoever was in charge, but the inevitability of a large-scale fight was firmly planted in the Commander's mind. Not needing to say anything directly and waste his breath, he began willing his engineering expert to work faster.

As Titus passed the blue statue just inside the main hall, he stopped and pressed his forehead to his sleeping healer.

He would thank Killian for his sacrifice one day, and the commander hoped it would be accompanied by many tales of future victories.

****

Thanks to the change in terrain, Shay had spotted the group from a considerable distance once he was outside the mist. About two mils east of the fort, the forest that surrounded the area turned into rolling hills of grass and sand with sparse trees. With his eyesight and the height advantage of climbing a tree, the enemy squad was easy enough to pick out as they moved in the direction of the fort.

The SALT confirmed that the scouting party had a variety of horde beasts consisting of bullans, ciaróg, and even a bultar. There was no doubt that this was a scouting party as it was led by a stone and not a shadow. A shadow would have pulled strings to avoid such a task, and a stone would jump at the chance to prove his worth.

Various weapons and armor were among the fighters, including the stone. Even at the distance, he knew that the stone was holding a makeshift weapon, not one made by the Creator. A common spear enhanced by the dark art used by their enemy would not hold up against a Sword's weapon, but it could still be deadly in the stone's hands.

It was the theory of many among the Clans that the former Arrows believed they should have been Swords - that their Creator had made a mistake in making them Arrows. When the false king whispered in their ear that they could be anything they wanted and change who the Maker had created them to be, they eagerly joined his attempted coup. Instead, they were treated as little more than slaves. Not having access to their gifts as Arrows and being unable to compare to their shadow brethren in combat meant both sides now looked down upon them. It was sad to see, but sympathy was far from Shay's mind.

They picked up weapons in rebellion and rejected their King. There was no coming back from that Choice, and infinite darkness was the only end to their path.

After getting the orders from the Commander, Shay gracefully jumped and swung down from his position at the top of a tall tree near the edge of the easter plains. He was already sprinting towards the fort when his feet touched the ground. Intercepting and meeting up with the privates would be quick, so he began reviewing the mapped area between the fort and the scouts within his mind. By the time he rendezvoused with his brothers, he had planned out the ambush perfectly.

To John and Wit, Shay materialized out of nothing to be standing before the two running brothers. Not allowing them to slow down, he turned and matched their pace, leading them to the spot he had picked out for their ambush that was just within the tree line coming in from the east. The timing would be close, but they should arrive before their prey and have enough time to prepare.

Being out in the open, Shay rightfully assumed that the stone would lead his minions to the darkest part of the forest as quickly as possible. While their leader would not need a break, Shay knew that some of the monsters in the party would need to catch their breath. Wanting to avoid detection, they would initially attempt to hide in the thickest part of the trees they could find.

The SALT had seen a small clearing within a thicket of trees that would be almost too ideal to pass up. He knew they would rest there before pushing on to the fort, and Shay intended to ensure their rest would become permanent.

As intended, they arrived at the clearing ahead of their prey. There were a few rocks and bushes but nothing that could be used for cover. Shay instructed John to take a position with his ranged gift behind a fallen log in the southwest corner of the clearing. His weapon and position would be the key to their ambush, allowing him the widest field of vision combined with his impressive firepower for ultimate destruction.

To ensure that neither Wit nor himself was in the crossfire, Shay placed Wit to John's left at the western edge of the clearing, and he took position to the large brother's right just within the southern tree line. The three Swords made a perfectly mirrored 'L' shape that would allow them to fire directly ahead of them without fear of hitting each other.

No more than a few heartbeats later, the stone entered the clearing and appeared to be fuming. He didn't yell but was not exactly quiet when he spoke to the horde creatures following him, "Move it, you worthless beasts! I can't believe I got stuck with such weak and...." The stone was cut off as two bullans with golden rings piercing their noses walked into the clearing and glared at the smaller stone.

The stone lowered his eyes and continued, albeit a bit more quietly, "Not you. I am talking about the others." He pointed to the group of ciaróg walking into the clearing behind the larger horde monsters.

Ciarógs were a common infantry type of horde that the legion never seemed to run out of. Each had a hard exoskeleton with a shell covering their backs. While they had four legs for sprinting, they used two of the legs to walk and the other two to interact with objects. Their arms were built solely to cut down their enemies as they had impressively sharp blades going the length of their underarms, culminating in a single curved tip pointing to the ground. The monster didn't have fingers, but all of its appendages rotated fully to allow it to defend and attack at nearly every angle. Its head was topped with large black eyes and antennae curving to their backs. The mouth of the beast was small, but it had pincer-like fangs that pulled food in versus actually chewing. When it bit an enemy, it was easier to decapitate the monster than to open its jaws.

Shay didn't think the leading ciaróg took the stone's belittling any better than the bullan as it took a swipe at the outstretched stone's finger with its bladed arm. It appeared to have scored a hit as the stone reacted like his arm had been chopped off. Once the stone had finished cursing and jumping around, Shay finally saw a small cut at the end of the stone's finger.

"You just wait until general Neart hears about this! I am in charge! This is mutiny," the stone shouted as he tentatively pointed his imperfect spear at the ciaróg who had cut him.

The bultan finally entered the clearing as well and looked like it was not used to the rigors of travel. Disheveled and haughty, it shoved past the others to sit on a rock in the center of the clearing. It immediately began brushing the three pitiful feathers on its head and adjusting its clothing. For one of the ugliest horde beasts, it seemed to pride itself on its appearance. Some Swords have claimed to have seen bultans killing each other over a colorful rock, only to have the winner slash its own face and place the rock in the cut.

Since there was only one bultan, Shay would prioritize it when the killing started. It wouldn't take much to dispatch the hideous creature, but he didn't want the monster to deploy its strange magic-like attacks. There was a lot of debate within the ranks of Swords as to how this horde creature could use black energy-infused attacks and defenses, but the fact of the matter was that they could, and Swords knew not to underestimate their effectiveness in combat.

After waiting a little longer to ensure there were no stragglers, Shay slowly rolled into position and readied his ranged gift on the log he was using as cover. Since the enemy was so close, he didn't need the optics with which his gift was created to engage targets at extreme ranges.

Instead, he gripped the barrel near the front with his left hand to steady the recoil and allow for the acquisition of multiple targets faster.

The SALT aligned his sites on the bultan in the center of the clearing. There was no need to confirm that his team was in position and ready. They understood their job and trusted each other to get it done.

Suddenly, the bultan stopped grooming and stuck its beak in the air like it smelled something. It knew something wasn't right, whether from its physical nose or its abilities, Shay didn't know. However, he did know it was too late.

Shay's shot started the ambush, creating a fist-sized hole through the chest of the alerted horde beast. Immediately, the clearing was lit up like a meteor shower in the dead of night. John's ranged weapon tore through the majority of monsters resting in the clearing. With Wit's and Shay's weapons taking down enemies on the fringes, the slaughter was over within a few heartbeats.

Every horde beast was lying on the ground with at least a few holes in them as the team approached with their primary weapons drawn. One of the bullans attempted a weak swing with a primitive-looking axe at John's legs from the ground. The large brother nimbly dodged it and immediately stomped viciously on the throat of the attacker. Kicking and grabbing at its throat, the bullan did not die well.

As his team was securing the rest of the clearing, Shay found the stone that had claimed to be in charge. He was attempting to crawl away, but Shay himself had shot both of his legs. He was bleeding out his energy, and Shay knew it wouldn't take much to push him over the edge of no return. As he slowly approached and drew one of his primary weapons, the stone rolled over, coughed, and shook his head as he spat, "You will not get anything from me!"

Shay pressed the tip of his blade under the chin of the stone and calmly responded, "Why would I want anything from a traitor?" Without so much as a second's hesitation, he shoved his elongated dagger up and into the skull of his enemy.

22

AS Bravo returned from their mission, they did a double-take when the fort came into view. They had left only a cycle ago but had returned to a whole new structure.

Where there was once a true fort with walls surrounding multiple buildings, there was now a twice-high U-shaped single wall wrapped around the single structure left standing. The tips of the U-shape were flared into platforms, which would be ideal for raining hell down on any that attempted to go through the narrow opening between them.

No other structures were seen, and the walls had been shortened in length or removed completely, so the reclaimed resources had been used to reinforce the walls and heighten them to truly unclimbable heights. At a distance, the main hall appeared like a pearl inside a narrowly opened clam. As Bravo approached, they saw that work still needed to be done. Some areas of the wall were unfinished, and Kurian methodically aligned stones and wood to fill the gaps.

"Welcome back," Titus called out from his position at the highest point of the wall centered at the back of the main hall. Shay had to strain his neck to see the Commander. The wall was another true work of art from Kurian as it clearly made it impossible, or at least highly unlikely, that the enemy could enter from any point other than the front. Immediately, Shay recognized its genius as it forced an invading army to take them on in small doses. No matter the army's size, a few Swords could hold them at bay for an extended amount of time.

“Commander, I am reporting a successful mission. All enemy dead, including a stone that was leading them,” Shay matter-of-factly stated to his superior.

“Well done. All of you,” Titus responded as he individually looked at each of the three Swords who had returned. He continued, “Shay with me for a full report at the bridge. Wit, take my position on watch in the tower. John, you will help Kurian with our preparations.”

The two juniors acknowledged their orders, and Shay walked alongside Titus on the short journey to the main hall’s doors.

“What are we dealing with out there, Shay,” Titus started.

“The scouting party was made up of two bullans, six ciarógs, a bultur, and a leading stone,” Shay paused at the door to the hall before adding, “It wasn’t a small group, and they were headed directly here.”

“So you are saying we have lost the advantage of going unnoticed,” Titus commented as he stroked his beard.

“Yes, sir. Stealth and time are now no longer with us. The western army marches on our position as we speak.”

“Western army? What makes you so certain that it is the full army? Is it not possible that it is just a roaming company?”

“No, sir. I am sure. The stone confirmed it without even knowing he had done it.”

“How so?”

“He mentioned their leader by name,” Shay paused before continuing, “It is our previous superior. General Neart.”

****

“There has been no word from the scouts, my lord,” one of

the newest of the general's advisors reported cautiously. Few would want to deliver bad news to the general, but it was truly unclear what news may set him off. The advisors had gotten together and developed a system where they drew lots each day to determine who would deliver reports to the general. It worked fairly well, especially since the newer ones seem to get 'randomly' chosen more often than not. Neart was, of course, fully aware of this from the beginning.

"Excellent," Neart responded.

The question of why the general would send some of their troops to likely get slaughtered went unspoken on everyone's lips. However, after reading the room and the hesitation, the general added, "Our enemy is better equipped and better trained than the majority of our army."

Thinking that should have been enough to answer the unspoken question, the general went back to reviewing his map. Only looking up when the silence stretched far too long. Anger started rising in the undead visage of the general. Red energy pulsed bright as he looked at each of his advisors, and the sudden realization that he was surrounded by idiots struck him again.

"They would have let us scout them if they had been prepared for us," a voice in the back of the tent said.

"Who said that," Neart nearly shouted.

The shadows and stones that were present parted like water to reveal an arm missing most of a hand raised in the air. Instantly, the general realized it was the fool that had let his post be overrun. His name came quickly to Neart as he fondly remembered removing the shadow's hand.

"Correct, Sham. Well done," Neart acknowledged with a smile.

Immediately, Sham's reaction was just as Neart had expected - shock that the general would give him a compliment. The expression on the shadow's face was quickly replaced with suspicion. Good. This one was both motivated and shrewd. It would be more interesting to use someone with a cautionary eye.

"Come up to the front. Idiots surround me, so it is good to have someone with a hint of intelligence."

Sham approached but cautiously. It wasn't more than a few cycles since this same leader had removed his hand, so he was watching the general like a beaten dog being given a bite to eat from the hand of his abuser. Neart knew this and also realized that Sham was not paying attention to the other shadows in the room and their reaction to a newcomer being singled out with praise.

Neart hated politics and the game that some made of it, but he didn't get to where he was without understanding the moves and how its players reacted. He could smell the ambition on Sham the moment he had entered his tent. The general didn't yet understand the play that he was making, but he knew exactly what the end goal was for this one. Using shadow's motivations to benefit his interests was a tactic Neart had learned from the king himself. He would use Sham's desire to ensure his advisors pushed themselves to be his second. The more his inner circle fought for a second's position, the less they would plot to become first.

"If you were in my position, lord Sham, what would you have us do next," Neart asked as Sham approached the map. The addition of *lord* to the shadow's name had caused a noticeable shift in the tent.

After only a heartbeat, Sham looked up at the general with a small glint in his eye. "I would not presume to claim such a title in such an illustrious audience as this," Sham responded as he waved at not only the general but the other advisors in the room.

Neart smiled as he thought this shadow might be even more intelligent than he had first given him credit for.

With a hint of an edge, Neart responded with, "Please, I insist."

Sham's eyes clearly showed that he was weighing his options and trying to find the best way to proceed. In the end, the general knew that Sham couldn't pass up an opportunity to highlight his capabilities to the shadows gathered, "The esteemed general was right to send scouts as their return, or not, gives us information we can work with. Since they did not return to give us any news, we can assume that the Swords are not ready for us. If they were, they would have let at least one scout return and let us know how impenetrable their defenses are and how it would be impossible for us to win."

The general merely stared at the one-handed shadow as he had done that first day of meeting him. Sham was clearly avoiding the question by reiterating what the general already understood. He was buying time to figure out the best political move. Neart was not known for his patience, and that was wearing thin extremely quickly.

Seemingly understanding the minefield he was dancing in was shrinking, Sham began answering the general's question more directly, "We need to send in a full force of our most mobile horde and shadows. Attack them immediately before they are capable of setting up defenses."

"Excellent! My thoughts exactly," Neart cheerfully said as he clapped Sham on the shoulder.

"I would like to volunteer to lead the force, general. It would be an honor to take back the fort," Sham said but quickly added, "In your name, of course."

Neart nearly laughed out loud at the nearly physical desire for power and glory that this one emanated. The shadow was almost drooling at the thought of being the one to destroy the invaders and take all the fame that came from such a feat.

"No, no, no. Your mind is far more useful with me here," Neart responded as he watched the spark of hope die in the eye of the shadow. He continued driving his strategy home by adding, "I need a shadow like you with intelligence to be by my side."

Looking about the room, he saw not only the eagerness of his advisors at the potential of leading the vanguard but also the venomous glances being shot at the shadow next to himself. Excellent. Hungry to prove themselves to *him* was exactly what he wanted from his advisors at the end of this interaction. The plan to send out the vanguard immediately and attack ahead of the main force was already in the works, and he had already chosen who would lead it. Playing the game with those around him was necessary to ensure loyalty and get his leadership team to come together against a common enemy. Neart did not care if it was a shadow or a Sword, as long as they united. He just used what was available to him.

"Of course, sir. I am here to humbly serve," Sham quickly replied as though he already knew what the general would say. Neart made to appoint the vanguard leader, but Sham surprisingly continued by adding, "However, since you value my opinion, I would like to humbly nominate Emer for leading the attack."

Neart controlled his anger as he turned to look at the one-handed shadow once more. The spark in his eye that he had thought he had just crushed was still there, only slightly hidden. How did this fool know who he had chosen already? Emer was not someone whom Neart publicly praised or gave the impression that he relied upon, but, in fact, was an excellent fighter and strategist. Neart had refused to let Emer know how valuable she was or let others see how much he depended upon the shadow. Yet, this new shadow had already deciphered Emer's value and moved to gain her loyalty. By giving Emer his recommendation, Sham will have sowed a seed of appreciation in the mind of Neart's top advisor.

Not seeing another way out, Neart didn't have any other choice but to lean into the recommendation, "Indeed. Emer is a good choice. She will lead the attack on the fort."

Emer was a fairly common-looking shadow with nothing of note about her other than a shorter stature and the slight madness that sparkled within her red eyes, which matched her red hair. As a former knowledge-seeker, her mind was constantly looking at what was around and attempting to give it some sort of meaning now that she was outside the influence of the Maker. While brilliant on the battlefield, the shadow would privately and audibly ask herself questions, only to become violent when she couldn't provide answers.

The new leader of the vanguard stepped forward and acknowledged the general but also nodded to Sham. Neart instantly knew that this would not do. He needed a way to bring this upstart down a peg, and he knew how to do it.

"Emer, you will take two companies of our fastest horde beasts and a full squad of legion," the general started.

"As you wish, my lord," came Emer's confident response.

Before Emer could turn to go, the general added, "You should also take Ronan."

Emer stopped dead in her tracks and slowly turned. Her skin slipped a little as the anxiety showed. "Should I go fetch him now, great general," Emer asked in an extremely less confident manner.

"No, you have much work to do to prepare the troops for battle," the general responded. He pointed towards Sham and continued, "My new advisor should be seen to have my authority and order Ronan to take part in the coming battle."

It was clear that Sham had seen several of the gathered advisors snicker a bit, and Emer looked immensely relieved. Not allowing an out, Neart stared down Sham and commanded, "Bring me Ronan. Bring me my SALT."

There was no hiding the shock that filled Sham's face. Even still, he didn't question the order and simply acknowledged it as he bowed before leaving the tent. The general couldn't help but grin as the newest advisor left. He didn't expect to see him again for some time, if ever.

23

A SALT shadow?!? Sham had never heard of such a thing. While possible, no one had ever spoken of a SALT rebelling with the legion. Having one on their side would make the task of regaining his fort and glory that much easier.

However, Sham immediately knew it was a trap. There was no way that he was going anywhere near this legion *SALT*. It didn't take much to understand that the general was attempting to punish him for his political maneuvering within the strategy session. He may not fully know what the general was up to by sending him out on this seemingly innocent errand, but Sham's warning bells were screaming at him the heartbeat that it took Neart to smile.

In truth, the entire meeting had been a boxing match. While the general was a brilliant strategist on the battlefield, Sham was no amateur in the political arena. All in all, he believed that they had come out even with trading social blows throughout the council. It wasn't a complete loss on either side, but it wasn't a victory either.

One thing was certain to Sham as he left: he would do what the general ordered but in the manner in which Sham wanted to do it. The letter of the order, but not the spirit of it. He would interpret how to get it done on his terms. To do that, he would need a good patsy. Someone to take the trap for him, but who would complete the task no matter the obstacle. He needed a gullible stone.

As luck would have it, the sentry who had initially let him into the camp and had taken punishment for it was walking not far away. Well, walking was not exactly how

Sham would describe it, as the stone was limping and seemed to have difficulty lifting its arms. Clearly, the punishment he had received was still causing a great deal of pain.

Could Sham pull off another scam on the same victim? The answer was obvious to him, as his confidence in himself truly knew no bounds.

Approaching cautiously and almost mimicking the stone's labored movements, Sham adjusted his path and speed so that he bumped into the stone crossing in front of him.

"Ouch! Watch where you are walking, idiot," the stone shouted. He quickly narrowed his eyes at who bumped into him and raised a finger menacingly at Sham before adding, "YOU!"

"Forgive me, sentry. It is hard to manage with my wounds," Sham replied as he raised his arm with a partially healed hand towards the outstretched finger of the accusing stone.

A slight smile escaped the mouth of the stone as he saw the missing hand. "Got what you deserved," he replied.

"Yes, absolutely. It was wrong of me to push you into the tent so quickly without formalities."

Sham could tell that the apology caught the stone off-guard. He mumbled a little as he dropped his arm and responded, "Yes. It was all your fault."

"Of course! I was in such a hurry to deliver my news that it got both of us nearly maimed. I am truly sorry that our mutual desire to eradicate the enemy caused us to forget our proper etiquette," Sham continued with his apology, using language that highlighted they were in this situation together as a team.

Slowly, the venom in the stone's eyes started to diminish as he considered Sham's words and the overplayed wounds that he exhibited. Eventually, he responded with, "It doesn't matter anymore. I am no longer a sentry and am demoted to camp fetcher."

Perfect. The camp fetcher was the lowest position held by any legion member. It was a gopher and practical slave to all others in the camp, including other stones. Anyone would be desperate to leave such a position, which meant that Sham had him right where he wanted him.

"What is your name, warrior?"

"I am Malachy."

"Well, Malachy, I have recently been added to the general's inner circle," Sham said as he witnessed shock and a bit of anger cross Malachy's face. Not letting his outrage take root, Sham continued, "I am looking for an intelligent, loyal, and competent second to help me. With what we went through together, there is no one else in this camp that I would trust more than you."

Suddenly, the stone's eyes changed from hatred to hope. Going from one of the lowest positions to being a second to a leader in the inner circle of the general would be a massive leap in the hierarchy. No one could resist such an offer.

"I am honored, lord Sham," Malachy bowed as he replied.

Wow. Sham didn't honestly think it would be this easy, but he would take what was offered.

"Thank you, Malachy. Together, you and I will make our way to the top of this army and, dare I say, liberation city itself! Before long, we shall dine with the king and take part in all the pleasure afforded to us," Sham exclaimed as he held out his good arm to embrace his newly appointed second. The thought crossed his mind that maybe he had played that a bit too aggressively, but the eyes of Malachy shined with greed as he grabbed hold of the outstretched forearm in a brotherly embrace.

"Before we get started," Sham continued, "there is one task that I need you to do for me."

****

* * *

Malachy limped away from the fortuitous meeting with lord Sham, happy that he was no longer in the position he had started that morning. He felt lighter and healthier with each step he took, but a new kind of dread filled him as he asked all shadows or stones in the area as to the whereabouts of Ronan.

While Malachy had never met the shadow, he was known to many and was nearly as feared as the general himself. While Neart was known as a harsh leader, there was never a doubt about where you stood with him. He would be blunt and direct with all members of the legion and even the horde. There was order and logic to most of his cruelty. Ronan was rumored to have neither. One story told of how he was joking and elbowing a companion next to him, then the next moment, he had put his thumb into their eye until there was an audible pop. No reason was given or complaint voiced, just the sound of his laughter and the wailing of a newly one-eyed shadow. Malachy hoped Ronan was in a less comedic mood today.

After only a few interrogations, he was pointed to Ronan's tent outside the legion area and just within the horde's own. Why the most feared fighter of their army chose to be among the creatures instead of his own was beyond Malachy's understanding. It was almost as if he preferred the filthy creatures' company to that of his fellow shadows. That said, now that he thought about it, the numbers of the legion's healthy fighters did seem unusually high compared to their typical city posting.

Regardless, the stone needed to be swift in his first task as a second to the newest advisor to the general.

When he arrived at the tent, he noticed a large amount of smoke pouring out. While many had fires within their tent, this was far more smoke than could be accounted for by a simple fire. A brief inhale as he entered caused the stone to have a small coughing fit as he instantly recognized the taste of Réama poison.

When properly *motivated*, the Réama could produce their internal poison externally to be smoked. Doing this would negate the harmful effects of being eaten alive but still allow the user to get the high that Réama victims experienced while they were being digested. It was an extremely delicate process to get the pure version of the drug while keeping the creature alive to produce more. What the messenger saw inside the tent was not that process. Instead, as he entered, he saw a Réama attempting to get out of a giant pot that was being held over a fire, causing it to be boiled alive in its own slime. The creature was too far gone to scream, but the look on its melted face said unspeakable pain. While inefficient, Malachy did have to admit that Ronan's process was technically working as he slowly started to forget why he was in such a big hurry.

Ronan sat in the back on several elaborate pillows with empty wine skins strewn about him, but he wasn't alone. On either side of him were Marows that he absently fondled as they touched his bare chest - all while he stared blankly at the new arrival.

Malachy stopped for a brief moment to admire Ronan's skin. In a word, it was perfect. If he had not known any better, he would have assumed it was one of the Host sitting in the tent. In complete contrast to the general, Ronan had perfected the art of his skin. He was handsome, tall, muscular, and without a blemish on his perfect teal skin. His hair was jet black and hung down to his muscled shoulders. Even the energy running through him was yellow instead of the red the stone knew was actually flowing beneath the projection. It was nowhere near the golden glow gifted by their Creator, and he still had red eyes, but Malachy had never seen one of the shadows with as close an imitation as what Ronan displayed outside of the king himself. His concentration to maintain such a skin had to be incredible. Malachy's own skin began to falter immediately after the first inhale of the drugged air.

After the brief pause to admire the shadow, the fresh reminder of his recent position and newly given authority pushed him back into the task at hand.

"General Neart orders you to his command tent immediately."

"Oh, he does, does he?" Ronan responded as he looked to the Marow on his left and began a detailed study of its face.

Malachy could have sworn that an angry red scar flashed across Ronan's face, but a second look showed only the near-perfect image he was projecting.

A longer pause ensued as the stone simply stood and stared at his first attempt at using his new supposed authority, melted like ice on a fire. His eyes must have shown the dejection that he felt because Ronan simply stared back with a new smile spreading across his face—not a welcoming or thankful smile, but one of a predator who was toying with its prey.

Between returning to camp fetcher and perceived glory, Malachy decided to go for broke and attempt to force the issue.

"The general is waiting. He will not appreciate any delays. We are leaving. Now." While the words sounded confident, the pitch and presentation were anything but.

Surprising Malachy, the response was immediate and extremely unexpected as Ronan shouted, "You are absolutely right! We must not keep the general or his advisors waiting." He quickly stood up, tightened his pant strings, and grabbed a cloak and tunic. Revealed underneath the discarded clothes was something that Malachy had thought was impossible. A ranged gift, but in the hands of a *shadow*. He had personally never had such a weapon, seeing how he was a former Arrow.

Ronan noticed his guest's interest and picked up the weapon with a gentle and almost loving touch. While initially it looked to be a ranged gift, Malachy now understood that this was decidedly not a Creator gift. Even in the smoke-filled tent, he saw that there was something just a little wrong with the weapon. Almost as if it were an attempt by a less talented artist to copy a masterpiece while looking through a warped window. It was exotic and wicked-looking. Malachy wanted it immediately.

The weapon was black from stock to muzzle, except for the grip and trigger, which were gold. Its scope at the top was made with such precise detail that the messenger didn't doubt it would display targets at extreme ranges. What confused the messenger were the various shiny strings and circles near the front that connected to multiple tucked wing-like appendages to either side.

Additionally, he quickly noted that, unlike original ranged gifts, this particular weapon did not shoot energy. Its ammunition was bolts made of pure black that appeared as though they were made from the night itself. Their lethality couldn't be questioned as the tips glinted even in the low fire light of the tent.

Pride filled every word as Ronan spoke, "It is not as good as my original and doesn't have the capacity or range of a real Creator gift, but that doesn't matter. The bolts were a gift from the king himself. In my hands, the bow is equal to any of my former brother's weapons."

When Ronan talked of his former brothers, he did not refer to the Host or the Sword clan. No, they were beneath Ronan. He was speaking strictly of those with his former designation - SALT. Malachy had heard the stories of the legendary warriors among the clans. They were said to take stalking and long-range fighting to another level. Very few existed, and even fewer were among the shadows as most remained with their Creator. Rumor had it that a single SALT could complete a mission that would otherwise have taken a battalion. He looked to Ronan with a renewed level of fear… and no small amount of respect.

Ronan noticed the small change in the messenger and

smiled once more before turning to his escorts, whom the messenger had all but forgotten since first arriving.

“My friends, please entertain our guest while I am away. It would be a terrible shame if you were lonely during my absence.”

Malachy was about to object, but both Marows smiled and reached out to the messenger to welcome him to the cushioned seating area. Having been in the tent for several minutes now and breathing the drug that permeated the air, his concerns about sitting and being between them were somehow hard to grasp, and the voice in his head warning of danger was nothing more than a breath in the wind.

Marows were creatures of beauty and danger. Their upper half was made to hide their lower by showing only feminine beauty with long flowing hair, stunning features, and unashamed nudity. They were known to lull their victims into false confidence by singing sweet melodies with hypnotic powers. The only warning a victim might catch as to their potential danger was viper-like eyes that held only malice for the world. Beneath the beautiful upper half, the lower was more akin to serpents, which held the lethality they were famous for. It is common knowledge among the legion that a Marow could constrict a fully grown bullan to the point where there wasn't a single bone left unbroken in its body.

None of that truly registered to Malachy as he was eased into the now vacant spot between the two beautiful beings. Was there a reason to go? Did he need to be somewhere? Who were these lovely creatures again? Could they have names? Did he care?

One thought that stayed with him was maybe Ronan wasn't so bad after all. Nothing like what others had spoken about him. He had been polite and offered his pleasures to a simple stone, right?

Of course, Malachy would take advantage of Ronan's

misplaced trust and take everything he could from him long before he came back. Maybe he could even take that beautiful weapon Ronan was so fond of. The thought made the stone smile at Ronan and, without a drop of sincerity, say, “I will be sure to take good care of them for you.” Ronan smiled back and actually winked at him. What a fool!

****

As Ronan was walking away from his tent and in the opposite direction of the general’s, he heard the messenger’s first scream. He was instantly curious about how many pieces of the idiot his pets would remove before he returned. Taking the long way to the general was not to insult his leader but to ensure the stone was punished in as many ways as possible - for as long as possible. He could not have a simple stone telling him what to do, and the general would have understood that.

Slowly, Ronan strolled to the outskirts of the camp. He thought he might go out again to try and find the elusive creatures that had stalked the camp since the arrival of that blubbering shadow from the west. Being a SALT, it frustrated him to no end that there was something out there that could remain hidden from his eyes. Tracks and signs were all he could find, and even those were incredibly hard to locate. However, it was a challenge, and Ronan desperately needed one after being surrounded by such incompetence for so long. With that thought, an image of the stone and the pain it must be enduring at that moment came to his mind. A handsome and genuine smile formed on his perfect skin. Maybe he would take the long way back, too.

Ronan never even thought to get the stone’s name.

24

IT was 6:15 PM on a Wednesday, and Henry did NOT want to attend the Bible study his parents were forcing him to go to. As an adult at 18, he should have the option. Unfortunately, his parents made it abundantly clear that he either participated in their church's activities or moved out of their basement. Since he had no money, no job, and wasn't in school, there wasn't much of a choice in that ultimatum.

As usual, he would wait until his parents' car was out of sight and call his buddy Eddy to hang out for an hour. While it was always a little awkward when Eddy only ever wanted to smoke weed, it was better than being inside with the group of Bible nerds who seemed to always come to these things.

Henry didn't mind if Eddy smoked as long as he wasn't constantly pressuring him to join in or was attempting to drive while high. Unfortunately, it was sometimes hit or miss with Eddy on both of those issues.

Smoking weed didn't seem like a big deal. However, Henry's parents would undoubtedly not only kick him out of the house if he was caught doing drugs but would be immensely disappointed in him. Deep down, he knew the disappointment would hurt far more than the loss of a roof over his head. He was unwilling to risk it over something that seemed to have very little benefit. Additionally, he had a stubborn streak that almost seemed to enjoy fighting peer pressure. When Eddy tried to get Henry to smoke for the first time in a group setting, Henry smiled the entire time as he twisted his friend's attempt back on itself to eventually have everyone else laughing at the frustrated and confused Eddy. He never tried to use that tactic again.

Hanging up his phone in exasperation after trying to reach his flaky friend for the fifth time, Henry started to feel raindrops on his head. Great, he thought. What else could go wrong tonight?

Not having any other choice, he stepped into the church and was immediately greeted by a cheery boy with pimples covering his face under thick glasses, "Hey, Henry! Welcome back. I haven't seen you in a while. What have you been up to?"

"Hey, Caleb. Not much. Just been doing stuff."

"For sure! I have been super busy packing up for college. It will be weird being so far from my family, but Saint Joesph's University has the best theology program," Caleb said to a disinterested Henry.

"Yeah, sure. I heard that about... that place."

"By the way, where are you going to school?"

"I am going to take a year to find myself," Henry responded, looking down at his phone. He had gotten a lot of practice with that partial-truth answer. Everyone had asked him the same thing for the past year. The full truth was that he didn't have the grades to get into college. He had spent his high school years playing video games, hanging out with friends, and occasionally going to baseball practice. It was well known that Henry was the star of the team as one of the best pitchers in the state, but his coach eventually kicked him off for missing practices. Henry didn't think he needed practice and it was a waste of time. No one could hit against him, so he didn't see the point of practicing with the others.

"That's cool, man. I hope you find it."

"For sure," Henry quickly answered. Hoping to watch a movie or mess around on the internet for an hour, he followed it up with, "Hey. Do you know what the wifi password is?"

Caleb chuckled and responded, "Wifi? In this old church? You are kidding, right?"

Wonderful. He was officially stuck in the church with no internet and nothing to do.

"Come on, man. Bible study is starting. We don't want to miss the guest speaker! I heard he is awesome."

With nothing left as an excuse, Henry walked towards the music that had just started in the main chapel area. He politely made an excuse not to sit with Caleb up front as they entered together, and instead, he took a seat in the back row near the exit.

After watching the thirty or more kids standing and waving their hands in the air to the music, Henry started to think he had made a mistake. These were definitely not the kind of kids to surround himself with. It was almost painfully awkward to watch. He began to think about what his friends would say if they rolled up to look for him and saw him with this group.

Convincing himself that it would be better to wait out in the lobby than here, Henry stood up as the music ended. Henry paused momentarily when the youth pastor came up on stage to start introducing the guest speaker. He remembered what Caleb had said earlier, and a part of him wanted to hear what the big deal was.

"Amen! Thank you so much for that, worship team," the youth pastor Allen started.

"Thank you all for joining us tonight. I see a number of new and old faces in the audience, and I am excited to have you all here for this special guest speaker."

Henry felt like Allen had looked right at him when he mentioned old faces, even though the dimmed lights made that unlikely. In truth, he used to come into the youth group consistently throughout his first few years of high school. That changed when he started hanging out with his baseball teammates, who welcomed him into the popular group due to his athletic prowess. Each week from then on, he pulled away from the youth group kids to spend time with his new friends. Eventually, the excuse of baseball practice stopped working with his parents, and he started the weekly hangout with Eddy, the team's catcher and his best friend. Until tonight, he had gotten away with it, but he knew it was only a matter of time before his parents caught on.

Feeling suddenly guilty about his lies to his parents, Henry sat back down as Allen continued, "I am thrilled to introduce you to our guest speaker tonight: Captain James McCarthy."

As he ended his announcement, Allen pointed to the fittest-looking man Henry had ever seen. Everyone began clapping as the stout soldier took the steps and walked to shake Allen's hand. It was clear that the man was a soldier from his bearing, plus the high and tight haircut helped. The Captain set his bible on the podium and looked out to address the youth gathered. He opened with, "God is good!"

The crowd, minus Henry, responded with the same in one voice, "All the time!"

Henry's mind laughed a little at the people gathered. It was always something he had trouble with in church. They followed a certain script, and he felt like it was a bit too cultish for his taste. He preferred to keep his independent thoughts and reactions.

"Thank you, Pastor Allen, for welcoming me and inviting me to speak to your group. I am very honored to be here and share my story."

The guest speaker seemed to gather himself before sharing his story: "I joined the Army right out of high school with no real alternatives. After spending some time in the infantry, I re-enlisted with the option to attend special forces training."

Special Forces? That caught Henry's attention, and he

immediately sat up in his seat.

“I passed selection and was assigned to a unit deployed to South America. I would tell you where and what I did, but then I would have to kill you,” Captain McCarthy said with a wink that got a good laugh out of the crowd. He continued, “I fought in many battles against some of the most evil people this planet has ever produced. In one such fight, I was separated from my unit and ended up living in the jungle for twenty days before being rescued by a kind farmer who smuggled me back to my team with severe risk to his own life.”

Henry was hooked. He couldn’t believe how incredibly awesome this guy was and the crazy stories he must have. Without even a second thought, he silenced his phone as Eddy started returning his calls at that moment.

“I give you this brief introduction so that you understand that I have been in multiple life-and-death situations. My team and I fought on several continents. We battled with enemies sworn to end our lives and nature that seemed to want its own pound of flesh,” James said. He took a moment before continuing, “I tell you these things because I need you to understand that I speak from experience when I say - each of you is in a fight for your own life right now.”

There was a pause in the room, and Henry guessed that he could have heard a pin drop from twenty feet away before Captain McCarthy continued, “Just like there was a physical enemy that did their best to kill my team and me, there is an enemy that is circling you who wants nothing less than your death. This enemy plays with an unprotected mind. Bending and twisting truths to pull you away from your support and lifeline. It gathers armies to lay siege to your very heart.”

Henry didn’t know how, but he knew this soldier was speaking to him directly. Thoughts of all the nights he had made excuses for not going to youth group or flat out lying to get out of going to church on Sundays. The creeping feeling that it was boring and there was so much out there to offer entertainment and fun had won more often than not in his life.

"The enemy has many tactics at his disposal. I know because I have personally experienced them myself. Alcohol, violence, gambling, and especially lust - I struggled with all of it throughout my life," James confessed.

As soon as the Captain had mentioned lust, Henry immediately wanted to get up and go hide. He felt a sudden wave of shame and disappointment that was almost overwhelming. However, another force glued him to his seat. Henry didn't know why, but he needed to hear this man.

"Right now, I know that some of you out here in the audience may struggle with these same things or similar attacks under the same banner. There is something that you each need to know. God loves you and wants to help, just like he helped me in my darkness."

The Special Forces soldier went on to explain how he had found God at the lowest point in his life, where all he felt was emptiness. James had sought comfort and distraction in any form, wanting relief from the pit that held him. During one evening of indulgence, he physically felt a force attempting to take his mind several times. Inexplicably, he felt another force blocking the attempts again and again. The experience had terrified him. What were these forces, and how could they have such power over him?

Not long after, a fellow soldier had invited him to a local church. Not seeing anything else helping and knowing there was a fight going on that he didn't understand, he decided to tag along. The sermon that day had been about the enemy of God and how he operates in our lives. James immediately felt the pieces fall into place. There was an enemy, and he couldn't defeat it alone. He didn't have the training or weapons. He needed something greater than his experience and better than his rifle in order to defend himself. All the tools and intel he needed were provided and outlined in God's battle manual, which is what James called the bible.

Henry soaked up all this man said as though it was water for a thirst he didn't even know he had. A nagging voice in the back of his mind said he was fine and already had God in his life. He was a pastor's kid, right? He shoved those thoughts aside and immediately came to the sudden and stark realization that he didn't have God in his life. With all his father's teachings and his mother's lessons, it was suddenly made very clear that he had never truly chosen God.

At the end of the testimony, Captain McCarthy stated, "If there are any here who would like to come up for prayer, please come up to the front."

Henry was halfway down the aisle before his brain kicked in and rebelled against the idea of being in front of all these people he had rejected as uncool. An immense fear of being marked as one of them by his popular friends washed over him, and he was even angry at the thought of others saying he needed to be corrected. He wasn't so bad, right? There was nothing wrong with him that needed fixing; if there were, he could probably do it himself. He didn't need to confess anything or do anything to be a good person.

When Henry had stopped and closed his eyes to battle this sudden wave of thoughts and emotions, after a minute, there was an equally strong pull to open his eyes and look up. As he did so, the guest speaker, Captain McCarthy, stood directly before him. He never saw the man approaching, but there he was. Before Henry could turn around, James grabbed both shoulders and looked directly into his eyes. "I see the battle wounds, son. You are hurting, aren't you?"

Without another word, Henry broke down in tears. The

large, deadly soldier pulled him close and hugged him. When they were close, he whispered into Henry's ear, "God sees you and wants to save you. All you need to do is choose Him."

Through his tears, Henry shook his head yes. The Captain continued to hug him as he prayed, and Henry repeated it. Soon, the tears of shame and sadness were replaced with ones made from joy. Henry knew that his life would never be the same from that point forward.

25

EACH of his team was working diligently with their tasks, and Titus's skills were not needed at the time. It was his rotation in the tunnel to protect the tomb, with Wit circling out to help in the construction. While he stood guard, Titus contemplated Kurian's genius and dedication as the younger brother had worked non-stop to complete the new design of the fort. Looking at it now, Titus wasn't sure if it was truly a fort anymore. He believed it resembled a small castle as it was a singular building with a U-shaped wall cupping it. The majority of the walls were solid and would hold out some of the more stubborn of enemies, and the engineer was working to add some surprises as well.

They all knew that the defenses wouldn't hold out an army, but it was a lot more defensible than what they had previously, considering they were now down two Swords. The smaller opening with the three overwatch positions allows for few defenders to hold the entirety of the fort. Plus, they had the addition of peace of mind knowing that there weren't any hidden enemies within their walls. Collapsing the walls back to their current position allowed a thorough and complete review of all hiding spaces. For the first time since their arrival, each member felt as though they had complete control of their area.

Titus opened the door to the tomb and inspected its contents. While nothing else had changed or moved, the dark plant seemed to have grown beyond anything Titus would have imagined. Large, thick vines now reached around the upper section of the stone casket. Needle-like thorns seemed to cover the vines, and there were even small, sickly leaves growing randomly on the vines. Again, it struck Titus that this plant didn't have a physical exterior presence. Instead, the vines were cutting deep into the casket itself as though a master stone mason had come down to give the casket a deeply disturbing plant effigy. Not one of his brothers had actually seen the plant grow or change on the casket, so none could say if it was alive or not. It only got bigger when it was out of sight, growing in solitude.

However, the only other remarkable thing about the casket hadn't changed since that first beam of light that had shot straight up out of the hole directly above it. Titus watched as the flame didn't move and never changed color, almost as though a fire was present but dead. The constant red it portrayed was not ugly but nowhere near the beauty of the violet beam that had saved them during the loskang attack.

Since Titus was on guard duty, he ensured that he could physically respond to any threat that appeared, but he let his mind go into deep consideration of these two oddities that both held claim over a casket. It was impossible to open the casket to understand what was within, but Titus had suspicions that it was a true treasure of their King. Something was affecting the flame and the plant in equal measure. Something that was beyond him and simply out of his control. The dark tidings that the team had brought back during their excursion to the south only amplified his curiosity. From the sounds of it, the plant had won over the flame and had claimed the casket. But, in truth, even that was not clear. Just because the flame was no longer on the other casket didn't really mean that the two were at odds. In fact, the plant didn't seem threatened by the current flame in the slightest. Additionally, their King would not have sent them to simply watch an evil-looking plant grow on a casket. They were there, fighting and even going blue, for a reason. Their fight with the enemy was preventing or doing something, but it was unclear to Titus how he was helping. As a Sword, he was truly happy to be serving his Maker in the way he was meant to, but Titus felt as though he would be able to help more if he understood more.

Titus snapped out of his mindset as he already understood the answer to all of his questions. He was there to do the will of his King. If he needed the information to do the work, he would have had it. His faith in his brothers, the mission, and his King was unwavering. It was time to stop whining about what he wasn't told and start dedicating his efforts to the only thing that mattered. His orders.

"This is Titus. Calling all 1-1-8 to check-in. Over."

Titus waited a bit but didn't really expect a response. The fog that had appeared with the réamas had not waivered and continued to play havoc with their communications, not to mention their sight lines.

Just as Titus was about to try again, he heard a crackle come over the team's link, "Sir, we have con....up her.... Ov.."

Titus's mind filled in the blanks and instantly was locking the tomb door and sprinting up the stairs. Exiting the main hall's entrance, he scanned for signs of the enemy or his team. On the wall positions that were the tips of the U-shaped design, John and Wit held the high ground with their range gifts at the ready and were scanning for threats behind stone barriers. Kurian was the sole occupant of the unblocked gateway, standing with his shield held casually in the front. Titus sprinted up to join the sergeant and drew his sword as he half-asked and half-ordered, "Status."

"Sir, Shay spotted unknown movement in the trees beyond the no-mans land just before the fog got too thick. I believe my early warning system is ineffective in this fog. There is no telling where they are coming from and how many. The LT will continue to provide overwatch and intel, but we all know it will be limited."

"Understood," Titus responded and switched his communication to a direct link to Shay, hoping it would have a stronger signal. "LT, do what you can from up there, but your primary order is to secure the main hall. Nothing is to enter. How copy? Over."

"Copy, sir. I will stay put and keep an eye on the objective. Over."

Titus was grateful that the fog allowed the brief conversation. At least he wouldn't have to worry about sending one of the front gate brothers to relay the message.

The blasted fog is making their job much harder. There was nothing they could do, so Titus needed to forget about it and pray that it would lift soon. If not, they would be fighting on their back foot for the rest of their deployment.

"Sir," Wit shouted from his perch on the right side of the opening, "I hear heavy steps. Something is coming."

Almost as a response, a single shot from Shay's oversized rifle zinged right between Kurian and Titus. What was left of a very large bullan came crashing down within twenty hands of the gateway. It was still kicking and holding onto a thick club when Titus turned and gave a pleased thumbs up to his second.

Suddenly, the mist gave way to twenty more bullans charging at their position. John and Wit opened up with their ranged gifts from their positions up top, with John mowing down the initial charge and Wit selectively picking his targets using his rifle. In the initial wave, only four made it to the gate where Titus and Kurian were positioned. Bouncing between the attackers, Kurian's bladed shield seemed to be on a mission to make each bullan shorter as it sliced calves and cut legs nearly in half. Titus took the upper portion of the beasts by dancing around their attacks and blocking fists with his blade. The force of their attacks caused some of their fingers to be sliced off as Titus was not blocking with the blunt side of his weapon. Using each other's movement and working in perfect harmony, they made short work of the attacking monsters.

The silence that filled the space after the initial charge was broken by Wit when he said, "Well. That wasn't so bad, right?" Immediately, a long blast of a war horn was sounded out in the fog, and screams filled with bloodlust seemed to come from every direction. All Swords present at the gate stopped and stared at Wit, with John shaking his head in a perfect way that easily conveyed, 'You just had to open your mouth.'

"Kurian, we need to know what we are dealing with. It is time. Light them up."

Not needing any encouragement or clarification, Kurian triggered a remote he had attached to his forearm underneath his shield. The results were instantaneous as bright lights and explosions erupted on the edge of the no man's land near the tree line.

One of the first things that 1-1-8 accomplished when they took possession of the fort was to clear the debris in the area between the fort and the tree line. At the direction of Kurian, they had stacked the dead trees and stones into piles at regular intervals. Any attacking force would see them as valuable pieces of cover when approaching. They would be dead wrong. Within the piles, Kurian had placed a variety of explosive charges with varying degrees of effects. While most of his charges provided the usual death and destruction by flinging the debris in all directions, there were some that also provided brilliant light that was initially aimed at stunning and disorienting the enemy. The latter now provided a bit of reprieve from the fog as they burned hot and gave the Swords a brief glimpse as to what they were up against. Unfortunately, what they saw was not encouraging.

As the flames burned bright, the brothers of 1-1-8

witnessed their true predicament. The enemy had surrounded them and was comprised of varying horde creatures. This was not a roaming band of monsters. It was a coordinated attack on their position.

The one positive that Titus saw was that some flames seemed dancing among the trees. He imagined that a number of their attackers were likely on fire and attempting to have their comrades put them out. There was no telling the true impact of their trap, but seeing horde corpses litter the areas surrounding the previously hidden explosives was a good start.

"Commander. This is Shay. I see multiple shadows moving among the enemy. The legion is leading the assault. How copy?"

The communication link seemed to come in a bit stronger as the flames burned out the fog somewhat.

"I read you, Shay. Any sign of the general?"

"Negative. This appears to be a smaller force. I am betting this is their vanguard."

Smaller was a bit disheartening as Titus surveyed the surrounding area, which highlighted a thick line of bullans and ciaróg being supported by both bulturs and gúl. The hard-hitting bullans and ciaróg were easy enough to deal with individually, as they would be forced to enter the fort via the singular entrance. Unfortunately, the ranged capabilities of both the bulturs and the gúl were going to complicate things.

Gúl were wily, small creatures that hid their pale bodies beneath cloaks. Only their red eyes were seen beneath their hoods, but the Host had killed enough to know that their elongated faces with tiny arms and legs were what was beneath their covering. Having large ears and eyes with tusks for teeth, they appeared as though they were an attempt at recreating a shadow that failed miserably. With their bows and arrows made from the bones of other gúl, they preferred wounding their enemy from afar and watching as their victim slowly bled out. With their natural selection of killing any of their own kind to create weapons, only those who were excellent shots survived, making them a formidable ranged adversary.

Seeing what was out there, Titus immediately slowed his mind and began formulating a new strategy to deal with the threat before their enemy could counterattack. Due to the fact that the flames would be put out and the fog would overtake them once more, their ranged capability would be diminished to only a few hands in front of them. They could not indiscriminately shoot towards the enemy as that would waste their energy and have minimum impact. On the other hand, their enemy would know exactly where the defenders were and could carpet the area with their ranged attacks while sending troops in to engage in close quarters. The legion would care very little for any friendly fire losses and some of the horde would probably get energized by killing either friend or foe. Taking all of this into account and prioritizing the mission, Titus knew what they had to do.

As the flames began disappearing and the fog thickened, Titus used the final opportunity to give clear orders to his brothers, “Listen up! We are switching tactics. John and I will hold the entrance. Wit will fall back and hold the objective. Shay and Kurian are now Bravo and will be going outside the wall to neutralize the enemy’s ranged capabilities. All Swords confirm.”

After each team member responded through their link and quickly began transitioning, Titus called out to Shay and Kurian, “Happy hunting, Bravo.”

26

SHE didn't know where this fog had come from, but it was exactly what Emer could have hoped for. Her success was now pushing into the eighty-third percentile.

That said, Emer's initial probing attack went about as she expected. While not overtly successful, it was useful in gathering intelligence regarding the structural change of the fort. The information from Sham and the details provided by the réama that they had found along the way indicated that only a few Swords held the fort, and it would be nearly impossible for them to secure the entire area. Using this information, she had planned to overwhelm the walls. She had expected heavy casualties, but their victory would have been all but assured. Seeing the new structure of the fort caused her to pause and calculate a new strategy, which led to her forces being struck by the traps and wiping out nine percent of her fighters.

As a former knowledge-seeker, she calculated the odds of such events playing out to be about twenty-one point three, five, two percent. She reassessed her enemy and updated her future calculations to account for their ingenuity and skill. Her plans would need to be changed to reduce the new margin of error. Failure was not an option. Neart was not someone that you disappointed.

One of the positives from her probing attack was a clear understanding of the battleground and position of the enemy. Intelligence from the réama was still valuable as it told of the composition of the entrenched Sword unit. Emer again calculated the odds and knew the unit had its SALT up high with the Big and communications experts as gunners above the gate. That left the commander and engineer as the barrier holding her forces from overwhelming their defenses. She was confident they would try something different or reposition, but their single entrance provided a focal point for her attack. Directing her ranged units to concentrate fire in waves and pushing her troops in would give her the desired outcome. It was only a matter of time.

All that said, she knew there were always variables. Managing these would be the difference between success and failure. One of those variables was the shadow standing next to her at that exact moment. Ronan had obeyed and came along as requested, but he seemed less interested in following her orders and more in locating the Sword's SALT. She knew he was obsessed with proving he was the best and saw his former brothers as the only true tests of this theory. There was a hundred percent chance that this wild card would do whatever he wished, so Emer planned on using his desire for her benefit.

"You have leave to do as you wish, Ronan. Just do what you can to distract the enemy SALT. My troops will handle the others," Emer said to the incredibly handsome shadow without even looking in his direction.

Ronan smiled as he glanced towards Emer before turning and walking away. As he headed out toward his ultimate goal, the shadow leader added, "Take half of the legion squad with you."

Without even slowing, Ronan responded, "No. They will only get in my way."

Emer knew this would be the outcome, so she simply directed a shadow near her to gather three others and join Ronan. The shadow paled, and his skin slipped at the order. Between a rock and a hard place, he bowed to his leader before pointing to a few of his unlucky brethren and began following the unbalanced Ronan.

"I can't promise they will be returned, Emer," Ronan shouted with a hint of humor as he picked up his pace without even turning around.

Emer estimated that there was a fifty percent chance that the Sword would kill the backup shadows. Alternatively, she calculated a fifty percent probability that Ronan would kill them. Either way, the objective of removing the SALT from the battlefield rose by fourteen percent if she sent the shadows. She deemed that acceptable.

Now that her wild card was dealt with, she turned her attention back to the battle at hand. With a hand gesture, she ordered the assault to begin. A wave of arrows was released from her gúl archers. Using bulturs to charge the arrows with dark energy allowed the small-statured horde beasts to send their projectiles much further than they usually would be capable of. Most were directed at the fort's entrance, but there were a few squads that she had commanded to aim higher at the far side of the fort. While she didn't imagine they would hit the SALT, it was enough to distract him and allow Ronan a slight advantage.

She smiled as the first of her ground forces moved forward across the field. All variables were accounted for, and the odds were in her favor. Nothing would stop her from the glory that awaited her after this battle.

****

Shay used his skills to get him and Kurian through the no-man's land and arrive at the forest line without being detected. They had exited the fort at the front and worked around the wall to eventually cross the open area near the back of the fort. It almost mimicked their previous journey to close the caves together. Shay crossed in stealth and waited to see any signs of being spotted before calling his junior to him.

After they arrived, the two wordlessly made their way through the forest as they circled further away from the fort to attack their enemy from the rear. However, about half a mil into their journey, a bullan suddenly appeared in front of Shay from behind a tree. Shay's choices were to use his ranged gift and announce their presence or risk the beast alerting those around them.

Choosing the possibility of being found instead of the guarantee of it, Shay drew his daggers and started sprinting at the creature. Less than two steps into his path, a streak of spinning silver flashed by him and passed through the throat of the bullan, sticking into the tree directly behind it. The result was the bullan's body falling to the ground with its head following a heartbeat later with Kurian's shield stuck into the tree.

Impressed, Shay turned to his sergeant and asked, "Are you sure you aren't a SALT?"

Without missing a beat, Kurian retrieved his shield and responded with a snort, "And give up blowing things up? Unlikely."

Picking back up the pace, they quickly made their way to the rear of the invading force. As expected, there was no rearguard, and the enemy was focused solely on the fort. Shay understood that it was only a matter of time before the enemy realized that their forces were being assaulted from multiple sides and sent troops out to engage them. With that in mind, he ordered Kurian to begin setting some explosives and traps on the outer edge of the enemy. Shay would start picking off groups and stragglers in the meantime.

Leaving Kurian to start doing what he did best, Shay left to do the same. Blending into the environment and using his scouting skills, he quickly identified a squad of gúls and a bultur on the edge of the battlefield. Using the trees, the SALT moved like a phantom and approached the group.

Climbing a tree close to the group, Shay positioned himself above the enemy. Prioritizing his targets, Shay leaped out and onto the bultur, pushing one of his daggers into the bird-like creature's brain. Before his feet hit the ground, Shay had slashed the throat of the gúl that the bultur was engaging with. When he did land and withdrew his dagger from the head of the dead monster, he turned and immediately threw both daggers at two other gúls who had turned at the sudden sound of bodies hitting the ground. Both died almost instantly as the daggers pierced black hearts. Without even gathering his weapons, Shay engaged the final three gúls with his fists and feet. Crushing the head of one with a kick and another with an elbow. The final creature turned to run, but Shay quickly overtook it and snapped its neck with his bare hands.

Shay retrieved his daggers and started sprinting to his next group of targets. The entire fight had taken no more than four heartbeats. If he was going to make a difference in the battle at the fort, he knew he had to pick up the pace.

****

Ronan had to admit that he liked Emer as a leader. She was smart and talented. He knew from previous battles that she wasn't too bad at close combat either. With all that in mind, he thought about how sweet it would be when he eventually broke her. Any that he deemed strong were simply stepping stones on his journey. He would break and destroy all opponents until he showed the Creator he was the best. None could stand before him in battle; it was the Creator's fault for making him too good.

The three remaining shadows were dead silent as they followed him to the rear of the horde lines. They had initially dogged him with questions of where they were going and why they were retreating from the front lines.

One had even been brave enough to question Ronan's confidence in the battle and thought out loud about Ronan's legendary fighting prowess. He had left that one behind without arms, legs, eyes, ears, or a tongue. The process wasn't short, so he had to make up time by pushing himself faster to try and catch his prey.

Emer may be brilliant, but she didn't understand how a SALT operated. Only another SALT could comprehend their capabilities and tactics. His brother would be out on the edges, hunting and attempting to silently cripple the attacking force. When he was done, Ronan doubted that Emer's force would be capable of taking a grain of sand from the Swords. Unless, of course, Ronan could entertain the SALT long enough. He almost shivered in pleasure at the thought of taking down one of his brethren. It was finally time to prove who was the best of the best.

Sprinting just ahead of the shadows that raced to catch him, Ronan finally slowed at the sight of two slaughtered horde squads. While putrid and brutal, the scene brought a big smile to his face. His brother had not disappointed him. Now was the time to begin hunting the hunter.

Without letting his shadows take a break, Ronan broke into a sprint again. His steps landed without a sound, and the fog did little to hinder his sight. The mist seemed to enhance his abilities. It dampened his sound, and he almost felt lighter within it, as though it was pushing him to find his prey.

Soon enough, he sensed movement ahead and saw a Sword kneeling between two boulders. Getting excited, the fallen SALT circled his prey and watched for the tall tale alertness that a SALT would experience when being watched. After observing the Sword work for a few heartbeats and ensuring the following shadows stayed put, Ronan became disappointed. It wasn't a SALT. The Sword was only an engineer.

In frustration, Ronan revealed himself and walked up to

the engineer from behind.

"I am almost done, LT," the smaller Sword spoke to the quiet footsteps that approached.

"Unfortunately, I do believe you are done now," Ronan responded.

Without looking, the engineer rolled to the left and brought his shield up just in time to meet the downswing of Ronan's blade.

"Impressive, little brother," Ronan commented to the Sword. The shadow moved like lightning and used his sword's tip to pull the shield up, exposing the midsection of the engineer. Delivering a spinning kick and knocking the wind out of the smaller Sword, Ronan continued, "But not impressive enough."

Surprising the SALT again, the engineer regained his composure quickly and attacked. The bladed shield of the Sword swiped at Ronan with speed and accuracy. Eventually, one of the swings even nicked him, and a small amount of angry red energy trickled out from his shoulder.

"YES! That is so good, little brother," Ronan shouted in joy as he watched his life trickle from the wound.

"I am not your *brother*, traitor," the smaller Sword spat back.

"Of course you are! We are family, right? Were we not created by the same Maker? Do we not look the same and fight the same? Well, maybe not fight exactly the same. It is obvious that I will crush you."

"You are nothing like me, and I will prove it," the Sword said and immediately slid on his knees, spinning his shield to attack Ronan's legs.

The fallen SALT jumped and simply squatted on the outstretched shield. He tapped the engineer's head with the blunt of his blade and mockingly said, "That isn't how you treat your superiors, brother."

With a flick of his shield to attempt to disrupt Ronan's balance, the Sword gave another spin and slash.

Nonchalantly, Ronan used the momentum to flip backward and out of the reach of the shield.

“This is fun, little brother, but I need to find your better. Me and him have business, so you understand why I need to make this quick,” Ronan mockingly commented.

“I am not done yet, traitor,” the engineer shouted as he made an impressive toss of his shield at Ronan. He immediately dodged it and watched as it soared away. Confusion plastered his face as the Sword had just relinquished his weapon during such a mismatched fight. When he turned back to the Sword, he was doubly surprised at how fast the engineer had moved to close the distance and started engaging in hand-to-hand with Ronan. The element of surprise helped the Sword land a vicious uppercut. However, it wasn’t enough, as Ronan quickly brushed it off and turned the tables to place his adversary in a chokehold. Within a few heartbeats, he tossed down an unconscious Sword.

The shadows emerged from the surrounding area and encircled their leader after the fight. One eager shadow moved in with duel hammers to attempt to finish the defeated Sword, their sworn enemy. Before the shadow could complete the swing, Ronan completed a spinning kick to his head, knocking him to the ground next to the Sword.

“I have plans for this one. Pick him up, get ready, and stay out of sight,” Ronan commented to the remaining two shadows as he wiped the red energy from his lip and licked it. He turned away from them, stared into the woods, and finally added with a grin, “My prize is coming.”

27

JOHN was having the time of his life. The silent and stoic Sword smiled with glee as large beasts charged him, bent on his destruction and getting to the objective he was sworn to protect. The narrow passageway that he guarded, along with his commander, was too small to allow even two bullans to pass shoulder to shoulder. While some of the smaller horde beasts could come through the passage in groups, the enemy's vanguard had thought to smash them with numbers and brute strength. Both had no true benefit in the narrow entrance of the newly formed entrance to the fort.

By switching and allowing each other to take breaks, neither John nor the commander had taken any serious injuries. A few hits here and there had broken through, but nothing serious that would prevent either one of them from needing to be pulled off the frontline. Due to John's size, he was able to hold the enemy at a chokepoint with barely any movement. His axe swiping faster than the monsters could react to, John made a new wall of the attacker's bodies and limbs. While it was temporary, the added defensive barriers made of decaying monsters allowed them to control the flow of the battle even more.

The constant rain of arrows was a nuisance, but being in the narrow passageway with walls on either side allowed for very few arrows to reach them. When some got close, John adopted a 'horde shield' method in which he grabbed the closest monster, dead or alive, and held it above his head. It was a bit satisfying to use the enemy's weapons against themselves.

"Switch," the commander called as John finished dispatching two ciarógs. They had charged him on their spindly legs in a single line with bladed arms swinging. He assumed they hoped he couldn't react to four blades swinging widely at him. They were sorely mistaken as he simply decapitated both with his axe while shattering their weaker blades along the way.

Stepping back and letting the commander come in to fill his space, John sat and watched his leader go to work. While not as broad or big as he was, Titus moved with power and strength that was indicative of a Sword twice his size. John knew his leader was strong but had never seen the commander toss a full-size bullan like it was a toy. The poor beast saw the switch and believed the smaller Sword may have been an easier target. With its horns leveled at the commander, it charged. Using the creature's momentum against it, Titus turned to the side and lowered his shoulder while bending his knees. He launched the monster into the fort itself as soon as its stomach came in contact with his shoulders, but he quickly circled his blade up to nearly slice the beast in half just as its body was sent flying. Watching a bullan that was easily twice the size of his leader go flying and raining down acidic blood across the path to the main hall was beautiful.

Suddenly, John realized he had not seen a shower of arrows in a few heartbeats. He grinned as he believed the cause was the LT and Kurian doing work out in the enemy's midst. The large Sword was about to attempt a peak outside the walls when a javelin materialized from out of nowhere to plant itself into Titus's shoulder.

John silently jumped to defend his leader as a ciaróg and a bullan moved in on the downed Sword. Making short work of the attackers, John turned to step in front of any other beasts that hoped to press the advantage.

Using a specific whistle sound, John signaled to Wit that

they needed him now.

Instantly, Wit responded in their link, "Underst.... On m... ver."

John was glad to hear that Wit had heard him since the fog seemed to dampen not only their communications link but also direct noise. Clear communication in battle was essential, especially for a silent brother.

With no beasts in his vicinity, John did a quick turn to check on Titus and remove the projectile from his shoulder. Unfortunately, after checking it, the barbed head had passed through to the other side. Additionally, while trying to inspect the wound, John noticed that the weapon was emitting a dark and sinister aura.

Reacting fast, John spun back to the front just in time to intercept another javelin with his axe that came flying out of the mist. A voice spoke out from the mist, "Is your friend hurt? We can help you if you want."

John grunted and held his position.

"Cat got your tongue?" the voice asked in a slick-like-oil voice, followed by a shadow suddenly appearing while holding another javelin.

John had to smile back at the cocky shadow since a one-on-one battle would favor him in the narrow passageway. His smile diminished just a bit when three other shadows materialized. One holding two hand axes, another with a pole-axe, and the final with a thin sword. The thought of using his armor or ranged gifts crossed his mind, but as far as he knew, he was the only obstacle holding back an entire army from entering the fort. Using his armor would have to be a last hope option.

"John! I am here," Wit announced as he appeared near Titus, who was lying on the ground. Wit immediately lit up as he saw the four shadows standing there and shouted, "Oh yeah! This is what I am talking about! Macey and I are ready to rumble."

John whistled to clearly indicate Wit needed to get Titus

to the bridge. While grabbing their leader and retreating, Wit pouted and yelled, "You better leave some for me and Macey."

John responded by holding up a single finger.

"You should have let your brother stay, big guy. You may have had a chance with two of you," said the lead shadow.

John chuckled and confidently pointed at each of the four shadows and then to himself before waving his hand like it wasn't a big deal. Finally, he raised his hand in front of himself and waved them forward in a defiant challenge.

With a growl, the javelin-wielding charged John. Blocking the extended weapon with the haft of his axe and trapping the barbed head using the curve of the axe head, the Sword disarmed the attacking shadow and increased the inertia of the traitor by pulling him forward using his own weapon. John extended his fist and clotheslined the approaching enemy directly into his throat, crushing it and knocking him to the ground unconscious. The three standing shadows glanced at each other and steeled themselves as John smiled and again challenged them to come forward.

Not wanting to take John up on his one-on-one offer, the duel axe wielder and swordsman moved in close to press their weapon's advantages while the pole-axe female stayed back to strike at a distance. John began his dance as he spun and lunged out of the deadly strikes coming in from all sides. Much like Titus's strength was underestimated, John's brothers knew that many would be amazed at the Big's flexibility and speed. His body was a blur as he ducked and struck at the swordsman's leg, but the enemy quickly raised his foot out of range. However, John had anticipated such a move and released his axe handle from his high grip for a split second in mid-swing, extending to strike the backfoot. The swordsman went down in a wail as his left ankle and foot remained standing where they had recently been attached to the shadow's leg.

With two downed, John danced out of range of the swordsman thrashing on the ground and turned his attention to the axe wielder. Before he could move to engage, the pole-axe came flying in at neck level. Quickly raising his axe to block, the smaller shadow moved in to put one of his axes into John's ribs. Completing an extremely acrobatic maneuver, John both jumped and ducked simultaneously in midair. The hand axe flew under his parallel-to-the-floor body while the released pole-axe continued its original swing just above his head. While he escaped the worst of the attack, the duel-wielding axe shadow used his second axe to clip John's right arm. After contact was reset and both sides appraised each other, John switched his axe from his right to his left as energy leaked out from a grievous gash that opened his forearm.

To the surprise of his enemy, John began to silently laugh. The two standing shadows looked at each other for clarification, but John quickly provided it by pointing to his right hand and shaking his head, signaling that he wasn't right-handed.

Quickly, he threw the collected liquid energy that had pooled into his right palm from his wound into the eyes of the duel wielder, temporarily blinding him. Using that distraction, he bypassed the blinded close threat and closed in on the pole-axe wielder. John split the shadow in half with a quick and vicious downward strike. Immediately, the wound was so catastrophic that the shadow instantly became black dust that collapsed to the ground.

Dodging the follow-up attack by the axe wielder and creating separation, John held up his hand to his ear and smiled at the remaining attacker.

Wit came running out of the fog yelling, "Here comes MACEY!"

After a quick flurry of attacks, the axe wielder realized how much trouble he was in and began retreating.

Unfortunately, the other two shadows, who had not been ended, seemed to have crawled away in the fight.

When Wit and John were alone, the bigger Sword turned to his brother, gave him a quizzical look, and pointed to the smaller brother's weapon.

"What? Does that war cry not instill fear in our enemies? We thought it was a pretty good catchphrase."

John just shook his head.

****

Shay had lost contact with Kurian, but that wasn't surprising in this fog. He had wiped several squads already and started noticing troops being more alert and bullans searching the woods. The bait was out, and he needed to ensure Kurian was ready with the hook. Retracing his steps and circling the area, he came to a small clearing with two stone boulders. Instantly, his instincts screamed that something was wrong. As he looked closer, he witnessed a shadow sitting on the smaller rock with his back to Shay.

Cautiously, Shay summoned his ranged gift and took a bead on the shadow with black hair and a near-perfect skin. As he placed his finger on the trigger, the shadow spoke clearly and loudly without turning around, "I wouldn't do that. Unless you don't want your brother returned. Personally, I would take the shot, but I am no longer beholden to certain expectations. I am free."

The SALT froze, not just at the chilling words that this shadow spoke about Kurian but also at the sound of the voice. He knew that it immediately.

"Ronan," was Shay's only response.

At the sound of his name, Ronan turned around and stared at Shay with a genuine smile before returning the greeting with more enthusiasm, "Shay!"

Jumping down from the rock, the shadow gleefully

started, "Brother! It has been so long! I didn't want to hope it was you when they said a SALT was here, but here you are," the shadow said as he moved towards the Sword in a friendly manner, almost as if to hug him.

Shay drew his daggers in a flash and blocked the sword that oozed desecration, which had appeared out of nowhere. A quick exchange of blades, and suddenly, the dark sword dropped to the side of the insane traitor as he continued, "Oh, how I have missed you. It was always such a challenge to spar you." He winked with a knowing smile at Shay as they both knew that Ronan had won nearly every one of their sparring matches.

As quick as a viper, Ronan slashed again. Perfected metal striking out against each other rang out in the small forest opening as they fought with frightening speed and skill.

After disengaging once again, Shay asked, "Where is Kurian?"

"Your engineer? Was that his name? You know me, Shay, I never bother to learn anyone's name outside the brotherhood."

They came together quickly and renewed their deadly dance. Both were unable to get a clear strike on the other. Shay's daggers were striking quickly and blocking Ronan's wicked-looking blade. If anyone were to witness the battle from the outside, it would seem as though Ronan wasn't taking the fight as seriously as the Sword. Shay knew that wasn't the case, as his former brother was a master at hiding his strengths and weaknesses. While not evident, Shay was giving just as much as he was receiving.

"I have had enough, Ronan. Tell me where my brother is, or I end this now."

Both of them understood what Shay meant, as he was the only one of the two who still had access to the Creator's gifts. Summoning his armor or ranged gift would be the ultimate trump card in ending their fight.

"Now, now, brother. No need to get all excited. He is close

at hand and yours to take back to your doomed little mission..... if you beat me in an *honest* fight."

At that, two shadows appeared, holding Kurian between them. Tossing the engineer to the ground, they both drew their weapons and held them menacingly above the unconscious Sword.

Shay instantly knew there were more shadows around. He would need to find them to fully map out his rescue plan.

"You are considering locating my hidden shadows, aren't you?"

Shay controlled his facial expression so as not to give away his surprise and disgust. It pained him that one of the best had become the creature he now fought. They were once brothers, but even though this thing in front of him had all the same training and skills as him, they were now wholly different beings.

Ronan smiled and continued, "Do you see all the angles? Are you watching for the opening? Thinking outside of the box? Do you prioritize the mission and run to fight another day, or do you try and save your brother?"

"What about you, Ronan? What do you fight for now?"

With a laugh, the shadow responded, "I fight for ME! It is wonderful, Shay. No one to tell me who I can't kill or what I have to do. I am free!"

Shay chuckled as he responded, "No, you are not free. The prison may look perfect, and you have decorated it to have all the comforts and joys you could ever desire, but I don't believe you have fallen so far to confuse freedom with slavery."

"Me? A slave? Ha ha ha, no. I have no master, unlike you."

"That is where you are wrong. Your master is your ego. Your pride. My brothers and I gladly give our loyalty and love to one who is greater. We are free in His wisdom, whereas you have jumped into your cage that will eventually drown you in a sea of darkness."

The SALT knew he had hit a nerve when the jovial and sadistic shadow charged Shay with no emotion displayed. The attack was so fast that his sword appeared to be teleported from one position to another. Shay fended off each strike as best he could, but several made it through to cut Shay's skin. Not to be outdone, Shay countered and scored some of his own hits. Between the anger that emanated from Ronan and the hits Shay had won, the shadow's skin began slipping. The smaller, dark, ghoulish body flashed through the perfect skin Ronan liked to display.

Through the fight, Shay would throw a glance towards Kurian. The shadows guarding him were so engrossed in the ultimate grudge match between two of the best fighters the Creator has ever made that they failed to realize that their hostage was regaining consciousness. Wisely, Kurian didn't make any sudden movements; he only opened his eyes to stare at his senior and blinked to make him aware that he was ready to make a move.

Shay allowed a small cut on his chest from Ronan to repay the shadow with a similar cut on his cheek. Both disengaged and reset across the clearing from each other, with Ronan on the side of the shadows and Kurian.

"You are right, Ronan. We are the same in combat, and you may even be better than me," Shay started. Seeing a grin and Ronan regaining control of his skin, Shay added, "But we are ultimately different in all ways that count."

"How? Because you follow a controlling and demanding King," the shadow questioned back.

"He is much more than that, but there are many other ways. For example, my brothers and I care for and prioritize each other over ourselves."

"That is exactly why I will beat you here, Shay."

"Perhaps, but there is only one way to find out."

They charged each other, and a few steps before contact was made, Shay surprised Ronan by throwing one of his daggers in an extremely high arch that he easily dodged. Unfathomable by Ronan, the former SALT was not his actual target, as the weapon flew into the tree above Kurian. The piercing scream of a shadow being hit and the thud of the body hitting the ground was immediately followed by one loud *boom* from Shay's ranged gift. Both shadows standing over Kurian were lifted off the ground as the round of white energy passed through them and threw them a few hands away. Kurian was immediately up and had his own ranged gift in hand.

However, because of the fact that he had used his dagger and ranged gift to save Kurian, Ronan had easily closed the distance and took the opening to chop down on Shay's head. The only reason it was not an instant kill was because Shay used his ranged gift to slightly deflect the blow. It wasn't enough, though, as the legion blade cut deep into the warrior's chest from the shoulder.

Kurian shouted and drew his ranged weapon, but Shay only heard Ronan's whispered voice say, "Your dirty tricks won't save you anymore. Say it. Say that I am the best. Say I win, *brother*."

****

Titus was kneeling next to the bridge, regaining his strength, and was unaware of the pure white bird that flew in through the chimney. His eyes were closed as it dove through the small opening in the fire pit to land gracefully on the tomb's stone near the red flame. The white bird moved to the edge of the diamond-decorated bowl that held the dead fire. At the nearness of the bird, the flame did something it had not done since its creation: it moved. Barely noticeable, but the flame seemed to reach out to the beautiful bird in a determined Choice. In response, the dove transformed into a brilliant blue flame and moved to join the red. Together, they became a beautiful violet color that filled the room with heat, exploded light, and shot out into the dark night. Those looking on from a distance saw a visage of a flaming bird clawing its way to the sky before exploding in a magnificent show of flame and light, leaving behind a towering beacon of violet flame that radiated energy and strength.

****

As Ronan pulled his sword out from the lieutenant's upper chest and moved to deliver the killing strike, an explosion of light emanated from the fort. A violet-colored pillar of flame expanded into the sky, which was so bright that all present had to cover their eyes or risk being blinded.

Instantly, Shay felt strong as he basked in the waves of light and warmth flowing out from the Choice beacon. His wounds healed, and his armor was activated without his calling. The light had changed, and it felt like home—it felt like their King.

Just as suddenly as it had arrived, the pillar was gone. Shay and Kurian were in their armor and fully energized, but neither the shadows nor Ronan were anywhere to be seen. Apparently, seeing the healing Swords and realizing that they were now outmatched, they had used the distraction to retreat.

Looking out over the battlefield, Shay immediately noticed something else had also retreated. He breathed a sigh of relief to see that the fog that had plagued them for cycles was gone. Additionally, through the morning air, Shay clearly saw that the fort still stood, as was evident by the light show of ranged weapons now decimating a retreating army.

28

HOW could this have happened? The calculations showed this outcome at only six percent! Emer had done everything possible to boost her success rate, but it wasn't enough. It didn't make any sense!

The attack on the fort had proceeded just as she had planned, and word from her attacking shadows was that they were able to incapacitate the leader of the defenders. While the remaining Sword sounded like a brute, he would have fallen with time.

Additionally, the other half of the shadow squad had said that Ronan had single-handedly dismantled a duo of flanking Swords. They had done some damage to her Gúl archers but nothing that would have changed the calculations in their favor.

However, her most significant advantage was the fog that seemed to be concentrated around the fort. It limited her enemy's ranged capability and forced them to change their strategy. That one variable alone exponentially multiplied her chances at success by a factor of ten.

Adding everything up, Emer had to admit that this fight had some of the most favorable conditions for victory she had ever seen. But here she was - running towards her doom. She didn't doubt what awaited her when she returned to the army that was just ahead. Neart would punish her - extensively. A shudder ran through her body as she slowed her approach.

Where had that light come from? That single change in the battlefield had completely upended all her calculations to rip victory from her grasp. With no visible cover for her approaching forces, they had been mowed down like grass before a scythe. When she had attempted to retreat and regroup, the forest had come alive with explosions of light and gore. They ran directly into the Sword's traps that somehow had appeared behind them. It was practically incalculable! The force returning to the main army was down to a trifle fifteen percent of the original amount. Again, the odds screamed that she was running to her doom.

How could she explain the situation so it wasn't her failure? Could she blame Ronan? She looked over at the former SALT as he was laughing and riding the shoulders of a bullan, kicking the creature to go faster as he held his sword's handle like a saddle horn. Unlike a typical horn, the sword was buried in the creature's shoulder and had exited through its armpit.

No. Blaming Ronan would only lead to a more creative and painful death at his inventive hands. While Emer didn't like playing politics as she deemed such games boring compared to the mysteries of the universe, she understood it enough to know she needed help. That new shadow, Sham, seemed to understand such things and had even selected her to lead the Vanguard. Odds were that he was likely to be punished alongside her. Perhaps he would have a way for them both to escape the wrath of their sadistic leader. As she pulled her hood up and ducked into the bushes surrounding the approaching force, her calculations said she had no choice.

****

Wit was still a little upset at John that he had only left a single shadow. Plus, he didn't even get to fight the last one, as it had promptly retreated when he and Macey showed up. No matter what John said, or technically not said, Wit knew that the legion had now heard of him and his bestie, Macey, which is why they had all immediately retreated. Wit was consoled by the fact that the beautiful light that had suddenly appeared above the crypt had made him supercharged when fighting a few horde beasts that had come to cover the retreat of the shadows.

Once the horde creatures that had charged were no longer living, Wit and John turned their attention to the mass of enemies now clearly visible due to the blasted fog being burned away. Jumping up to their positions on the wall, they called up their ranged gifts and started deleting everything that wasn't them. Not long after they had begun their mass extinction event, the Commander joined them and began handing out passes to skip the line of life. Wit chuckled to himself as he thought that was a good one, and he would have to remember all of these sweet one-liners to tell the team later. John probably would do his usual groan of approval, but he bet Marcus would laugh when he woke back up..... Probably.

The feeling of loss was a small echo in Wit's heart as he thought about Killian and Marcus. They were good brothers, and he missed their company. Simultaneously, he was also a little annoyed that he had to remember everything awesome that he was saying and doing to tell them later. When they wake up, he would definitely have to give them a good talking to. He would be all like, "*Now, Marcus and Killian, you are not allowed to go blue again, you hear me? No more hero stuff. I am in charge around here now because of my awesomeness during all the missions you missed out on, so you will have to do what I tell you, okay?*"

They would probably say something like, "*Oh wow! You are so cool, Wit! It is obvious how you got promoted so quickly. Tell us again how you defeated the legion single-handedly.*"

"Wit! Pay attention," the Commander yelled, bringing

Wit back to the debriefing they were attending near the main hall's entrance.

"I am tracking with you, boss," Wit responded immediately. In fact, he truly was. He had the ability to listen to what was happening around him and catalog it for later review as a communications expert, even while scheming or daydreaming about other things.

"Like I was saying, thanks to Kurian's designs, we were easily able to hold the front gate against the attack and inflict heavy casualties. Between Alpha's position here and Bravo's campaign outside the fort, Shay estimates we inflicted an eighty-five percent casualty rate on the attacking force that originally numbered a thousand, based on the tracks of those that got away."

Wit couldn't help but whistle in appreciation. That was quite the achievement for a Sword unit of five.

Titus continued, "The fort held, but I understand it was a close call for Bravo." The Commander turned to the LT and said, "Give your report, lieutenant."

Shay stood and gave his report, outlining their initial success in setting up traps as well as stealthfully removing several squads of Gúl enforced by bulturs. Things got interesting when Shay spoke about his encounter with the shadow named Ronan. Wit had heard of the former SALT as he was fairly well known among the Clans. He was said to have been the best at single combat and one of the best, if not the best, ranged marksmen. Back when he was a Sword, it was also said that he pushed training with other Swords to an extreme and quickly got a reputation for winning at all costs.

Wit was glad to hear that his brothers had come out on top after the crypt made the right Choice and had that sweet light burst from it. Hearing that Shay was close to going blue was a slap of reality to Wit. He had always assumed that both officers were practically invincible. Remembering the awe-inspiring fights between Shay and

Titus during training made the thought of them taking shadow weapons to their respective shoulders hard to fathom.

The good news was that both had made it through by the grace and mercy of their Maker. Nothing short of their Creator would explain the feeling and the light that had turned the tide of the fight. Later, they discovered that the small flame above the tomb had turned to the same color of violet that had exploded into the sky. Additionally, the flame was now *alive*. There was no other way to explain it as it now moved like a fire should while providing warmth and energy directly to the Swords. Much like the bridge, the flame appeared directly connected to the Maker. It was still confusing to Wit, so not for the first time in the last few heartbeats, Wit missed Marcus. The knowledge-seeker would be all over this and would likely have had the puzzle solved before the end of lunch.

Titus did that thing again that made Wit believe he was partially psychic when he said, "I know you all want answers and wished Marcus was still with us." Their leader stopped and looked at each of them before continuing, "We don't have him, and I don't have any more answers."

Unable to stop himself, Wit burst into laughter and said, "Good pep talk, sir."

Titus gave him a warning glance that would have stopped a charging army before adding, "The one thing I do know is where that beacon came from." Everyone gathered knew exactly what he was talking about. The feeling emanating from the violet flame tower could only originate from one source: their Creator.

"Our King fights with us and through us. He never fails, so no matter what comes, the cost, or the fight - we are His Sword, and we will not fail Him."

In unison, the team shouted back, "Hura!"

"We have won a battle today, but the enemy amasses and

marches on us. We don't retreat. We don't surrender. We give no mercy. We offer no quarter. We are warriors. We are death to our King's enemies. We were Chosen to be here by the Creator of all, in this moment - in these battles. Who here is ready to show them why?"

"Hura!" came the reply from the team as they stood and raised their weapons.

Titus nodded and dismissed his team to begin preparations.

As Wit stood to leave, their leader grabbed his shoulder. Titus good-naturedly asked him, "How was that for a pep talk?"

"I don't call you boss for nothing, boss," Wit replied with a smile.

"Great. Glad you approve."

After a few heartbeats, the Commander continued to hold Wit's shoulder, so the private asked, "Was there something else, sir?"

"I didn't assign you a task yet."

Feigning shock, Wit asked, "You didn't?"

With a way too happy-looking smile, Titus said, "Nope. I saved something special for you, young private."

Pointing towards the entrance and the stack of still decomposing horde beasts and immediately starting to walk away, Titus said, "You have clean-up duty."

Wit caught a whiff of the bodies and immediately thought that he really needed to start controlling his mouth. Cleaning up was truly unnecessary, but the punishment task was not lost on him.

Looking at the rotting corpses, Wit whispered, "Can I at least get a shovel?"

****

Sham was sure he had seen the glint of eyes in the woods

as the army marched. A phantom foe was definitely tracking the army, but no scouts had reported anything, no matter how accurately he had pointed out the location of the eyes.

Something out here is hunting you. The words of Ronan had come back to haunt him often since the army began its march towards his former outpost. He tried to shake the feeling that he was being watched, but just when he had put it outside his mind, a glint of eyes or slight movement of leaves and branches that went against the wind would remind him. It was infuriating. Actually, if Sham was honest with himself, it was terrifying and made enjoyment in the war camp nearly impossible.

Constantly asking the scouts for updates on their surroundings sounded less and less like a good leader checking the army's status and more like someone paranoid. While paranoia was not uncommon among the legion, it was not good to show it and the weakness it portrayed. Then again, he absolutely just saw something move in that bush!

As Sham was about to call out to the lead scout again, he saw a ripple of sudden movement ahead of him. Stone runners began dispersing orders for a halt. Knowing that the army had not reached their destination for the day, it had to be one thing. The vanguard had returned.

Sham was about to head up and see if he could grab a runner to hear the news when a hand suddenly grabbed his forearm. Already paranoid, Sham drew his sickle into his good hand and turned to strike.

"It's me!"

Sham stopped his sickle from completely removing the offending appendage as he saw a hooded Emer beside him. The sickle bit into her skin slightly, and the darkness in Sham wanted to continue his swing and remove her arm for frightening him, but he held onto pragmatism and slowly lifted his blade.

It was obvious to anyone with eyes that the attack had failed. The desperation that burned in Emer's eyes was entertaining to Sham, but a new fear immediately pushed that thought out. He had sent her and selected her as the commander of the vanguard. Whatever punishment awaited her would fall on his shoulders as well. He cursed to himself, but he also wouldn't let this be the end of him. He could think of a way out.

"Sham, what are we going to do," Emer questioned like a whining puppy.

Unable to control his anger, he bit back with a "Shut up and let me think!"

After a minute of collecting himself, he asked Emer to tell him everything that had happened. She proceeded to give a full, detailed report of the battle and the new flame that burned the fog away. Everything about her report made no sense to Sham, as even the fort structure seemed to have changed. He almost considered that they had attacked the wrong place, but it was obvious from the report of a SALT and the physical location that the Swords had reconstructed his fort.

Thinking quickly, Sham realized that all those changes may be to his benefit. A plan began to form in his mind as a small wave of separation made its way through the marching ranks of legion and horde beast. Apparently, Neart knew exactly where his vanguard's commander would run to and sent a runner to get them both.

Traveling as slow as he dared, Sham trotted with the runner and Emer in silence to the quickly erected command tent. Just as his plan locked into his mind, they entered the tent. Neart stood with his back to them, speaking with another stone messenger. The general spoke in whispers, but Sham picked up the words king, beacon, and all haste. He filed that information away as the runner sprinted out.

The general turned to the new arrivals as soon as the stone exited the tent. With a cruel smile that spoke volumes about the coming punishment he had already settled on, Neart said, “Welcome back, Emer! I am surprised to find you with my newest advisor and not reporting to me directly about the victory that was sure to have been complete.”

The surprise Neart mentioned must have been hidden very well, as nothing about his eyes said he was the least bit surprised to find Emer with Sham.

“My general, I am....” Emer started before Sham interrupted, saying, “It is my fault, great general.”

Neart turned to Sham and said, “Oh? I don’t doubt that part of this catastrophe is your fault, but please enlighten me.”

“As I am sure you are aware of right now, the attack on the newly enforced fort by the vanguard was not what we had anticipated.”

“If you mean we didn’t anticipate an utter failure, then yes - it was not as we expected.”

“Not exactly, your greatness.”

A slight pull of a facial muscle exposed due to a rotted hole on Neart’s un-skinned face was the only evidence of his annoyance.

“While Emer certainly failed at overcoming our hated enemy’s new defenses,” Sham started as Emer shot him a panicked look. He understood it sounded like he was about to throw her to the beasts, but that wouldn’t bode well for him either. If he was to survive, he also needed her to come out of this - which is why he added, “She also discovered a great resource that will ensure the downfall of the same defenses.”

Neart perked up a little but was hesitant. Clearly, he desired to punish the pair, but he seemed to want a quick victory slightly more. Quickly coming to some kind of decision, he asked, “What resource?”

Having set the bait, Sham continued more confidently, “An entire army of kreehauns in the mountains directly next to the fort."

"Interesting. Tell me more."

"Since the Swords have limited numbers and have pulled themselves back into their new defenses like a frightened turtle, we can distract them in the front while the kreehauns dig us an entrance in the back."

Looking past Sham at Emer, Neart asked her, "Is this true? How did you find them?"

"It is true, my lord," Emer answered, wisely ignoring the second question.

Sham quickly filled in the details as he weaved lies about casually mentioning to Emer that there were caves to the northeast of the fort that he had never bothered to explore. Apparently, Emer had sent a few scouts to discover what was within, and they had returned with the news of a giant army of kreehauns simply hiding in the mountain. Very unfortunately, the same scouts were killed in the retreat, so it would be impossible to corroborate the story.

"Is any of this true," Neart questioned the dark corner of the tent directly behind Sham.

An oil-slick voice emanated from the shadows, "How would I know? I was too busy distracting myself with true battle."

Sham didn't want to turn around as he immediately recognized the voice. He would not forget the insane and wicked shadow that had threatened him upon his arrival at the camp.

Ronan emerged from the darkness and elbowed Sham in almost a conspiratory way while winking at Emer. He continued as he walked past both to throw himself on pillows that lay on the skin of some soft beast. "I was too busy playing war games with my brother to have noticed what scouts did or said."

Neart rubbed his head as he now had no way of knowing if what Sham said was true, but also no way to refute it. The fact was that if this were true, it would be a great tactical benefit to him.

"Very well. The three of you will go to the mountains and gather this force while I take the army to attack the front. Understood?"

Emer was the fastest to respond with, "Yes! Absolutely, sir. We will not fail you."

Sham agreed, too, but wasn't as happy as he had just given up the one trump card that would give him an edge while simultaneously signing up to travel with the chaotic lunatic. He tried to console himself that it was a life-or-death matter and that he could find more advantages as long as he still lived.

After both Sham and Emer left the tent, Neart turned to his barely leashed killer and said, "If anything goes wrong, end them both."

With a surprised look, Ronan turned to his leader and said, "Wait. Is there a scenario in which you want them to live?"

"Good point. When we are done, kill them."

With a big and beautiful smile in direct opposition to Neart's large, rotting corpse of a body, Ronan happily responded, "That is why I love working with you, general. You always know how to have fun."

29

IT was 4:47 on a Thursday, and Henry couldn't believe it! The day had finally arrived, literally a week after his 26th birthday. He often mentioned to his friends and family that today was the best birthday gift he could have ever hoped for, and no future birthday would compare. Today, he would marry the most beautiful and loving person he had ever met - Hana.

They had met at a Saturday night church event and immediately hit it off, spending the entire evening talking exclusively to each other. By the night's end, they had set a date to go to church together the next morning. Henry had reflected many times on that Sunday's service. He specifically recalled looking over at her and watching her sing a worship song with eyes closed and hands raised. At that moment, Henry knew that he would love her for the rest of their lives.

While Hana was truly beautiful physically, her love of God had been the most attractive part of her to Henry. From the second they had met, there was an undeniable glow of love that emanated from her. Having struggled the past six years to find purpose in his life, Henry found her to be an ever-flowing cup of God's love in the desert that was his current existence.

It was hard to believe they met less than a year before today, their wedding day. Some family and friends had questioned the speed at which they moved, but Henry never second-guessed his choice to express his love to her only a few short weeks into their relationship. That action quickly led to a proposal a few weeks later, as soon as Henry had saved enough for a ring. He had to chuckle to himself as he thought about his proposal. He had planned an elaborate scavenger hunt to end with him on his knee and ring in hand. It didn't quite go as planned, with the weather not cooperating and complications in finding clues he had hidden. The day nearly ended with both of them hunting for hidden clues that may or may not have been washed away in a rain storm. In truth, all of that didn't matter, as the result was what counted. Sure enough, by the end of the day, he got a 'yes' from the most wonderful person he had ever met. Hana may have been hesitant to express her love at the beginning of their relationship due to past experiences, but there was no hesitation in her answer to Henry's proposal.

All that said, their relationship was not always easy, as they both brought their own issues as well as their strengths into it. Henry's future bride had not always been a believer and had pursued and been pushed into various poor choices. Stemming from an early childhood when her mother left the family, Hana believed she was unlovable and unworthy of love. She would accept relationships that were both unhealthy and harmful, which also pushed her boundaries beyond what she knew deep inside were unacceptable. Being immigrants from Korea, her family seemed too busy or didn't know how to handle such situations.

Deciding that there was no future in the small Ohio town she was eventually raised in, Hana traveled across the country to California. Unfortunately, she couldn't escape her pattern of poor choices with men and immediately got involved in another abusive relationship that would eventually leave her broken and practically homeless. Seeing no other option, she eventually began working as an exotic dancer at a club, where she felt as though she had fallen into a pit of darkness in which there was no escape.

Hana chose to look towards God in that darkness, believing that only a miracle could save her.

With newfound strength in her faith, Hana hatched her plan to get out of her current circumstances and pattern of decision-making. With every spiritual step she made toward God, she moved physically as far away as possible from the things that clawed her back into the cycle she fought to break free from. Her retreat landed her in Oregon, where she decided to pursue a career in helping others and entered a school for counseling. After graduating with honors, Hana continued living in Oregon, using what she learned to heal herself and those who sought her help.

Even though she had begun the process of healing, certain triggers connected to her past would cause arguments and frustration in both Henry and Hana. However, as quickly as they rose, they worked together to overcome them and draw closer to each other. Henry learned to be patient and loving instead of his default of stubbornness, and Hana began working on being vulnerable with him.

On the other side of the equation, Henry attempted to get his life back on track after becoming a Christian and even considered joining the military to follow in the footsteps of his father and the man who had saved him, Captain McCarthy. Unfortunately, a diagnosis of an undiscovered heart condition had put an end to that career path. While his relationship with his family and newfound faith grew in leaps and bounds, he felt he was professionally and academically years behind everyone else. Afraid he would end up working at a gas station for the rest of his life, he took the first entry-level job he could find at a bank.

Working as a foreclosure agent, Henry was responsible for evaluating homes and their loans to see if it was worth the bank's efforts to continue seeking payment or make moves to foreclose. During his time in the position, he often needed to evict individuals and families from their houses. Being there for less than a month was enough to have depression seize his whole identity. He became angry. Not just at this work but at the world and even with God at times. Violence became his escape as he dove into the world of martial arts and shooting ranges. Unlike those who attended classes looking for ways to defend themselves, Henry often was the first to attack.

Suddenly waking up one day and realizing that he couldn't keep living like this, he quit his job with no backup plan. The feeling of freedom from that decision almost immediately evaporated as he realized the gap he had been so afraid of before had grown. He now had no money and no prospects.

Since his conversion, Henry had become good friends with Caleb and decided to confess his hopelessness. His friend immediately perked up and told him about a training program his company did for those who wanted to learn computer coding. Taking his friend up on the offer to sponsor him, Henry entered the program and immediately took a liking to the work. Not only did he like it, but after graduating from the program, the company offered him a lucrative position due to his obvious skill in the field.

"Hey, dude! People are starting to get to their seats. Almost show time," Caleb said with a wink as he poked his head into the dressing room where Henry was getting ready. Henry's groomsman came in and closed the door behind him.

As Caleb sat next to Henry, he pointed to a window and asked, "You sure you want to do this? We can jump out that window and be out of here in seconds."

Henry heard the humor in the comment and replied, "Only if I can take Hana with me."

"Well, then you would have to get married another day, and it would just be a hassle," Caleb sarcastically sighed before adding, "Might as well marry the woman of your dreams and ride off into the sunset to live a happy life as soon as possible."

"Exactly. Glad you get it."

Caleb switched topics and asked, "Did you see Eddy out there? I think he is trying to hit on your sister again."

Henry chuckled before adding, "I wish him good luck and God's speed. Jules just got her black belt and is excited to show off her skills."

With Henry's brother, Jace, the best man, Eddy was the final groomsman in the wedding party of three. Caleb, Henry, and Eddy had all become good friends, eventually. Henry's conversion meant he started attending youth groups and bible studies instead of hanging out with his dope-smoking best friend. It seemed as though Eddy missed his buddy, even if he would never admit it, and began coming to church with Henry. The three young men sat together during services, and Eddy eventually accepted God and, more reluctantly, Caleb into his life. While he had given up many of his vices, women would be his downfall as he shamelessly flirted with single women every chance he got.

Almost on cue, a powerful thump was heard from the main hall. Soon after, Henry's dad, Carl, entered the dressing room and pointed at the groomsmen, asking, "Caleb, can you please clean up your foolish friend off the ground? He attempted to kiss Jule's hand, and apparently, she reacted by throwing him over her shoulder."

Caleb stood and asked, "In her dress?"

With unmatched self-control, Carl didn't even smile as he replied in a serious voice, "Was she supposed to change first?"

"No, sir. That isn't what I meant. I... will go get him," Caleb stuttered before going out the door.

When Caleb left, Henry said, "You know you intimidate him, right?"

Carl chuckled and said, "The kid needs a bit more of a spine if he wants to eventually be a missionary like he claims."

Henry nervously pulled out his tie and tried to make a bigger knot like he had seen on YouTube about 5 minutes earlier. Seeing him struggle, his dad came up from behind and helped him out before asking, "You ready for this, son? Your life will never be the same after today."

Looking into the mirror at his father behind him, he replied with conviction, "I have never been more ready for anything in my life."

"Good," Carl responded as he finished with the tie and ended with, "You look ready. I am proud of you, son. Hana is an amazing woman who will be an incredible partner and spiritual backup for the rest of your life like your mother was to me."

Henry turned around and hugged his dad before saying, "Thanks for putting up with me and helping point me down the right path, Dad. I wouldn't be here without your or mom's help."

They both got quiet, as it was still painful to think about his mother's passing, but Carl eventually broke the silence by saying, "She would be proud of you and would have loved Hana."

"I know."

The room grew silent as they processed both their sadness and joy. Henry's mom had fought cancer his whole life, with good years and bad. It had eventually returned, with treatment no longer having the same effect when Henry had turned twenty-four and finally started to get his life on track. She had fought hard again but had passed peacefully a few months after the re-diagnosis.

On her deathbed, Arlene had said that it was her greatest joy to see each of her children growing their faith, and she jokingly swore to slap them silly if they didn't meet her in heaven. It was heartbreaking to see her pass, but there was a peace that came over each of them afterward that made it feel like she was still there and telling them to live their life. He swore he could still hear her sing hymns sometimes, and he did not doubt that she would approve of Hana.

Almost as if his father read his thoughts, Carl quickly hugged his son one more time and said, "We are almost ready for you out there, but before you leave - your future bride tasked me with bringing you this." From within his suit, he pulled out an envelope with a single word beautifully handwritten on it: Henry

"I think she wants you to read it before you walk down the aisle. Take your time, and know I will always be next to you." Since his father would officiate their wedding, he literally would be next to him during the ceremony, but Henry appreciated the sentiment.

Once his father left, Henry sat down to look at the letter. Lovingly, he opened it carefully so as not to tear the envelope. He knew immediately that he would want to keep every piece of this letter for years.

Unfolding the single piece of paper, Henry began to read:

Dear future husband,

I love you wholeheartedly and am thrilled to spend our entire life together.

I am praying for you. You will never be alone.....

30

SHAY breathed hard from the exertion of the limit-pushing battle that he had been embroiled in for what felt like an eternity. His opponent didn't make mistakes and had unending energy. He was a blur of deadly steal, fists, and feet as he danced around Shay. Only the heightened senses credited to his SALT designation allowed him to even remotely have a chance at defense. Offense was not even a consideration.

Summoning his calm and understanding that there was no victory in continuing what he had been doing, Shay did something that instantly confused his attacker - he closed his eyes. Believing that Shay had truly given up, the attacker knew an opening when he saw it and moved in for the kill. Using that eagerness to his advantage, Shay waited until the last minute when his opponent was fully committed to the attack before opening his eyes and barely deflecting the incoming sword thrust. Letting the sword pass between his arm and body, Shay hooked his arm into the armpit of the attacker and trapped his sword arm betwixt their bodies. Utilizing the momentum from the attacker's thrust and the trapped arm, Shay ducked and turned to throw his opponent's body over himself and to the ground. With his sword arm trapped and Shay's dagger pressed firmly to his throat, Ronan had no choice but to admit defeat and tap out.

The training circle erupted in a chorus of cheers and shouts as the gathered Swords watching the sparring match were amazed at what they had just witnessed.

Everyone knew that Ronan had only ever been defeated by no more than two others within the Clans, making him one of the most famous of the already legendary SALT warriors. Shay had never defeated Ronan before, so to see the SALT break into that upper echelon of top-tier fighters was something each of the gathered Clan members would remember until the end of time.

Shay smiled as he reached down to help his brother get up off the ground. "Good fight, brother! You had me all throughout that match. Until the end, of course." Shay added that last bit with a wink at the senior SALT. Ronan didn't accept the gesture, and a strange glint passed across his eyes that made Shay want to step back and withdraw his hand. However, the look passed so fast that Shay questioned if he saw it.

Ronan ignored Shay's hand as he acrobatically flipped off the ground to stand beside the victor. As he patted Shay on the back, Ronan responded, "Well fought, my young apprentice! I will make a true SALT out of you yet."

While Shay was absolutely not Ronan's apprentice, and their Creator made them SALTs, Shay passed off the underhanded comment as it was common with the legendary warrior. It was understood throughout all the Clans that Ronan tended to act as though others were beneath him. He was never cruel, but to those outside his direct superiors or other SALTs, he would not fraternize with Swords and seemed almost indifferent to all others. Those he did speak with, or more likely sparred with, often received his backhanded compliments. All of those he let in his circle would say that it was only his quirky personality and no harm was meant, Shay being one of them.

Shay often trained with Ronan and spent time with the Commander SALT, as he was a wealth of information and battle wisdom. Being both a Commander and a SALT truly set him apart from others, and that status often pulled others to him like a mini-planet. Shay had been honored to be selected to train with the legend back when Ronan first took notice of him. While it was inevitable that they would meet, seeing how they were both SALTs within the command structure of General Neart, it was not a guarantee that Ronan would care to bring Shay into his circle. Shay's appreciation didn't erase his unease at how his training partner conducted himself around others.

The senior SALT often liked to joke with those in his circle, but it seemed a little more dangerous rather than funny. Wit had always been pulling pranks, but no one had ever gotten hurt, and even Shay had to admit that some of the things the young communications expert did were a little funny. On the other hand, Swords had been struck with ranged gifts or knocked unconscious due to Ronan's *pranks*. Shay would often internally excuse it as all part of the training process and that Ronan knew best. Plus, since they all were within the King's realm, they couldn't truly get hurt, and the knowledge he received was invaluable.

The training that Shay and the small group under Ronan received was brutal but effective. Everyone in the group admired Ronan and his battle prowess. Individuals within the group had defeated Ronan in sparring once, but it was never repeated. The senior SALT made sure of that. He believed his status as a Commander and a SALT made him the ultimate warrior. It seemed as though it was his mission to prove it.

Once the crowd congratulated Shay with pats on the back and cheered after his unexpected victory over Ronan, they dispersed to return to their training or home units. A single look was all it took for everyone in the audience to avoid giving condolences to the defeated SALT.

"I have to know. Why did you close your eyes?" Ronan asked after the audience had dispersed.

Shay smiled as he responded, "You don't know? You? Ronan? The legend?"

With a jovial laugh, Ronan shot back, "I am a legend! The

best that ever was and ever will be. Hence, I need to know why you did it so I can be even better next time. I need to know about all your dirty little tricks."

Sharing fighting tips and working to improve each other was part of the Clan's culture. They worked together to achieve perfection in everything they were created to do. That said, the last part of Ronan's comments made Shay reflect on that brief glint in his superior's eyes. Shay hesitated to share information with another Sword for the first time since his creation.

Shay finally answered Ronan, saying, "If you fall for it again, I will let you in on it. I think I want another win before giving up my secrets."

A hungry look came across Ronan's face as he said, "Is that so?"

Again, something behind his superior's eyes rubbed Shay wrong as he spoke. A feeling he had never expected to sense from someone within the King's realm screamed at him. Trying to pinpoint exactly what it was, realization struck him like lightning and stole the breath from his lungs. It was danger. Such a feeling was unheard of. How could his brother be a threat? They shared a deep love and connection that stemmed from their King. It would be extremely insulting and hurtful if Ronan ever understood what Shay felt at that moment.

Ronan continued, "I was going to invite you to the General's private gathering tonight as the only other SALT, but instead, I may need to spend some time analyzing our fight to take you on next time."

"A private gathering? Who is coming, and what is the purpose?"

"I don't have all the details, but it is a *very* exclusive guest list. Word is that even one of the Lords will be there."

"A Lord? Here? Should they not be in the presence of the King or managing their realm?"

Ronan winked as he said, "Very curious, right? I bet you

wish you were coming now."

"I am just a lowly Sword. What reason would I have to rub elbows with a Lord? Besides, they should be attending the King and the court."

"Word around the General's group is that big things are shifting, and this Lord has plans to benefit us all. Plans that would see us using our skills instead of tirelessly training."

Ronan clearly implied that there would be an enemy to fight and kill. Shay was unsure who that enemy could possibly be.

Instantly, he knew that he didn't like what he was hearing. The same wrongness he sensed within Ronan earlier seemed to come from his words. Nothing was logically or technically wrong with what the senior SALT was saying. Still, the ominous feeling that had fallen over Shay ever since the end of their match only became heavier with every spoken word. Danger was standing in front of Shay, but it was incomprehensible.

Doing his best to act nonplus, Shay said, "I appreciate the consideration, brother, but I think I am happy not to be invited." He waved his farewell and started walking back to his unit. Something urged him to move quickly, and he heeded that instinct as he started to run.

Ronan shouted to the retreating SALT, "I will see you again for that rematch, my young apprentice."

The threat that dripped out of the words felt like a poison trying to infect Shay's mind. He had to get back to his unit and speak with Commander Titus. Ronan was right; things were shifting in the King's realm. Shay immediately knew that those changes would rock the very heart of the Kingdom.

****

Ronan didn't like being a babysitter, but he liked toying

with the two babies ahead of him. He had recently launched an arrow at Emer that had passed directly next to her neck, making a small slice. It had wedged into a tree, and when the shadow had jumped and turned to look at him, he had merely shrugged and said, "Oops. It slipped."

Before that, he had disappeared and practiced his hunting skills by sneaking up next to the one called Sham. To the shadow's credit, he hadn't jumped or reacted like Ronan had expected. But, the tiny shimmer in Sham's skin was all the confirmation that the former SALT needed that he held a special place in the shadow's fears.

Since they had begun their travels, Ronan hadn't engaged in much conversation with the two shadows as they were already dead in his mind. Of course, he would still have fun with them in the meantime, but there was no point in taking an interest. Instead, he reserved his mind's thoughts for the prize hidden away in the Sword's fort, which they were now close enough to see in the distance. Shay was there. Ronan thought it was possible that his young apprentice was looking at him at that moment through the scope of his ranged gift. Even for a SALT, this distance would be an impossible shot, and the three shadows would be hard to spot. Ronan stopped and waved with a smile anyway. No reason not to be friendly before he added the trophy of his brother's blue body to his collection.

The next time he fought Shay, no brilliant light or other distractions would prevent him from winning. Proving he was the best, once and for all. That was the entire reason he had joined the king in their attempted coup. It was an opportunity that he could simply not pass up. The ability to fight the best warriors in all the realms in real combat where eternal sleep was on the line. No more training. Real stakes for real warriors.

During the initial battles, Ronan sought every warrior who had previously defeated him and watched as they all went blue to his blade. He knew their previous victories in training had been flukes and that real combat would prove him the better fighter. Unfortunately, they had been tossed out of the realm before he had a chance to locate Shay. While Ronan was the absolute best fighter in every realm, he understood immediately that any campaign against their Maker was doomed. Their former brothers outnumbered them two to one and had all the advantages provided to them by the Creator. The king had convinced many to fight with him, but a surprise attack would be their only advantage. Ronan had to laugh at that. The King surprised? You would have had to have been an idiot to believe that was even an option. All of that didn't matter, though. The new king was true to his word with Ronan when it came to the promise of being able to use his skills to prove he was the best.

Once again, Ronan looked off into the distance at the final obstacle to that title. Finishing off Shay would mean that no living being had ever defeated him. A true warrior with no equal. The joy of that thought brought a shiver to Ronan's body. Perhaps he could simply kill these two now and move to challenge Shay again? Who knows if their promise of reinforcements was even real? Sham seemed like an oily eel that would use lies like slime to slip out of any noose you put around him.

Having locked in his Choice to end this and find his destiny, Ronan started coming up behind the two with his sword drawn. Sham announced that they had arrived as he was about to end this waste of time, and the two shadows breath in a surprise attack.

Just ahead of the group, a large cave opening appeared. Ronan did not sheath his blade as he bumped past the two to stare at the large cave. Using his scouting skills, Ronan instantly knew they would not find what was promised. An army's worth of footprints were seen leaving the cave, with none returning. Whatever kreehauns lived within the mountain were long gone.

"Please, lead the way," Ronan commented as he bowed with outstretched arms towards the opening, encouraging them to move ahead of him.

In an odd physical display, Sham hooked arms with Emer and started marching past Ronan with a nod to the former SALT. As they entered the cave, Ronan drew his crossbow, took quick aim at the back of Sham's head, and released. To his surprise, Sham used Emer's hooked arm to swing the shadow into the path of the incoming projectile. Being somewhat taller than Sham, the arrow pierced the female shadow's shoulder blade and flung her to the ground as Sham ran further into the cave and ducked behind a bolder.

Ronan smiled as he drew his sword and moved to enter the cave. He chuckled as he once again thought this shadow was more eel than warrior. No matter. The former SALT would enjoy seeing Sham turn to ash in his hands.

As he passed by the pleading Emer, he made a swift slice to separate head from body and end her pitiful screeching. Choosing that exact moment to appear from behind a bolder, Ronan noticed that Sham had stones in his hands. Somewhat confused and amused about what the shadow hoped to accomplish, Ronan moved towards the stone-wielding shadow. Before he made two steps, Sham launched his stones, not at Ronan, but at the ceiling.

Stopping at the sound of a loud *crack* above him. Staring up, Ronan slowly took a few steps back. His walk turned into a full sprint back toward the opening as rocks began falling from the cave's ceiling. Dodging the raining boulders, the former SALT lept out of the cave and somersaulted to freedom just in time as the opening completely collapsed behind him.

Ronan started laughing uncontrollably as he didn't doubt the survival of Sham within the caves. An eel indeed.

Perhaps once he was done with Shay, he would need to hunt a new type of prey.

31

TITUS felt the army approach before he saw it. The sheer number of horde and legion fighters that approached shook the ground. It was clear that the army coming for them would not be as easily defeated as the group they had sent running just a few cycles prior. Not only that, but his former superior, one of the best tacticians in all the clans, was leading the same army to his doorstep, intending to end Titus and his remaining brothers. Once again, Titus was in awe of his King's faith in him and could not stop smiling at what some would assume was an inevitable defeat that eventually came marching into sight.

With the communications now operational since the revival of the flame, Titus had immediately requested support after the original attack by legion forces. While the leaders back in the Kingdom were happy to hear they were still holding, they could not promise aid. Battles were happening all across the borders, and resources were being triaged to those who required them at a given moment. Since their situation was stable, they would need to wait until things changed or resources became available. For now, they would be on their own.

Looking at the beasts and monsters now arrayed against him, Titus suspected their situation had changed enough to warrant support. He watched as a turtair and farhatchs appeared as they trampled entire trees to the ground. Neart had not held back anything for this campaign. Titus wasn't sure if he should be honored or not.

Tutairs were a sad abomination, if Swords truly thought

such beasts deserved pity. Walking on four legs, they were the size of a two-story home. Their bodies were covered in a hard shell that could protect them from the energy of Sword's ranged gifts, with only their legs and heads coming out as potential targets. To make them more formidable, shadows often reinforced those extremities with metal crafted by servant stones. Each tutair was unique in the atrocities done to it by the shadows to ensure it served their purposes. Considering that this one had a large blunt metal spike coming out of its head, Titus knew they had made sure it would behave like a battering ram to smash down his defenses. The screams of pain erupted from the monster as shadows whipped it forward were haunting. All that said, Titus could feel no pity for the beast as it would easily convert a scream to laugh if given the chance to crush him or his brothers.

While much smaller than tutairs, farhatchs were also used in siege combat. They were particularly adept at throwing large boulders, or anything they could grab, at impressive distances. Used as a form of artillery for the legion, the creatures resembled Swords and legion in body shape with two arms, two legs, and a torso. However, their heads and sheer size were what set them apart. Having no neck and a giant single eye, they looked like a puss-filled boil had decided to sprout a body. Seemingly taller than any in the Voice clan, their muscles matched their height, making them large and powerful. Not having the best flexibility, they were terrible at close-quarters fighting, but the single powerful eye made them incredibly accurate at range.

Aside from a few noticeable absences, all the other horde beasts also seem to be present. Titus couldn't spot a single kreehaun or loskang in the army. He had wondered if the two major engagements outside of legion control had wiped the area of such monsters. Not to say that more would not suddenly emerge, but Titus would take the victories as he saw them.

Seeing enough, Titus moved to the communications hub that Wit had set up in their last remaining structure, the main hall. When he got there, Wit had anticipated the request and was already working his way up the command chain to someone who could give them support.

"General Tomaltach, hold one for 1-1-8 actual," Wit said as he nodded towards Titus and patched him into his communication link to the command center back in the Kingdom.

"General, this is Commander Titus. It is good to speak with you again, sir. Over."

"Same to you, Commander. Sounds like you and yours have been taking a beating down there. How is your team holding up? Over."

"Happy to be here, and we have been handing out the beatings more than we have taken, sir. We have lost two Swords but continue to hold the objective. Over."

"Sorry for your loss, but glad to hear your spirit is still in the fight. What do you need, Commander? Over."

"Sir. We have an army at our doorstep. Legion-supported horde numbering in the thousands has undoubtedly encircled us at this point. Our defenses are solid, but I can't be certain for how long that will remain to be true. General Neart is leading the attack force. What resources can you offer? Over."

There was a pause before the General responded, "I understand your situation, Commander. Unfortunately, there are no resources available right now. Swords have been deployed at scale across multiple fronts, and the Arrows are stretched to the breaking. I can not promise support at this time, but I will do everything I can to get you something. Over."

Titus was a bit taken aback. He knew that his team had been deployed to the front, but he had no idea that 1-1-8 was just one of seemingly a multitude of squads dispatched. Having so many teams engaged would absolutely stretch Command's ability to support every squad in the field.

Not seeing any other choice but to continue to hold their assigned objective, Titus replied, "Understood, sir. 1-1-8 will hold the objective, no matter the cost. Over."

"Good luck, Commander. Keep up the fight and honor the King. Over and out."

Taking a minute to absorb all the new information he had just received, Titus eventually turned to see Wit staring at him with a wide, goofy smile.

"What is so funny, private Amadon?"

"Not only are we behind enemy lines with no support, but we are surrounded by a large army led by one of the most brutal leaders the Clan has ever produced."

"Yes. And?"

"I am totally getting a promotion after we win this."

Stifling a laugh, Titus responded, "You make it out of this without going blue, and I will put in the paperwork myself."

"That is why I love working with you, boss!"

****

Neart looked out across the barren landscape that separated his army from the entrenched Swords and his eventual goal. The day had come for him to crush his enemy. He would defeat the Swords that protected the prize he planned to give his king. Long ago, he had promised his new king that nothing would prevent him from delivering many such tombs. Each one would provide power to his king and was precious to their former King. While it was impossible to physically injure their Maker, the legion was dedicated to disrupting His plans or hurting Him in any way possible, if nothing else, but to prove that they could.

After checking in with a few stone runners to ensure that Ronan checked in with him immediately after making himself known, Neart grabbed a white cloth and attached it to a stick. He couldn't wait any longer for his capricious former SALT to appear, either with the promised kreehauns or alone. It was time to start his attack.

He walked confidently into the open ground between him and the fort and started waving his white flag. It was possible that Titus's SALT would put an energy round through his head, but Neart knew Titus and how his mind worked. He was a curious one and wanted to understand. Neart would use that to his advantage as he knew Commanders were not ranked high enough to have been told what these battles were truly about. On the other hand, Generals, such as himself, knew every disgusting detail. He knew immediately that Titus would be patient if it meant learning the truth.

Once he was about halfway into the field, he stopped and waited. It wasn't a long wait as, within a few heartbeats, Titus appeared from the walls and walked towards him. Titus looked exactly as Neart remembered, bringing back a brief memory of Neart considering inviting the young Commander to join him in their initial attempted coup. Seeing him now made him not regret the choice as he knew deep down that not only would the Commander have refused, but he now had the opportunity to show this upstart how real war is waged.

"Titus," Neart stated as the Commander approached.

"Neart," came his reply.

"No general? Has the Sword clan fallen so low that they no longer recognize their betters?"

"You lost that title a long time ago, traitor. Speak your words quickly. I have to slaughter your beasts in a few heartbeats."

"Such hostility," Neart said as he shook his head like a

disappointed parent. He added, "There is no need for anyone to die. My beasts or your brothers."

Without missing a beat, Titus responded, "Oh, good. You have come to surrender? I accept."

Laughing, Neart responded, "No, I am afraid not. But you don't need to surrender either."

Not grasping what Neart was offering, Titus remained quiet and signaled with his eyes for Neart to continue, which he did by stating, "You don't need to surrender, and I don't either. All that you need to do is leave. You have my word that your entire team, including those that may have gone blue, will have safe passage back to the Kingdom."

Titus answered quickly and succinctly, "No."

Not surprised at the answer, Neart said, "I understand. I truly do. You are a Sword, and you have your orders."

"Glad you remember what your oaths were. Before you broke every one of them, that is," Titus said as he turned to leave.

"Oh, I remember them. I remember many things that were told to me back in the Kingdom. Including what it is that you so vehemently guard and why."

Titus stopped with his back to Neart. The general knew he had him, and it was time to sink in his claws, so he continued, "Isn't it strange that the King trusted me with the information but hasn't trusted you with it? Even after you remained on His side." Neart clicked his tongue disapprovingly before continuing, "He may not trust you, but I do. You were always my most valued officer. Smart, strong, quick, and vicious - as you should be. As I trained you to be."

Neart's former pupil slowly half-turned to look up the mountain, not fully turning to meet the general in the eyes.

"Join me, and I will tell you everything. I will tell you how to seize power and how we can hurt the King who gave us Choice with no freedom. Join me, and you will be the most feared commander in all the realms. One who will have the trust and respect of every being outside the Kingdom. Every creature, save me and the king, will bow before you. The freedom to choose your path is right here and now."

A look of hesitation and perhaps curiosity came over Titus as Neart spoke. Smiling, Neart asked, "Tell me, is the flame now alive and violet in color in the crypt?"

The young Commander wanted information and couldn't help but ask, "What do you know?"

"I know all about the flame and the plant that grows daily on the tomb. I know that the horde is called to it, and it will use them to grow stronger. I know that the plant will win over the tomb. I know you are protecting the very thing using Choice to try to end you and your brothers. I know you were sent here to be defeated because the King can never trust you."

It was fast, but Neart caught a twitch in Titus's face. Something he had said had landed true. He pushed forward to drive doubt further into his opponent's mind, "My scouts tell me that you have visited the tomb to the south. You and your team have seen what becomes of *every* tomb. There is no reason to protect something that is actively trying to kill you and who doesn't want your protection! See sense, Titus. At least consider leaving with your team and live to fight another day."

Neart didn't think that Titus or his team would abandon their post, but his seed of doubt would take root. Doubt would cause mistakes, and mistakes would lead to defeat.

Everything Neart said could be true, up to a point. Titus would sense any direct lies, so Neart was sure to include truth in the mix. Unable to determine what was true and what was a lie would only add to the doubt that was surely feeding on the Commander's curiosity.

"Think it over, Titus. I will give you one cycle to give me your answer."

Neart then did his own turn and started walking back to

his army. Of course, he did not intend to allow Titus or his men to escape or wait an entire cycle before attacking. With or without the kreehauns, he would begin the assault at first light. It would be just enough time for the doubt to cause some mental confusion or for Titus to attempt to get more answers instead of planning for the defense of the fort.

However, before Neart had taken no more than ten steps, he heard Titus yelling, "Neart! Why wait?"

Sensing the danger, Neart leaped to the right as an energy round cut through the air and struck the left side of his skull, splitting the bone above his ear from front to back. Since it wasn't a fatal shot, Neart started running and zig-zagging back to the safety of his lines and the forest. A few rounds struck his shoulder and legs before he was able to reach his forces. Bullans jumped to the general's defense and encircled him. Two went down before the general was out of danger of the cursed SALT.

Touching his skull and feeling his energy bleed out of his many wounds, Neart angrily shouted, "Attack!"

32

THAT certainly kicked the hornet's nest, Titus thought as he rapidly retreated to the cover offered by the fort's walls. A hail of arrows and boulders landed all around him as he traversed the open area between the meeting ground and the fort. He didn't zig or zag in a vain attempt to avoid the onslaught, as the best defense of an untargeted attack was to run as hard as he could to cover. Running around would only mean he was out in the open longer. Still, one of the arrows a Gúl shot struck his leg and slowed him down a bit. Due to his slowed pace, he was an easier target for a farhatch's boulder, which crashed near him. The projectile managed to trap Titus's leg to the ground after a bounce, all while arrows continued to rain from the sky.

However, as the latest barrage was about to impale the Commander, Kurian sprang from behind the fort walls. With his shield raised, he stood over and covered his leader and himself from the enemy's arrows.

As soon as there was a break in the attack, John lept from the fort's walls with his axe raised to slam down and cut the boulder cleanly in half. It was done with such precision that the axe blade had stopped within a hair of Titus's leg.

Freed and still his normal color, Titus and his brothers scrambled back to the fort as a new volley of arrows and rocks came crashing down from the sky. They closed the recently added gate behind them as boulders struck the walls.

"Thank you. Both of you," Titus said directly to his two subordinates who had rescued him.

They both nodded and quickly moved back to their positions.

Titus continued his appreciation over the team's link by complimenting Shay's shot.

"Thank you, sir, but I had hoped to put him down for good. He was faster than he looked," Shay responded.

"While removing him would have been nice, showing that we would not be manipulated and we would not go down without a fight was the goal. I believe they got the message."

Horns began blowing from deep within the tree line, and the intensity of the enemy's attacks increased. Boulders of all sizes smashed into the walls and fortified positions the Swords currently occupied. More accurate arrows dropped from the sky, preventing the Swords from engaging the enemy for too long. As expected, the first wave of attackers burst from the trees. A combination of various horde creatures were seen racing across the open field. John held the top left position above the gate, and Wit had the opposite. Both began engaging the first wave of enemies. But perhaps a more apt description would be cannon fodder as the monsters began falling by the hundreds.

Titus was not fooled by the tactic their former leader was using. Horde beasts were nothing to Neart, and he would gladly sacrifice thousands for one Sword. He was attempting to wear down the defender's energy early to ensure they wouldn't have the capacity to use their gifts later. The general knew all too well Titus and his brothers only had a single bridge, and it would take time for each Sword to refill, one at a time. If he kept up the pressure, eventually, there would be an opening he could exploit. If they played his game, it would come down to which would give out first, Neart's troops or 1-1-8's energy. Titus didn't want to bet on that race. Unfortunately, he also didn't yet have a solid alternative.

Using the time to quickly move to the bridge to fill his

own reserves after healing his wounds, Titus replayed each word Neart had spoken. The former general's words were filled with half-truths, and Titus knew it. Psychological warfare was exactly what he would expect from his former superior, and he anticipated such tactics when he went to meet with the leader. What Neart didn't account for was Titus's capacity to do both. He planned to hear his adversary out, but he had pre-arranged the attempted assassination. Removing the leader of the siege would have been a boon far greater than anything he would learn from the traitor.

While tainted, the information gave Titus some pieces to the puzzle that was helpful to his objective. Of course, he gave no credence to Neart's attempt at driving a wedge between Titus and his King. It was actually laughable. In Titus's mind, 1-1-8 was saved especially for this mission as they were best suited to handle their former leader and not due to a lack of trust. Neart couldn't have known that Titus manipulated Neart perfectly to get more information with every glance or facial cue.

While his team had already deduced that the plant was calling to the horde beasts, the added detail that it would use them to grow stronger and faster was useful. His team's top priority would be ensuring no horde creature entered the tomb.

Just as useful as what Neart had said was what he did not say. There was hardly any mention of what was in the crypt and the flame. Using the new information and compiling it with what had happened since their arrival, he believed that the flame and the plant were manifestations of Choices made by the being within the crypt. The Choices would enhance and call to the armies of darkness, whereas the awakened flame seemed to align with the Kingdom or, maybe more specifically, with the King Himself. Titus wasn't sure how to use the information provided, but it felt like he was finally getting a better picture of what was happening.

Regardless of epiphanies, he needed to formalize a strategy to see his remaining brothers stay on this side of the blue. He considered and dismissed a hundred different strategies within a heartbeat. From a constant rotation of brothers to the bridge to designs of a counterattack, there wasn't a solution with the right criteria for success. Titus saw his men overrun and cut down in various ways as he ran through scenarios in his mind. What he needed was a new factor. Something that would change the battlefield entirely.

The answer struck Titus as he finished filling his reserve. He contacted Kurian immediately to relay his idea and see if it was possible.

"I can do it, sir," Kurian responded with confidence. That was immediately followed up by a less confident, "It will take time, and I will need to bring Shay with me to watch my back and clear any enemies while I work. Will you be able to hold?"

Knowing the truth behind the question, Titus fully understood that if both Kurian and Shay were gone, the situation wouldn't allow the remaining three Swords to rotate out of their position to restore themselves at the bridge. They would be depleting themselves with no ability to recharge. The enemy would swarm the final two defenders if they tried to rotate or heal. It would be a new race, but one between the energy stores of the defenders and the abilities of Shay and Kurian. That was the type of race that Titus would bet on.

"Go and move like the wind," Titus ordered as he felt the warmth of Choice activating within himself.

****

Shay and Kurian moved swiftly up the hill again towards the mountain entrance they had traveled to twice before.

Something about the mountain called them both, but not in a pleasant way. It now seemed as though it was a force that was bent on claiming the two specific Swords. Kurian's only response to these intrusive thoughts was - *bring it on*.

The remaining defenders had used a fair bit of their energy to create an opening for Shay and Kurian to move past enemy lines seemingly undetected. There was no guarantee that they were not seen, but there wasn't anything they could do about it either. If they failed to complete their objective, defense of the fort would be nearly impossible. Kurian had faith in the defenders, Titus's plan, and their King.

He was glad to have a tactical genius leading them. Titus had taken a small detail of their after-action report from their last trek into the mountains and turned that into a strategy that could save them and their primary objective. As Titus had put it, they needed to change the battlefield to their advantage. What he was about to do in the mountain would definitely do that, Kurian thought with a smirk. He just hoped he stayed this side of blue long enough to see the aftermath.

They were nearing the final remaining entrance to the cave when Shay quickly gave hand signals to indicate an enemy was near and for Kurian to hold his position. The lieutenant then seemed to dematerialize into the scant trees and bushes. Kurian would never understand SALTs. They were almost the exact opposite of engineers. Where SALTs were true long-range masters who could sneak up on an enemy and pluck a hair from their head, few could hold against an engineer at close range or hide from their elaborate performances using explosives.

Kurian didn't wait long as Shay rematerialized right next to him while sheathing his blades. The engineer didn't miss that both had a few drops of black blood on them.

"A small group of gúl and bullan were scouting the area. We are clear to move to the entrance," Shay whispered as an explanation.

Of course, the SALT cleared a squad without a single sound in a matter of heartbeats. Wait, was it a squad? Shay didn't say the number. Kurian realized he didn't want to know the number as it would probably depress him, but he was equally happy to have such a warrior watching his back as he worked.

The duo sprinted through the last bit of cover and approached the entrance. Or at least what should have been the entrance. What greeted them caused both to lose heart instantly. The one remaining opening had caved in and sealed the mountain.

Shay turned to Kurian with determination and said, "Tell me what you need to make this plan work."

It wasn't a question but an order. Shay was forcing Kurian to quickly move on and start working on plan B. Every Sword understood their plans were like the wind - getting where it needed to go but changing its path based on what was in front of it. They needed to be fluid with their plan to ensure they completed the objective.

"We can go to the caved-in entrance where we caught that kreehaun. It shouldn't be as thick since we cleared some of the rubble on the other side, and it is closer to our objective."

Kurian could tell that his senior sensed the hesitation as Shay asked, "There is a *but* in there. What is it?"

"I can clear it by hand, but it will dramatically extend the time needed to complete my work. But, if I use charges to clear the entrance...."

Shay finished Kurian's thought: "We will get swarmed before you can get set inside."

"Exactly."

After only a brief moment, Shay responded with, "We will decide what to do when we get there."

Without another word, the two started moving toward the other sealed entrance and gave Titus the update. While not pleased, their leader understood and told them to keep him updated on their progress.

It didn't take long for them to arrive at the correct entrance due to a mix of Shay's scouting and tracking skills combined with Kurian's innate understanding of tunnel construction. Kurian began a detailed inspection of the entrance. Quickly, he realized that the Creator was with them as it was clear that the combination of their previous efforts on the other side to clear some of the rubble and the blood of the kreehauns crushed had made the removal of the barrier by hand doable.

The engineer turned to give Shay the good news when a small arrow made of a black material that Kurian had never seen before seemed to grow from his shoulder and throw him to the ground. He was almost confused for a heartbeat before training and instinct took control, and he scrambled for cover.

Kurian's confusion didn't come from being hit; rather, Shay had not warned him of the enemy's presence. Pulling out his shield to cover himself from potential angles of attack, he scanned the area to find Shay lying behind two stones with his ranged gift resting between them. Before Kurian could communicate, Shay fired two quick rounds using low energy to make as little sound as possible.

Believing that the enemy was surely dealt with, Kurian was surprised to see Shay roll out from behind the boulders as two more black arrows landed right where he had been previously. They had threaded the needle between the stones.

Looking at the projectiles in the ground and reviewing the one in his shoulder, Kurian realized they were not arrows but bolts. He immediately understood that this was not a gúl or other horde attack. It wasn't a normal legion soldier, either. Ronan had returned.

Knowing he couldn't pull the bolt out in reverse as its head was barbed based on the other bolts he now saw,

Kurian attempted to push the bolt the rest of the way through his back. Doing so elicited a screaming pain that the engineer had never felt before. Something about the bolt itself was agony, and all movement of it within him was like a thousand arrows piercing his body. Horrified at the sudden darkness that he felt, Kurian braced himself to try again. He knew he would likely go blue if he didn't immediately get the bolt out.

Before he had the chance, Shay's voice came over the communication and said, "Ronan wants me and will likely not care about you now that he took you out of the fight. I will draw him away, but you need to complete the objective. Are we clear, sergeant?"

While Shay spoke with directness and authority, Kurian understood that the truth was that their entire mission and their collective honor depended on him getting the job done. Wounded and likely going blue with their mission riding on his shoulders, Kurian thought he would have to slap his twin when he saw him again for putting him in this position.

Taking a deep breath, Kurian gritted his teeth and sprinted towards a boulder, leading with his shoulder that contained the protruding bolt. The offending projectile continued its path through his body and out the back to land on the ground next to him. He was pleased that he didn't scream or pass out from the pain that racked his body.

"Pressure creates diamonds, LT," Kurian eventually responded after getting his breath back. Moving towards the tunnel, he added, "I got this."

33

WIT enjoyed a good fight, but this was a tad bit ridiculous. Sure, the wholesale slaughter of creatures made of chaos and darkness was fun, but it just was such a pain to keep count of his kills. They all had to keep making up new rules like 'this beast was worth two or shadows was worth five'. Doing so much math while holding back a flood of monsters bent on your destruction gave Wit a headache. That said, he thought that he and John were about even though. He was pretty sure, anyway.

Titus was holding the rear in the LT's position, and both front defenders would do a killing sweep of the side walls to ensure no enemies could use ladders or stacked bodies to reach the top. It was clear that they would run out of energy soon, and there wouldn't be a chance to restore themselves unless they retreated into the hall. Of course, they would be overrun within heartbeats if they tried that.

Wit didn't mind going to primary weapons as Macey was itching to break some bones. What he would mind is going blue early. Considering that, he thought it best to keep the bad guys on the other side of the walls for as long as possible.

John whistled that an enemy was on the right.

Whipping to the right wall, Wit fired his ranged gift at the leaping loskang. The blast reversed the flying beast, and it fell to the ground below. He turned to his brother with a smile and three fingers up as he said, "That counts as three."

A skeptical look was all that he got as a response.

"That was the first one we have seen, and I killed it, which means I get to decide the points."

John continued to pin down a squad of shadows as they attempted to advance, and he gave an unhappy grunt.

Wit laughed at the larger brother's grumpy demeanor and picked off a few more before sensing his energy quickly depleting.

"Sir, any news from Bravo," he asked Titus through their link.

"Nothing you haven't heard yourself, private."

"Not to tell you what to do or anything, but maybe you could get them to move along? I am running low down here."

"I am as well, but they know their mission and will get it done."

Titus didn't have to actually say 'or die trying' as that was obvious to Swords. Wit knew they would do everything they could, but time was short.

Suddenly, almost in response to their conversation, Kurian came over the radio. Even with the fog mostly gone, communication around the mountains was still patchy like they had experienced when first arriving. Even still, it came across loud and clear that they were still working on getting into the tunnels. Deflated, Wit and John heard the acknowledgment of their leader.

Almost as if that bad news wanted friends, Titus told John and Wit that he had run dry on energy and would now be moving to primary to hold the walls. Wit wasn't far behind as he drew out Macey.

"Time to go to work, my friend."

John confidently nodded in response.

"I wasn't talking to you," Wit said with a smirk.

Turning red in embarrassment, John jumped down with his axe to hold the entrance.

Laughing, Wit joined and elbowed him as he said,

"Wouldn't want to have this undeniably bad moment with anyone else, buddy."

Wit couldn't believe his eyes as a small smile crept onto John's face. As he was about to call it out, John opened the gate. Without the ability to handle the enemy at range, they needed to resort back to using the gate as a funnel to bring as many enemies to a narrow passage as possible.

The horde beasts saw the opening and ran towards the gate. On the other hand, the shadows seemed to believe it was a trap and held back to let the horde take the brunt of whatever awaited them on the other side of the now-open gate. That suited the Swords just fine, as the name of the game was to delay. It would be over quicker if the entire army rushed the now-depleted 1-1-8.

All that said, it wouldn't be long before the perceived danger would prove smaller than the legion anticipated. The uncomfortable truth was that Wit didn't see how they would hold for long enough. Impossible odds. He loved that thought. Nothing was more dangerous than a cornered animal - especially if that animal was armed with weapons and a member of the most feared army in all the realms. He and Macey were looking forward to seeing how they would pull this one out.

****

Shay moved quickly and activated his camouflage. It wouldn't do much good against this particular enemy, but he would take every advantage he could. Thoughts of their last encounter came into his mind as he replayed the fight and analyzed every aspect to find a weakness in Ronan's movements to exploit. Unfortunately, he couldn't find any. Ronan truly was one of the best.

However, this fight would absolutely not be the same. Shay had the energy to spare and both his armor and ranged gifts to call upon. His opponent did not. While Shay didn't want to extend himself too far as he still needed to protect Kurian, his advantages over Ronan should be enough to finish the fight quickly. The SALT's strategy was to close the gap and use his armor to end the rogue warrior once and for all. Some may not see that as honorable, but honor came from their King, and Ronan was as far removed from the Creator as one could be. There is no honor in putting a rabid dog down.

As Shay approached the position from which Ronan had launched his attack from atop a hill, he did have to admit that the distance was well beyond any current known weapon from either horde or legion. He had traveled close to a mil to reach his destination and had dodged a few incoming bolts along the way. Each one had originated from the same position; however, upon arrival, all was quiet, and there was no sign of his prey.

Not wanting to expose himself to the obvious ambush, Shay retreated back into the scant cover of trees and brush on the mountainside. He performed a quick but methodological search of the surrounding area to pick up any tracks. Shay and Ronan were similar in their long-range capabilities, but Ronan held a slight advantage in closer-quarter fighting. Where Shay shined was in tracking, which held true as he picked up his former brother's trail. It was well hidden, but slight environmental changes subtly pointed him to his quarry uphill.

Eventually, Shay located Ronan's position, even though it was well hidden between rocks on a plateau above. The SALT was just barely able to see the bow protruding from the position above him. Ronan had clear high ground, enabling him to fire down at Shay as he approached, all while having superior cover. Without any good angles to use his own ranged weapon, Shay would need to approach on foot from an unexpected position. Perhaps he could take him from above? He would need to circle wide, but he may be able to climb the rock face to reach a ledge just above Ronan. Running short on time and options, Shay retreated once again and began to move around.

As he reached the cliff that he would use to climb up and around, Shay suddenly felt alarm bells scream in his mind. Lunging to the left to get behind a tree, a sharp pain came from his right leg. Looking down, he saw one of Ronan's bolts in his thigh. The silence of the mountainside was shattered by a cackle from nearby.

"What happened, SALT? Did you get injured again," Ronan questioned in mock disappointment as he stretched out the final word. His voice echoed off the rocks and seemed to be coming from multiple places.

Calming his mind and choosing not to play into the traitor's game, Shay grabbed the bolt and attempted to pull it free. The bolt was shallow, which meant it wasn't shot by any weapon and was likely thrown by his sadistic opponent. Even still, it took much of the lieutenant's energy to pull it free and heal his leg. Much more than normal, which was a concern as he no longer had the ability to summon his armor without risking going blue. His plans for dealing with the shadow was now ruined. Drawing his daggers, Shay mentally shrugged off the minor defeat and moved to find his opponent.

"Did you like that feeling? Is the darkness consuming you? It is exhilarating, is it not," Ronan's voice called out again. Shay was still having difficulty locating his target but decided to engage in the hopes of drawing him out.

"What are those vile things?"

"They are a present from my king. As one of the few shadows capable of true damage at long range, he saw it fitting that I would be gifted with such a weapon," Ronan replied before asking, "Do you not recognize it? You have lived near enough to one for long enough."

Shay thought for a moment before he understood what Ronan spoke of. Only one such dark entity was filled with horror and anguish.

"The plant growing on the tomb."

"Well done, my young apprentice! My bolts are indeed made from the very thing you so adamantly protect. Funny, no? Your King sends you to guard something that desires your death more than I."

"It is not for me to decide. I follow my King. I follow honor. Unlike you, traitor."

Ronan's chuckle sounded closer this time as Shay moved between the trees. A soft wind swayed the branches and leaves. Silence, more than anything, announced the attack that came from above.

The shadow's blade led the way as Ronan flipped down from his hidden position on tree branches. His circular movement allowed him to swing his sword upward, even though he was coming down. Shay blocked and used the force to perform his own backward flip to create space. The SALT assessed his enemy with daggers crossed in front of his body as Ronan landed and spun to sit on a rock with his typical bored expression.

"We both know how this ends, Shay."

"Indeed," came Shay's response, which surprised Ronan a bit.

"Why fight it? I will end you quickly, and you can go to your statuesque slumber knowing you were one of the best."

"I think you misunderstand how this will end, Ronan."

With a smile that didn't reach his red eyes, the shadow asked, "Please enlighten me."

But before Shay could speak, Ronan kicked dirt at his eyes and advanced with lightning strikes to the SALT's legs and arms. Blocking each and not allowing himself to spread his defense too wide in any one area to be open for a killing blow, Shay retreated until a tree prevented it. Stabbing one of his daggers into the rear of the tree and using it as a pivot point, Shay swung around the tree and landed a kick to Ronan's head. A hit like that would have knocked down even the strongest horde beast or legion, but Ronan merely shook it off and renewed their deadly dance.

Shay had to admit that Ronan was one of the best fighters created by the Maker. His moves were precise, and Shay felt his defense breaking down. Partially due to the bolt made of darkness, but it seemed as though Ronan was being energized in the fight. The shadow's pride was growing as Shay's energy waned.

"No light or ally will save you this time, my young apprentice. You will fall to my blade, and I will prove that none can defeat me."

The SALT blocked more strikes and retreated to create distance, but it was evident that he was losing as shallow cuts all over his body began leaking energy onto the ground. He refused to show weakness and rose to stare into the eyes of his traitorous brother.

"Is that what this was all about? Fear?"

"Me? Afraid? Don't make me laugh, brother. I fear nothing."

"Are you not afraid of being defeated? Not being the warrior you believe yourself to be?"

In anger, Ronan shouted, "I am the ultimate warrior!"

Using an almost sad tone, Shay responded in a hushed voice, "We are nothing without the King."

Ronan heard the rebuke but became enraged when he saw Shay close his eyes and sheath his daggers. This was a clear reminder of the defeat the shadow had previously received at the hands of the junior SALT.

Not to be fooled twice, Ronan moved in cautiously. Shay didn't move and stood there in silence as the shadow circled. With lightning speed, the shadow pierced the SALT through the back. Shay gasped as the blade exited through his chest. He kneeled as a torrent of golden energy flowed out of the wound.

Seeing victory take hold as Shay's legs began turning to

the impossibly hard blue of a defeated Sword, Ronan took the opportunity to advance and whisper into Shay's ear, "I wi.."

Shay wrapped his arm around his opponent's neck, using the last of his energy and flexibility. Flipping him over his shoulder without loosening his grip, Shay placed his head on Ronan's chest and squeezed the shadow's neck. The blue took Shay's chest and arms, solidifying into an impossible-to-escape tightened noose made of an indestructible Sword's body.

Ronan panicked as he realized the situation and attempted to punch, kick, and even bite the solid blue arm that now held him. However, nothing he did would change his destiny.

As the blue crept up his own neck, Shay spoke to his traitorous brother, "Your fear blinded you to the truth. It was never about winning. It was about your willingness to lose everything for something greater. Someone greater." He turned his head to see the sky one last time and, in that moment, saw a streak of flame come from the North to land atop the fort.

"The King will always win."

34

"ARROW 3 calling any Sword unit. Please respond. Over."

Titus pulled his sword from the corpse of a ciaróg that had used its bladed hands to claw up the massive wall at the rear of the main hall. He shoved the body down on top of another that had been right behind, causing both to fall and nearly explode upon impact with the ground. The Commander had watched the insect-like monsters slowly scale their way up but didn't have the energy to kill them before they reached the top.

Turning to the next batch of enemies bringing a ladder, Titus responded to the newcomers with, "Arrow 3, this is 1-1-8 actual. We are glad to hear from you and would appreciate any assistance. The situation is as follows: three Swords are within the walls, and our energy is depleted. An entire army surrounds us and is attempting to overrun our position. There are two Swords in the mountains, the status of which is currently unknown. We would appreciate fire support outside the walls and as needed for the mountain team. How copy? Over."

"Solid copy, Commander. Unfortunately, we are depleted as well. No spare energy for ordinance at this time."

Titus almost angrily responded, 'Well, thanks for stopping by then,' but his frustration was quickly interrupted by the Captain of the bird-like craft, who continued, "However, I am transporting a few passengers who are itching for a fight. Over."

Immediately after the Captain finished, a new feminine voice spoke, "1-1-8 actual. This is elements of Sword 2-1-2 requesting to join the fight. Over."

Titus responded, "Happy to have you 2-1-2. Tell us what you need. Over."

The calm and polite voice responded, "Roger, Commander. We are approaching from your west. We would be very grateful if you could clear a spot for us to land. Over."

Switching from the communication line with the newcomers to the squad's, Titus ordered John to relieve him in the rear and Wit to hold the front. He would clear a landing zone himself just outside the western wall.

Once his brothers were in position, Titus leaped from the west wall to land among the monsters clamoring to reach the Swords within the fort. Seeing one of their enemies suddenly land amongst them caused a slight pause as they tried to comprehend what had just happened. It didn't last long as Titus got to work.

Like a scythe cutting through the grain, Titus reaped his bloody harvest. Moving faster than most of the beasts could track, the Commander cut down those that could potentially cause trouble to the incoming reinforcements. Targeting the larger beasts, Titus spun and sliced his way to a farhatch who had given up on long-range to brave an up-close battle with the Swords. It seemed pleased as Titus charged it and raised its fist to smash down on its incoming enemy. To Titus, it seemed like the monster was moving through water as he jumped between two bullans to roll and spring up towards the farhatch's head and its single-eye, with his sword's point leading the way. The tip of his blade went perfectly through the iris of the one eye and exited through the back of the creature's skull. Its raised fits help it fall backward on top of a few small gúls attempting to run away behind it.

Spinning back to cut off the legs of both bullans he had just bypassed, Titus continued to move fast and kill any enemy within his vicinity. Before long, a swath of land was littered with bodies, and Titus had dropped a beacon as he moved back to the gate with the remaining creatures leaving the area to race after their attacker.

Even while fighting and retreating, Titus called out to the reinforcements, “Arrow 3. We have placed a beacon on your landing area. Confirm visual. Over.”

The answer came as Titus cleared the gateway and fell back behind Wit, who continued to hold the entrance “1-1-8. We see your beacon and are moving for a quick drop. Over.”

Wit glanced at the landing area that was carpeted in bodies before commenting to Titus with a wink, “May not be sanitary, but it will definitely be a soft landing.”

No sooner had he spoken than the large transport swooped in and positioned itself perfectly centered above the beacon. Ropes dropped from the rear as the ramp opened up from behind. Two forms descended to the ground with such speed that it almost seemed they had simply jumped out of the aircraft.

The two new Swords held position for a few heartbeats to ensure they could cover the retreating Arrow. To the credit of the team aboard, it was only a single heartbeat before the ship jetted away, and the Captain announced they would move to do what they could for the mountain team. Titus expressed his appreciation just as two large boulders came flying into the area very recently occupied by the ship. If the Arrow had held the position for only a moment more, or if the Swords exiting had taken their time, Titus knew that the ship would have been swatted down.

Using his mind’s ability to slow and assess, Titus surveyed the new arrivals as they began moving to the gate. The first would easily compete against John for the largest Sword in the area. His helmet made his face indiscernible, but he carried an odd-looking device strapped to his back that seemed extremely heavy at a distance. Impressively, as Titus watched, the brother moved with such ease and swiftness that he had to now question his original assessment of the device's weight. The Commander thought it might be part of the Sword's gifted armor, but that was dismissed as it was clear that the brother was only in his soft armor and tunic. Realizing that the only answer was that it had something to do with the Sword's ranged gift, he moved to assess the second member of their rescue team and the likely source of the feminine voice.

Even with the helmet covering her face and gifted armor summoned, it was clear that the much smaller sister was no virgin to combat. Still, with some distance between them, Titus saw the many scars on all areas of her body that were not covered by armor. Scars, while rare on Swords, were possible as energy to heal may not have been available for long periods of time, which would eventually cause the permanent lines.

As the pair moved to the front, the sister's voice came over the communications, "2-1-2 to 1-1-8 actual. We are moving to the center and are requesting permission to push the enemy back in a counter-offensive. Recommend your team begin rotating to the bridge. Please confirm. Over."

His first thought was that he must have heard her wrong. Push an entire army back? While he didn't doubt their skills, how would they accomplish such a task independently? He responded, "2-1-2. Granted, but how? Clarify your action. Over."

With a smirk that translated clear as day through his link, she simply replied, "Watch us."

From his position, Titus saw the smaller Sword nod towards her comrade. The larger Sword moved to stand in front of a charging platoon of horde monsters of various types. A weapon appeared to his right, attached to the pack through an extension tube. Gripping the handle, he held down the trigger to his gift. What came next was one of the most glorious sights any of the remaining defenders of the fort had ever seen. Flames.

Not just any flames came from the man's weapon, but the flame of the Creator. It poured forth from the brother as though it was water and he was merely caring for a garden. Like water, the energy-infused flames seemingly washed the filth and grime from the Creator's land. Titus and his squad's ranged gifts would leave blood, bodies, and lots of cleanup. Comparatively, this brother's weapon simply made it as though the enemy was never there as they disintegrated into screams and ash. The Maker's own magical eraser.

The sister was not idle either. She moved towards the advancing horde like a hungry lioness charging a cocky elephant who had yet to notice its doom. Drawing her blade, she advanced with lightning-fast movement and struck with uncanny accuracy.

Her primary was a sword half her height that was razor sharp on one side only and ended in a single, angled, pointed tip. It was meant for a push-pull cut, and it appeared to glow slightly, highlighting the beautiful imagery etched into the blade. Her ranged gift was a seemingly simple pistol, which likely didn't have the range of other Sword's gifts, but it would allow her faster transitions for close-quarter combat. Titus began wondering if he should push out to help but noticed that the two were, in fact, working in concert and decided it was best not to interrupt their strategy.

Watching, he began to pick up their tactic. The sister would push forward and engage ranged targets, only to pull back to be within range of her brother, who would clean up the enemies that attempted to chase her down in close combat. Where the larger of the two was a blunt instrument that stopped the masses, the sister was a scalpel - cutting away the enemy's leadership and individual threats. Of course, that did not mean that she was incapable of handling even the worst that this dark army could summon. She danced a beautiful and graceful death ballet that left bullans slack-jawed. Well, maybe not really 'slacked-jaw' and more like 'no-jaw' as pieces of much larger and seemingly stronger fighters flew away as they attempted to get in her way.

They both were a masterful and wonderful display of the Creator's power and imagination. Not only were these two the perfect weapons to turn this battle, but Titus couldn't imagine a more lethal combination. They worked like a deadly low tide - pushing the ocean of enemies back in leaps and bounds.

"Commander, permission to be in love, sir," Wit suddenly said. Titus had been so mesmerized by the newcomers that he had almost forgotten the young private was next to him. He looked over and saw Amadon dumbly staring at the sister, dancing from enemy to enemy, leaving only chaos and destruction in her wake.

With a quick smirk, Titus replied, "Denied. Now move to the bridge quickly and then relieve John." The last part was made on the open channel to ensure both Swords would hear.

Battered and bruised, he and John continued to hold their position as enemies still continued to move in from different angles to attack the fort. However, the defenders' spirits rose, and their blows had new energy due to the show of force by their brother and sister.

Before long, a horn sounded within the tree line, and the enemies began retreating to regroup. Titus used the break to call in the two arrivals to ensure they would not be overrun outside the walls and to reassess the situation. A full counteroffensive would be too risky to their mission's objective.

As the two returned to the gate, Titus first approached the sister. Because she was doing the majority of the communication, he knew she would be in charge.

"You have the Creator's timing. What is your name, sister?" Titus said with a smile and an appreciative head nod.

His first statement wasn't a question. It was nothing less than the Creator Himself who had ensured these kin arrived when they did. This is evident by the beacon, further cementing Titus's thoughts on the flame.

"The Creator never fails." responded the sister as she removed her helmet and dispersed her armor. "I am Lieutenant Nessa, and this large use of space is my Big, who goes by Seargent McCoy."

To put it lightly, she was beautiful. Physical beauty wasn't abnormal, as all Host members were perfect physically, but somehow, the Creator had made her special. Her looks were paired with the lethal skills that were just displayed. Titus knew that the Maker had definitely built this sister uniquely. Even though her face was scarred with what looked like an animal's claws slashing across her left eye to her jaw, it only enhanced her beauty. Her long black hair flowed out as soon as the helmet was dispersed, and her piercing golden eyes shone brightly. While she had obviously just been through heavy combat and had used her gifts extensively, she looked fresh and full of the King's energy.

"Well met, sister. I am Commander Titus, and those are some of my brothers," Titus said as he pointed to John and Wit, as the communication expert was just now returning to the wall to replace John. Titus also mentioned the two up in the mountains and the two they had lost.

"I am truly sorry for your losses, Commander," Nessa began, "I am one of three remaining on my original squad of nine Swords deployed to an outpost. We understand the pain of seeing kin go blue."

"Only three remain? How is it you are both here? Surely one is not enough to hold your objective?"

"No, we were reinforced with new Swords. In fact,

Sergeant McCoy is one of our reinforcements. He was not part of my original team. Most of my squad and even a few reinforcements took the blue heroically, like the warriors they are."

Titus looked at the larger brother, realizing he had just now noticed his presence. He was lying down with his pack to his side. If Titus had not known better, he may have assumed McCoy was sleeping. Noticing the Commander's attention, the brother gave a half-hearted salute and began chewing on a blade of grass he had grabbed from somewhere during the fight.

A brother of few words, Titus thought with a chuckle. He and Wit would get along great - or Wit would end up blue.

Titus responded to the fare lieutenant, "Of course. We shall hear your tale another time. For now, let us regroup and re-energize. Please use our bridge as soon as John is finished."

Nessa ordered McCoy to take a position at the gate so the two officers could speak and plan their next moves. Walking together, Titus asked how they came to be here. The lieutenant told him that their outpost had suddenly gone silent after cycles and cycles of battle. Suddenly, an Arrow appeared, telling them they had new orders and would have to follow 'the beacon'. When she had asked what beacon, their tomb had suddenly shot out a flame. Jumping aboard the Arrow, they followed it, and here they are.

Based on this new information, Titus surmised that this would be a temporary reinforcement. These two had their own mission and would need to return to their team. "How long will you be joining us?"

"Not long. The orders were to help strengthen your position, but my team will need us soon. The transport has just enough energy to bring us back and return to re-fuel within the Kingdom."

"Understood. Rest for now, but we will have much to

discuss and do during your stay."

"Thank you, Commander," Nessa said with a salute.

"Oh. One thing, lieutenant."

"Yes, Commander?"

"Apologies in advance, but I would appreciate it if you didn't kill Wit. I sort of need him... Sometimes."

35

KURIAN heard the beautiful and melodic songs coming from just outside the tunnel's entrance. He cursed and moved back into the cave, quickly finding mud that he shoved into his ears to help shut out the noise. If he wanted the best chance at survival, he would find something to cover his ears and wait at the small entrance he had dug out. Ambushing the horde beasts that hunted him at the tiny opening would ensure he walked out of there in one piece. That said, his survival was not the priority. He needed to complete his mission at all costs.

Having been in these same exact tunnels, Kurian had the layout memorized. He knew each path he had to stop at and each turn he needed to make. The path to his objective was clear in his mind.

Sprinting to the first intersection of tunnels, Kurian placed a charge on the tunnel he did not need. It was perfectly placed to ensure a full collapse of the side tunnel and leave a singular path clear. To his immediate frustration, as soon as he finished and was preparing to move on, the melodic sounds suddenly grew louder. He knew they were now in the tunnels. Marows had come hunting.

To be fair, he didn't know if it was *only* Marows, but he was fairly confident that not many of the horde could fit through the entrance he had made. The snake-like bodies of the Marows and their hypnotic songs echoing in these tunnels would be hard enough to deal with without his armor or ranged gifts; he really didn't want to have to fight additional enemies as well. It would be a waste of precious time he knew he no longer had.

Communication around the mountain was difficult to begin with but was impossible within the tunnels. He truly didn't know if his team was still fighting or if he would eventually return to a fort that had been overrun. Of course, Kurian would have to devise a strategy to take it back, but that would be difficult, to say the least.

Trying to shake off images of his brothers going blue, the engineer set himself the task of placing another charge on another branch of the tunnels. He was a professional; it was time to show it by completing his objective.

Finishing the final branch in the main tunnel, Kurian approached the giant cave at the heart of the mountain with a lake at its core. Even with little to no light, the sergeant could tell that the lake was beautiful and still. With nothing to disturb it, the lake sat quiet and crystal clear. He could make out small cave creatures swimming and crawling alongside the water. It would be a shame to break the peace of the few creatures that inhabited this realm, but the King's mission would not be denied, and even these small creations would understand such a command.

Kurian looked at the cave walls and found the least damp area to begin his climb. The cave ceiling was not high, at only fifty hands, but it was wide, and he would need to set charges in a wide circle at precise positions. Many stalactites hung above the water, which would be helpful as an anchor point as he worked.

While not the best free-climber, it was still a skill that all Swords possessed to ensure they were capable of handling any situation. Kurian had long ago found a trick to make the task of climbing less cumbersome. His strategy was simply to slam his shield into the wall and use it as a platform to stand on and find a new grip. Removing the shield beneath him, he would swing higher and repeat the process. This was especially helpful to him now as time was the priority, and a stable platform would enable him to work swiftly. Completing this task was important, but it was even more important to do it fast.

Unfortunately, the one drawback to his climbing method was the sound it created. In a closed cave, he might as well have wrung the dinner bell for his enemies. He was halfway up the wall when the first Marow entered the cave. Its evil eyes quickly zeroed in on the climbing Sword. Immediately, it started emitting the tones that were made to lull him into a sleepy or submissive state. Thanks to the mud he had stuffed into his ears, it had almost no effect on Kurian.

Choosing to ignore the threat, the engineer renewed his efforts to reach the lake's ceiling. Unfortunately, the Marow would not be denied as it unfathomably began crawling up the wall behind him. Kurian really thought that wasn't fair as he had assumed he at least would have peace while he worked high above his enemy.

Moving slowly but surely, the advancing monster kept singing its song and staring hungrily at the Sword. The monster didn't truly desire to devour the Sword, but the hunger was due to the constant need to destroy what the Creator had made. Seeing the solo Sword in a seemingly vulnerable state lit a fire in this creature that it longed to satisfy.

A Sword was never truly vulnerable, but Kurian had to admit that it was not an ideal scenario. He had no energy for armor or ranged gift that would instantly end the fight, and his primary weapon was currently being used to keep him from falling into the depths of the lake.

When the Marow approached, Kurian did the only thing he could by finding a solid grip and holding his shield in an offensive stance as he hung from the wall. He needed to end the creature quickly and get back to his work. The Marow advanced and sweetly smiled through fanged teeth.

He had to admit that it was a beautifully symmetrical face with golden hair flowing behind it, so it was a shame that Kurian had to slash it as it drew near. It wasn't as beautiful with the black blood flowing over its facial skin and dissolving it. An ear-piecing and hideous screech replaced the sweet siren's call as it reared back and bared its fangs at the hanging shield bearer.

Instead of waiting for another attempted strike, Kurian went on the offensive by swinging towards the Marow and slamming his shield into the wall once more just above the monster to land a quick strike to the already wounded face. Black blood exploded over both of them and immediately began eating away at them both and the wall. While Kurian didn't mind the acid biting into him too much, the real issue was how it was deteriorating the wall he was currently attached to.

The wall broke down without much warning, and his shield was dislodged. Since Kurian was still above the Marow, he slashed at the monster once more as he dropped past it into the water below. Due to the strike and its own grip loosening, the monster fell with the Sword.

Kurian swam up and moved to get to solid ground as soon as he hit the water. Not that he had trouble fighting in the water, but he didn't relish a Marow's serpent body's clear advantage in the current situation. Unfortunately, the monster quickly recovered as well and was quickly upon him. It first wrapped its tail-like lower half around the arm holding Kurian's shield. While not usually a big deal as he could transition and fight with another, the water slowed his movement just enough to allow the creature to fully envelop his upper body while keeping the weapon away from itself.

Attempting to keep his wits about him, Kurian quickly tried to see the way out. His training demanded that there would be one as long as he considered every possible angle and outcome. Just as he saw the path out, the creature started singing directly into his ear. With sudden panic, Kurian realized that the fall into the water had removed the mud he had placed in his ears. To his horror, that panic was soon replaced with calm. He knew logically that he shouldn't be that calm, but his body began feeling sluggish, and his mind was not far behind. His thoughts flooded with the creature's beauty and confusion about why he would fight such a pretty thing, even while his body was squeezed with unmeasurable pressure.

Kurian turned to study the creature so close to his face as they floated in the water. He didn't know why, but a clear and vivid thought came to his mind. Not a thought, but an order. It was a ridiculous thing to do, but the order was unmistakable and came from a place within him that demanded action.

The Marow came closer and opened its fanged mouth as if to kiss Kurian with their heads just above the water, and the Sword returned the gesture. However, the Sword went higher at the last heartbeat and bit down as hard as he could on the feminine nose. The screech that came from the Marow shattered the silence of the cave. It also broke through the Sword's haze, which his mind seemed entangled by.

Both combatants realized what had happened at the same time, and before the now gruesome-looking creature could begin its song once more, Kurian used his body and the awkward position of the Marow to dive them both underwater. Since the creature could not use its lower body to swim back up and Kurian's legs were far more powerful than the small arms of the Marow, they dove deeper. The water silenced the sound, and the scream it had emitted before the dive left the monster's breath short. It wasn't long before it was desperate to surface and unwound itself around the Sword.

Not allowing the Marow the opportunity to break the surface, Kurian grabbed its tail as it finally uncoiled to swim away. Now free and gripping the beast, Kurian continued to swim down. Desperation in the Marow could be felt as it did everything it could to wriggle out of or break his grip, but nothing would prevent him from holding his enemy underneath the water. Determined, he held firm and swam against the creature doing everything it could to survive.

After a few moments, the peace of the surface was finally broken as Kurian emerged to breathe again. The body of the Marow did not resurface as the Sword made his way to the shore, spat out the foul taste in his mouth, and quickly resumed his climb up the wall. He had wasted enough time, and there was work to do.

****

Neart was angry. He had been surprised by the ambush and betrayal of the peaceful meeting standards typically abided by when two leaders discussed terms. While he never held much stock in the tradition and often broke the peace himself by ambushing the other leader when it suited his strategy, he had thought he understood his enemy well enough to manipulate. Clearly, he had miscalculated Titus.

Even that initial small misstep could have been handled, but he could only watch as the defenders received reinforcements and the fresh Swords routed his forces. Things were not going in his favor, which meant someone needed to be punished.

Once his sadistic craving was satiated in gore and pain by two of his advisors and a full platoon of horde beasts, he could finally think. The scouts recently reported that some of the Swords were outside the protected fort and doing something in the mountain. Based on the number of defenders seen, Neart knew that two were outside on the loose. He didn't know the identity of the other but assumed with certainty that one of them would be the SALT. That would also explain why he had not heard from Ronan or his promised reinforcements. Either Ronan had gotten distracted by the presence of the other SALT, or they were all dead. Neither option was helpful to the general.

Ronan was a skillful and the finest fighter Neart had ever seen, but he was easily distracted. A true agent of chaos that was only helpful in specific situations. At that moment, he wasn't being helpful at all. Anger threatened to overcome the general once more, but he calmed himself as he touched the black blood still staining his sword and relished the recent memory of the agony he had given.

Returning to the battle at hand, Neart needed to come up with a better strategy. The war of attrition would be in his favor if the other two Swords did not return. With a bridge, seven Swords in one place could hold a high-ground fort indefinitely. He either needed to end this fight quickly or ensure the other two never returned.

Taking stock of his resources, the legion's leader knew that the horde was nearly infinite as there were always more appearing. He didn't know how they were created as there didn't seem to be procreation within their ranks, but he didn't complain at a nearly inexhaustible army. On the other side of the spectrum, the shadows under his command were finite. They were better equipped to handle the Swords, but they would be best used as finishers and be wasted if he used them too soon.

Making the most of what he had, he decided it would be best to send the bulk of his shadows into the mountains to deal with the two Swords. Simultaneously, he would throw every horde beast at the defenders to keep them exhausted. Once the two were dealt with and whatever strategy they had hoped to implement was destroyed, he would move in to clear the fort.

As Neart gave his orders, he looked at the single Turtair milling about within camp. Suddenly, a brilliant idea formed in his mind. He knew how to crack open the

Sword's defenses and claim his victory. The king would arrive in a few cycles, and the general smiled as he thought about personally welcoming him into the fort and gifting him the hidden prize within.

36

WIT had thought he knew pain before, but now he understood what true pain was. To be so close to the beauty of the sun and be unable to do anything as it burned you into dust was the only way he could describe how he felt at that moment. He would do anything to make it stop. Going blue seemed like a vacation at that moment. All he wanted to do was talk to *her* - Lieutenant Nessa.

Unfortunately, a brute with no sense of romance was sitting on him and covering his mouth as they sat near the gate. Wit had never really known that another Sword could be as wide or big as John was, but they both felt about the same when they were sitting on top of him. He wasn't in any pain from the brother atop him as he was used to Titus ordering John to do the same. The pain came from the longing in his heart that needed to escape his mouth. As the new brother prevented him from speaking, those words were burning inside his chest.

Even though the order to sit on Wit had come from Nessa herself, Wit took it as a challenge to prove himself instead of a rejection. While he had to admit that the order was a bit rude, he would prove to her that he was the Sword of her dreams. The fact that there were no romantic relationships between members of the Host didn't sway him. He just wanted to be near her and spend endless hours talking. Wit saw a future of the two of them talking to each other, holding hands, traveling all the realms, doing pranks on other Swords, and slaughtering hideous monsters. It was beautiful, and he just needed to convince her of that.

As Wit was held hostage, Titus briefed the team on their plan and the strategy for handling the army that surrounded them. Nessa provided her suggestions, and they fine-tuned the plan based on the beauty's extensive experience in combat. She complimented Titus's idea as bold and said she wished that her first leader had not gone blue so early in their deployment. He was known as a creative tactician like Titus, and the two leaders would have enjoyed each other's company.

The two leaders turned quickly to the gate as a yelp of pain came from McCoy. It was followed immediately by Wit quickly yelling, "I am here and would greatly enjoy your company, my lady!"

"Did you just bite me?" McCoy asked as he looked at his finger as if in confusion.

Before Wit could say anything more, McCoy slammed a newly gauntleted fist on the ground right next to his face. The large brother leered down at Wit as he continued, "Don't do that."

To emphasize his point, he actually flicked the smaller brother in the forehead with an armored finger. It was revealed to Wit that the primary weapon of the Seargent was actually the gauntlets themselves. Each knuckle on his glove had a sharpened point that would easily punch holes into the larger brother's enemies. Thinking back on the arrival of their reinforcements, Wit remembered how McCoy had moved quickly and easily on the field. Imagining the brother in a fistfight was truly frightening. His size, uncanny speed, and indestructible fists would make him a terror. Suddenly, Wit was happy that the brother was on his side - if not on top of him.

Changing his strategy, Wit thought he would win McCoy to his side. He was lovable, after all.

"My brother, have you ever…" Wit started but was quickly interrupted by the behemoth turning his head and putting a single finger to his lips.

Wit wasn't a creative genius like Kurian or as knowledgeable as Marcus, but he knew when to speak and when to be silent. Looking at the spiked gauntlet slowly come away from the brother's mouth made it very clear that this was a silent moment.

"Can I trade you for that brother?" Wit heard Titus ask Nessa in humor.

Wit couldn't hold it back as he replied, "I will volunteer!"

As Wit braced for the incoming flick that was sure to come, a horn blasted in the distance, and a roar of beasts could be heard as the regrouped legion army broke from the cover of the woods. Switching back into work mode, all Swords prepared to fight. McCoy stood and gripped Wit's hand to bring him up. With a nod, Wit jumped into his position above the gate.

Swords were professional when it counted and would place the mission above all else. Wit was no exception as he looked at the incoming beasts and the arrows that blotted out the sky. Freshly energized, he called his ranged gift and aimed at the leading creatures made from nightmares.

"Points are decided by the Sword who made the first kill," Wit shouted to McCoy, who stood in John's previous position.

"Fair enough," came the reply from the Sergeant.

Wit smiled as he thought he would finally win one. Having seen McCoy's ranged gift and its limitation in distance, Wit would be able to kill enemies first and determine a point structure that would benefit him.

Silent as the night, Nessa climbed up next to Wit and fired a single round from her pistol to end a gúl taking the field at a ridiculous distance.

"They are worth one," the lieutenant said.

Turning to look at Wit and his mouth in the shape of an O, she reached over and lifted his chin to close his mouth. Before moving to her position alongside his side of the wall, she smiled in his direction and winked.

Wit decided that this was definitely not the day to go blue.

****

Kurian understood that he had spent far too long on his mission, but there was nothing left for him except to continue. He knew that his brothers would do everything needed to hold, but it had nearly been a cycle between Ronan's ambush at the entrance, having to dig himself a tunnel, and finally setting the necessary charges. Hope and faith that he would see his brothers still in the fight kept him moving. Still, there was no time left to spare as he sprinted back down the tunnel towards the entrance.

Immediately upon having that thought, two Marows appeared from side tunnels. Without hesitation, Kurian triggered the charges for those specific tunnel branches. While he had planned to wait until he had cleared the tunnel before triggering the explosions and alerting the enemy of his presence, there was no sense in going blue now in hopes of avoiding it later.

One of the Marows was crushed instantly, but the other avoided its collapsing tunnel and slithered into the main path ahead of Kurian. It advanced and began humming its hypnotic songs. The Sword noticeably slowed his run and started stumbling towards the tempting creature.

As Kurian got close, the monster sweetly smiled at him while its tail started towards his leg and began wrapping him up in a lethal embrace. While keeping its torso at a distance, the tail slithered up the engineer's legs slowly and moved to try and wrap his arms to restrict his movements.

Faster than a hawk's dive, Kurian slammed his bladed shield down and severed the portion of its tail attached to himself. Black blood spewed out from both of the severed pieces as the Marow screamed in pain and retreated faster than Kurian could follow up with a kill strike.

Kicking off the piece of the monster that was still attached to himself, the Sword was grateful that he had stopped for a quick moment at the lake's edge to reapply mud to his ears. That said, even without the monster's hypnotic sounds, it was still a vicious fighter he had just wounded. Cornering it within the tight confines of the cave would come at its own risk, but Kurian needed to get out quickly to help his brothers.

As he advanced, the creature continued to retreat, eventually hitting the tunnel's wall while continually hissing at the Sword that had just wounded it. Kurian wasn't interested in playing with the beast, so he threw his shield at the creature's neck. The Marow saw it coming and ducked quickly to avoid it. The shield ended up securely sticking into the wall directly behind it.

The creature was suddenly filled with confidence as it stretched itself back up and looked at the Sword's weapon stuck to the wall. Her enemy was now defenseless. It turned with a new smile towards the Sword, who had hurt it and killed its sisters. That smile remained, even as Kurian came in hard with a jumping sidekick to launch the Marow backward and into his bladed shield's edge at just the right height. The monster's smile only faltered when Kurian knocked its head off his shield to join the rest of the body that now lay separate on the cave floor.

Frustrated that he was continually late, Kurian picked up his pace once more to reach the exit of these cursed tunnels. He hoped there would be no more disruptions but kept his senses tuned for any more ambushes.

Kurian reached the exit soon after without any further complications. He was tired, dirty, low on energy, and still hurt from the initial bolt that had pierced him. He chuckled as he crawled through the opening he had created to enter the tunnels. It was just another day in the office.

When he exited the tunnel and shook himself off, he sensed something wasn't right and positioned his shield before him. He watched a shadow emerge from the brush about twenty hands in front of the tunnel.

'Okay, not bad. I can handle a single shadow,' Kurian thought to himself.

However, he immediately cursed himself for the thought as two more appeared. It would be hard, but he had seen worse fights.

Only after twenty total shadows appeared around him in a half circle, completely enveloping him against the cave's entrance, did he decide that this would probably not go well.

"Just give up," the initial shadow yelled to him with a smirk.

Kurian yelled his reply with his own smile, "What? To you all? Do you not have more traitors around? I think you may need them."

The lead shadow wasn't phased by Kurian and simply asked, "We already found and dispatched your partner. No one will save you. Why not surrender? We will make it quick."

Shay gone? Unlikely that this group could have pulled that off, but Ronan was another matter. Could he have lost his battle? Is that why he never joined him? Possible, but, again, hard to believe. The fact that Ronan wasn't leading this group meant something as well. Kurian would need to figure out what had happened. In the meantime, the shadow said one thing was likely still true. No one was coming to help him.

Kurian turned and scrambled up the side of the mountain to reach a spot just above the cave entrance. The shadows turned at one another and snickered. His climb wasn't exactly graceful, and there was no avenue of escape where he had placed himself.

The leader spoke again and asked, "Do you think the high

ground will help you? I thought Swords were trained better than this." He then turned to his legion comrades and waved for them to begin their advance on the single Sword.

"I have a riddle before we get started," Kurian announced from his position.

Weary but curious, the leader replied, "Oh, really? What might that be?"

With a smile that rivaled Wit's famous grins before he pulled some type of prank, Boomer asked, "What's my name?"

In answer, the engineer activated all his placed charges inside the mountain, as well as those that were planted all the way up the mountain. While the charges outside the mountain were instantly seen via a massive trench that suddenly appeared with the explosions, the ones inside the mountain were a bit slower, which caused a tiny piece of doubt in Kurian's mind. Letting out a breath he didn't know he was holding, his success was evident as the mountain noticeably grew shorter when it internally collapsed on itself.

He saw in his mind's eye the charges above the massive lake at the heart of the mountain going off, starting at the rear. Like a wave, the rock and debris above the still and peaceful lake would plummet into the depths below, displacing the water. Simultaneously, all other tunnels would be sealed, not allowing the water to go anywhere but out the path Kurian had chosen, which happened to be beneath him and directed toward the advancing shadows.

The somewhat loose rocks exploded out and struck some of the shadows. Those who remained unscathed immediately began swimming down the hill as the water flowed down the trench that had just been created and towards the fort below, which rested on a small hill.

Kurian could just barely make out the fort from his position on the mountainside. He witnessed the water begin covering the barren land between the fort's hill and the surrounding trees. The chaos the water created among the attacking forces was obvious as an entire army was swept away.

Boomer breathed a sigh of relief as he saw energy rounds strike enemies that were close enough to the fort and on the hill to stay on their feet. Even from a distance, the sight of a giant flame coming down from one of the walls toward legion and horde alike caused the engineer to become curious. When did they get that?

37

"FINAL score is seven hundred and thirty," Wit yelled out from atop the wall with a smile.

McCoy's response on the other side of the gate wiped the smile from his face: "Eight hundred and twenty."

"What?!?"

The Big's only response was a shrug.

Nessa's feminine voice spoke up by adding, "One thousand, one hundred and ten."

Titus saw that Wit wasn't capable of a response as he stood dumbfounded. Eventually, the communications expert sputtered out, "How?"

The female lieutenant explained how she had dipped back into the midst of the enemy to clear leaders and large foes before using the wall and McCoy's help to climb back up into the fort. Her exploits were growing rapidly on this extra deployment.

Once her after-action report explaining her high score was complete, Wit turned to his leader with almost a hopeful and questioning look.

He had to think and replay the battle a bit, but Titus eventually responded, "Six hundred and fifty."

Wit sighed with relief that he hadn't lost to everyone, but Nessa had to correct the Commander by saying, "Sir, are you counting correctly? Farhatchs were worth twenty."

"Oh. In that case, I have seven hundred and eighty."

A deep groan came from Wit. Titus consoled his private by saying, "I am sure we will be surrounded by an uncountable, bloodthirsty army again soon."

"You are just saying that," Wit replied with a slouch.

"Neart isn't done with us. He won't stop until he wins or is ended himself."

Wit responded with a hopeful, "You promise?"

"Definitely."

Nessa interrupted by reporting, "Looks like we have someone coming down the mountain."

Titus switched to his team's link and sent out, "Alpha team calling Bravo. Is anyone reading me? Over."

"Bravo-two reporting in, sir. Over."

"Good to hear from you, Sergeant. Great work up there. Where is Shay? Over."

"Unknown, sir. We were ambushed by Ronan, and he moved to draw him away from the mountain. Over."

"Understood. Return to base. We will have to come up with a plan on how to follow the lieutenant. How copy? Over."

"Roger that, sir. I am returning to base. Over and out."

With the water surrounding the fort quickly being soaked into the ground and dispersing, Kurian shouldn't need to swim to get back. However, the mud that the massive amount of water had created around their position would make it difficult to traverse. Of course, that was the original plan anyway.

Titus's strategy had accomplished two things. Firstly, the massive amount of water cleared the battlefield of enemies just outside the fort. While killing as many as possible was surely a benefit, the true goal was to restart the siege on more favorable terms for the defenders. Since the ground around the fort was dead with no vegetation, Titus knew that the ground would soak up the water quickly to form a mire of mud that would slow any attack to a snail's pace. Any delays on the attacker's side would make the Sword's mission that much easier. They could swap positions and recharge at the bridge without fear of being overwhelmed in any one area. Of course, even this would be temporary, but the name of the game was delay and attrition. The longer the defenders survived and the more attackers that died, the higher the chance of victory. Anything that kept the enemy at bay increased their chances of completing the mission. Mud and muck would definitely do that.

Kurian didn't take long to reach the fort as he avoided deep water as much as possible. Upon his return, he gave his report to Titus and the last seen position of their missing brother. After introductions were made, the returned engineer immediately began pestering McCoy on how his ranged gift worked. While such things were sometimes beyond the understanding of Sword, an engineer would be determined as a seeker searching for answers when it came to understanding how things worked.

Once the team was settled, Nessa pulled Titus aside. Before she could speak, he said, "You are leaving, correct?"

With a hint of regret, 2-1-2's lieutenant confirmed, "Yes. My team needs me and McCoy. We did what was requested and I believe your team is secure enough for us to return to our own."

"While we are sorry to see you go, I give thanks to the Maker for your arrival."

"It was a pleasure to work with you and your team. I wish you all the King's blessings. Is there anything you need before we call in a pickup?"

"Thank you. You as well," Titus replied before stopping and answering her question, "Yes, I believe there is something you can do for us. Could you find our wayward SALT?"

In shock, Nessa replied in humor, "You have a SALT? How in the world did you lose one of those?"

"Unfortunately, we weren't the only ones with such a resource, and I am afraid the traitor was determined to find Shay."

"There is a rogue legion SALT out there?" Nessa said incredulously.

After a moment, she answered, "You have a high degree of faith in me and McCoy's skills to go out there looking for two SALTs, but we will do our best."

With a chuckle, Titus said, "I think you earned every bit of faith in the last cycle."

The two leaders returned to the gate and announced the departure of 2-1-2. The brothers of 1-1-8 shook the hands of their kin and expressed their appreciation. When Nessa got to Wit, Titus considered ordering John to sit on the private again, but he was surprised when Wit simply shook the sister's hand and said with a straight face, "Thank you for the assist, lieutenant. You were amazing, and it was an honor to have been fighting alongside you."

Everyone present was taken aback by their normally clownish brother's professional and sincere words. Nessa also seemed shocked, even though they had only known each other for a short time. She glowed extra bright for a split second as Wit bowed to kiss her blood-encrusted hand.

Without another word, Wit turned to allow the two reinforcements to exit through the gate that was directly behind him. Nessa didn't say a word as she started off, but McCoy gave the communications expert a friendly punch to the shoulder before following his leader.

Titus came up to the private and was about to comment on the young brother's growth and professionalism when he suddenly shouted to the retreating forms of 2-1-2, "We will meet again, and we will be together, my sun and stars!"

Ah. There it was - the Wit they all knew.

However, against all odds, both Titus and Wit saw the lead Sword turn and blow a kiss towards them. Wit's smile as he turned to his leader seemed to light up the whole realm. Titus could only laugh at the inconceivable turn of events.

****

Ronan was lying on the ground with his face pointed to the sky. He had tried everything he could to slip his head free of the vice-like grip that held his neck in place. The former SALT had screamed at and punched the stupid face of Shay for marks. Eventually, he had given up and even had to laugh at his predicament. Shay had done the unexpected and had lost but had also won. It was infuriating and impressive at the same time.

The trapped shadow had thought of every possible potential of escape, but nothing reasonable came to his mind. He was truly and thoroughly trapped for the remainder of time. Well, that wasn't exactly true. Every Sword and legion member knew that the King would eventually blow His war horn to return His army back to full strength. At that time, Shay would return to his former self, and Ronan would be free to continue their fight.

That said, Ronan didn't exactly want to be trapped in this stinking shit of a realm while held in a chokehold for an unknown amount of time. There was much more he could accomplish and do in the meantime.

A thought crept into his mind: *Do you?*

Of course, he did! There were many other Swords he could hunt to show all realms that he was the ultimate warrior. He knew that there weren't any more threats that could even come close to defeating him with Shay now gone, but that didn't matter.

Doesn't it?

Ronan wanted to scream at this intrusive voice. But truth was hard to grasp as a shadow since that sort of thing was relative now. Truth and meaning are what he decided they were. Meaning could be found in many things if he so chose.

Is it?

Fury began boiling in the trapped shadow. 'Yes!' the legion member shouted at the voice in his mind. The King doesn't have control over his life anymore, and he has true freedom.

The voice in his mind laughed in a mocking tone and said, *Is this freedom?*

Ronan had to admit that was a good comeback, as he truly was trapped with no hope of escape. Wait. Shouldn't the voice in his head be his own? Why was he arguing with himself?

Am I your voice?

Mentally, Ronan responded, 'What else could you be?'

I might be something greater than you. Something that wants the same thing as you.

'Nothing is greater than me,' Ronan snorted but added, 'What is it that we both want?'

To show the realm and the Creator who is the greatest.

Ronan liked the sound of that, but it also had a ring of familiarity to it. It was as if he had heard it before.

'Who are you?'

I believe you know already.

Attempting to get a better view of his surroundings, the former SALT contorted his head in the grip that held him. Eventually, he could see most of the area to his right. From behind a tree stepped the most handsome individual had ever seen, completely covered in finery, shining with a light that seemed unreal, and adorned with a radiant crown. Instantly, he knew who had come - his king.

"My lord! Why do you play games with my mind? Come and free me."

"Do you give orders to your king, Ronan?"

That response immediately shut up the shadow. Trying to frame his words more pleasingly to his potential savior, Ronan took a moment to collect himself.

“You are truly one of my finest warriors, Ronan. But do you know why I allowed Neart to keep you and not take you to be my own personal weapon?”

Having been around legion leaders many times, Ronan remained silent in the hopes that his king would answer. Unfortunately, the king was not a simple leader and returned silence with silence.

Eventually, Ronan replied, “I had assumed you believed my loyalty was to the general or that we would work well together.”

The king tapped his lip in thought before responding, “While that could be true, that is not the full answer. In truth, you were not ready to give me everything.”

Ronan couldn’t believe what he was hearing. He had given everything to join the rebellion and turn on his Creator.

Returning the conversation back inside Ronan’s head, the king said, “*You gave up the Maker’s gifts to pursue your own interests. You wanted to be the best and to defeat any who could stand against you. Your captor said it well in that you were never willing to give it all for someone greater because you believed you were the greatest.*”

Angrily, Ronan mentally shouted back, ‘What other victory is there outside of proving I am the best?’

“True victory,” came the verbal reply.

Calming himself, Ronan asked, “How can we achieve victory against our Creator?”

With a small chuckle, the king responded, “Our victory is found by hurting what the Creator loves.”

Understanding what he meant due to his rank and information gleaned within the legion, Ronan responded, “The Created.”

“Indeed.”

Taking a moment, a hopeful Ronan finally stated, “I can’t help you if I am trapped here for the remainder of time.”

The king smiled and said, "I suppose we could fix that, but you must give me your full loyalty. No more doing what you please. I have allowed you time to fulfill your goals. Now you will fulfill mine. Your singular purpose will be my purpose. Are you prepared for that?"

Knowing there was no way out without the king and the fact was that he truly didn't have a purpose anymore, he might as well give the king what he asked. Instantly, Ronan knew there would be no escape from the king's grip. He would be jumping from one cage to another. That said, the new cage would at least allow him to move.

With his own smile, Ronan responded, "So be it. Should you free me, I will be your weapon. Your will is my will."

"Excellent," the king said aloud and in the shadow's mind before continuing, "I am afraid that this will be painful." The tone was remorseful, but the slight glimmer in the king's eyes said something else.

What followed was the most excruciating moment of Ronan's existence. Far greater than his severing of bonds with his Maker. He didn't even have the capacity to scream as the king worked to literally remove parts of the shadow's face in order to free his head from the blue statue's grip. His jaw, his nose, his ears, and most of his skull were reformed. While the king was skilled in the removal of parts without ending a shadow, he wasn't as skilled in putting them back together. By the time he was finished, Ronan couldn't yet speak and was nearly blind. However, he was free. The same could not be said of his blade still stuck in the chest of Shay.

Handing Ronan both a mask made to look terrifying with images completely opposite of what the Creator is famous for and a long dagger made from the same material as his crossbow bolts, the king said, "I made them from a tomb to the south that I came across on my way here. Take them and never be without the mask." He then turned towards the fort below them and crossed his arms behind his flowing robe as he continued, "I have a mission for you in a more fertile land that will put an end to this nonsense."

Standing erect for the first time in nearly a cycle, the newly reborn shadow turned to his master and, with his face now hidden behind the horrifying mask, mentally responded, 'I am my king's blade. It is my pleasure to serve.'

38

IT was 1:15 pm on a Tuesday, and Henry was tired of working. He had hit his recent deadline for integrating another product into the company site and was waiting for marketing to sign off on the images he planned to use. There wasn't much left from his side besides another seemingly pointless meeting.

Inspiration hit him out of nowhere, and Henry decided he wanted to play hooky. More importantly, he knew he didn't want to do it alone. Hana wasn't going to be able to get out of work, so he decided to make it a boy's day and take his two sons, Hunter and Logan, out of class early. They would hit the batting cages and maybe get some ice cream. Hunter was a little young at five years old and maybe frightened at the cages, but Henry believed he would rise to the occasion.

Living so close to the school had its perks, as it was only a four-minute ride from his home office to the school. This didn't give Henry very long to come up with an excuse to get both the boys out on short notice. However, Henry decided to go with the truth, as he was their dad, and he paid for the school. He hoped it sounded as confident when he tried to explain it to the office secretary as it did in his head.

As he pulled into the parking lot just outside the front entrance, he noticed that a beat-up car barely held together by duct tape was parked on top of the curb and in the fire lane at the school's main entrance. The way that it was parked blocked Henry's view of the entryway. That said, this wasn't unusual, as many parents tended to flaunt the parking rules at the school. When Henry found a spot just opposite the poorly parked car, he suddenly heard a loud *BOOM*. After quickly checking his initial surroundings to determine the cause, he heard a second and third *BOOM* in quick succession. Henry's stomach dropped. He knew exactly what that was. Gunshots.

Within seconds of the last shot, Henry attempted to reign in his thoughts as images of his sons and the other children in the school lying in a pool of blood ran through his brain like a freight train. There was no time to think or plan; he needed to get in there.

Exiting his vehicle and drawing his concealed Springfield Hellcat 9mm pistol, he pulled out his cell phone and dialed 911. The emergency dispatcher on the other end answered with the typical "911, what is your emergency?"

"Active shooter at Cascade Elementary School. Send the police immediately! My name is Henry Joffer. I am armed and am going in."

"Sir, no! Do not attempt to go into the school. Police are..."

Henry didn't hear the rest of what they said. He threw the phone onto the ground and approached the oddly parked vehicle and school entranceway. He said a quick prayer in his mind, asking God for speed and accuracy for him and protection for all those within.

Having never felt anything close to actual combat, Henry's whole body shook as he rounded the vehicle with his gun drawn up. He did what he thought was best and quickly cleared the interior of the vehicle as well as the immediate area to ensure no second shooter was waiting for kids to make a break for it.

All he saw within the car were a few shotgun shells and what appeared to be pages and pages of scribbling with drawings of an extremely demonic-looking masked creature.

When he approached the front entrance, he noticed that the locked security doors, made mostly of glass, were shattered. To the immediate left of the entrance, the principal's office and secretary's desk were located beyond another glass panel. It, too, was shot out, and only a bloodied hand peaked out from behind the desk.

A rage filled Henry that he had never felt before. He knew he needed to stay calm, but the rage seemed to do just that. Instead of the shaking he experienced outside, he now had a singular purpose and the will to see it done. A warmth and feeling of electricity seemed to course through him. The shooter intended to hunt children, but instead, they would soon feel what it would be like to be prey.

He took the same route that the shooter did as he ducked through the broken glass panes of the ineffective security door. On the other side, he knew a singular hall ran the length of the square-shaped building. The entrance was just about in the center, so he visually cleared the left before quickly moving to the right. Henry liked to think that the choice was random, but the truth was that both of his son's classrooms were to the right. He would move to secure them before attempting to clear the rest of the building.

As he moved quickly down the hall, attempting to cover the multiple entrances in front while trying not to think about the possibility that he was wrong and the shooter was behind him, a door suddenly opened just ahead. Time seemed to slow down as a barrel of a shotgun came through the classroom door and into the hall, followed by the hands and the body of the shooter. Having seen too many movies, Henry shouted, "Drop the gun!" and hesitated just as the shooter fully entered the hallway.

The shooter did not drop the gun. Instead, he quickly turned and lifted the barrel towards Henry. A large sound accompanied a flash in his direction. After that, his mind went blank.

When Henry opened his eyes, he saw his sons' faces crying. He instantly tried to go to them and draw them into him for comfort, but he didn't seem to be able to move his body at all. Teachers and what looked like police officers were trying to hold back the boys, but they were strong, and Henry could tell the adults were having trouble. An immense sense of pride swelled up in him as he thought of his boys and their strength. He wasn't sure why they were so upset, but he knew they would be alright.

As Henry was suddenly lifted higher onto a gurney, he noticed an EMT placing a blanket over someone just down the hall from him. It looked like there was a lot of blood. Henry didn't know exactly why, but he felt relieved and again looked in the crowd to see his sons once more. Unfortunately, he felt exhausted and had difficulty keeping his eyelids open.

Two police officers securing the scene started chatting as the ambulance pulled away with Henry inside.

"The secretary will live, and the first classroom was empty due to a field trip. He got the shooter as soon as he exited. That dude saved a lot of lives in there. What was his name?"

"I think the dispatcher said it is Henry. Those are his kids back there."

"That's rough. Hope they know their dad was a hero."

"Was? You don't think he will make it?"

"Nah. Shotgun to the gut? I would be surprised if he made it to the hospital."

"Still. He took out the shooter after being shot, right? Seems like a tough S.O.B. to me."

The first officer gestured towards the two boys, saying, "For their sake. I hope you are right and he pulls through."

39

NEART was lying prostrate at the feet of his king while fuming at the incredulous loss he had just suffered. He hated bowing and kneeling in front of anyone, but he knew he wasn't in any position to bend the hierarchal rules demanded by his leader. In better times, he would have dipped his head slightly to welcome the only being in authority over him. Unfortunately, these were not better times, as evidenced by his inability to squash the Swords that guarded the treasure.

The king reviewed Neart's maps and asked only a handful of questions. He was apparently curious as to why his greatest general, who commanded the largest horde army, was being held at bay by four or five Swords. The hulking, undead-looking general stopped his mind to consider an answer that would shift the blame to the appropriate parties. Not finding any good approaches, he figured there was no point in lying to an entity capable of getting into his mind.

"No excuses, your majesty," Neart finally responded.

"Indeed," came the king's only reply.

Thumbing through more of the general's notes and maps, the king said calmly, "Oh, general. What shall I do with you?"

"Whatever you desire, my lord. I am your's to command."

Touching a soft glowing hand to his beautiful mouth, the king replied, "Indeed?"

Laughing with a handsome voice, the king added, "Come now, Neart! I am not here to punish you."

Quickly crossing the command tent to the general, the smaller king grabbed the giant shadow's shoulders and easily lifted him to his feet.

"If I punished every general that a group of Swords stopped, I would have no generals left," the king exclaimed with a mischievous smile. He quickly added, "You will, of course, send me the leader responsible for not finishing off the Swords in the mountains. Punishment must be applied to someone after all."

The general nodded in agreement and said, "As you command, my lord."

"Excellent," the king replied with a joyful clap before returning to the table with maps and reports. "Now, tell me how you plan on removing the parasites surrounding my prize?"

Suddenly grateful that he had come up with another plan before the giant river suddenly appeared and decimated his forces, Neart began to explain his strategy: "We will use our remaining forces to attack the front gate while sending our turtair to get close to the wall in the rear."

"A turtair? Just waltzing up and knocking down the wall. That is your big plan?"

Neart quickly continued in an effort to brush off the king's underwhelming enthusiasm, "The job of the turtair will not be to smash open the wall but rather distract the Swords as to what is happening beneath it."

Waving his hand in a gesture that clearly indicated for the general to continue, the king sat back in the large chair at the center of the room and on the opposite side of the table to Neart.

"While the Swords did wipe out the majority of the kreehauns in this area, I did bring a small number of them myself. Using the turtair's attacks against the wall to overwhelm the alerts and sensors the Swords may have underground, the kreehauns will dig a tunnel beneath the wall and directly into the rear of the main building to allow a small number of shadows to take a foothold within the fort."

"Very devious. I like it! But how will the kreehauns approach the wall without being seen?" the king questioned.

"My shadows are already at work on that," the general said as he walked to the entrance and opened the tent door wide.

Even without moving from his position, the general knew the king could hear and see his men's bloody work.

In the heart of the camp, the single turtair was screaming in agony as shadows worked their blades underneath it. They carved out a large section of the beast's underbelly while avoiding lethal blows. It was a masterful work of art as they installed crude planks below the gaping wound to allow kreehauns to climb inside the walking tank. Metal plates were placed above to ensure the turtair's blood didn't disintegrate the passengers. It would work, for a time.

"When the turtair begins its assault on the rear wall, the kreehauns will drop beneath and start opening up the way for our soldiers."

The king slowly stood and started clapping before adding, "Brilliant! Simply brilliant. That is why you are one of the best, my dear general. Now, get me that shadow you promised. All this screaming has made me..... hungry."

"I am honored to serve you, my king, and will go fetch him immediately," Neart responded. Waiting for a moment, he decided to take advantage of the positive momentum and said, "There is one small issue with my plan that I would appreciate your grace's more benevolent assistance with. My plan was hinged on the belief that I would have a large contingent of fighters ready to move in on two fronts. To my disgust, the tactics of the enemy have dwindled my forces. I now find myself without the necessary power to overwhelm them. Would any of your majesty's forces be available to me?"

Getting up and crossing to the tent's entrance to stand beside the general, the king grabbed his shoulders again and turned him to face the east. Even from a distance, the general could easily see a massive army approaching. From just one glance, it was apparent this was no typical army either. It was the *king's* army, which was completely made up of shadows. True fighters.

The king drew Neart in and whispered with a perfect smile, "What is mine is yours. We are legion."

****

Titus acknowledged the bad news from Lieutenant Nessa. She had found Shay alone on the mountainside. Her report indicated that the amount of residue from a seriously injured, if not deceased, shadow near his oddly positioned statue indicated that they wouldn't be bothered by Ronan. Titus had no doubt his friend and second made the fallen SALT pay dearly.

Arrow 3 agreed to take Shay back to the kingdom after dropping off 2-1-2 at their outpost. Both leaders said their final goodbyes as the ship flew back west, where it had originally come from.

The leader of 1-1-8 looked about his surroundings as he took in what he and his brothers had given to defend this ever-shrinking plot of land. He thought back on his conversation with his second and his inability to stop second-guessing his choices. Titus couldn't help but feel a deeper camaraderie with Shay, even now after he had taken the blue. Dishonoring his brother by throwing out his own advice would be beneath a Sword. He knew they were here for a purpose and their King had already ensured victory. The Choices he made may have brought them to this desperate position, but it was equally true that his Choices had given them the best possible path to success.

He would move forward for the love of his King and trust that there would always be an answer, even if he couldn't fathom the question.

Titus announced the news to his team through their communication. Instead of highlighting their loss, he chose to use Shay's sacrifice as a rallying cry. They would complete their mission because their brother, the best warrior they had ever known, believed his sacrifice would propel them to victory. As he finished, he announced that it was time to honor that Choice in their deeds as a fresh assault began.

As expected, the horde beasts had trouble moving in the giant mud pit that now surrounded the fort. Water had washed away the enemy but had soaked into the barren soil soon after, creating a mire that was impossible to fully run through.

Wit and Titus were at the front, with John holding the rear. Kurian would be the runner who would stand in for his brothers as they replenished themselves at the bridge.

The two at the gate were easily picking off all manner of horde monsters as they approached. It wasn't hard, as they would get stuck roughly every fifteen hands.

"I almost feel bad for them," Wit remarked as he shot down a slew of ciaróg that seemed to fair a little better than their hoofed or clawed brethren and had reached about ten paces into the mire.

Titus quickly racked up kills from a group of bullans attempting to force their way through the mud. He gave his junior a side-eye before returning to kill more.

"Don't get me wrong, Commander. I will gladly kill them all in any way, but they don't get to experience Macey up close. It really is a shame."

Right as Titus was about to ask questions he probably shouldn't have, John whistled that an enemy was approaching. Kurian ran to check and confirmed that a single turtair was on its way out of the woods and heading to the rear of the fort.

"Will the wall hold against that monstrosity," Titus asked his engineer.

"Yes, sir. There is no way that thing could knock down something I built."

"Good. Keep me posted."

A turtair could be difficult to deal with as it was mostly armored against their ranged gifts, but it wasn't exactly a fighter they had to worry about. Used only as area or building destroyers, they were seen as far too slow to be a concern in actual combat. It was welcome to come give itself a headache against the walls, as long as it didn't damage them.

"Sir, it is giving off a weird scream," Kurian reported.

"Understood. Legion enjoys modifying the beasts. Keep me updated if you see anything odd about it."

With nothing left to do but go back to killing, Titus tried to put Boomer's report out of his mind. However, in the back of it, a thought seemed to nag at him: something about that scream didn't sit right. He felt the wrongness from the scream, but he couldn't place a finger on the why.

Over the next cycle, the creature had arrived and was indeed smashing his head against their wall, all while continuing its ear-piercing scream of agony. Having switched with John to give him a break from the noise, Titus continued to ponder the scream. The turtair did have a giant spike on its head, which would have caused immense pain when surgically attached, but it looked old to the commander's eyes.

Due to the sound of the beast, Wit wasn't capable of watching the rear for long as it caused him great discomfort due to his heightened hearing. It wasn't a problem as keeping the rotation between John, Titus, and Kurian was plenty.

Titus had asked Kurian several times if anything was wrong with the wall, but the engineer had inspected it more often than Titus asked for updates. The wall was sound, even if his alert system was practically useless.

Trusting that his engineer knew best, Titus continued shooting at enemies that advanced and watched as the giant monster smashed his head against the wall. Borrowing a page from Wit, Titus could almost feel bad for the creature. Reality quickly squashed that thought as he knew that the monster would do anything simply to have the chance to crush or destroy his brothers and what they protected.

Glancing out at the tree line behind the turtair, Titus suddenly saw movement. Small glimpses of branches moving or tree swaying were all it took, but he knew instantly that something was afoot.

Turning to look to his brothers on the other side of the main hall to shout a warning, he felt more than saw their bridge fall. It felt like a sudden severing of a small connection from inside himself to their King. They all sensed it and, as evidence, simultaneously whipped their heads to the center of their fort.

"John, hold the front. Wit and Kurian to the main hall, now!"

He watched as each member responded instantly without needing further instruction.

Titus turned back to where he had seen movement only a heartbeat ago. His gut dropped out from him as rows and rows of shadows advanced out of the trees at a sprint. Wanting to warn his Big, the remaining defender at the gate, Titus turned back the opposite way only to realize that no warning was necessary. The same scene was playing out in front of John. A new flood soon overtook the barren ground surrounding the Swords of 1-1-8. A flood of death and darkness.

****

* * *

Kurian cursed at himself as he rammed into the main hall doors. He knew what had happened and was furious at himself. It was his fault that the enemy had gotten within the walls. He had sensed the warnings that had gone off underground but had immediately chalked it up to the giant beast's attacks.

Standing before him within the main hall was failure in physical form as shadows glanced up from their handiwork beneath them.

"Oops! Was this important to you?" one of the three shadows mockingly asked as he stepped on the broken bridge towards the advancing Swords. The same bridge that was their lifeline and the only remaining piece of Killian left at the fort.

Wit blew air out his mouth and glanced at Kurian before responding to the shadow, "Oh boy. You have done it now."

Kurian advanced and started blocking the hard strikes from one shadow's war hammer. Deflecting and dodging was easy enough with the shield, but Kurian was out for blood.

The engineer sliced his opponent's thigh but, in doing so, allowed an opening for his opponent to strike his offhand. Fortunately, as he braced for the hit, Wit's mace flew in and smashed the shadow's hand that gripped the weapon. Unable to keep a hold, the shadow's hammer dropped harmlessly to the ground instead of shattering the Sword's arm.

Unfortunately, Wit's sacrifice came at a cost as another shadow saw an opening to hit the private's ribs with a wicked-looking cutlass. The grievous wound was healed but at great cost to Wit's energy reserves. No bridge meant he couldn't use any gifts without going over his limit, and healing would be difficult.

Moving to create space, Kurian dug his heels in and pushed his shield into the shadow, which lifted him into the air. The bladed edge sliced the opponent's neck as

Kurian rotated his shield, which held the shadow while simultaneously smashing the opponent into the wall. Leaving his enemy on the ground, knocked out and bleeding, the Sergeant turned back to engage the two who were ganging up on a wounded Wit.

Not wanting to waste any more time, Kurian brought his ranged gift out and shot both shadows point blank. His limited range but high power gift ensured that both shadows were quickly dealt with. Most likely, they would heal, but they were effectively out of this fight.

Before Wit and Kurian could move to find the enemy's tunnel, which was likely somewhere in the back of the main hall, Titus came bursting through the front door. As he crossed the threshold, a shadow leapt at him from behind. Sensing the threat, Titus pivoted and used his sword like a bat to both swat the enemy away and sever her into two.

Kurian saw Titus's eyes show a hint of disappointment as he turned to see the bridge at the feet of his two brothers. Quickly shifting gears, their leader asked if Kurian could still salvage this by closing the tunnel. With his own show of disappointment, he explained that he had used all of his charges in their flooding strategy, and there hadn't been enough time to create more.

Each member of the present team realized that there was no strategy that would force the enemy back outside the walls. With no way to re-energize themselves, it was now a matter of when, not if, they would go blue.

Titus immediately called out to John on their link, "Retreat back to the final defensive position."

A regretful grunt came as the larger brother's reply.

All three Swords in the main hall looked out to the entrance. John was fully surrounded by a layer of at least two deep shadows. Kurian took a step in their brother's direction but was immediately held back by Titus. The painful acceptance in his leader's golden eyes was evident as he ordered them to retreat back to the crypt. Kurian knew that the mission came first, but stepping back into the hall and moving to the stairwell was one of the hardest things he had ever done.

Titus called out to John on the team channel, "It was an honor to serve with you, private. I look forward to fighting beside you once more."

There was no response other than John's gruff acknowledgment and the battle noise emanating from the gate.

As the three Swords descended the interior stairwell, Kurian saw Wit speak into his link. It must have been a direct link to John, as Kurian didn't hear it directly in his. That said, they were close enough that he picked up Wit's final words. In a serious tone, the typically goofy Sword whispered, "Brother, I can't wait to hear you laugh one day. Until then, silently drag them all screaming with you."

40

IT was 2:15 pm on a Tuesday when Henry's ambulance arrived at the hospital. He was rushed into surgery, and his wife was immediately contacted. Hana, Hunter, and Logan arrived soon after using a police escort. After arriving, they were placed in a waiting area outside surgery.

The family wasn't waiting long before a doctor in green scrubs came out of the double doors and took one look at Hana. It was all that was needed for her to break down in tears and wailing as the boys looked at her in confusion.

Henry Joffer died at 3:23 pm on a Tuesday.

41

TITUS and his two remaining brothers were trapped. For the last cycle, the heavy doors were the only thing separating them from the army of former elite soldiers and vile monsters whose sole goal was ending their lives. It was not the best position, but it was not the worst. They could not have had a door, which Wit pointed out as they all braced against it. The comment was timed with a battering ram smashing into it once again.

There was no escape from their position within the crypt, but that was never a thought anyway. 1-1-8 had their orders, and it was to defend the tomb. Each of the remaining team members would rather go blue than abandon their post.

The leader of Swords slammed his back into the door once again as the battering ram flung him back a few hands. Looking toward the tomb, he saw that the black plant had nearly overcome the entirety of it. When the three of them had entered, they saw a horrifying scene play out where kreehauns willingly threw themselves on the tomb to instantly be drained of every ounce of acidic blood, which caused a violent growth spurt in the plant. It had expanded to only have the bowl holding the violet flame remaining that was not covered in dark vines filled with sickly leaves and dagger-like thorns. The tomb was almost unrecognizable compared to what they had seen when they first arrived.

While considering the ramifications of the etched plant's expansion, the battering ram hit harder than before and threw all three Swords across the room. Before they could recover, the door finally exploded inward. The swarm of shadows was overwhelming as they simply threw their bodies at the beleaguered defenders.

Not being able to use their weapons effectively and not having enough energy to summon their armor, the three did what they could to fight off the inevitability. However, even after putting down several attackers, the sheer number was enough to subdue the three in the tiny space.

Within a few moments of the Swords being pinned to the ground, they heard a slow clap as the legion's king entered the tomb, followed quickly by the hulking general Neart.

The king stopped clapping as he neared the prisoners and exclaimed, "Well fought! Of course, I would expect nothing less from Swords."

He walked towards Titus, and as he got close, he tossed a thumb behind him and, with a conspiring wink and a chuckle, said, "You had my general quite flummoxed out there. Not many can get under his skin.....or what's left of it."

With a shadow holding his face to the ground, Titus attempted to look at his sworn enemy and asked, "What do you want, traitor?"

"What do I want?" the king asked himself before answering with, "You and what's left of your brothers are gone or at my mercy, and I am currently at the heart of what you so desperately tried to keep me away from. I suppose I could use a nice foot massage?"

The last part was likely meant as a dig at the Swords, but two shadows suddenly stepped forward, one going on his hands and knees while the other began undoing the king's sandal to give him a massage.

"I want for nothing, Commander," the king finally said after a few heartbeats.

After another pause, Wit finally broke the silence and said, "I could use one of those. My feet have been killing me for the past few cycles as I slaughtered your army."

Even though Titus couldn't see what was happening, he heard the kicks and punches landing on the defenseless brother. Kurian shouted for them to stop, but they continued until the king raised a hand after a few more hits. The only sound afterward was Wit gasping for air and groaning.

Titus saw that the king was about to speak, but Wit somehow was able to speak one more time and interrupted by saying, "No, you idiots! I said my feet."

Both Titus and Kurian couldn't hold it in and began laughing hysterically.

"How very droll," the king said and pointed at his ear, then towards the direction of Wit.

The communications expert went quiet as he held back a scream, but the silence only allowed Titus to fill in the blanks as to what was happening. Soon enough, his theory was confirmed as Wit's tongue and ear landed at the feet of the king.

The king picked up the two appendages and showed them to Titus as he asked, "I do hope he didn't need these."

Shadows in the room chuckled as Titus seethed.

"Where was I.... Oh, yes. You wanted to know what I wanted, and I explained that I had everything. I believe there is a far greater question to be asked. What is it that you want, Titus?"

Without missing a beat, the Commander answered, "To kill you."

Showing perfect teeth, the king smiled and replied, "Indeed? Do you desire to be greater than your King? The last time I was in His presence, I believe He said only He would defeat me. Do you secretly want to be a king yourself?"

Titus had to admit that the king was very good at manipulating words and appearance. Everything about him screamed desire and power. His appearance was as stunning as anything created by the Maker. Long hair, a perfect smile, and golden skin that glowed with a radiant light. The robes he wore were made of gold and adorned with beautiful diamonds that told everything around him that he was a creature of immense power and deserving of praise. Any lesser creature would look at him and believe he had the authority to grant desires, but Titus knew it was all a lie.

"I am a Sword. I am a living weapon and would be honored to be wielded by my King as your instrument of death."

"Such loyalty! I am impressed. You are a brilliant tactician, an inspiring leader of warriors, loyal as no one else, and an unmatched fighter. The true full package that could lead entire armies to victory against any who dared oppose you. No one is worthy of standing against you..."

Titus started blocking out the words and images of glory that invaded his mind. All the honey in the world couldn't mask the poison that this so-called king was attempting to feed him. He wasn't a fool and understood the power this former leader within the Kingdom wielded. The traitor would whisper innocent enough words, but they were comprised only of false pride. Titus also knew that 'the offer' would soon follow.

"...generous, and might I say quite handsome. With all these features, does it not make sense to be free to do as you wish? To be something greater - perhaps even as the right hand of a true king? Bow to me once, only once, and you will never need to bow to any other again. What do you say?"

There was only one response worth giving as Titus began laughing once more. Kurian quickly picked up the laugh, and even Wit made a sound that could only be described as a garbled chuckle without a tongue.

Fury ran through the king's face. He stood and commanded his soldiers, "End them."

“No,” a calm and truly magnificent voice said from the center of the room where the tomb sat.

With that single word voiced with true authority, every shadow, Sword, traitorous general, and rebel king in the crypt and beyond the fort kneeled with bowed heads. The power of the one true King poured out from his voice, and there was no possible other physical reaction.

Titus wasn’t worthy enough to hear that mouth speak, let alone be in the same room as the speaker. All he could do was bow and avert his eyes from the glory that shone around his liege. While doing so, he was able to see the traitorous king. In the true light shining from the King, the Commander saw the truth behind every lie, including the one under which the false king hid. Instead of a king in his prime with fine clothing and his own glow, the Sword saw a snake poorly masquerading as a man. Titus could imagine that the snake was once beautiful, with stunning scales that reflected the light around it. Wounds on its back spoke of missing wings that it could have previously used to fly and dance in the early light of its Maker. Knowing little about lords, he only understood that they were there to help rule realms while delighting and honoring their Creator. What lay low in this dirty crypt now was a pathetic reflection of what Titus could only imagine was the initial lord of the morning, Lucifer.

“My Lord. Do you not see how the plant has completely wrapped the tomb? It is ugly and reeks of poor use of Choice. This one is not worthy of you. Let me take it away from your sight,” the snake said while still hiding its eyes from the light that filled the room.

The piercing eyes of one who longed for the death of a sworn enemy slowly turned to the serpent. For a brief moment, Titus believed the King would draw His weapon and end the foul beast. However, He simply stated, “The horn of battle has not been sounded. But you now have no authority in this place. Be gone,” the King commanded.

In response, the snake and every shadow in the room simply disappeared. Titus immediately understood that it wasn't just this room either. A command spoken by the King had the authority to rewrite reality itself. The Commander knew that every legion fighter and horde monster was no longer in or around the fort.

Alone in the crypt with their King, the Swords bowed low and remained silent as the Maker lovingly touched the tomb. Eventually, the King acknowledged His Swords and told them to rise and come forward.

As the three brothers approached, their King reached down and picked up Wit's ear and tongue. He gingerly placed the ear back on the Sword's head, and it was instantly healed. Before re-attaching the tongue, the King lovingly and jokingly said to Wit, "I specifically gave you this for a reason, as I enjoy hearing you talk," he winked and added, "Try not to lose it again."

As Wit elbowed Kurian with a grin that was a mil long, the King next singled out Titus as He said, "Come. See now what you protected in my Name and see for yourself if it was worth it."

Titus moved forward and kneeled as he watched the flame sputter, with the red hint slowly flickering and eventually fading away. All that was left was a blue flame above a tomb covered in a sickly plant made of pure evil. While Titus stared, he could have sworn he saw the flames take the form of the Maker bird that stared back at him with the same eyes that he had seen on the King, who now looked to the coffin-like tomb.

Leaning into the tomb while placing a hand on the stone, the King spoke to the plant itself, "As it was for Me, Death, you have no power over this one. I claim Henry as ***mine***."

With the final word whispered, red blood began flowing from the King's pierced hand that rested atop the tomb. It began slowly, yet fully, flowing through the dark etchings throughout the stone. The blood appeared like molten lava, filling and searing away the black plant, leaving behind clean stone once more. While not fully weakened or defeated by the experience, it was evident that this process was not without a payment made by the King.

As the final black stain was covered by His blood, the blue flame above the casket began to pulse and grow brighter. Suddenly, with a violent explosion of light and stone, the casket broke apart, and what was once cold and ugly was no more. In fact, the entire fort was no more.

Titus stared in awe around him as he realized they were no longer in the crypt but raised in the hall where the throne stood. While the throne was still there and raised, it had also changed. It was now masterfully gilded with precious gems of all realms. The hall and fort weren't impervious to the changes as they were replaced with a beautiful open-air temple. To either side of him, alabaster pillars shined with the light emitting from the King and the flame. With no roof above them, a gorgeous night sky was putting on a firework show of shooting stars. The blue flame was still centered just beneath and in front of the throne. Some might view the flame as awaiting the judgment of the sitting King, but in truth, the opposite feeling of joy, like an expectant mother, was radiating from every inch of the new structure.

The land itself began transforming in response to the King's actions. Where only darkness and death had shown moments before, life began springing forth. The ground was no longer stained with the acidic blood and gore of past battles but rather dressed in grass, flowers, and creations of boundless beauty that only the Creator could imagine.

Looking around the now temple that housed the flame at the center, Titus saw that even though it was giving off brilliant light, it was not outshining the King. Instead, it seemed to reflect His own light through a new lens to harmonize and amplify the great light. Gingerly, the King placed His hand on the surface of the flame with another smile that was beautiful and full of love. Peering past his King into the flame, Titus could just make out the shape of an awakening Man. Like the breaking of a dam in his mind, understanding flooded Titus. He internally answered his King's comment confidently - yes. 1-1-8 had served their King in the most profound of ways.

As the Prince of the Kingdom awoke and stepped out of the flame, he immediately cried with joy as he ran to his Father. The King's smile as he wrapped His son up into an embrace that put the brilliant light show in the night sky to shame.

After a few moments, the King walked with his son towards Titus and his brothers. He nodded toward the kneeling warriors, and Prince Henry spoke, "My Father says you are my guardians. Even while I made your task difficult through my use of Choice, you held and allowed me to expand the Kingdom. I am humbled by your actions."

"My Prince, we may not have always known what we protected, but we are pleased to have brought joy to our King by serving."

The King stepped forward and touched Titus's head, "You have honored me with your actions. Well done, good and faithful servants."

Titus was nearly buzzing with energy and joy at the King's touch and words. He wasn't the only one, as his two remaining brothers visibly glowed behind him.

"However, your work is not done. My son has asked specifically for your assistance with some of my other lost children in this realm, and I am inclined to grant his request as this war is far from over. Ready to get back in the fight?"

Without hesitation, Titus ceremonially drew his weapon and laid it in his palms before lifting it as an offering. Meaning every word, he responded, "I am my King's Sword. I am honored to serve."

Epilogue

Sham couldn't believe his luck as he finally saw moonlight creep through the cracks of the rocks as he worked to dig himself out. He had been wandering around the tunnels, looking for a way out after he had escaped the clutches of that insane shadow, Ronan. He sincerely hoped never to see that creature again unless it was with Ronan on his knees before Sham. That was a fun image to conjure, no matter how unlikely.

With no light within the mountain's vast tunnels, Sham had no idea how long he had been crawling around, trying to find an exit. Each passageway he remembered from his previous trips ended in a cave-in. He knew that the Swords had caused them, and they were likely the cause of all the kreehauns being gone or killed. He had hoped to find his army waiting, and he would use them to gain glory, but every tunnel and cave was empty. Before long, Sham knew he was completely alone and trapped.

All that changed when the mountain exploded. He had felt the ground shake, and the sound was overwhelming as massive Sword charges went off and echoed throughout the tunnels. Sham was lucky to have been in one that didn't collapse as a number of them did, based on his exploration after the event.

Eventually, Sham located a tunnel that had closed but had something else as well—water. The shadow realized that this tunnel was likely his best chance to escape. If he found flowing water to help him loosen stones blocking his path and potentially follow the water out, he could finally free himself from his prison.

Working what felt like cycles, the faint light was just the victory he needed to push the last rock out of place to allow him to wriggle his way out. The tunnel he found himself in was still soaked in water and clear of all debris. He was unsure what had caused it, but he also did not care as he saw an exit just to his right.

Stepping out, Sham was amazed and disturbed at the transformation he saw. Trees and brush around the exit seem to have new life in them. The typical clouds and overall darkness he had come to recognize as neutral territory were no more. Sham knew he wasn't welcome in this land, and there would be no horde or legion around to get support. He needed to leave immediately.

Skirting around the fort that had transformed into a temple, Sham made plans to get back to legion territory. He also started making other plans to use his experience to gain favor. While it was challenging to think of how he could possibly spin this situation to his benefit, he had confidence that he would figure something out.

As he moved silently through a dense forest, he quickly turned to his right at the sound of breaking branches. Stopping and drawing his scythes, he checked to see who was there. However, after seeing nothing, the familiar paranoia came over him. He was sure that his stalker had come back. Fighting back the anger and fear that threatened to overcome his senses, Sham started sprinting with no thought of how it may look. In truth, he was terrified. Frantically looking from side to side to spot his stalker, he didn't see the tree branch directly in his path and was knocked to the ground.

Before he could open his eyes, what felt like large daggers pierced both his forearms as he lay in the dirt. Screaming in agony, Sham looked to his right and left to see who had attacked him. What he saw made him shiver and lose his ability to hold his skin.

Slowly, like a smooth sheet being pulled from a bed, a cloak of invisibility was removed from two giant golden lionesses on either side of him. Their fangs had shattered his forearms, and they firmly held him in their mouths with no hope of wriggling free.

Unsure of what was happening, Sham attempted to kick at the beasts holding him. He theorized that a quick strike would make at least one of them release an arm, enabling him to attack with one of his scythes. That hope was shattered immediately as they adjusted and forced him into a kneeling position.

"I would not try that again, murderer," came a voice within Sham's mind.

Panic took hold of him as he heard the voice. He had killed many, so being called a murderer was not unwarranted, but the panic was from the fact that very few had the power to invade the mind of a higher being such as him, and none of them were friendly.

Using his physical voice, Sham terror strickenly asked, "Who are you, and what do you want?"

"Who am I? I am lord of my realm, by grace and wisdom of the Maker. I am the protector of my people. I am A-odah," the voice replied as the speaker revealed itself before finishing with, *"But today, I am the King's justice."*

As the name was pronounced, a lion appeared in front of Sham. Besides being a male, his size was twice that of the already impressively large females. And if that was not intimidating enough, the male looked like he was on fire. His body was not that of fur or the golden color of the females who held him but of red scales that captured light. Tendrils of orange power seemed to stand out from his neck and head to create a beautiful mane unlike any other Sham had seen. The shadow had difficulty looking at the dominating creature as he emitted such bright, fiery light.

Sham didn't have to guess who A-odah was referring to regarding who he had murdered. Not only was the creature passing along images of the winged lamb he had slaughtered when first arriving at his fort, but the lion itself had massive wings that paired perfectly with the ones that had hung over his throne room.

"Yes. My partner and friend, Bán, had come to bear witness to the arrival of a Prince. She didn't realize that you scum had already infested the area."

Sham nearly screamed in a begging tone, "I didn't know!"

The lion angrily responded, *"Would it have mattered to you if you had known? Would you have treated her with respect and let her go? Or would you have enjoyed tormenting her that much more?"*

The shadow couldn't hide his reaction in his mind as he instantly thought about how he would have likely tortured a high-level dignitary from another realm for more information before sending it to the king for more entertaining torture. It was evident on the lion's disgusted face that he saw what would have become of his dearest friend.

"By order of the King and Maker, I have authority to pass judgment on you, Sham of the fallen ones," the lion-like lord pronounced inside Sham's mind.

Sham thought that there was still some way out of this. There was still an angle. Something that he could use to get out of this situation. Maybe he could convince them to imprison him and then escape? Maybe they would try to kill him, and he could pretend to die. Did these beasts know how a shadow died? Could he act his way out of it? Perhaps he would lose a lot of energy, but he would return eventually. Yes, he could get out of this and return to climbing to the heights of legion's upper echelon.

However, without a chance for Sham to offer some options, A-odah looked as though he had come to a conclusion and stated, *"You shall be given the same respect that was awarded to Bán."*

Sham shouted, "Noooo!"

The plea fell on deaf ears as the two lionesses immediately ripped both of his arms off. A-odah played the memory of Sham cutting the wings off of Bán, which he had taken from the shadow's own mind.

Falling to his knees as his red energy oozed out of both shoulders, Sham looked up at the giant fire lion and straight into his cold blue eyes that held nothing but contempt. Slowly, A-odah raised a paw and extended one single claw out. It was razor sharp and appeared very similar to Sham's scythes. The thought of his weapons quickly brought the memory of how he had cut the throat of.... He fought to say stupid animal, but the force of the lion in his mind refused to let him say anything but the lamb's name, Bán.

With that final word in his mind, the claw swiftly sliced through the neck of Sham and severed his head from his body. There was no returning, and the shadow felt himself drift into the void that was nothing but blackness. A forever prison of blackness.

****

A-odah took no pleasure in the fallen one's destruction, but, as a leader, he appreciated the balance that the King's justice had brought. He finally would be able to return home and mourn his friend.

"My lord, are we to return to our realm," his youngest huntress, Ciúnas, asked.

"We shall return, but you will remain," A-odah replied inside her mind.

He was pleased that Ciúnas didn't question his decision and only bowed her head in response and waited for further instruction. She was becoming an excellent huntress very quickly.

"The King has commanded that we track, protect, and return the silent one," the lord said. He continued with instructions, *"You will track and locate him. Once you see an opening, take it and escape with him back to the Kingdom. We will come to help if called. Understood?"*

"Yes, my lord."

All three lions came together and nuzzled their heads against one another in an affectionate embrace.

A-odah roared, and a portal was created. The other huntress went through to their home, and he walked behind her before looking back and commanding Ciúnas, *"Go. Hunt."*

Ciúnas nodded as she cloaked herself in invisibility once more. A-odah's own eyes saw her as a shining golden beauty when she gracefully ran towards the east and towards the infectious wound that the fallen ones called 'liberation city.'

Glossary

- **Creator, Maker, King** - The Creator of the realms, Maker of every inhabitant, and King to all.
- **Sword Clan** - Warriors created for the sole purpose of battling the King's enemies. Each member is unique, but they have a unified purpose and will to see that their beloved King's commands are followed. They can heal themselves with their Maker's energy and use that same energy to power their gifts. Without energy, they are incapable of moving, and their bodies turn into blue statues until called upon by the King once more.
    - **Swords** - The ground forces of the Sword Clan that directly complete the missions assigned. They were born with weapons in hand and have trained since the beginning for every possible combat scenario.
        - **Type of Swords:**
            - **General** - Leaders capable of planning massive campaigns against multiple foes within the blink of an eye.
            - **Commander** - On-the-ground leaders of Sword units with the ability to take in all information around them and form perfect tactics and strategies.
            - **Scout And Long-range Termination (SALT)** - Rare specialists with abilities in tracking and more extensive use

with long-range gifts. They are the very pinnacle of fighters in almost every aspect.

- **Engineer** - Extremely skilled in both building and destroying, the team's engineers are the explosive experts who can create a palace and blow it up for fun.
- **Healer** - Often referred to as Doc, these Swords can share energy with others to heal them and keep them in the fight.
- **Communications** - A specialist with above-average hearing and is responsible for maintaining communication links within the team and with the leadership of the Sword Clan while on missions outside the Kingdom.
- **Knowledge Seeker** - The investigator of the Swords who will leave no stone unturned and learn everything there is to know about all subjects. They are relied upon to retain information and find answers to the team's questions.
- **Battle Integral Gunner (Big)** - The weapon expert of the unit who is blessed with an unusually large amount of energy reserve to handle specialized weapons that commonly have high energy requirements.

- Sword's Gifts - Gifts are ranged weapons and armor that can be summoned by Swords in time of need. They are powered by Creator energy that flows within each Sword. Each gift was given to the Sword after their creation, which is why they are called gifts and can no longer be used by shadows.
- Link - a term used to describe the internal communications network between Swords.

- **Arrows** - Additional members of the Sword Clan that are in a support role. While they have no weapons or gifts, some pilot airships have armaments capable of large-scale lethal force.
    - **Ships** - Shaped like a large robin with short wings, the ships are the transport and aerial support used by Swords to travel to and from each realm. They use Creator energy to both fly and use their armaments, so they constantly need to return to the Kingdom to re-energize.

- **Voice Clan** - The other half of the Clans that support the King. These larger and winged individuals minister to the King and perform other duties required within the Kingdom.
    - **Speakers** - Messengers of the King who bring the voice of the Creator to his subjects.
- **Horde** - Created by the power of Choice, they are monstrous creatures whose only thoughts are for chaos and destruction of everything the King has created.
    - **Kreehaun** - Short-sighted creatures with

sharp claws and fangs adept at digging tunnels and finding ways to destroy their enemy from below.

- **Bullans** - Large and muscular with bovine-like heads, they are used as shock troops to push through strong defenses.
- **Marow** - Half beauty and half serpent, they are deadly with their siren song and constricting power that rivals the strength of all horde beasts.
- **Gúl** - Smaller creatures that hide their hideous forms beneath cloaks and use their short bows and arrows to attack their victims from range.
- **Réama** - Monsters made of a slime-like substance that will inject a strong narcotic into their victims as they slowly digest them within themselves. They have a floating and moving spherical core, which is their only weakness.
- **Bréag** - A hive-minded creature that is made up of thousands of tiny beings who are four-legged, have tails, and protrude razor-sharp claws.
- **Ciaróg** - Humanoid-sized insects with blade-like arms, a thick shell on their back, and pincers to pull the prey into their mouths.
- **Loskang** - Amphibian monsters with powerful legs and a single stripe of poison on their body. They use spears and are ambush hunters who enjoy poisoning their prey to watch their suffering.
- **Farhatch** - One-eyed ogres who are all muscle. They aren't used for close combat by the legion but are excellent artillery when throwing heavy objects.

- **Turtair** - Giant-shelled monsters who will smash buildings beneath them or ram their head against anything as long as it allows them to destroy anything made by the King.
- **Bulturs** - Bird-like-headed beasts with humanoid bodies that are users of dark energy. They are infamous for their supporting role in protecting and furthering the range of other horde creatures.

- **Legion** - Former members of the Sword Clan that rebelled against their Maker in a failed attempt to overthrow Him.
    - **Shadows** - Once Swords, they are now sworn enemies of the Creator and revel in all things opposite of their brethren. While they project beauty onto their bodies through skins, they are actually decaying underneath and rotting from the inside due to using their pride as a source of power. Even without their gifts, they are formidable warriors.
    - **Stones** - Former Arrows that turned against the King alongside shadows. They do not have their own weapons and are mostly used for less glorified positions, but they are still capable in battle.
- **The king** - a former Lord of the Kingdom who plotted to overthrow the true King and take His place on the throne by convincing the Swords to take up arms against their own Creator.
- **Measurements**:
    - **Hand** - equal to the length of one of the Sword or legion's hands.
    - **Mil** - 5,000 hands.
    - **Cycle** - one rotation of the celestial body within a realm.

Printed in the USA
CPSIA information can be obtained
at www.ICGtesting.com
CBHW010339171124
17423CB00012B/147